SENTINALS JUSTICE

BOOK THREE OF THE SENTINAL SERIES

HELEN GARRAWAY

Published by Jerven Publishing

Cover by Jeff Brown Graphics

This is a work of fiction. Names, characters, organisations, places, events, and incidents are either products of the author's imagination or are used fictitiously. Any resemblance to actual events or persons, living or dead, businesses, companies or locales is entirely coincidental.

eBook ISBN: 978-1-8381559-6-4

Paperback ISBN: 978-1-8381559-7-1

Hardcover ISBN: 978-1-8381559-8-8

Sign up to my mailing list to join my magical world and for further information about forthcoming books and latest news at: www.helengarraway.com

First Edition

For Kaye

My dear friend,
crafting partner
and sounding board.

Thank you!

CONTENTS

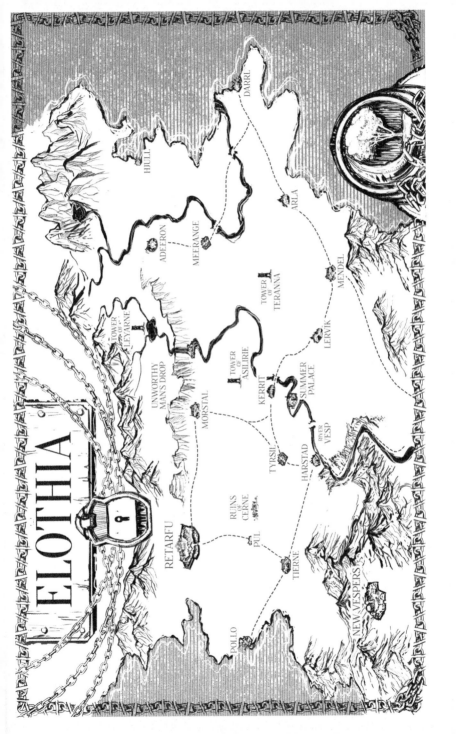

1

ADEERON, ELOTHIA

Birlerion curled in on himself, more for warmth than any protection it could afford him. Aching with the unrelenting cold, he couldn't stop trembling. The cold ate away his reserves faster than the Ascendant could beat it out of him. He hurt everywhere. Tor'asion's fists were brutal, and he was beside himself with fury. Birlerion hoped he had worked his anger out by now. He couldn't take much more.

The only thing that kept him going was the knowledge that the Captain had escaped, and the longer he held out, the longer the Ascendants were distracted from their purpose. The Captain should have listened to him; he had always known Torsion was no good, and Tor'asion was worse.

His head ached, thumping in time with his ribs, and it hurt to breathe. Blood oozed from the jagged cut above his left eye, crusting on his face, and pooling onto the stone floor. He watched it seep between the cracks of the paving stones into the soil below.

Flinching against the sudden light, he tensed as the healer entered his cell. Muttering under his breath, the healer forced Birlerion's head back, roughly stitched the wound that bisected his eyebrow and left. Birlerion wondered why they didn't leave him to bleed to death.

Alone again, the darkness soothed him.

The Ascendants thought it would drive him mad, but he found solace in the dark. He wrapped his belief in the Lady around him like a warm blanket until the door opened and the light brought the next attempt to break him down.

Flaring torchlight flooded his cell and the guards dragged him out. The sudden brightness made his sore eyes water and his headache worse. He couldn't stand. His legs wouldn't hold him up, and he hung limply between the guards and shivered. Squinting through swollen eyes at the man staring at him, the realisation was slow to form. A new visitor. His battered mind hunted down the name. Ah yes, Var'geris.

He was sure he looked a wreck; he certainly felt like one. His left arm was splinted, it was difficult to breathe, and when he pissed, his urine was pink, which meant more damage somewhere.

Tor'asion had enjoyed the sound of his ribs cracking. Only the guards holding him up had stopped him trying again, along with the fact that Tor'asion had injured his hand. Birlerion would have laughed if it didn't hurt so much.

Voices surrounded him, meaningless, just noise, until Var'geris crouched down beside him and pulled his head up by his hair, making Birlerion's eyes water. *Funny how something so simple can still cause pain*, he mused.

"You know it doesn't have to be this way. Your suffering is pointless. There is no help coming. No one knows where you are. Pain and deprivation; that is all you'll suffer until the day you die."

Birlerion remained silent. Nothing new there, then.

"You are worthless to us if you do not yield. We need the Captain, not you. You will listen to me because you have no other choice. Listen and obey. You will look at me." Var'geris yanked his head back, forcing Birlerion to watch him. "Look into my eyes, and listen. Only to my voice. It's all that you care about; just my voice."

Birlerion stared at him and thought about Leyandrii, remembering how she had looked the last time he had seen her, with Guerlaire by her side. Beautiful and bold and with determination in her green eyes. She had never given up on them and neither would he. She had saved his life. Turning inwards, he remembered the smile on her face as she greeted him, concentrating on his memories and blocking out the present.

Var'geris stood scowling down at the man before him. The once powerful Sentinal who had persistently prevented them from reaching the Lady's Captain was now reduced to a shivering pile of filthy, blood-spattered rags. It was useless. The man was completely unresponsive, almost catatonic. Tor'asion had done more damage than he realised. The healer had warned against more beatings unless they wanted the Sentinal dead. He had splinted the man's arm and strapped his ribs, but there was little he could do for the rest of the damage, except rest and warmth, and it was unlikely the man would get any of that.

Var'geris instructed the guards to return him to his cell and strode off.

Birlerion lay on the stone floor, no longer feeling the cold. A soft voice breathed in his ear, but he ignored it, lost in his memories.

"Birlerion? So this is where you are. Oh, my poor, poor Birlerion. What have they done to you?" The voice grew insistent, wheedling its way into his reminiscing.

Warm arms embraced him, and Birlerion stirred. Images

of the auburn-haired younger sister of the Lady Leyandrii flooded through him, reminding him of better days.

"Birlerion, stay a little longer. Don't give up. The Captain is coming. He is coming for you."

"W-what?"

"You are doing so well. I am sorry. Birler is needed now, let Birlerion rest. He will be all the stronger when he is needed."

Arms hugging himself tight, Birlerion struggled upright. He shook as tremors rushed through him in waves; shudders he couldn't control. *"Marguerite?"* Memories slowly penetrated his battered mind. Birler? He hadn't been called that name since he had turned Sentinal over three thousand years ago, when Leyandrii had asked him for his help and he had committed his life to her. Give her up? Never!

"Hush, she will always love you, as will I. But for now, Birlerion needs to rest. Birler has his own skills that will help you. He knows how to survive."

Survive, Birler thought, confusion muddying his thoughts. He had to survive until Leyandrii could spare Guerlaire or maybe his brother, Tagerill, to rescue him. What his father would say when he found out, made Birler wince. *At least Warren,* Birler corrected the thought, *his father would not stop until his son was found.* Birler's heart eased at the thought. His father would make sure someone would come for him.

"Stay strong, Birler. Help is coming. I will stay with you." Marguerite held him, soothing the shudders, and Birler sighed back down to the cold floor, lost in memories evoked by the voice from his past.

2

SOMEWHERE IN ELOTHIA

Tor'asion knelt before the simple altar, the rising star of the Ascendants resplendent in red and gold before him. His dark head was bowed, his black eyes closed.

They were so close. It was their destiny; it was meant to be. He had searched and searched the archives, the catacombs, the Watch Towers. He had spent his life searching, as had his father and *his* father before him. His ancestors were depending on him to open the way for their return. They waited beyond the the Veil, eager to claim Remargaren.

They had followed the trail, haphazard at times, but they had pieced together the Ascendant's message. They could read it in the stars and now the final piece: The Lady's Captain, a man called Jerrol Haven. A child he had befriended accidentally and nurtured into a close friend, held the key, and he was almost theirs. Such an unassuming man, yet he had eluded them so many times. His guards were prescient and had proved troublesome, especially the Sentinal, Birlerion. Tor'asion tensed at the thought of the man who had stood in his way.

Drawing in deep, slow breaths, he tried to control the

anger threatening to engulf him. He still couldn't believe he had let Jerrol escape from the Watch Towers. Jerrol had been in their power, helpless. Grinding his teeth, he made himself a promise. Birlerion would pay for distracting him.

The Ascendants were closing in. They would have Jerrol soon enough, and then it would all be theirs as their forefathers had ordained. They would rule Remargaren and the goddesses power would be theirs. The thought of unlimited magic instead of the dregs they struggled to use now made his heart race. A pulse throbbed under his eye and he took a deep breath. Soon. There had been sacrifices and more would be made, but it was all in aid of the final commandment. They would fulfil the demand and reap the rewards. It was only a matter of time.

Tor'asion stood and stared out of the window over the icy landscape of Elothia. His severe face tightened as he considered their hasty retreat, the lines on his face deepening as he massaged his aching knuckles. If it hadn't been for Jerrol getting in their way, his fists shook as he tried to control his anger. He had underestimated him. He hadn't realised what the role of the Lady's Captain really meant. They would have succeeded if not for Jerrol and that Sentinal. They would have been in control of Terolia and Vespiri.

But still, they had one last throw, and they wouldn't fail this time. No one knew he was an Ascendant. Jerrol had no idea; he had never suspected him of being anything other than his friend and mentor, Torsion. A harmless scholar. He would return to Vespiri and resume his disguise. He would not fail a second time.

He turned as one of his brothers entered the room. "It's time," Var'geris said, glaring at Tor'asion. "Are you sure this is the right interpretation?"

Tor'asion smiled, the certainty flushing him with strength. "Oh yes, I'm sure," he said as he indicated for his brother to lead the way. Pausing at the entrance to the circular room where four men were already seated, Tor'asion scowled. There should have been eight of them but Jerrol and those Sentinals had managed to overcome two of their brothers. Tor'asion clamped his lips tight as another flash of anger seared through him. He needed to control his emotions; his frustration was getting the better of him.

All the brothers were tall and slender with black eyes like himself, the mark of an Ascendant, except the squat ex-chancellor, once called Isseran, on the end. Their faces were angular with sharp cheek bones and square chins, distinctive and yet similar at the same time. Tor'asion relaxed his shoulders as he realised they were all looking at him.

"Tor'asion, what say you?" Pev'eril asked.

"The time approaches. Focus on the Veil."

"We have been," Var'geris said through gritted teeth, "but it has been repaired, and we can't get in to shred it. I thought you were going to deal with the Captain? Your self-indulgence has cost us dearly. You had him in your grasp, and you let him escape."

Tor'asion raised his hand. "The Lady is not to be under-estimated, nor her minions. Success grows as we gain more power. We still have some control of the Watches; enough for our purposes, at least. Terolia has met our needs. Let the Terolians be a distraction for the king. Our allies will harass them. Elothia will provide what we need to prepare. In the end, we will have all. We can wait."

"Haven't we waited long enough?" Iss'aren whined.

"My dear Iss'aren; you shall be reinstated, never fear." Tor'asion smiled as he observed the small man who had once held the chancellorship of Vespiri, second only to the king, and still he had let the power slip through his fingers. "Your talents will not be wasted. It's time you returned to court. I have someone for you to entertain."

"My talents would be better spent ruling Vespiri. It should have been ours by now. Instead, we are freezing our arses off up here. Why are we here, Tor'asion?" Iss'aren snapped.

Tor'asion tutted. "You seem to have forgotten the bigger picture, Iss'aren. Vespiri is but the stepping-stone. Why not rule Elothia as well?"

"A stepping-stone for you, maybe," Iss'aren muttered under his breath as he glared around the table.

Tor'asion kept his face calm, controlling his spurt of annoyance. "We will capture the Lady's Captain, and he will unseal the Veil. He will come to us, never fear. I expect to hear of his arrival in Elothia any day now. Var'geris, return to Retarfu. You need to join Sul'enne and spend some time with the grand duke. He must be prepared for Haven's arrival. I will return to Old Vespers and ensure he performs as expected. The rest of you focus on the Veil. There must be a way in."

"If there was, we would have found it by now," one of the brothers murmured.

Tor'asion glared at Ain'uncer. "Focus on the towers; you know them well. There has to be a way in using the Watchers."

"You and Ain'uncer spent months there. Was your time as a scholar not well spent? Why return there now? What did you miss?" Iss'aren demanded, his face cold and cynical.

"I didn't miss anything," Tor'asion snapped. "The Captain woke the Watcher. He must be the key. We will return the Captain to the towers, and he will shred the Veil. Make sure we are in control when we do."

"What about the Sentinals? We have one now; what have you found out? You've spent enough time with him." Ain'uncer glared at Tor'asion.

Tor'asion grimaced, flexing his hands in memory.

Ain'uncer was still smarting from his close call at the Watch Towers. His fight with the Sentinal still rankled. Birlerion had nearly killed him, he had held off a unit of King's Rangers and then he had fought Ain'uncer, determined to protect his Captain. Ain'uncer had only survived because Tor'asion had helped drag the Sentinal away.

"They are troublesome and difficult to overcome. They seem immune to *Mentiserium*. It has no effect. Birlerion even resists Var'geris, but he is weak; he can't hold out forever."

"It takes too long. This Birlerion wasn't the one we wanted. We don't have time for this," Ain'uncer argued.

Tor'asion scowled. "I know. Jerrol is the key, and he is the only one we need alive. If Var'geris can work his magic, maybe we can use Birlerion to trap him."

Iss'aren stood. "Is that it? The Kirshans have failed to capture the Captain; you had him in your hands, and *you* failed. What makes you think you can force Haven to do what we need this time, even if you *do* trap him?"

Tor'asion stood tall. "He will pay for the loss of our brothers, but he has weaknesses like all men. If you play your parts, Remargaren will be ours! The time approaches: our ancestors will return and take up their rightful position, and we will all bathe in their glory."

"You had better make sure your plan works this time, Tor'asion," Ain'uncer bit out. "Our ancestors grow impatient. We have one chance at this. Don't fail."

"I won't," Tor'asion said, his black eyes glittering as he watched his brothers leave to do his bidding.

3

KING'S PALACE, OLD VESPERS, VESPIRI

Jerrol Haven, Captain of the Lady's Guard, Commander of the King's Justice and Keeper of the Oath sat behind his desk and eyed the large pile of paper awaiting his attention. He had forgotten the amount of paperwork that went with a desk job. If anything were to drive him back into the field, it would be the paperwork for sure.

He pulled the pile towards him and began sorting it into priorities. Without thinking, he reached for the quill and came up short as it slipped out of his remaining fingers. His right hand was strapped in bandages, concealing the damage. He flexed his hand, and the skin pulled tight against the stumps of two of his fingers. A reminder of his last run in with the Ascendants. He would not forget the Ascendant called Ain'uncer, who had attacked him and mutilated his right hand.

Healer Francis would be nagging him to exercise his hand more. With a huff of frustration, he stooped and picked up the quill in his left hand. It just didn't feel right. He wondered if his sword would feel any better. He stood, awkwardly drawing his sword. He would have to get his aide, Jenkins, to adjust the belt to his right hip.

Jerrol gripped his sword in his left hand. The grip fit perfectly and it vibrated gently in his hand. He just didn't have enough strength to feel in control. He needed to strengthen his left side in general; he would learn to be as good with his left as he had been with his right, he vowed to himself.

Sheathing the sword, he sat and considered its previous owner. Guerlaire had been the Lady's Captain before him. He had been lost with Lady Leyandrii nearly three thousand years ago when she had sundered the Bloodstone and banished all magic from the world, including herself and her family.

Leyandrii had bestowed the sword on Guerlaire, and Guerlaire had passed it to him. Only he had lost it at the Watch Towers. Ain'uncer had taken it along with two of his fingers. He was fortunate that Leyandrii had returned the sword to him; pity she couldn't do the same for his fingers or his Sentinals.

The loss of two of his Sentinals shivered through him and he stilled as the guilt roiled in his stomach. Not only had he lost his Sentinals, but also his good friend and mentor, Scholar Torsion, who had been studying the records at the Watch Towers with Taelia. Jerrol had been so focused on rescuing Taelia, he hadn't spared a thought for Torsion. Why the Ascendants had taken him, Jerrol didn't know.

Deliberately, he turned his thoughts to Taelia, and sliding his hand into his pocket, he felt the ring he had purchased. He imagined her beautiful face with those brilliant turquoise eyes brimming with love just for him. He still couldn't get over the fact that she felt the same way about him as he felt about her. Just thinking about her eased his tension. He needed to hold her; she seemed to alleviate all his worries when she was near. Unfortunately, she was tucked away down at the Chapterhouse in the city. He needed to find time to see her.

Heaving a deep sigh, he returned to his paperwork. Ten minutes later, he cursed and threw the quill across the room. It skittered across the floor and out his open door. It was impossible. His writing had never been particularly neat, but now it was illegible, a spidery crawl across the paper.

At the sight of the quill, Niallerion, the Sentinal on guard by the door, left his post and peered into Jerrol's dim office. Only a small window, high in the wall let in the light. The rest of the walls were covered in maps of the countries of Remargaren.

"Is everything alright, Captain?" Niallerion asked. His silver-green uniform, identifying him as a Sentinal as if his silver eyes weren't proof enough, shimmered as he stood in the doorway. A vacant desk stood in the brightly lit outer office behind him, awaiting Jerrol's assigned aide, Private Deron.

Narrowing his eyes, Jerrol rose. "I think it's time Private Deron took up his duties," he said as Niallerion backed out of the doorway. He needed a scribe, an aide, and he needed him now. He had expected young Deron to be fit for duty by now.

Deron had been struggling to cope with the life-altering injury he had suffered defending the palace a few months before. Jerrol had been keeping an eye on him since he had returned from his own life-altering experience in his defence of the nomadic people of Terolia and the subsequent ambush at the Watch Towers. He needed hands, not legs to help him, and Deron had two of those.

He crossed the open space of the outer office, and Niallerion took position behind his shoulder. The thin, dark-haired Sentinal guarded him religiously, and although Jerrol trusted him, he missed Birlerion. There had been something reassuring about having Birlerion behind his shoulder, but he had been lost at the Watch Towers, along with Serillion; two Sentinals lost when they had so few.

Jerrol tried to recall what he knew about Niallerion as he left his office and walked around the outer walls of the palace towards the parade ground. Niallerion was one of Birlerion's contemporaries; one of his friends. Birlerion had constantly wished for him to be found, wanting his keen intelligence to help solve their difficulties.

Remembering a rare evening in the Terolian desert when he had actually been able to talk to his Sentinals, he cast a quick glance over his shoulder. "Have you figured out that onoff yet?"

Niallerion wrinkled his brow and huffed. "Birlerion was right. There is no solution; it is pure energy."

"Well, he did create it out of thin air."

"Still, everything should have an explanation, even magic."

"Did you all have magic like Birlerion?"

"No. Magic wasn't a skill you just picked up, it was inherent, though not everyone used it. I hadn't realised how much Birlerion could do."

Jerrol grimaced as his thoughts returned to the lost Sentinal. All the Sentinals were vocal in their belief that Birlerion lived, though he was out of reach in the hands of the Ascendants. Serillion, he had truly lost. He had died protecting Jerrol, and although Jerrol knew he was safe with the Lady, his loss still hurt. The Sentinals were also adamant that he should be more careful and should not be gallivanting around the countries of Remargaren without protection.

Since Jerrol's return to duty, Niallerion had appointed himself in Birlerion's place. Pale faced and gaunt looking from the recent events in Terolia, his uniform baggier than it should be, he was obviously tougher than he looked.

As they walked around the building, the newly arrived sentinal trees came into view. They towered over the barracks. The smooth silver trunks gleamed in the bright sunshine, drawing the eye. They were majestic and ancient, and a reminder that the Lady Leyandrii hadn't left them completely unprotected.

"How are your trees settling in?" Jerrol asked.

"Fine. It was a short transfer from Marchwood. It's good to have them here. Quieter than the barracks." Niallerion's silver eyes were bright as he inspected his tree. "Marianille hasn't been so uptight since her tree arrived, so that is good."

Jerrol winced. "I wish I had better news for her, but we just don't know where to look for Birlerion."

"She knows that, really. It's just frustrating doing nothing. If it wasn't for Birlerion, she would be fine," Niallerion replied. "She is taking her frustration out on the rest of us. I recommend you do not go near the sparring ring; you won't come out again."

Jerrol laughed. "I'm glad to see she hasn't run out of opponents."

"No chance. The guards have got a book running as to who will land the first blow. No one's succeeded yet."

Jerrol grimaced. Nor would they, he was sure. Birlerion had often said that his brother, Tagerill, crackled with energy; his sister Marianille was no different. She was a force to be reckoned with, and her anger at not being able to find her brother was honing her skill; making her deadly. *Lady protect the fool who underestimates her.*

Rubbing his face, Jerrol led the way across the parade ground towards the infirmary. He was still amazed when he thought about the fact that he had awoken these men and women from a three thousand-year-long sleep and recruited them back into the Lady's Guard. They were all tall, silver-eyed and very well trained, if a little enthusiastic on occasion. They had a presence about them; you noticed when they were around, *and when they are absent*, he thought ruefully, and it wasn't just because of their height, which towered over his measly five feet whatever.

The Sentinals he had awoken were still adjusting to the new Remargaren. A lot had changed in three thousand years. Their families and friends had lived and died a long time ago. It was impossible to imagine what they were going through, and yet they had sworn allegiance to the king and picked up where they had left off. At least they knew about the Ascendants and the powers they had; information that Jerrol badly needed.

Arriving at the infirmary, Jerrol paused in the doorway and watched the healer's assistant, Mathieu, trying to encourage a very young-looking private to take a few steps using a pair of wooden crutches. The boy didn't look old enough to be a soldier. He had messy straw-coloured hair and his skin was the washed-out complexion of a convalescent. His balance was all over the place, and he was twisting his body unnaturally to compensate for the lack of his left leg.

Murmuring to Niallerion to remain outside, Jerrol stepped through the doorway. "Private, you look like you've been drinking too much," he said as he approached. He prodded the boy's gut. "Tighten up your core. You're all over the place."

The private instinctively straightened as Jerrol entered. Letting go of his crutch, he tried to salute and overbalanced into Jerrol's arms. Jerrol steadied him while Mathieu retrieved the crutch. "Forget the salutes, private. I will understand, alright?"

"Yes, sir," Deron replied, blushing crimson. He straightened up, pulling in his stomach.

"That's right; you control your body, not the other way around." Jerrol glanced at Mathieu, who was watching closely. "My aide is derelict in his duty. I was expecting him at his desk this morning. Is there any medical reason why he can't come with me now?"

"He needs to keep practicing with the crutches. As you say, he needs to build strength in his core; otherwise, he is fit for office duty," Mathieu replied.

Jerrol grinned wryly and waved his bandaged hand. "I need someone who can write and you don't need legs for that. Come with me, private. Your duty awaits you."

"Yes, sir," the private gasped, and gripping his crutches, he stomped after him, Niallerion close behind.

Mathieu turned as Healer Francis entered the main room of the infirmary. He gave Francis a grin. "At last, I thought we'd never winkle him out."

Francis nodded thoughtfully. "Keep an eye on both of them. Make sure they don't overdo it; the commander especially."

Mathieu grimaced in agreement and left the infirmary to follow them down the corridor. They made slow progress, Jerrol adjusting his stride and explaining what he needed as they crossed the parade ground. Deron perked up, his eyes bright with interest.

By the time they neared Jerrol's office, Deron was faltering, and steadying himself against the palace wall. Jerrol smiled at him. "Well done, lad. We'll build up your stamina, don't worry."

"About that." Mathieu stepped forward. "Slow and steady both of you, don't overdo it. Commander, make sure you and the private report into Healer Francis every day."

Jerrol grinned. "Yes sir," he said with a mock salute.

"I mean it. You don't want Healer Francis tracking you down."

Jerrol shuddered. "Not if he's anything like Healer Tyrone from Stoneford," he said in a conspiratorial whisper to Deron.

"Well, then, you've been warned."

"Yes, yes, I am sure you have more important things to be doing than harassing us," Jerrol said, shooing him away.

Mathieu laughed and left them to it.

"Right," Jerrol said, "this is your desk." He waited for Deron to manoeuvre himself behind the desk and into the chair. Leaving him to sort out his crutches, Jerrol entered his inner office. He swept the papers up from his desk and returned to drop them on Deron's. He stooped and picked up the quill from the floor. "Only I am allowed to throw quills. Please make sure there is a sharpened quill on my desk every morning; a chore I am currently incapable of performing." Jerrol held up his hand, a touch of frustration in his face.

Deron nodded. "Yes, sir."

"This lot needs sorting into categories and priority. Priority one is messages from the king; the chancellor, Prince Anders; or Commander Nikols; priority two is messages from the watches; three is personnel; four is requisitions and so on. Once you've sorted them, we'll go through them together, and you can get an idea of how to manage them. Eventually, I expect you to answer the majority of requests and only escalate those items that you can't answer or I need to deal with. If in doubt, ask; there is no wrong question, alright? Corporal Jenkins will deliver any messages for you until you get your strength up."

"Yes, sir," Deron said, casting a wary eye at the tall Sentinal standing guard by the door.

"Ah yes, this is Sentinal Niallerion. You'll meet the other Sentinals over time."

Niallerion grinned, and shifted the broadsword strapped across his back. Deron's eyes widened and then returned to Jerrol.

"Good, call if you need me." Jerrol returned to his office and sat behind his empty desk.

He reached for Zin'talia, his Darian mare. They were bonded mind to mind, and he missed her snippy comments. Stretching his mind out as far as he could, he searched for her, but it was just an echoing emptiness, their telepathic connection silent. The Ascendants had absconded from the Watch Towers not only with Birlerion but with her as well; they had much to answer for. Jerrol rubbed his temples in frustration. Where had they taken them?

Jerrol was frowning at the wall when the private stomped back into his office, a bunch of papers scrunched up in his hand as he gripped his crutches.

"Sir, these documents need your immediate attention," Deron said as he sat in the chair in front of Jerrol's desk, drawing the commander's attention away from the wall as his crutches clattered to the floor. Deron winced, and then leaned forward, pointing at the papers as he began to ask his questions. They worked their way through the documents discussing options. Occasionally Jerrol dictated responses. They were interrupted by Corporal Jenkins poking his head around the door.

"Beggin' yer pardon, sir, but I've been instructed to advise you that it's lunchtime," he said with a swift grin as he prepared to leave.

"Jenkins, stay a moment," Jerrol said, easing his shoulders. Jenkins was his latest recruit. The corporal had helped rescue Jerrol from the Watch Towers and had subsequently assigned himself as the commander's aide, probably to make sure Jerrol did as he was told. He was surrounded by mother hens. He smiled at the thought.

Jenkins quirked an eyebrow at him. "Yes, sir."

"I want you to run as messenger for me. Deron has the missives. I want you to observe how they are received and whether there is an immediate response or not. Do you think you can do that?"

"Of course, sir," Jenkins responded.

Jerrol nodded. "Excellent," he said, turning to Deron. "Time for lunch as the good man says. Come on." He rose and waited as Deron retrieved his crutches and offering a hand helped lever the boy upright.

"Get some lunch, Niallerion. You need feeding up; you still look far too thin. I am not going to be attacked in the dining hall," Jerrol said sharply as Niallerion began to protest. He was still arguing with Niallerion as they approached the hall.

Deron hung back as they approached the door.

"Stout heart," Jerrol murmured. "Most will treat you as a hero, glad to have you back."

Deron swallowed and entered the hall, head held high. There was a general hum of conversation and the clatter of crockery as they made their way down the hall. Long wooden tables crossed the room, leaving a walkway down the centre and at either end. The serving hatches lined the far wall, the kitchens behind them.

Jerrol scanned the tables looking for familiar faces, but he was preempted by a gruff voice off to his right. "Bob, lad, I'm glad to see you up. Come join us."

Deron's face lit up. "Sarge. Where are you sitting?"

"Over here, lad." The man stiffened as he saw the commander beside him. "Sir." He saluted.

Jerrol nodded. "At ease, sergeant. Carry on, private. I'll see you later."

"Yes, sir."

Jerrol continued into the room as the men crowded around Deron; they seemed to be in good spirits. Jerrol tried to avoid the men's eyes so they wouldn't have to acknowledge him; he had forgotten how awkward it was as you rose up the ranks. Maybe he would lunch in his office going forward.

He grabbed a tray and selected a spoon and a bowl of soup. Eyeing the bread, he selected a couple of pieces and, balancing the tray, he made his way to the officer's table. He slid his tray onto the table and went back and helped himself to a mug of tea before returning to his seat.

Deron was being joshed by his mates. Colour stained his cheeks as he accepted their rough offers of help more gracefully than he would have accepted Jerrol's. Jerrol drank his soup and gnawed his bread, resting his right hand in his lap under the table.

"Would you like some company?" Healer Francis asked as he slid his tray onto the table.

"Please." Bread still in hand, Jerrol gestured to the seat beside him.

"I hope you are eating more than a bowl of soup," Healer Francis said as he made himself more comfortable.

"I was debating about what to have. Everything needs cutting up," Jerrol admitted. "I'll be glad when this is off." He waved his bandaged hand under the healer's nose.

The healer peered at him over his glasses and nodded. "Come see me this afternoon, and we'll take a look. Well done with Deron by the way. Just what he needed, a purpose."

Jerrol grinned. "It was pure selfishness. I need someone to write for me. No one can read my scrawl." He stood and returned to the serving line, selecting a second course.

Plumping for the chicken, chops being beyond him, he balanced the tray and returned to his table.

"Chop the meat up for me, would you?" he asked Francis, who wordlessly leant over and cut everything up for him.

"Thanks," Jerrol murmured as he stabbed a piece of chicken with his fork.

Deron observed the commander from his seat in the hall. He watched him struggling with his tray and accepting help, yet it didn't diminish his authority. Every man in the hall was aware that the Commander of the King's Justice was in the room. His difficulties only made him more human. It didn't lessen him or the awe the men felt.

Deron mused over the fact that although the commander was not particularly tall, nor imposing, there was a presence about him. Only his silver eyes that gleamed in the dim hall, like the other Sentinals, marked him as different. He kept having to push his floppy brown hair out of his eyes, but there the difference ended. Deron struggled to identify any other noteworthy feature; he looked normal, nondescript, all except for the eyes.

Twisting his lips, Deron grimaced. And the uniform of course. The silver green jacket of the Lady's Guard, which all Sentinals wore, shimmered as he moved, catching the eye. Maybe it was the archaic-looking uniform that drew attention instead of the man. He wondered idly why the commander wasn't in the colours of the King's Guards.

One of his mates slid a tray in front of him and he relaxed as he began to eat.

When Deron stomped his way back to his desk, the commander was deep in conversation with Lieutenant-Commander Bryce, his deputy. They were arguing over a piece of paper on the desk between them. The stocky officer was well respected in the palace, having stepped into the commander's duties when the commander had been sent off on the mission to Terolia by the king. Bryce was a career soldier, originating in Stoneford Watch and had relocated to Vespers at the commander's request.

Deron discreetly observed them. Compared to Bryce, who was the epitome of a military officer, smart and fit, the commander looked washed out. Lines of strain were apparent on his face; his cheekbones were prominent, and dark shadows like bruises curved beneath his silver eyes.

Bryce had obviously come to a similar conclusion as Deron heard him say, "Jerrol, don't overdo it. You can't solve all our problems in one day."

"I know; there is just so much that needs to be done."

"And we'll get it done between us, but not if you make yourself ill."

"Don't. I already have Francis breathing down my neck. And anyway, only I can wake the Sentinals in East Watch. They have waited long enough while I recuperated. There is no reason to delay any longer. I know what I'm capable of."

"That's what *I* said, but now I know better. Fortunately, I have Olivia to keep me sensible, but what about *you*, Jerrol? Where's Taelia? You need her beside you."

"I know, but she's busy in the Chapterhouse. I'll see her, don't worry."

Bryce stood. "Make sure you do. You have to make time for yourself in all of this chaos."

Deron concentrated on his work and began copying out the responses the commander had dictated. He would help alleviate the pressure on the commander in any way he could. Jenkins was soon running all over the palace and into the city of Old Vespers.

.   .   .

Jerrol's thoughts returned to Birlerion as Bryce left, a constant worry at the back of his mind. It had been three weeks since he had disappeared, taking the Ascendants with him. Birlerion's actions were the only reason Jerrol was alive today, and his mouth tightened at the thought of what he might be suffering through, but without knowing where he was, there was little he could do.

He flexed his hand again, thankful that Chryllion's sentinal tree had healed the worst of the injury whilst he had been recovering in Stoneford, but he still needed to strengthen his grip and toughen the skin.

His ruminations were interrupted by the arrival of Adilion, one of the younger Sentinals Jerrol had awoken in Terolia; though they were all over three thousand years old. Adilion had broken his collarbone as they had tried to help some enslaved Terolians escape a collapsing mine. Reporting back for duty, he was eager to help. He looked fresh and healthy, his silver eyes bright in his deep brown face. Like most of the Sentinals, he seemed to fill the office. His height and breadth took up all the space, along with his enthusiasm.

Jerrol was glad of the interruption. "Before you join the roster, I need you to go to Mistra and warn Maraine and Kayerille about possible retaliations. I think any threats will just be posturing, a distraction to try and divide our forces, but we need to make sure they stay alert just in case."

Adilion nodded, his blue-black curls bouncing. "Do you want me to stop off at Marchwood and check the nursery?"

"No, don't worry, I will be going there. You can travel with us as far as the border if you want; we'll be leaving in the morning." Jerrol watched the eager young Sentinal leave and turned his thoughts to the Watch Towers. Who should he send up there? He ran through the list of available Sentinals; there were so few. He called in Niallerion, who was still standing guard outside his office.

"I need a Sentinal guard for the Watch Towers, do you think Darllion would go? Who would you recommend?" he asked, frowning over the map on his desk.

"If Tianerille and Venterion are recovered, I would recommend them. Without Birlerion to advise us, Marianille ought to stay in Vespers. She was one of those closest to the Lady. She can advise the king."

Jerrol pursed his lips considering his options. "I'll speak to them tomorrow, good idea." As he returned to his paper-work, Niallerion drifted back to his post.

Marianille was not only the sister of Birlerion, but also two other Sentinals; Tagerill and Versillion, and she was proving to be as astute and as skilled as her brothers were. Elegant and poised, she fit into the king's court with ease and was as different to her brothers as she could be. She was tall, slender and undeniably beautiful. Her strength was fluid and hidden, and she wielded the broadsword as easily, if not better than the men.

Jerrol had been surprised to find out that she was older than Tagerill and Birlerion and had graduated from the rangers two years before them. She was relentless in her belief that Birlerion still lived, and Jerrol clung to her convic-tion; her assurance was solace to the guilt he felt, having led Birlerion into an ambush. She was also the most vocal in the need to search for Birlerion, not that there was any resistance to the request; they just didn't know where to search.

4

SENTINAL BARRACKS, OLD VESPERS

J errol woke, stuffing his fist in his mouth to stop the screams. The cool night air pressed in on him, drying his sweat as he lay panting, listening to the echoes of his shouts fading into the night. Had anyone heard him? His nightmares were getting worse. The images from the Terolian mines invaded his mind; the people he had sentenced to death, their pleading eyes turning to accusation and drilling into his skull. Twisted sheets trapped him and his heart rate spiked as he tried to unravel them.

Unclenching his fist, he raised his palm, allowing the glow from the shards of the bloodstone he had absorbed to illuminate his room and banish the darkness and the remnants of his dream. He controlled his breathing, thinking about Leyandrii, the goddess who had originally sundered the bloodstone to protect the world of Remargaren, who was guiding him to find the fragments. He had found two, which now resided within him and enabled him to create a silvery flame in his hand, but there was one more piece to find.

Extinguishing the light, he rose and dressed and then, silently, made his way through the corridors. Marianille, the Sentinal on night duty, followed, watching him with concern, which eased as she realised their destination as they crossed the shadowy parade ground. The night was dark and thick; no moon tonight.

Jerrol acknowledged the salutes of the roving guards as they passed and entered the infirmary. A small light burned in the office at the end, and he hoped it would be Francis on duty.

Healer Francis looked up from the book he was reading as Jerrol hovered in his doorway. His sharp eyes inspected Jerrol for a moment. "Commander, please have a seat. I was just making some tea," he said as he put his book down and rose. Jerrol sat, head bent, staring at his hands as Francis pottered about. He placed a mug in front of Jerrol and sat back down in his chair.

"Tell me."

Jerrol sighed and raised his head. Where to begin? Thoughts and images tumbled in his mind. "I went to Terolia, searching for Sentinals to wake and to prevent the Ascendants from destabilising the Families," Jerrol began. He rambled on about the Ascendants' mind control techniques and the increasingly deserted villages. Francis let him talk until, finally, Jerrol faltered to a stop. "We found the mines."

"What did you find at the mines?" Francis prompted.

"What I found was worse than death." Jerrol closed his eyes. Francis was about to prompt him again when Jerrol continued. "I can't get their faces out of my head. It's their eyes. I've never seen such despair, and I couldn't help them." Jerrol stared bleakly at the mug in front of him, not seeing it as the memories from the mines overwhelmed him and the anguish at his failure to save the people clawed at his innards. Bitter tears welled and he blinked them away.

Taking a deep breath, Jerrol continued speaking, his voice low. "There were hundreds of them. I've never seen so many desperate people. They must have been clearing the villages for years, replacing people as they died. Their own people," Jerrol exclaimed, anger colouring his voice. "They enslaved their own people and treated them worse than animals, and all for what? To dig up dirt.

"They had them digging day and night, even though there was nothing to find. They sent children down narrow shafts, in baskets, expecting them to dig while hanging at the end of a rope in the dark. The people," Jerrol paused, his voice failing, "they were emaciated; men, women, children; you could count their ribs. The children's bones were so fragile they could snap at the slightest touch." Jerrol gritted his teeth and pushed out the words. "I couldn't save them. Their eyes haunt me. Such despair, to be replaced by a flicker of hope, only for it to be snatched away at the last moment." His eyes filled with tears again. He wiped them away angrily.

"What happened to them?"

"We were overwhelmed; there were too many of them. A mass of despairing humanity, all deserving love and care, all deserving to live. It was like they were sucking the life out of us to replenish their meagre reserves. Not deliberately, don't get me wrong; they were desperate." Jerrol's voice cracked as he tried to control the emotions battering him. "We couldn't cope with them all." He leaned back in his chair, his face strained and drawn.

"The people were so weak and downtrodden, they only needed a skeleton guard." Jerrol laughed darkly, and Francis shivered at the lack of emotion in his voice. "A skeleton guard for a skeleton crew. We dealt with them." Jerrol shrugged as if they were of no concern. Then he dropped his head into his hands. "I instructed the Sentinals to keep those poor people in the caves. It was too hot outside; the heat of the sun would have had them dropping like flies. They were already dehydrated. I didn't even let them see the sky. That was all they wanted," he said to the floor, "but I was afraid we wouldn't be able to control them to get them back undercover. I deprived them of their one request."

"For good reason," Francis interjected.

"By what right did I stop them from standing outside in the sun? They were free. I had freed them. Some had never even seen the sun before, yet I still treated them as captives."

"You treated them with care, and you were trying to protect them; it was for their own good. Once they'd grown stronger, rehydrated, then they could go out," Francis said. "It is exactly what I would have recommended, had I been there."

"They never had the chance," Jerrol said, his voice low. "The Ascendants blew up the mines and buried most of them alive. We got some of the stronger ones out. They were helping us to cook up some gruel. I didn't think they would be able to eat anything more solid after all that time."

Francis nodded. "You know that not all of them would have survived? Malnutrition and heat are not a good combination; you were right to keep them out of the sun. You couldn't know that the Ascendants would blow up the mines. You didn't kill them. The Ascendants did."

"The screams." Jerrol swallowed as he looked up at the healer, strained and exhausted. Francis tightened his lips but let Jerrol continue speaking. "I can hear them screaming, over and over and over. Their voices cut through me; yet after the mountain collapsed, it was deadly silent; not a sound. So why do I hear them screaming?

"The mountain collapsed in on itself. We were fortunate that we had set up camp outside." Jerrol scrunched up his face and rubbed his temples. "The smell, you know—that much death stinks. I can still smell it now. They had fortunately become used to it and didn't notice. We should have got them out quicker. I should have helped them."

"Jerrol, you can't second guess yourself. You are not the monster; the Ascendants are. You provided the right help. They would have collapsed and probably died if you had let them out into the heat. It was better that they stayed in the mines. The sun would have damaged their eyes that were so used to the dark. Water was what they needed to begin with."

"Then why do they invade my dreams? Their eyes accusing me of failing them, reliving their suffering, their screams."

"Because you are a good man, Jerrol. You are horrified by the treatment of those people; most sane people would be. You empathised with their situation; you tried to help, and you thought you had saved them. Your reactions are normal; you've seen horrific things, suffered severe trauma. You feel their loss. Don't forget that you are grieving, for them and Serillion, for Birlerion. Compounded, it is amazing that you are still functioning at all. It takes time to get over traumatic events like that.

"You can't suppress your grief; it will just come out in other ways. Your brain is a tricky thing, very clever. The pressure must be released somewhere, otherwise you will do yourself more damage. The health of your mind is as important as your physical health, and you know that or you wouldn't be here talking to me now." Francis sat back in his chair and studied him. "Jerrol, don't take the blame for actions the Ascendants took or you'll do their work for them."

Jerrol lifted his head, startled.

Francis continued now that he had Jerrol's attention. "I remember once there was a terrible storm in Woodbridge, deep in the Marchwood Watch. That's where I originally came from. I was apprenticed to the Watch healer, just starting out. There was terrible flooding; trees down, whole villages washed away. We were overwhelmed," he said, deliberately using the same word Jerrol had. "We couldn't cope with the injured or the dead.

"The healer set up a triage. We had to decide who was worth treating and who we had to leave to die. There just weren't the people or the supplies. We saved who we could. That was when I first learnt the power that I would hold in my hands as a healer; power over who would live and who would die." He peered at Jerrol. "The people we put aside to die—their pain and anguish haunted me for many months, and then my teacher said to me: You are not all powerful, you are just a man, but a man with knowledge and some aptitude." Francis' lips quirked. "If you use it right, you can save many who would otherwise have died. I decided that saving some lives was better than saving none. You can't save everyone. Yes, it's terrible when someone dies, but we didn't cause it. It is not our fault. We must accept that we did our best.

"Hard lesson to learn, while not letting it dehumanise you. You must be able to help the next person. They deserve help just as much." Francis leaned forward, his eyes shining behind his glasses. "I am not belittling your grief; what you have seen I have never experienced, but you are not alone. You are never alone, and that is your strength. Share your grief, share your burden; you will be the stronger for it."

Jerrol heaved a big sigh and smiled tentatively at the healer. "Thank you," he said. "I mean it. Thank you, Francis."

The healer grinned. "Now, go back to bed and get some sleep, and let me get back to my book."

5

KING'S PALACE, OLD VESPERS

The next morning, Niallerion stood guard in the outer office. The commander's aide sat at his desk deep in some correspondence. Although Deron had been in awe of the Sentinals to begin with, he now routinely ignored the Sentinals keeping him company. Unless he was working himself up to ask them questions, which often were unexpectedly astute. Niallerion was sure it was because Deron found them fascinating.

"Why do you call the commander, Captain?" was Deron's question for today.

Niallerion grinned. "The Captain plays many roles in court; the king's claim on him is as his Commander of the King's Justice just as the Lady's claim is as her Captain of the Sentinals," he replied. "No matter what the king demands of him, he will always be the Lady's Captain."

"Is it true he annexed Terolia for the king? He just told them what to do and they obeyed him?"

"It was not so simple, but yes, King Benedict now rules Terolia," Niallerion said, staring out of the office window as the amusement drained from his expression.

Deron nodded, his gaze drawn to the Sentinal. Niallerion

stiffened under his inspection, wondering what he saw. Relief was uppermost in his mind when the Captain came out of his office, preventing what he was sure would have been another astute question.

Jerrol looked across at Deron. "We'll be down at the Chapterhouse."

Deron nodded as he left the office, heading for the stables, Niallerion in tow.

"What do you think of Old Vespers, so far?" Jerrol asked Niallerion as they walked around the building.

"It's alright; a bit crowded. Takes a bit of getting used to with so many people in one place."

"I suppose we've grown over time," Jerrol said.

"Not only that, the city is unrecognisable. Without the Lady's palace and the old Justice buildings, it is disorienting."

"Why do you suppose none of the buildings survived? I believe Vespers had to be rebuilt from the ground up."

"No idea," Niallerion said with a shrug.

Jerrol took the reins from Adilion, who was waiting by the horses, and swung himself up into the saddle of yet another borrowed mount. Niallerion watched as Jerrol's gaze grew distant. The Captain was searching for his Darian mare. From his frustrated expression, he still couldn't find her. The hope was that, if the Captain could contact her, she could tell him where the Ascendants had taken Birlerion and give them somewhere to head for. The Ascendants had stolen her away, along with half a unit of Kings Rangers and Birlerion. Niallerion sighed as he followed the Captain out of the palace courtyard with Adilion beside him.

They fell silent as they rode into the city, and Niallerion's thoughts moved onto the Sentinals that the Captain had woken in Terolia. Eleven more Sentinals to bolster those he had woken in Vespiri, but still a fraction of the number there were supposed to be. His gaze swept the surrounding fields, pausing on a sudden movement. He relaxed as a roosting bird took flight and continued his inspection of the unfamiliar landscape. His gut tightened at the sight of Old Vespers. Nothing looked as it should, and they were too few of them to be able to spend the time learning it anew.

Jerrol pulled up beside the gate to the Lady's temple. "I won't be a moment," he said, slipping off his horse and entering the gardens where Birlerion's sentinal arched over the Lady's temple. The sentinal tree stood tall and proud, silver bark gleaming, crowned by emerald green pointy leaves. This was the tree that had sheltered Birlerion for over three thousand years, suspended in sleep until Jerrol had awoken him. He lay his hand against the smooth trunk, and the bark warmed beneath his palm. *"I am so sorry. We are searching for him. I promise I won't stop until I find him."*

The tree shuddered under his palm, and Jerrol had a brief impression of utter despair and loss. He took a deep breath as he tried to discern whether it was the tree's feelings or whether the tree was sharing what Birlerion was experiencing. *"Do you know where he is?"*

There was a succession of impressions; a stormy sea, grey stone, darkness and despair, and cold, a bone-chilling cold that sapped the energy, and then more darkness, impenetrable and consuming.

Jerrol removed his hand and stood back, shaken. A sense of urgency ran through him. Birlerion needed help, and he needed it now. He patted the tree. *"We'll find him, I promise."* He reached for Zin'talia again, the bark warming under his hand in acknowledgement as he searched the vaults of his mind, extending himself further. *"Zin'talia? Where are you? If you don't hurry up, I'm going to find another horse."*

"*Don't even think of it*," she gasped in his mind, horrified, her voice faint. "*Jerrol? I'm coming.*"

"*Zin'talia? Thank the Lady. I've been so worried. Where are you?*"

"*I'm coming. I'm up near Ramila. They tried to get me on a boat, but I told She'vanne there was no way I was going north. It's too cold.*"

"*Is Torsion with you? What about Birlerion?*"

"*Torsion managed to escape, I think. I don't know where they went, but they hurt Birlerion, Jerrol. They hurt him bad. They were so angry with him. They blamed him for you escaping. I was so relieved you got away. Are you alright?*"

"*I'm fine. Worried about you.*"

Zin'talia snorted in his head. "*Those shepakes. They couldn't hold me. How dare they try! She'vanne said Birlerion wouldn't survive the night, but he did.*"

Jerrol's stomach clenched at the thought. "*Do you know where they took him?*"

"*They had a boat at Amsar, but where they went, I don't know.*"

"*Be careful, Zin'talia. I'll send Adilion to meet you in Ramila.*"

"*Alright, I'll meet him there.*"

He strode back to his horse and led him round to the Chapterhouse courtyard. Jerrol paused by Adilion's stirrup. "Once you've found the Atolea and spoken to Medera Maraine, I want you to meet Zin'talia. She is north of Ramila. I need you to bring her home through the waystone."

"Of course," Adilion murmured.

Jerrol ran a hand through his hair and stared up at the two Sentinals. "If you had a boat at Amsar, where would you go? North is the logical direction, isn't it? Into Elothia?"

Adilion nodded.

"Elothia," Jerrol murmured under his breath as the Sentinals watched him, somewhat bemused. Realising the Sentinals were staring at him, he grimaced. "I'll only be half a chime," he promised as Adilion raised his eyebrows in surprise.

Jerrol crossed the cloisters and entered the Chapterhouse building, Niallerion close behind him. Jerrol smiled at the Duty-Scholar on the door. "Could you tell me where I might find Scholar Taelia?"

"At this time of day, she'll be in the lower chambers," the doorman replied.

Jerrol nodded his thanks and led the way deeper into the building.

Behind him, Niallerion released a dejected sigh. "I still can't believe so many of Guerlaire's records have been lost. He thought he was protecting them, building these archives."

"They may still be preserved. It just takes time to dig them out."

"They haven't reached the main floor yet; these are just reception rooms and study booths."

Jerrol led the way through the dim corridors until they reached the stone stairs that led down to the lower chambers. "I thought Darllion gave them a map?"

"He did, but there are processes to follow, apparently."

Jerrol scowled. "Maybe I should fall into a few more chambers and speed them up." He paused at the bottom of the steps as candlelight softened the grey stone chamber. "Tali," he whispered as he saw her; a slight, young woman dressed in the silver robes of a scholar, with a mass of cloudy, brown curls. Crossing the room, she was in his arms before she could reply, and she relaxed into his embrace.

"Jerrol," she breathed as he loosened his grip.

"I'm sorry, I shouldn't assume you feel ..."

"Hush," Taelia interrupted him. "Yes, you should. I've missed you. The king needs to allow you more free time; a girl could get jealous," she murmured against his lips, kissing whichever part of his face she could reach.

"I've missed you too," he said, sighing into her hair. Breathing in deeply, he relaxed. The tension that had been singing through his veins melting away.

Reluctantly, she leaned back and raised her head from his chest. "I've been expecting you. I had a dream."

Jerrol tensed. Her dreams tended to mean more than other people's dreams.

"I dreamt I was in a strange palace, and I was waiting ... for you."

"For me?"

"Yes, you asked me to wait for you, and I said I would wait for as long as you needed me to; forever, if need be." She smiled up at him and kissed his chin.

"Tali." Jerrol cleared his throat, which was suddenly croaky with nerves. He tightened his embrace and her smile faded.

"Yes?"

"Tali, will you join with me?" he asked in a rush. "I love you so much; you are the only person who keeps me sane."

She smiled in delight, scattering kisses over his face. "Yes, yes, yes," she replied as she hugged him tight and then kissed him again.

Jerrol couldn't stop the grin that spread over his face at her response as he rummaged in his pocket. "Here," he said as he slipped a twisted gold band onto her finger. "Two strands of gold entwined forever around a gem the colour of your beautiful eyes, and a silver pearl the colour of mine."

"Oh," Taelia sighed, her brilliant eyes brimming with tears. "I wish I could see it."

"Don't cry, sweetheart, just know that I'm always with you." Gently, he wiped away her tears and then he hugged her close, relieved that she had said yes.

"I've always known that."

"I have to go to Marchwood, but when I return, I expect you to have picked the date."

"If I had my way, it would be here and now," she said. "It's the only way I can guarantee it will happen before the king sends you off again."

Jerrol grinned and kissed her nose. "I doubt he'll send me anywhere. I'm on light duties, remember?"

"You're off to Marchwood. Riding all the way there isn't light duties."

"Well, it's not particularly heavy-duty; we're using the waystones."

"Rather you than me. Make sure you visit on the way back. I expect my future husband to be very attentive."

"Ah, I see my chosen wife is going to be very demanding." Basking in the warm glow of her love, he looked down into her sparkling blue eyes, which sadly couldn't see him, and he hugged her tight. Not wanting to leave her, he breathed in the scent of hair again; finally, he was where he belonged. Niallerion shifted on the steps behind them and Jerrol sighed. "I have to go."

Taelia smiled and cupped his face in her hands. "I'll let you leave as long as you come back to me."

"I will always come back to you; I promise," Jerrol said.

"Good." She kissed him. "You're mine. It's taken you long enough to realise it, but we belong together. I'll be waiting!"

"The sooner I go, the sooner I return."

"I suppose so."

He grinned, seeing the same reluctance in her expressive face that he felt. He kissed her once more, easing back as the kiss deepened. If he didn't leave now, he wouldn't be able to. Turning back towards the stairs, he saw the wide grin on Niallerion's face; a reflection of the smile on his own face, he was sure. He tried to straighten his expression but failed, dismally.

"Congratulations, Captain. Congratulations, Taelia," Niallerion called as he backed up the steps.

Taelia laughed, her face glowing, and Jerrol's grin widened as he mounted the steps behind the tall Sentinal.

6

CHAPTERHOUSE, OLD VESPERS

Adilion raised an eyebrow at Niallerion as the grinning Sentinal returned with a much happier-looking Captain. "Well?" he murmured as the Captain wordlessly took his horse and led it out of the court-yard. Niallerion winked as he followed.

The waystone, an ancient magical portal enabling instant transportation between one place and another, was situated behind the Chapterhouse and obscured by a small copse of trees. A soft chime resonated through Jerrol's body as he approached. He hesitated remembering the day Birlerion had created it, and his chest tightened. Considering that he had only known Birlerion a few months, memories of his missing Sentinal surrounded him. He stiffened as Niallerion gripped his arm.

"Captain?"

"It's nothing," Jerrol replied.

He was prevented from entering the waystone by the arrival of an excited mackerel-striped Arifel. The small fluffy creature was a cross between a kitten and a lizard with wings, and it fluttered around Jerrol's head. Jerrol coaxed the little creature down, and Ari perched on his arm, chittering with excitement, his thin scaly tail wrapped around Jerrol's wrist.

"What is it?" Images of the Watch Towers and his friend, Scholar Torsion, filled his mind. "Torsion? Has he arrived at the towers?" Jerrol asked, his knees wobbling as relief rushed through him. Throat suddenly tight, he ducked his face into the Arifel's fur. "Is he alright?" he asked. Some good news at last.

Ari chittered, and new images of Torsion falling off his horse and the guards helping him up passed before his eyes. The weary scholar didn't look too steady on his feet.

Jerrol cuddled the little Arifel as he considered. "Adilion, go and ask the duty scholar to send a message to the palace. Advise them that we are going to Stoneford and won't be back until tomorrow. Then go to Marchwood and collect Tianerille and Venterion; explain that Torsion has arrived at the towers, and I'm hoping he has news of Birlerion. After I've woken the Sentinals in East Watch, Niallerion and I will waystone to Stoneford, meet us there and we'll go on to the towers together."

Decision made, Jerrol released the Arifel and stepped through the waystone. The instant transition from one place to another, which upset most people's stomachs, no longer affected him, and he stepped out into East Watch with Niallerion at his shoulder.

Jerrol passed Niallerion his reins and approached the majestic sentinal trees, still amazed that the Lady's Guards had slept within them for so many years. Memories of his first meeting with Birlerion all those months ago in Old Vespers shivered through him, and he reached out to touch the bark of the first tall sentinal tree, standing proudly beside the manor house. A stocky man stepped out blinking in the brilliant sunlight. His alert silver gaze took in his surroundings and his tense shoulders relaxed.

Jerrol could wake them without difficulty now, though Royerion and Generille were the last Sentinals he knew of in Vespiri. Royerion's black hair and hooked nose reminded Jerrol of the swarthy Terolians from the neighbouring country, but his face was a pale brown and creased with lines and wrinkles; here was a man who was used to being out in the sun.

"Royerion." Jerrol held out his hand.

"Captain, welcome to East Watch."

"Welcome home." Jerrol released Royerion's hand and reached to touch the second sentinal, and a beautiful woman shimmered out.

Generille's smooth complexion was framed by long blonde hair, and her brilliant silver eyes sparkled as her face relaxed into a smile. "Captain, I'm so glad to meet you. Lord Marcus has been keeping us advised. We've been expecting you." She hugged him before turning to embrace Royerion. She kissed him soundly before linking her arm through his. "You need to get out in the sun, my love. You're looking peaky."

Royerion grunted in response.

Generille glanced around her and spotted Niallerion beside the horses. With a yell of *Niallerion!* She ran across the courtyard.

Jerrol smiled as he watched their reunion, their happiness infectious. Jerrol and Royerion walked over to join them. "It's so good to have you both here. I'm sorry it's taken me so long."

"I heard you've been kept busy," Royerion said as he strode forward and gripped Niallerion's arm. "Niallerion. You need to eat more, lad."

Jerrol grinned as Niallerion rolled his eyes.

Lord Marcus appeared at the top of the steps, drawn by the commotion. He was a middle-aged man, short in stature but fit and competent. Marcus paused at the top of the steps and grinned at the gathering of distinctive Sentinals before him. "I don't think I've ever seen so many Sentinals in one place. Welcome to you all." He picked out his Sentinals without hesitation. "Generille, my dear, welcome to East Watch, and Royerion, you are both very welcome. We have been eagerly awaiting this day."

Generille flew up the steps and hugged the surprised man. "Guardian, finally! We are so glad to meet you. Royerion, come up here, quick."

Royerion grinned at the lord as he approached, shaking hands more sedately. "Thank you for your welcome. We look forward to assisting you with the security of your Watch."

"Your help will be greatly appreciated. There is a lot to do. Please join me; I was just working in my study."

Jerrol smiled. "I'll leave you to it. Niallerion and I need to travel up to the Watch Towers; we hope for news of Birlerion." He looked around the smiling faces, all of which grew grave at the mention of the lost Sentinal. "With you two awoken, that gives us all the Sentinals we know of in Vespiri." His smile faded. "So many lost."

"We will work together, Captain. We will be enough," Royerion said. "We will work with the others and secure Terolia. We are familiar with the Families of old. I doubt much has changed. And if it has, we will learn." He gripped Jerrol's arm. "Leave it with us. Find Birlerion and deal with the Ascendants once and for all."

Jerrol gripped his arm in return and nodded before leading the way back to the East Watch waystone and taking a deep breath he stepped forward. He walked out of the Stoneford Waystone and Niallerion stepped out behind him.

Jason, the grey-haired Lord of Stoneford Watch, and his Sentinals were waiting for them. Jason gave him a sharp inspection before pulling him into a hug. "Adilion already explained about Torsion," he said, indicating the young Sentinal who had arrived before them. "Do you know what happened?"

"We're hoping Torsion can tell us that."

"We can't feel Birlerion. Something's changed," Chryllion, one of the Stoneford Sentinals standing at Jason's shoulder, said as he scowled in concern. Niallerion stiffened, his gaze turning inward; his lips tightened as he confirmed Chryllion's statement. A general air of tension hung over them all.

Jerrol frowned. "Is it a distance thing? They've taken him further away?"

"No ... I suppose it could be." Chryllion rubbed his temple. "I don't know. It's not like Serillion; it isn't the same feeling. We think he's still alive, but whatever's happening isn't good."

"Then we won't waste time. Jason, warn Tyrone; we'll probably bring Torsion back here. He didn't look too great from what Ari showed us, though I don't know what his injuries are. Chryllion, I'll create a waystone up at the towers, make it easier for you and Jason to keep an eye on them." Jerrol grimaced at the two Sentinals Adilion had collected from Marchwood. "Tianerille, Venterion, I hope you are ready; there is a lot that needs putting right at the towers."

Tianerille's laugh was more like a growl. "Don't worry, Captain, we've rested enough; we are ready." The two Sentinals had been recuperating in Marchwood since Jerrol had woken them in the rock strata under Terolia; the same place where he had found Niallerion and Marianille.

"Let's go and see what Torsion can tell us." Jerrol mounted his horse and led the Sentinals down the road. It was at least a day's ride to Velmouth and then they had to climb up to the towers. "Keep alert, we weren't intending on riding anywhere," Jerrol said, his voice sharp as they turned onto the road to Velmouth.

It was dark by the time they reached Velmouth, but Jerrol was insistent that they keep moving, ignoring Niallerion's concerned gaze.

"Captain, stop a moment." Niallerion pulled his horse in front of Jerrol. "You're cold, wrap your cloak around you. We weren't expecting to be travelling all night. We ought to stop and rest. For the sake of the horses, and Tianerille and Venterion. They haven't ridden for a while."

Jerrol pulled up, staring at Niallerion and then the other Sentinals.

Venterion winced as he met his gaze and shifted in his saddle. "Much as I hate to say it, a chance to stretch out lazy muscles would be a relief."

Tianerille was quick to agree, stretching out her back and wriggling in her saddle.

"Of course, I'm sorry. I never thought," Jerrol said.

"We all want to get there as fast as we can, but we won't be able to function if we don't rest." Tianerille wiggled her fingers. "And who knows, I might even be able to resolve some of Venterion's aches and pains. A nice massage wouldn't go amiss, now, would it?"

Venterion's silver eyes gleamed as he grinned back at her.

"You should have said earlier. We could have stopped at the inn," Jerrol said.

"It's only a mile back down the road. Let's return there and start again in the morning. We'll stay just for a few hours, until dawn," Niallerion suggested.

Jerrol allowed Niallerion to lead them back. He followed, concentrating on trying to relax; his muscles were so tight, they ached. On arrival at the inn, Niallerion found them rooms and they shed their gear and relaxed in the empty parlour.

After a glance around the room, Tianerille moved behind Jerrol and began massaging his shoulders. "So tense, my Captain, it's not good for you." He relaxed into her hands, and she worked the knots out of his muscles.

"I can't help it. The towers evoke memories I don't want to think about."

"Then we'll have to change that. For now, let your mind drift and think about your young lady. Yes, we heard; congratulations, by the way."

Jerrol chuckled as he tried to relax. "Where did you learn to do this?"

"My father was a healer. He taught me many tricks to help with injuries and stress. He said I'd see both as a ranger; he was right of course."

Jerrol's head hung down as Tianerille massaged his neck, his mind drifting in a haze of contentment, when dinner arrived. He almost groaned out loud when Tianerille stopped her magic.

"I'll be rubbing Venterion's butt later if he asks me nicely."

Venterion chuckled as he sat at the table. "If you want the favour returned, you'll be nice to me."

Tianerille laughed and sat beside him, her arms as thick as his as she rested them on the table and inhaled the aroma. She sighed. "I've missed this. You don't realise how little sensation is around you until your senses are overloaded with a delicious stew."

"I'm sorry to be pitching you straight in without any time to adjust," Jerrol said, fumbling the spoon in his left hand as he helped himself to the potatoes. He gritted his teeth and clenched his mutilated hand below the table, his massage-induced sensation of lazy relaxation already lost.

"Best way, probably; doesn't give us time to overthink it," Venterion replied. "It sounds like the Ascendants are causing as many problems now as they did in our time. The Lady expects us to stop them."

"Well, we stopped them in Vespiri and Terolia. Elothia is probably next. I believe that is where they're retreating to, taking Birlerion with them. I'm hoping Torsion can tell us where they went," Jerrol replied.

"Who is Torsion?" Tianerille asked.

"A scholar from the Chapterhouse. He specialises in antiquities. I've known him for years, since I was a young lad in Stoneford. He was my mentor; he sponsored me into the Chapterhouse when I first came to Old Vespers."

"And he was at the Watch Towers when everything happened?" Tianerille asked.

"Yes, he had been assigned up there for a few months. He was supposed to be alleviating the condition of the Watchers, but I didn't see any sign of it."

"I heard he and Birlerion clashed," Niallerion said.

"Yes, they took an instant dislike to each other," Jerrol admitted.

Tianerille frowned. "Birlerion is usually a good judge of character, Captain."

"I think it was because Torsion reminded him of some-one. But Torsion is the only person who may know what happened to Birlerion, so that's why we need to speak to him." Jerrol rubbed his face, suddenly exhausted.

He forced himself to eat, toying with his food, but he could barely keep his eyes open, and as soon as he could, he went to bed. Niallerion had been right. They wouldn't have made it to the towers without him falling out of his saddle.

Venterion watched him go. "We'll take the watch between us. You go and rest, Niallerion. Tomorrow looks like it will be a tough day."

Niallerion nodded. "He blames himself for losing Seril-lion and Birlerion. Along with the Ascendants attacking him, it's not surprising he doesn't want to return to the towers."

"We'll be with him, and he has to face it sometime. I guess tomorrow is as good a time as any, and anyway, it's not his fault; the Ascendants are to blame," Tianerille said. "He is a sensible man. He'll realise it soon enough. Go on with you, Nialler; you're shattered."

"Yes, ma," Niallerion said and retreated before she could clout him.

7

WATCH TOWERS, STONEFORD WATCH

Jerrol woke with the dawn and dragged himself out of bed, even though his preference would have been to turn over and go back to sleep. His brain thought otherwise, and unwanted memories and images spun off each other and kept him awake. After tossing and turning for a while, he couldn't stay in bed and rose. He needed answers.

Venterion and Tianerille both looked fresh and alert and were already waiting outside with the horses by the time Jerrol joined them. Jerrol wondered if they had deliberately feigned exhaustion the night before to make him rest. He scowled as he mounted his horse, but there was no point complaining; they had been right.

The nearer they got to the towers, the more he tensed. He didn't want to face Serillion's loss again. He had failed to protect his Sentinals and the guilt ground through him as he rode. Clenching his hand, he tried to disguise the tremor that was beginning to shudder through him.

Tianerille moved up beside him, and Jerrol stiffened.

"Did you know I was posted to Greens when I was a

ranger? The lord of the Watch back then, Lord Warren, was an amazing man; generous, kind, and far-sighted. He knew how to run a Watch.

"One day, when I was out on patrol, we came across this Terolian. Swaddled in those desert robes, we had no idea who it was; he had scarves wrapped around his head and face. He was riding the most beautiful black stallion; a Darian, for sure. He was gorgeous. There was a blanket over the horse's withers. I expect they were feeling the weather.

"Didn't recognise him, of course, not until he spoke, and even them, it wasn't until he dropped his scarves that I realised it was Birler. He was exhausted, barely keeping his seat. There was an arrow in the back of the saddle. Terolian saddles had those raised backs, fortunate for Birler.

"He was being chased; had been all the way from Terolia. Days he had been travelling, determined to reach Greens. We dealt with his pursuers and returned to Birler. He was so exhausted, he couldn't get back in the saddle. I had to give him a leg up." She smiled at the memory.

"Well, you should have seen Lord Warren's face when we all trailed in. Birler had been determined to get home and warn his father about the Ascendants' threat against his family, and he did. The Lady watches over him, Captain, as she does you. He'll be there waiting when we find him. Don't you worry, he'll be there."

Jerrol eased his shoulders. "Thank you," he said, somehow soothed by the story. It sounded just like Birlerion.

They clattered into the Watch Towers courtyard late that evening and the sergeant rushed up to greet them. "I was going to send a message to the keep. The scholar arrived yesterday, all beat up."

"Where is he?"

"In his room. He ain't left it."

"Is he badly hurt?"

"Just bruises I think; he was more shocked than anything."

"Very well, I'll go and see him. Sentinals Venterion and Tianerille are here to take over the management of the Watch Towers. You and your men will report to them."

"Yes, sir." The sergeant watched the Sentinals warily.

"Venterion, see what you can find out from the sergeant. Tianerille, you come with me. Let's see what Torsion can tell us." Jerrol led the way to tower, his steps slowing as he approached the entrance. He halted as the aroma of dry stone hit him. His heart rate accelerated and he broke out in a sweat as he froze.

"We are here for answers," Tianerille's steady voice said from behind him. "Once we have them, you and Niallerion can return to Old Vespers and leave the towers to me and Venterion."

"Answers," Jerrol repeated and, taking a deep breath, he entered the building.

They found Torsion in his room on his hands and knees scrabbling about in a box of papers. He jerked up as Jerrol opened the door, an expression of undisguised horror spreading across his face as he leapt to his feet. "Jerrol, what are you doing here?"

"I'm here to see you, of course. Why else would I be here?"

"You were hurt," he said, his eyes flicking down to Jerrol's hand.

Jerrol held up his gloved hand up. "Everything heals in time," he said. "What about you? The sergeant said you were not well."

Torsion tottered over to his bed, where he dramatically collapsed. "I barely escaped with my life. It was terrible."

"So I see," Tianerille said dryly.

Torsion flicked her a resentful glare. "You don't know what it was like! If it hadn't been for She'vanne, I wouldn't have escaped. They were focused on that Sentinal; I told you he was no good, Jerrol. Why didn't you listen to me? He was fighting off the rangers and he wouldn't let anyone into the tower to help you."

"He was defending me. It was a good job someone was," Jerrol said, running a hand through his hair as he tried to contain his spurt of disbelief. Was Torsion really trying to accuse Birlerion of being an Ascendant?

Torsion's gaze slid over him and he changed tack. "He was hurt, so they took him with them. I told you he was one of them."

"Don't be ridiculous, Torsion; you know better than that. Birlerion is no Ascendant, and you know it. Ain'uncer took him because he couldn't escape without taking Birlerion with him."

"Jerrol, look, I know he's one of yours, but I've told you, you can't trust them."

Anger flared through Jerrol, burning off his tension. "Don't you dare. I told you before, Birlerion is the Lady's and he is my friend, and if you have nothing to say that will help us find him, then don't speak."

Tianerille slipped passed him. "You've damaged your hands, what happened?" she asked, grasping Torsion's hand and smoothing her fingers over the swollen knuckles and faded bruising. Torsion tried to snatch his hand back, but Tianerille tightened her grip. "They were caused by you punching something or someone, repeatedly."

"I had to fight my way out, I told you. I couldn't stay there. It's not my fault they took him."

"Where were you when you escaped?" Tianerille asked, releasing his hand, and Torsion tucked it under his arm.

"Amsar. They were boarding a ship. I managed to overpower my guard, and She'vanne helped me escape."

"And Birlerion?"

"They had already tossed him in the hold. I couldn't help him."

"Where were they going?"

"I don't know. North, up the coast."

"Why did they come back for the guards and horses?"

"I don't know."

"What *do* you know, Torsion?" Jerrol asked, a bite to his voice.

Torsion flapped his hands. "It wasn't my fault. When I was woken by the racket your Sentinal was making, I had no idea what was going on. My first thought was to make sure Taelia was alright, but I got caught up in the fracas in the courtyard."

"You didn't come up into the tower?"

"No, I told you; I couldn't get passed Birlerion. When he was overpowered, I thought it would be over, but there was a blinding flash. He did something, knocked us all out. When I came too, I was in a cart with him. He was out cold; I couldn't get him to respond." He flicked a nervous glance at Tianerille as she hissed. "I pretended to be unconscious and I overheard them speaking. They're after the grand duke; they were going to Retarfu."

Jerrol frowned. "Retarfu? Why not the Summer Palace? The grand duke would have relocated by now."

Torsion shrugged. "That was what they said. When we pulled up at the dock, I managed to slip away while they were unloading Birlerion. I had to fight off some of their guards, but She'vanne appeared and we escaped. It took us weeks to get back here."

"Why didn't you go to Stoneford? It was closer," Tianer-ille asked.

Torsion scowled. "I wasn't thinking straight. I let She'-vanne choose where we went. As I said, it's taken us weeks to get back. Now, do you mind? I've had a terrible experience. I need to rest."

Tianerille smiled, though it didn't reach her glittering eyes. "That's right. You ought to stay in bed; the best place for you. The Captain will create a waystone, and I'll escort you to Stoneford. Their healer will soon have you sorted."

"That won't be necessary, a good night's sleep and I'll be fine."

"Oh, we don't want to take any risks. I think you ought to see the healer. But for now, rest. I'll send some food up for you." Tianerille hustled Jerrol out and shut the door on Torsion's protests. She wouldn't let Jerrol speak until they reached the ground floor.

"There's something not quite right about him," she said.

"Do you think he's been enspelled? The Ascendants have discovered *Mentiserium.*"

"It's possible. You need to be careful about believing anything he says. The only thing that rang true was him not being able to get past Birlerion. He was annoyed by that."

"We still don't know where they were going."

"North, into Elothia. There's not much in the north of Elothia. It shouldn't be hard to find him."

"It's the cold season. It'll be snowed in."

"Which means they've gone to a large town. They wouldn't get through the snow off the beaten track."

Jerrol stared off into the distance. Retarfu was in the west, clear across the other side of the country. If he went there, could he find a way into the north?

"You should create your waystone, Captain. Time for

you to return to Old Vespers. I'll take Torsion back to Stoneford. They can keep an eye on him there."

"Healer Tyrone at Stoneford has some experience with *Mentiserium;* he will be able to tell if Torsion is affected," Jerrol said as he walked out of the building. He stared around the courtyard, his mind churning as much as his gut was.

Niallerion approached. "You've got your work cut out here, Tianerille. Venterion is not impressed."

Tianerille laughed. "He'll be happy sorting it out, then. Come on, Captain, make your waystone; you need to get back."

King's Palace, Old Vespers

King Benedict of Vespiri and Terolia paced the floor of his study. He stopped by the window and stared out over the terrace that led down into the formal gardens. Dreary grey stone dominated the view as the rain continued to sift down.

He turned away from the window, a frown creasing his brow as his steward, Darris, announced Commander Haven. His frown deepened as he watched Jerrol enter and kneel before him. How such an unassuming man could be the cause of so much trouble amazed him sometimes. "Rise," he said. He wasn't going to talk to the top of the man's damn head. "Sit."

"Thank you, sire." Jerrol sat before the king's desk.

Benedict's lips twitched at his commander's wary expression. "I suppose you heard that I received a formal response to my letter to Grand Duke Randolf of Elothia?"

"Yes, sire."

"He had the temerity to accuse Vespiri of violating his borders."

"What did he say about Elothia's incursions?"

"He said they hadn't crossed the border."

Jerrol huffed. "Lord Jennery's reports have said otherwise."

"I know," Benedict said as he sat behind his desk and steepled his fingers. He stared at Jerrol for a long moment as if making a decision. "I want you to head up a delegation. A diplomatic mission to shore up our relations with Randolf. We can't afford to go to war. Not while these Ascendants are still stirring up trouble."

Jerrol straightened up in surprise. "You want to send me to Elothia?"

Benedict nodded. "You are my best hope of avoiding war. You know Randolf; you've dealt with him before. You've already demonstrated your skill at diplomacy. You can explain to him about the Ascendants, warn him what to look out for. Let's preempt any move they can make on him. Bryce can continue managing the King's Justice while you are gone. It shouldn't take more than a month. I've sent for Roberion. He will take you in his ship."

Jerrol stared at the king in shock. How had he managed to arrange all this without him knowing. "How long have you been planning this, sire?"

Benedict scowled. "Since you returned. Healer Francis says you are fit for the journey. In fact he said it would be a good opportunity for you to rest. A diplomatic mission should be peaceful enough for you to manage."

Peaceful? Jerrol could imagine how boring it would be. Last time they had kept him kicking his heels for weeks before the grand duke deigned to speak to him. Though seeing as Randolf himself had sent the missive to Benedict, maybe it wouldn't take so long. He realised he had been silent too long as the king raised an expectant eyebrow. "Of course, sire," Jerrol murmured.

"Take these." Benedict handed Jerrol a folder. "It

contains a copy of all the recent correspondence. Also, the background on Randolf's key supporters and detractors."

"Commander Nikols has been busy," Jerrol said as he rifled through the thick wad of papers.

"It's all the information we have. You have until Roberion arrives to study it."

"Yes, sire."

"You will also be escorting Scholar Taelia to Retarfu. Randolf requested a scholar versed in ancient engravings. Scholar Deane Liliian would have sent Torsion, but he is in no fit state to travel, or so I understand?"

"No, he can't go." Jerrol rubbed his eyes. "He looked exhausted. He needs to recover from his recent ordeal. Venterion was going to take him to Stoneford. Healer Tyrone will look after him."

King Benedict stood and paced back over to the window. Rivulets of water streamed down the glass, blurring the view. He turned back to Jerrol. "Then it will have to be Scholar Taelia. Randolf's request said they had found evidence of Sentinals. Randolf wants to find out more about them. You may tell him what you know but not that you are the Lady's Captain. That we keep under wraps."

"If there are more Sentinals then we need to wake them."

"My thoughts exactly," Benedict replied. "Your priority is persuading Randolf that we are not a threat. After that, you can help Taelia search for the Sentinals. But you return after a month, no longer. I need you here."

"Of course, sire." Jerrol stood, bowed and made his escape.

The king's shoulders relaxed as the door closed behind him. He rubbed a weary hand over his face and returned to his desk. He stared blindly at his papers for a moment before leaning back in his chair with a sigh, his frown firmly in place. The Veil. The Lady Leyandrii had created a Veil of protection around their world to guard against the threat of wild magic. The Ascendants wanted to bring it down, to shred it, so they could control the magic for their own purposes. The king shivered. They had tried to overthrow him, and then subjugate the people of Terolia. Were they behind the deteriorating relations with Elothia? He hoped not.

Jerrol paused outside the king's study before squaring his shoulders and heading for the stables. He needed to see Taelia. Niallerion followed close behind, and retrieving their damp cloaks from a footman and their horses from the stables, they set off for the Chapterhouse.

They found Taelia down in the catacombs, busy working with Mary; a young novice whom Taelia was mentoring. Mary smiled at Jerrol before she left them alone, joining Niallerion in the upper room out of earshot.

Jerrol engulfed her in a desperate hug.

Taelia hugged him in return, before leaning back and gazing up at him with a slight frown on her face. "What's wrong?"

"Benedict said that the Deane received a formal request from Grand Duke Randolf for the services of a scholar expert in ancient engravings."

"Which is within his rights," Taelia said.

"I am to escort you to Retarfu. I am Benedict's Ambassador for peace."

Taelia's face brightened. "You are? I am so glad. The trip will be so much more fun if you are there."

"I'm not sure Elothia is the safest place right now, Taelia."

"It's as safe as anywhere. Lillian said they had found signs of more Sentinals. Isn't that exciting?"

"Convenient, maybe," Jerrol murmured.

Taelia tilted her head back and stared at him. Her turquoise eyes narrowed, even though she couldn't see him. "You don't think there are more Sentinals? Why would they say there are?"

"I sincerely hope there are more. Niallerion said there were more posted to Elothia, so there should be signs. But I've never heard of any trees. The Elothians have never mentioned them before."

"More reason for me to go. We have to find them and wake them. You can't leave them sleeping."

"I'm just worried about where the Ascendants went. The only word we have is that they went north into Elothia. I should be searching for Birlerion, not kicking my heels in the corridors of a palace in Retarfu."

"If the Ascendants did go north then you might hear of it in Retarfu. At least you would be in the right country."

"True." He paced across the chamber and back.

"What is it? What is worrying you?"

"I don't know. I don't want to take you into danger."

"The grand duke is suing for peace. He is actively in negotiation with Benedict. They are sensible men, and sensible men do not go to war. And anyway, it's not your decision, my love. The grand duke petitioned the king and the Chapterhouse for my services. It is their decision."

"I'm worried it's not safe."

"If it's not safe for me, then it definitely isn't safe for you. Have you told the king your concerns? I'm surprised he is letting _you_ go."

Jerrol sighed and folded her into his arms. He rested his head on her shoulder and kissed her neck as she snuggled close, holding him tight against her. "I have no proof, and as you say Benedict and Randolf are talking. If I don't go then there is more likelihood of war. I just don't like it."

"I'd rather have you negotiating for peace than anyone else, Jerrol. And just think of all that time for us to be together! How can you turn that down?"

Jerrol's breath huffed out on a laugh. "You'd never forgive me if I did."

8

ADEERON, ELOTHIA

Var'geris' black gaze examined Birlerion as he stood in the sparring ring and waited. Birlerion held a sword in his right hand; the edge blunted, useless. Even more useless was his left arm, which was splinted; the result of an earlier session with Tor'asion. Bruising of all colours marred his pale skin, evidence of their many fruitless sessions.

One result of the repeated beatings and attempts at *Mentiserium* over the past month was that Birlerion was finally more malleable. In fact, he was a different man, unrecognisable as the Sentinal they had first brought here. Less assured, younger even, yet when threatened, his reactions were feral, untamed. His eyes had lost their silver sheen and were a deep, dark blue, where they were not bloody. The young men watched their opponent warily. The battered man's reputation preceded him, and none of them were keen to try his sword. A sharp order had the men advancing, but Birlerion stared at his opponents without much interest.

Even with the beatings, they had found it difficult to enspell the Sentinal. Var'geris wasn't convinced they had succeeded, but Birlerion was now docile and obedient. No matter what they did, they had been unable to get him to tell them anything. Resentment roiled through Var'geris as he scowled at the Sentinal. No matter how much time Var'geris spent with Birlerion, he got no information out of him. He had talked himself hoarse, but the man just stared at him as if he didn't hear a word. Tor'asion had done more damage than they had realised.

As Var'geris watched, Birlerion decimated his opponents. He had not lost any of his fighting skills. Only the blunted sword was preventing their deaths, though at least one of his opponents cradled a broken limb.

"He will obey whomever you put in command of him. Use him as you will; he is useless to us. We can't send him back now," Var'geris said as he turned away. "We cannot delay any longer; we've wasted enough time. The grand duke is expecting us in Retarfu."

The brute of a man they called the Tasker smiled. "I am sure we'll find a use for him. He has already demonstrated his skill, damaged as he is. At a minimum, he will make a worthy soldier in the grand duke's army."

Stepping back at the Tasker's order, Birler waited. The Tasker snapped his fingers and five more recruits joined him in the ring. Birler stiffened into a semblance of his fighting stance. He focused on the new threat and concentrated on surviving.

He was good at that.

9

KING'S PORT, OLD VESPERS, VESPIRI

A few days later, Roberion of Selir arrived on the morning breeze in a tall ship with its sails in full glory. Sailing into King's Port, his ship caused all sorts of excitement. The sailors efficiently furled the sails and brought the vessel to anchor safely. Such a ship rarely visited the port. Normally it was just troopships or Jerven shipping line boats delivering their haul of fish and goods from Birtoli. Nothing as elegant as the frigate now gracing their harbour.

Roberion grinned as his men pulled him ashore in a skiff, revelling in being a sea captain of note. Glancing back at the sleek lines of his ship, he thrust his chest out proudly as he disembarked. He knew his fellow Sentinals would burst his bubble soon enough, but he was going to enjoy it while he could.

The hired carriage rumbled up the Port Road towards the town of Old Vespers and thence onto the king's palace. Leaning forward, he inspected Old Vespers as it passed; he had never visited before, having stayed behind in Terolia to help the devastated people relocate after the terrible events in the Terolian Mines.

Once folks were settled, Roberion had remembered the Captain's words from one long night in the Terolian desert. The Captain had said that the Lady provided many miracles and that they should rejoice in them if they had the chance, or words to that effect. So he had. He had bought the *Lady's Miracle* with monies he had found accruing in his name, and here he was in response to the king's order.

Roberion couldn't have been more pleased with his welcome to Old Vespers. Marianille, Darllion, and Niallerion all crowded around him, and he could hear Fonorion on his way, released by the king, the Captain not far behind him.

He hugged them again. Marianille, slender, alert and beautiful. Niallerion, still looking thin and gaunt but present. Darllion, grey-haired and sensible. He had missed them all.

Just as he was asked the question, 'But why are you here?' for the third time, Jerrol came skidding out of the palace.

"Captain," Roberion shouted and engulfed him in a huge hug.

"Roberion, welcome," Jerrol gasped as he managed to escape the hug. "I'm so glad to see you."

The evening meal was quite a celebration. The king declined the invitation to join them, saying they all had much to catch up on; he could meet Roberion the following day. He left the Sentinals to celebrate in peace. Bryce reluctantly took bodyguard duty, missing out on the reunion, but was satisfied that Fonorion therefore owed him one.

It was quite late when Jerrol stood, waving his mug in the air. "A few words, just a few," he said with a laugh as the Sentinals jeered. "Alright, alright," he said as he waved them down. "Seriously, nights like this are too few. We rarely get to appreciate each other.

"It's not often we're all together at the same time, and I just wanted to say I appreciate all that you do for me and the king. Thank you," he said, solemnly nodding at the Sentinals. "This is a time of conflict, no more peaceful than when you left. We hope the end is in sight and Remargaren can be at peace, as the Guardians meant us to be. Rejoice in your brothers and sisters, as we rejoice in you all. Our thoughts and prayers are with those who are lost; we hope they will return to us soon. Lady's blessings to you all," he said firmly before sitting back down with a thud. There was a small silence and then uproar as the Sentinals all began talking together.

The next morning, Adilion arrived with Zin'talia in tow. Jerrol hugged her silky neck and breathed in her musky scent, absorbing the affection she bombarded him with. She was a pure white Darian, with a flowing white mane and tail, though she was looking somewhat grubby and travel-stained.

"I am so sorry. I never meant to be so long. It was further than I remembered," she murmured in his head.

"You are here now. I've missed you."

"And I you. There was nothing I could do, Jerrol. I am so sorry. I couldn't help Birlerion."

Jerrol stroked her neck. *"It's not your fault."*

"If it hadn't been for him ..." her voice faltered.

"Shh, we will find him. His sacrifice will not be in vain. I promise."

"Good," she said, a vicious bite to her voice. *"They have no respect for life. They don't deserve the Lady's grace. That Ain'uncer, he was livid that they had lost you."*

"What about Torsion, did you see how he escaped?"

"No, I don't know how he managed it. Must have been when they took Birlerion onto the ship. He wouldn't co-operate. It would have been the only time they were distracted. That was when I managed to slip away; the other horses didn't want to board, either."

"At least you are here now. Let's get you stabled. We will be travel-ling to Elothia soon."

"Not by ship, I hope?"

"Roberion is here, so yes, by ship."

"I don't want to go on a ship; they are smelly and they leak, and they don't stay still." Zin'talia continued to grumble as a stable boy rushed up to lead her to the stables. Her complaints filled Jerrol's head until the stable boy procured her favourite baliweed and began to groom her, which shut her up.

The next two days were spent with Nikols and King Benedict going over their arguments. They had spent the time trying to fill Jerrol's head with as much information about Randolf's government as they could. His head was ringing with names and associations, and whatever Benedict could think of, which would sway Randolf towards peace.

Jerrol was glad when the *Lady's Miracle* set sail, and he could have a rest.

Two days later, Jerrol stood with Roberion, looking out over the bow of the *Lady's Miracle* at the smooth waters as they drifted in the becalmed sea. The silence of the night was only interrupted by creaking ropes and the gentle slapping of water against the hull. The moon shone down from a star-filled sky, and not a cloud marred the twinkling array above them.

They had left the port of Vespers headed for Pollo on the Elothian western seaboard. After two days of sailing north, the wind had suddenly dropped, and Roberion had ordered the men to get the oars out.

Jerrol thought back to his last audience with the king. As if he wasn't under enough pressure already, the king had repeated the importance of the mission. After that meeting, he had tried to convince Niallerion to remain behind. Niallerion had been adamant he should come too, but as Jerrol had said, they had few Sentinals as it was, without putting two at risk in Elothia. Marianille would be perfectly capable of looking after Taelia and him. Niallerion's parting argument that he would have taken Birlerion, was, Jerrol thought, a little below the belt, but Niallerion had been beside himself, and in the end, Jerrol had given in.

"Roberion," Jerrol said, his voice a mere whisper on the night air.

"Captain?"

Jerrol smiled. "I want you to be the captain tonight. Would you perform the joining ceremony for Taelia and I? A moment out of time just for us, under the Lady's moon, where the sea meets the sky under her peaceful gaze?"

Roberion stared at Jerrol. "I would be honoured," he said. "Are you sure you want to do it now?"

Jerrol was certain. "Oh yes. This is for us and no one else. You were right. There is nowhere better than the middle of the ocean to really appreciate the Lady."

Roberion smiled. "Of course."

Jerrol went to find Taelia below decks. "He agreed if you are still of a mind."

She smiled up at him. "I couldn't live another day knowing that I had missed the chance to finally become one with you." She twirled. "Look, I even have a gown," she laughed, displaying her scholar robes.

Jerrol frowned. "I should have warned you so that you could have chosen a dress."

Taelia leaned against him. "Don't be silly. I don't need a dress. I just need you."

He bent his head and kissed her lips; they tasted so sweet. "Come, before we do something we shouldn't," he murmured, leading her up the steps to the deck.

Word spread around the ship like a prevailing wind. The sailors had placed lanterns around the main deck, and a trail led up to the Quarterdeck, where Roberion stood waiting. Marianille and Niallerion stood next to him, grinning broadly.

Smiling down at the couple before him, Roberion couldn't think of a more deserving man and woman. They had persevered through so much and yet had so much more to face.

Taelia was radiant as she stood beside Jerrol, her beautiful blue eyes sparkling with happiness. Jerrol clasped her hand and she gripped his back, fairly humming with delight. Roberion's lips twitched as he watched Jerrol run a finger around his collar; his silvery-green uniform glowed, surrounding him in a soft aura of light. His silver eyes were luminous as he looked up at Roberion, a shy smile on his face.

"We stand here, in the presence of the Lady, to join these two people together as one." Roberion began, pausing as the waters around the ship began to glow. The sailors peered over the side and exchanged nervous glances before staring up at the moon, which was pulsing brightly.

Jerrol smiled at Taelia. "The Lady watches."

"As the line protects," Taelia replied, completing the age-old catechism.

A soft silvery glow surrounded Jerrol and Taelia, and Roberion knew they didn't need his words. Raising his arms, he intoned: "Do you, Jerrol, take Taelia to be joined as one in the eyes of the Lady?"

"I do," Jerrol replied, gazing into Taelia's turquoise eyes. Her cold fingers shook in his.

"Do you, Taelia, take Jerrol to be joined as one in the eyes of the Lady?"

"Oh, I do," Taelia replied vehemently, staring at Jerrol as if she could see him.

Roberion almost laughed. "In the name of the Lady, Land, and Liege, may these two be joined, forever as one," he declared, a smile spreading over his face.

The silvery green glow brightened around Jerrol and Taelia as Jerrol dipped his head and they kissed. The sailors all whooped in celebration as Roberion grinned at Marianille and Niallerion, wiping away a surreptitious tear.

Taelia came up for air, laughing as Niallerion and Marianille crowded around them in congratulation, admiring her silver robes which flowed around her. The little Arifels, Ari and Lin, popped into view, chittering in the air above them, their delicate wings flared and glittering in the moonlight. Sailors stared with expressions of awe tinged with a little fear at the spectacle. They knew their captain was different, he was a Sentinal after all, but to see a mythical creature hovering in the air above them emphasised how different. A few fell to their knees praying to the Lady, others gasped as the Arifels descended to perch on Jerrol and Taelia's offered hands.

Raising a toast, Roberion allowed one drink apiece, strictly abiding by the rules of the ship. Who knew when the wind would fill their sails? Once the ceremony was over, the sailors snuffed out the candles, had one final glance at the magical creatures and returned to duty. The *Lady's Miracle* glowed in the silvery moonlight, mysterious and serene, surrounded by still waters.

A little later, Jerrol and Taelia cuddled under a blanket, up on the poop deck. A brilliant moon and a spray of sparkling shooting stars lit up the sky in celebration. Jerrol described the view as eloquently as he could. "I think the Lady approves," he said, breathing in Taelia's sweet scent.

"Do you remember when we first met?" Taelia asked, her voice soft.

Jerrol laughed. "How could I ever forget? You dropped from the sky like a Lady's blessing."

"That's not what you said at the time."

"Well, you were a bit heavier than I expected, and I was only a scrawny lad at the time."

"But you caught me, and you never let go."

"Never," Jerrol whispered, hugging her tight.

"I wish I could see you just once."

Everything around them stilled for a moment, and then Jerrol stiffened as a great pressure constricted his head and then suddenly released him and all around Jerrol went dark. He heard Taelia gasp and he froze as his sight left him. Taelia twisted in his arms as she frantically looked around her before she stilled in turn.

"Oh." Her voice wavered.

"I love you," Jerrol said, trying to put all his love for her into his expression. As he bent to kiss her, he felt the pressure as his sight returned and knew she could no longer see. He hoped she had seen enough.

He wiped the tears from her cheeks. "Come," he said, helping her stand. The blanket falling onto the deck. His hand trembled in hers, and she gave him a small smile as she followed him down the stairs. The sailors politely looked elsewhere as the newly joined couple made their way to their cabin.

Jerrol stood in the centre of the cabin and held out his hand. He still couldn't believe he was joined heart and soul to this beautiful woman. Taelia unerringly gripped his hand as she stepped into his embrace. Sliding her hand up his chest and around his neck, she pulled his head down, and their lips met. The kiss deepened and became more urgent, the heat between their bodies rising. He began undoing the tiny buttons of her gown, her fingers reciprocating as she felt for his. He shrugged out of his jacket; he had fewer buttons. His shoes followed, as did hers.

She smiled against his lips as her fingers slid up his body and she moved on to the next set of buttons. The heat of his skin beneath the fine material of his shirt tempted her closer, and she stroked his skin as his shirt parted and her lips found his chest. Soft fingers explored in wonder as her lips left a cool trail across his skin.

Jerrol groaned, his skin sensitised to her touch. He shivered in response, yet the heat seemed to be collecting in his groin. He needed to touch her, yet he couldn't get near enough.

"How many buttons does this gown have?" he whispered, frustrated.

"Silly." Her breath tingled against his skin. "You don't have to undo them all." She wriggled, and the gown slithered to the floor, leaving her thin petticoat which slid smoothly up her skin and over her head in one smooth motion revealing the most wondrous sight his eyes had ever seen. His hands smoothed over her pink tipped breasts, revelling in the touch of satin smooth skin.

"Ah," she gasped as the sensations led to more exploration and burning hot lips left a trail of sultry kisses over her skin. Her fingers ventured hesitantly to his waist and struggled with his belt. His hands covered hers, the lack of fingers ignored as he helped ease the buckle off and then the remaining buttons. His trousers fell and he stepped out of them. Her hands fluttered over him as he pulled her close and their skin met along the length of their bodies. She felt him straining against her thigh, hot and pulsing.

"You are so beautiful," he whispered as he scooped her up and laid her on the bunk, kissing her face and neck as his hand drifted down her body.

"It's not fair, I can't see you," she growled huskily as her body shuddered in response to his every caress. She cupped him as he hovered over her.

He groaned as she squeezed him gently. "You don't need to see me," he gasped, "you can feel all that needs to be felt." Their bodies moved more urgently as the desire built. She gripped him tight, pushing up as he penetrated deeper. She gasped, and the world exploded as their bodies arched and melded together, Taelia drawing him in as far and deep as possible. She was never, ever letting him go.

Taelia was laying on top of him, trying to pretend she would never move again, when he started laughing beneath her. "This must be the most perfect position ever," he said, chuckling with delight as she frowned down at him. His fingers swirled her nipples.

She wriggled, trying to keep him within her. "Stop laughing," she grumbled as he slid out. He laughed even more as he drew her down and she swallowed his chuckles as their lazy kiss grew urgent again and their touch awoke each other's bodies for much more urgent activity.

During the night, unnoticed, the wind picked up and filled the sails, keeping the sailors busy. A blushing bride climbed back on deck with her husband the next morning. They climbed up to join Roberion, who smiled knowingly at Jerrol. Jerrol grinned and hugged his wife. Taelia lifted her face to him. "What?"

"Roberion is throwing me knowing looks," he murmured into her ear.

Taelia blushed and laughed softly. "Good," she said. "I hope you look very pleased with yourself."

"He does," Roberion laughed, infected by their obvious happiness. "As do you, Mrs. Haven."

Jerrol laughed as he hugged her, watching the ocean, his hair ruffled by the breeze. He lifted his face and inhaled the fresh salty air and the never-ending view. He stored the memory; an amazing one to balance all the terrible ones he had been collecting lately.

10

POLLO, ELOTHIA

The *Lady's Miracle* approached the port of Pollo early the next morning. Jerrol and Taelia reluctantly left their shared cabin for the deck above after a second wonderful night of exploration and sheer bliss.

Roberion's men unloaded their horses and belongings and helpfully pointed out the custom's hut at the end of the Jetty. Jerrol smiled his thanks and confirmed Roberion would return in a month to collect them.

Leaving Roberion to unload his cargo, Jerrol took Taelia's hand, and they walked down the swaying wooden planks. Taelia lurched as the swells unexpectedly made the jetty rise, and Jerrol slipped his arm around her waist, anchoring her safely to his hip. She smiled her thanks and his heart melted. He couldn't resist kissing her. Taelia sparkled with happiness beside him.

Marianille followed them with a grin on her face, and Niallerion staggered ashore behind her, glad to be off the ship. Raucous seagulls swooped expectantly, shrieking over their heads as they wheeled and dived on the sea breeze. Taelia laughed as Marianille described the seagulls, big enough to carry off a small child, according to her.

Jerrol steered Taelia to a seat on a bollard on dry land. "Wait here a moment; the hut is so small we won't all fit. The sea is behind you, so take care you don't fall in." Jerrol left her chatting with Marianille as he took their papers into the hut.

Niallerion waited by the door, still swaying as he held the reins of their horses, and Zin'talia whisked her tail at Jerrol as he passed.

"Dry land," she murmured. *"But does it have to be so cold?"*

Jerrol chuckled. *"What? A mighty Darian, afraid of a little chill?"*

"I come from the desert. You know I prefer the heat!"

"You'll survive. We have to climb that hill. That should warm you up." His gaze rose to the rising ranks of grey stone buildings that marched their way up the sides of the valley leading away from the port. He grimaced at the sight and entered the customs office, which was in a bare wooden shack only furnished with a wooden table and chair.

A scrawny man in a cloth cap with a scarf tied around his neck sat at the table. His clothes hung off him as if he had recently lost a lot of weight. "Papers," he said in a bored voice.

Jerrol handed over their papers and waited.

The man stilled as he read them. His eyes returned to the top of the page, and he read them again. He glanced up and met Jerrol's amused eyes. He lurched to his feet. "Sir, my apologies. I wasn't aware you were arriving today."

Jerrol smiled. "Well, as you can see, we have arrived."

"Your honour guard is not due here until tomorrow. May I suggest you await them at the Grand Duke Hotel? It's up on the main street. The port would be honoured to host your stay. Let me show you the way," he said, handing back the papers.

"That won't be necessary. We have our horses, we can

make our own way. We just need assistance with our baggage."

"Of course, I will see to it. But you must wait for the guard. The grand duke expects to greet you in Retarfu personally." The man puffed out his chest as if it was his own doing.

"Very well," Jerrol said, trying to conceal his annoyance. Benedict must have set expectations. Sighing under his breath, he backed out of the hut, folding his papers over as the port master edged past him.

The port master hurried up the road, gesticulating urgently. Jerrol watched him with a slight frown, before walking over to Taelia. "It seems we are to be feted. Our arrival is unexpected. The king's emissaries are to be escorted to Retarfu tomorrow by the Duke's own guards, and we are offered rooms at the Grand Duke Hotel for tonight.

"I suggest we start as we mean to go on, Scholar Haven. We could treat this as part of our joining celebration. A night in a distinguished hotel. Marianille will attend you, responsible for your comfort and safety. Niallerion is my man, and me, I'll just tag along as the king's representative." He smiled, his eyes sparkling with anticipation.

Taelia laughed. "I am happy to celebrate at the king's expense. I expect the king's representative to be very ingenious, if discreet," she said, ignoring Marianille's snort of laughter.

"In that case my lady, may I escort you to the hotel?" Jerrol asked with a flourish, helping her up from the bollard. Marianille fell behind with Niallerion, leading her own horse and Zin'talia.

They walked up the main street, allowing the port master time to reach the hotel before them. Voice low, Jerrol described to Taelia where they were. "Looks like the buildings along the wharves are all warehouses. They back onto what I can only guess is where the wharf rats live; an area I think we should avoid it if at all possible."

The smell wafting from the buildings to Taelia's left was of decaying dead things, the stench of stale beer, and rotting seaweed, and Taelia held her handkerchief to her nose; a pungent combination they were glad to leave behind as they climbed the slowly steepening incline.

"I can see why they built the town up here and not down there," Taelia said a little breathlessly as they reached the top. She breathed in the fresh sea breeze with relief. "I can hear a bell chiming. Is there a temple over there?" she asked, pointing to the north.

Jerrol looked to where she pointed, listening intently; he couldn't hear the bell, but he didn't doubt her. "We can check at the hotel. I'm sure they will show us."

"Good. Where are we now?"

"We've reached a crossroads. A narrow track leads to your temple to the north, the main road continues east, and more residential areas feed off to the south. There are a few boarded-up shops, and there's a hardware store of some sort, but to be honest, I don't think you'll be doing much shopping here. It looks like this town has fallen on hard times," Jerrol said, watching the way the people openly stared at them.

Taelia frowned at him as she pushed her hair out of her face. "I thought this was one of the major trading ports; surely it should be vibrant and busy?"

"Well, it's not today. Let's get out of the street. We're causing some interest with the locals. The hotel is straight ahead of us."

Taelia nodded in quick agreement, and Jerrol led the way to a square three-storey building that took up two plots of land and extended out to the rear. It was clad in white-washed boards that had collected enough road grime and weathering to give it a grey tinge. They walked up the steps, which were made of grey wooden planks. Taelia clutched Jerrol's arm tighter as the planks gave a little under them and they passed through the wooden door that was standing open into the dim interior of the Grand Duke Hotel. Niallerion and Marianille took their horses around the side of the timber-clad building and through the stone arch into the stable yard.

"Commander Haven, welcome, sir. Scholar Taelia, welcome to the Grand Duke Hotel. My name is Thorsten. I am the manager here. We have prepared two rooms for you and a private parlour on the second floor, if that suits? Your companions can room over the stables." The manager gabbled so fast, they barely made out the words.

"Thank you, Thorsten," Jerrol said, looking around the reception area. The walls were clad in a faded red paper and the floors were bare wooden boards, which once would have been polished to a high shine but were now dull, darkened with age and use. "Our baggage is still down on the docks if you could send someone to retrieve it."

Taelia's nose twitched, sensitive to the dust swirling around them. She sneezed.

"Of course, it would be our pleasure." The manager snapped his fingers and a young boy sprang forward to take the saddlebag from Jerrol. "For your own safety, we advise you to stay within the hotel until your escort arrives. There has been some unrest in the port, a result of news of Vespirian attacks on the border. People are a little on edge and we wish to avoid any unnecessary incidents."

"Incidents? I can assure you we are very well-behaved Vespirians. We will not cause any incidents," Jerrol replied.

The hotel manager swept his hand towards the young boy holding Jerrol's saddlebag. He was dressed in a rather grubby, blue uniform. "Carsten will show you to your rooms." He glared at the boy, who bobbed his head and led the way to the stairs.

Taelia clucked as Jerrol tucked her hand in his arm, and she leaned into him. "Well, he is very efficient. He couldn't get rid of us fast enough. I must admit I have not had much experience of hotels, but is that a normal greeting? Do they not like guests lingering in the foyer?" she asked.

"Seems not," Jerrol replied as they followed the young boy. "Carsten, do you have many guests staying here at the moment?"

The boy stared up at him, his eyes wide. "People come in on ships," he said, eager to get them to their rooms. He hurried up the stairs, hopping from one foot to the other as he waited for them at the top. "Your rooms, sir, this is a suite with two bedchambers as requested and the parlour is between." He opened the door to the parlour and ushered them in. He did his funny bob again, and he was gone before Jerrol could thank him.

"Well, something's not right here," Jerrol murmured as he released Taelia's arm. He checked the bedchambers, pausing at the side of the window to ease the net curtain aside. It smelt musty. The grimy window looked over the back of the hotel. Niallerion was talking to someone just inside the barn. He glanced up and casually scanned the windows, nodding as he caught sight of Jerrol.

"These rooms haven't been aired in months." Taelia frowned. "I can smell the dust."

"I agree. I think all the furniture was covered. They've opened the rooms, especially for us. Be careful as you enter the bedchambers; the floors are wood and there is a rug in the centre just waiting to trip you up. Come have a seat. There are two armchairs and a settee. Which do you prefer?" Jerrol asked.

"Well, you'll want the one facing the door, so the other chair, please."

"Am I that obvious?" Jerrol asked with a grin as he escorted her to the chair.

She sank down and eased off her shoes with relief. "If I'd known we were going mountaineering, I would have worn my boots. Any chance we could get some tea, do you think?"

"We'll ask as soon as Carsten returns."

"Good." There was a relaxed silence. "What do you think's going on?"

Jerrol sighed as he sat opposite her. "We can either take the welcome as a deliberate insult or take it at face value. Roberion's ship is faster than a general cargo ship, but then we were becalmed for a day. After all, they don't know we were joined on the way here." He paused. "We don't have to use both bedchambers, of course."

Taelia smiled, hearing the amusement in his voice, and rose. "I've decided I want your chair, husband dear," she said as she climbed into his lap.

He hugged her close. "Excellent choice," he murmured as he kissed her. They were enjoyably occupied when she suddenly lifted her head.

"Someone's coming. I suppose I should act with some decorum." She sighed as she rose. "I'm not mussed, am I?" she asked, conscientiously trying to straighten her hair.

She giggled as she sat back in her original chair.

At the tap on the door, Jerrol bid them enter. "Ah, Carsten with some tea; he must have heard you, Taelia."

The crockery clattered on the tray as the boy trembled, and he stared at Jerrol, aghast.

"Please place it on the table. We'll serve ourselves," Jerrol said smoothly, covering the awkward pause. "Is there a method for requesting your services? Or do we have to venture down to the reception?"

"If you please, sir, pull that cord there. A bell will ring in the kitchens and they'll send me up." The boy escaped out the door.

"Interesting reaction, don't you think?" Taelia asked as she moved over to the table. Her fingers fluttered over the contents and set the cups into saucers.

Jerrol laughed. "I wasn't serious about him hearing our conversation, but I obviously hit a nerve. We'll have to be a bit more careful, as you said."

"Not tonight, though," Taelia said, smiling mysteriously at the teapot.

Jerrol moved behind her, pulling her back against his chest and tucking her hair behind her ear. "Why, Mrs Haven, what do you mean?" His whisper tickled her ears and she shivered in delight.

"You'll see," she smiled as she raised a cup and saucer. He sighed and released her to take it.

"You know this should really be our time. I am sorry, I didn't think this through properly."

"Don't worry. I'm keeping a tally. I am an excellent book keeper. One gown, one party, a house, your undivided attention; it's beginning to mount up, husband dear," she said as she returned to her chair.

She grinned with delight as he choked on his tea. "Tali!"

Marianille entered the parlour as Taelia's peal of laughter filled the room. She raised her eyebrows as she watched them. It was obvious that these two were not going to behave; their happiness with each other was palpable, not that she could really blame them.

"Marianille," Jerrol said as he frowned at Taelia, which was a waste as she couldn't see it, but she broke into chuckles at the tone of his voice. Jerrol couldn't help smiling with her. "My, ah, Scholar Taelia seems to find this hotel amusing," he said, trying to sound severe.

"I'm not surprised. It is rather unusual. We seem to be its only guests."

"Really? No wonder we are attracting such close attention," Jerrol murmured. "I suggest we go for a walk, if your feet can stand it, Tali."

"Yes, lets. It is so stuffy in here."

"That may not be a very good idea. The manager was very insistent about us not leaving," Marianille said.

Jerrol grinned. "I'm sure he'll survive. We only want to visit the temple, that is harmless enough."

Taelia spoke up. "Do you know if our luggage has arrived? I have some boots I'll change into."

"I'm sure it has. They were lugging the chests up the stairs just now."

"We have two rooms to choose from, as we forgot to tell them about our joining," Jerrol said.

Marianille grinned. "Somehow, even if you had, I don't think they would have listened. Everyone seems confused by our arrival. No one was expecting us, and it has caused quite a commotion. Would you like me to escort you to your room, Scholar Taelia?"

"Thank you Marianille. If you could provide me with a quick layout of the room, I'd appreciate it. I'll be fine after that."

"Of course."

Jerrol was standing by the window when they returned. He looked over as the door opened. "Ready?"

"Yes." Taelia raised a booted foot and grinned.

"Your cloak, my love," Jerrol breathed as he settled her cloak around her shoulders.

She flashed him that look, and he shivered. Taelia tucked her hand in his arm and smiled as he moved closer.

"Lead on," Jerrol said, a slight tremor in his voice.

Marianille cast them a swift glance and opened the door.

"The temple is where Scholar Taelia thought. The stable boys were encouraging us to visit. I think the people around here need all the help they can get."

"Interesting, seeing as the hotel manager was trying to keep us in the hotel," Jerrol said.

"Apparently, it is dedicated to a local deity, the Lady Margrete, a Guardian of the Land. Lady Margrete manages the seasons and their affects on the land."

"A variation of Marguerite?" Jerrol murmured.

"I would think so." Marianille said. "It's been a harsh winter. The snows came early, and the grand duke has not left Retarfu. There is concern that supplies will not last the winter; they are already running low. The people haven't had the chance to prepare, and the growing months are shortening."

"But that's terrible. What is the grand duke doing about it?" Taelia asked, keeping her voice soft.

"Nothing," Marianille replied just as quietly.

"Nothing?" Jerrol frowned.

"Nothing that will help these people. He has a conscription effort going. Most young men have been drafted into the army. You'll notice most here are women and the men are either very young or very old. There are few left to run the port."

"Why does he need to conscript?"

"The Vespirians are going to attack," Marianille replied.

Jerrol gave her a sharp glance. "That explains why the port master was so upset about our early arrival. Are we in immediate danger?" he asked.

"We're not supposed to know. But the stable boys couldn't wait to tell us. I think we're the most excitement they've had in months. As long as we stay alert, I'm sure we can handle the locals."

Jerrol exhaled. "Let's visit the temple. It may show we are not heathens."

"I'll let you tell the hotel manager."

Jerrol laughed. "You leave all the fun stuff for me."

In the end, they managed to slip out the hotel without the manager seeing them, and they blithely strolled down the road to the temple. Jerrol watched the surrounding buildings with an informed eye. He could see the truth of Marianille's report.

"The houses are a reasonable size. They are similar in structure to Vespiri; you know, square with an apex at the front. But to be honest, most are in some need of repair," Jerrol murmured to Taelia as they walked. "Especially the roofs. Tiles are missing, roofs are sagging. Simple to fix if you have the expertise and the tools. The conditions must be terrible."

"And the money," Taelia said.

"Indeed. The temple looks in good repair. It has a yellow dome, Tali, a small one. But it's still a dome. I wonder how they built it." He led her inside, and it felt quite warm after the biting chill of the wind. Jerrol felt a stir of interest in the air.

Taelia lifted her head and Jerrol placed her hand on the wall. "Here, the outer wall," he said as they walked around the stone walls.

"It's old," murmured Taelia. "It's been here at least a thousand years, if not longer." She trailed her fingers over the stone as she walked. "Jerrol? What's this?" Taelia called.

Jerrol spun as he realised he had stopped in front of the altar whilst Taelia had continued walking. He dragged himself away from the small statue in the alcove. "What have you found?" he asked.

"Look, isn't this the same verse that is in the temple in Old Vespers?" Taelia was kneeling beside an inscription on the floor, worn through the middle as people had walked on it daily. Jerrol knelt beside her, his blood stirring.

He read the archaic Elothian script, the letters resolving themselves before his eyes.

"Art thou of Remargaren, you ask?
Blood of Elothia.
Realms balance,
Divide, Unite.
Salvation will come
'neath Land's watchful gaze.
Marguerite awaits
The tardy Keeper.
Wait and watch
The change to come.

"Why are they always saying I'm late!" Jerrol complained, his voice echoing off the walls.

Taelia chuckled. "That is not what it says in the Lady's temple."

"Then it's not the same. Anyway, this proves its Marguerite's temple. I heard she was more prevalent up here."

"I didn't realise you read ancient Elothian," Taelia murmured, her attention diverted as she ran her fingers over the stone.

"See, and you thought you knew everything there was to know about me," Jerrol replied as he was drawn back to the altar. A leather-bound book sat on a stand; he ran his fingers over the smooth surface and he flexed the page. It was thin yet sturdy; a much better medium than he was using in

Vespers. He wondered if it was made especially for the temple or for general use. He searched for any other leaflets and drifted over to a board hanging on the wall. Notices of all sizes, some even in hues of blue and pink he saw in wonder, were pinned to the board. The paper felt the same. He returned to the altar.

Taelia muttered to herself as she moved from one engraving to another. Marianille followed behind her.

Jerrol knelt and reached to touch the statue in the alcove. A flash of light blinded him; a vision of a young woman laughing, her arms full of flowers, chestnut-coloured hair burnished to copper in the brilliant sunlight flowing loose around her shoulders.

"Marguerite," he said out loud. The woman stopped laughing and stared directly at him as the flowers slipped from her grasp.

"Sir, please, we ask that you do not touch." A sharp voice spoke behind him.

Jerrol snatched his hand back and the vision was gone, but the girl's startled face was burned in his memory, her vivid blue eyes boring into his.

Jerrol rose and turned. "My apologies," he murmured as a small rotund priest approached him.

"Desecration, that is what it is. No respect these days. What is the world coming too?"

"I meant no disrespect, I assure you. Please tell me about Lady Marguerite. This temple is dedicated to her, is it not?"

"Yes, Lady Margrete. You are not pronouncing it correctly. The Guardian of the Land."

Taelia drifted closer, listening with interest.

"Well," the priest thrust his chest out a little as he realised he had an audience. "She was the Lady's sister and Guardian of all Elothia and the Land."

"Please tell us more," Taelia murmured, smiling at the priest.

"Hum, yes, well. Legend has it, that she was sacrificed by her family into a union with the Land itself. She can control the ground we stand on with a mere thought, raise the highest mountains, split the ground, or cause the hottest elements to rise into the air. The seasons pass or linger at her whim, and here we pray for mild winters and long summers. Unfortunately, our prayers haven't been answered recently."

"Why is that do you think?" Taelia asked.

"I don't know; our prayers are fervent and plenty."

"You said she was sacrificed by her family?" Jerrol cast Marianille a warning glance at her hiss of protest. "What happened?" he asked.

"Well, that was thousands of years ago, and we only have legends and myth to go by. I can't say how true they are." The priest observed the attentive faces and continued. "Hmm, well the most popular myth says that the Lady Leyandrii asked her sister to bond with the Land. It was at a time of upheaval when the ancient keeper could no longer manage the demands being made on him. The Lady believed her sister would be able to take on the guardianship and protect the lands.

"Back then, the plains of Elothia were grass-covered and plenty. The snowline was much further north and the land thrived; the crops were bountiful under the Lady Margrete's guidance, and the clear air sustained us all.

"She left the mortal world to join with the Land, never to be seen again. A sacrifice, truly. She destroyed her temple at Cerne and left only ruins that were gradually overgrown and lost, as a sacrifice to the love she had to leave behind."

"And the least accepted myth?" Jerrol asked as the priest fell silent.

The priest shrugged. "There are many stories, so

farfetched they are not worth repeating." He frowned. "The problem is that they are only hearsay; there is no proof. But then there isn't much proof for the other legends, either. It's all held in place by faith."

Jerrol laughed. "The impossible is not always as unbelievable as people seem to think. Maybe if we believed no matter what, the Ladies would listen more."

The priest snorted. "Faith is personal to the believer. I am here to guide and instruct, not propagate theories."

"I don't think Marguerite would mind; she strikes me as progressive."

"Her name is Margrete."

Marianille's voice echoed behind him. "The Captain is correct; she prefers the name Marguerite."

The temple trembled, and Jerrol grinned. "I think she is agreeing."

The priest cast about in a panic. "We must leave. If the roof collapses, we could be killed."

"Father, the Guardian would not hurt her followers."

"These buildings are not very stable. We had a land tremor about ten years ago, and there was terrible devastation down by the wharves. Many families were made destitute as a result."

"I expect those buildings were shoddily built. This temple is well built and in good repair; there should be no concern. It is probably one of the safest places in Pollo. If anything like that should ever happen again, make sure your flock come here," Jerrol reassured him.

They were interrupted by the panicked voice of the port master. "Commander Haven, I've been looking all over for you. You shouldn't leave your hotel unescorted."

Jerrol stared at him in surprise. "My dear port master, we are quite safe in the Guardian's temple."

"These are difficult times. The roads are not always safe." The port master looked appealingly at the priest for help.

The priest huffed. "It's not so bad as you make out. There are few here that would attack visitors. Why, they are the lifeblood of the port, and we have few enough as it is."

"Yes, but they are from Vespiri," the port master replied in a hushed voice.

"So?" The priest shrugged. "Why would the Vespirians attack us? We have nothing. There is nothing for them to take; it's already been taken." The priest trailed off at the port master's expression. "Yes, well. I must get on. Thank you for taking the time to visit our temple. Guardian's blessings on you all." The little man retreated.

"Let me escort you back to your hotel," the port master blustered, though how he would be any protection if they were attacked Jerrol was at a loss to know. But for the sake of the port master's anxiety levels, he agreed, and they allowed themselves to be hustled out of the temple and back down the road.

11

GRAND DUKE HOTEL, POLLO

The hotel manager, Thorsten, was hovering in the reception area as they arrived, his agitated expression relaxing as they entered the foyer. "Ah you found them safe. Commander Haven, I apologise for any inconvenience, but it is safer if you all stay within the hotel."

"Yes, so I understand," Jerrol replied. "But please do not concern yourselves. We just wanted to pay our respects at the temple."

"Good. Well, your dinner will be served at the sixth chime in your rooms. I hope you will enjoy it." Thorsten snapped his fingers, and Carsten slunk out of a doorway and led the way up the stairs.

As they reached the first landing Jerrol grasped Carsten's shoulder. "Stay a moment," Jerrol said and tilted Carsten's chin towards him. "What happened to your face, boy?" he asked, his voice sharp with concern.

"N-nothing. I wasn't watching where I was going," the boy stuttered, his eyes desperate. He shrank away from Jerrol's hand. "Please, sir. I done nothing wrong."

"I know you haven't. I didn't mean to snap at you," Jerrol

soothed. "I was concerned that you had been hurt. Has someone treated it for you?"

Carsten twisted his hands together and stared at the floor. "With what, sir?"

"What is it, Jerrol?" Taelia asked, listening hard.

"He's got a right shiner," Jerrol muttered under his breath. "Lead on, lad. We ought to return to our rooms."

They entered the parlour, and Marianille shut the door firmly behind her to prevent the lad from running.

"Ah, Niallerion, where have you been?" Jerrol asked as he spotted the Sentinal standing by the window.

"I was going to ask the same of you," he replied, his gaze resting on the boy. "Hey, Carsten. What happened to your face?"

"My very question," Jerrol murmured as he led the boy over to the table. "Let me look at you. Do you have a headache?" he asked.

Carsten went to shake his head and winced.

"Tali, did you pack any pain relief powder?"

Taelia raised her brows. "Of course I did," she said as she went into her room. She came back slowly, a packet in her hand. "Jerrol, someone's searched through our things."

Carsten flinched under Jerrol's grip. "You won't be in any trouble if you tell me who told you to go through our things and why," he said, keeping his voice gentle.

"She can't see; how does she know? Is it magic?" the boy blurted, his gaze darting between them.

"Of course not. Being blind, she needs to know where things are so she can find them," Jerrol said with a soft laugh. "You must have moved something. Who told you to search our things?"

"Master Thorsten. He said I should do it cos I let you leave the hotel. But it was the port master who said to look for papers."

"Any particular papers?"

"He wanted to see if you had anything from a king."

"And when you didn't find anything, he punished you?"

Carsten nodded gingerly.

"Where do you live?"

The boy stared at him. "Don't get me in trouble with me mam. My money's the only brass we got. Please, sir, I'll do anything you say. I can't lose me job."

Jerrol poured a glass water and shook the powder into it, stirring it briskly. "Drink it," he said. "All of it."

Carsten swallowed the draft without complaint.

"What time do you finish?" Jerrol asked.

"Not till midnight. I got to clear all the grates and lay the fires first."

"And when do you return to work?"

"Five in the morning, sir."

"Every day?"

"Yes sir."

"And how much do they pay you?"

"Two coppers a se'nnight, sir. It's all we got; me mam, m'sister, and me."

"How old are you?"

"Ten, sir,"

"Very well, off you go." Jerrol released him from the catechism.

Niallerion spoke quietly. "They have him spying as well. There are narrow crawl spaces in the ceiling. He can hear every word we say in here."

"And even if you try and help him, his place will be filled by another desperate volunteer immediately," Marianille said.

Jerrol twisted his lips in agreement and then he changed the subject. "It must be time to prepare for our wonderful dinner. I wonder what delights they have in store for us."

"And how many people are going to starve because of it," Taelia said.

"A sobering and worrying thought," Jerrol replied.

"I'll see if I can find out," Marianille promised.

"Where have they billeted you?"

"We have rooms over the stables. Niallerion, you'd better eat in the kitchens. Get them to keep me a plate," Marianille said.

They sat at the small table, candles already lit as the dark clouds drew the night in early. The wind was picking up and a loose board tapped repeatedly against the window.

Jerrol smiled at his wife. "Hear that wind? I am glad we are not on the *Miracle* tonight," he said, stroking her hand.

Taelia laughed. "I doubt you would have noticed," she replied, a gleam in her eye just for him.

Jerrol laughed in return. "I'm sure I wouldn't have."

Dinner arrived on a trolley pushed by a scrawny-looking man in a long-tailed black uniform. He placed a tureen in the centre of the table and proceeded to ladle a sweet-smelling soup into the bowls in front of them.

Jerrol watched the ladle with a slight smile.

"Oh, that smells delicious. Pray, what is it?" Taelia asked, looking up at the man.

The man swallowed as her bright eyes looked straight at him. "Sweet potato and leek, madam; a local specialty." He handed over a basket of bread and wheeled his trolley back out.

"It *is* delicious," Taelia murmured as she cleared her bowl.

"Would you like some more?" Jerrol asked, amused.

"Please. You never know what the next course might be, and after all, I need to build up my strength," she said, swallowing a laugh.

Jerrol gave a crack of laughter that made her grin as he

stood and ladled some more soup into her bowl. "Just hope you never have to face any of their fish gruel," he said as he sat back in his chair and picked up his spoon in his left hand. Even though he hardly noticed the damage to his right hand now, he tended to default to his left for most things. "It's full of fish bones." He shuddered delicately. "Supposed to give it more flavour."

Taelia nodded. "Makes sense. You always simmer chicken bones to make a broth for the same reason."

"But you don't leave them in it."

"True."

"More bread?" he asked as he placed a slice of the dark rye bread on her plate.

"We ought to leave it in case the staff need it."

"I have a feeling the staff wouldn't see any of it anyway. Don't fret. Marianille will let us know," he reassured her.

"When do you think our escort will arrive?"

"Depends where they are coming from, but probably tomorrow."

Taelia bit her lip. "And then onto Retarfu."

"Yes. I have the introduction to Grand Duke Randolf. I wonder if his daughter will be to court."

"Preferably not."

"Indeed, she was not particularly pleased with any of us by the time she left. With the death of Crown Prince Kharel, it left her exposed. Having shown her sympathies lay with her husband and the Ascendants, she couldn't back track from that. She had no choice but to return to her father." Jerrol stared off into the distance. "I know she was upset, but do you think she would encourage her father to go war?"

"Are you sure the grand duke will?"

"I hope not. He knows Benedict. I'm sure he wouldn't want to clash unnecessarily. He should be trading for goods not war. He needs to be preparing for winter." He frowned down at his empty bowl.

Taelia reached for his hand. "You'll make him see reason. After all, he wouldn't have granted you an audience if he wasn't prepared to listen."

Jerrol caressed her hand, drawing circles around her knuckles. "But why request *your* presence? Doesn't he have his own scholars?"

"I suppose we'll find out when we get there." She smiled at him, letting her hand drift down his thigh. He shivered beneath her fingers, and her smile deepened.

Jerrol and Taelia sat drinking their coffee as the dishes were cleared. Jerrol watched his wife with pleasure, a small smile hovering over his mouth. He dismissed the manservant with soft thanks and shut the door.

He pulled Taelia up out of her chair and hugged her close. Kissing her, he scooped her up in his arms and strode into one of the bedrooms before putting her down. He closed the door and slid the bolt before returning to stand before her.

He extended a trembling hand to tuck a stray curl behind her ear, leaned forward, and breathed gently as he kissed the edge of her ear. She quivered in delight. He kissed his way across her eyebrow, to the end of her nose, which made her smile, and continued all the way to the other ear, his hand caressing her face. "You complete me," he whispered as her fingers attacked the silver fastenings on his jacket.

And that was all it took. They shed their clothes and embraced. The touch of skin against skin set them on fire, and their bodies responded immediately to the touch of a fingertip, a tongue, or a lip. Jerrol led the way to the bed and lay down, surrendering to her completely as her hands worked her magic and he was lost in an overload of sensation and lust, his body responding to her slightest touch.

Jerrol lay replete with Taelia sprawled over him. She wriggled to keep him in place and then kissed the hollow of his throat as he slid his fingertips down her satin smooth back. The hair on his arms stood up on end as he shivered. She had captivated him, and he was her prisoner forever. Wrapping his arms around her and breathing her scent deep into his lungs, he rolled her over. She lifted her face and kissed him thoroughly as she wrapped her warm body around him, and he relaxed into the comfort of her arms as they snuggled down to sleep together.

12

GRAND DUKE HOTEL, POLLO

The next morning Marianille checked one room, found it empty and went to the other. She discreetly knocked on the door. There was no answer. Taking a deep breath, she opened the door and strode in to wake them. The words died on her lips as she saw them drowned in sleep, peacefully entwined around each other. She didn't want to disturb them.

Flipping a mental coin, she shook Jerrol's bare shoulder. "Captain, you need to wake; our escort has arrived."

Jerrol opened an eye, assessed his current position and sighed, his breath ruffling Taelia's hair. She was curled into his body, and he didn't want to move. "Very well, I'll be there shortly," he murmured, his reluctance obvious.

"You'd better be or I'll send in Niallerion," Marianille threatened.

Jerrol sighed again and stretched. His body ached deliciously, stirring pleasurable memories and promises of ravishing, but he heard the guards arriving in the courtyard below and levered himself up. He washed and dressed before turning to wake Taelia.

He woke her with a well-placed kiss, and she rose to the surface laughing, her arms reaching for him.

"Time, Scholar Haven, to rise and shine. Our escort has arrived."

"That sounds so nice. Scholar Haven," she said as she stretched luxuriously, her fingers caressing his neck as he leant over her, her face reflecting the pleasures they had shared. She sighed, staring up at him, her blue eyes sparkling with love and contentment. Truly you would never know she was blind. She smiled. "Good morning, my love."

"Good morning to you," he replied, kissing her on the lips.

She swung her legs over the side of the bed. "This is just a delay. You owe me big time," she said as she rose and moved over to the washbasin.

"Deal," he whispered as the door snicked shut behind him.

She smiled as she raised the washcloth to her face and inhaled the scent of him. Taelia closed her eyes. She was in so much trouble; she knew she wouldn't be able to keep her hands off him.

Jerrol and Taelia were sedately finishing their breakfast when Captain Ragthern of the Second Chevron arrived in their parlour. A waft of cold air preceded him, and Taelia shivered. He saluted briskly. "Sir, Grand Duke Randolf the fourteenth sends greetings. Your escort is ready. We leave in ten minutes. Your baggage is being transferred as we speak."

"Stay a moment, captain," Jerrol said as Ragthern turned to leave. "Grand Duke Randolf the fourteenth? I thought we had an audience with Grand Duke Randolf the thirteenth?"

"He died. His son ascended the throne four months ago.

Get ready. We leave now." He saluted again and turned on his heel before leaving them staring at an empty doorway.

"What?" Jerrol said into empty air as he sat back in shock.

"A man of immediate action," Taelia said as she placed her cup back in its saucer. She dabbed her mouth with her napkin as Jerrol rose.

"Lady help us, we're meeting the son. I have no idea what he is like or what he wants," Jerrol said, aghast. "Our hopes just went up in smoke."

"Maybe the son will be more reasonable?" Taelia suggested.

"I suppose we will have to find out. Shall we?"

"I suppose we ought to. Best not to upset the captain straight away," she murmured with a slight smile as Jerrol wrapped her cloak around her.

"Jerrol, they do not want you to ride us. Why is it wrong to ride? They have brought a carriage with them." Zin'talia's peevish voice filled his head.

"I don't know. I'll find out," Jerrol replied.

As they left the hotel, Taelia raised her face to the weak sunshine that was trying to break through the thick clouds. Her breath plumed on the chill air and Jerrol stiffened beside her. "What?"

"They have a very antiquated carriage for us," he murmured. "It is going to be a most uncomfortable journey."

"Oh dear." Taelia twinkled at him. "But surely any journey with me would be a pleasure?"

"Of course, my dear, just don't expect to walk straight when we get there."

"Why, Commander Haven, what do you have planned for me? And in a carriage as well."

"Behave," he murmured as he escorted her to the carriage.

She laughed as they came to a stop.

"Captain Ragthern, are you expecting us to ride in that to Retarfu?" Jerrol asked.

"Yes, sir, the grand duke sent it especially."

"Now, why would he do that?"

The captain flicked a glance at him and tightened his lips. "If you and the lady would board, we'll make a start."

"We brought horses with us. We could ride; it may be quicker," Jerrol offered.

"Your horses will stay here until you return. You won't need them at the palace."

"You should be riding me, not in a carriage," Zin'talia said.

"Zin'talia. It looks like Niallerion will have to ride you."

"Why? Why can't you ride me?"

"You were the one who wanted to come with us. Allowing Niallerion to ride you is the only way to get you to Retarfu," Jerrol replied. He caught Niallerion's eye. "Make sure you ride Zin'talia," he said in an undertone.

Niallerion nodded and moved towards the stables.

Jerrol assisted Taelia into the carriage, and then walked around to the front, where the horses steamed in their traces. He peered up to where Marianille sat on the roof. "Marianille, all good?" he called.

"Yes, sir," Marianille replied, her face expressionless.

Jerrol grinned at her discomfort before returning to the door and climbing into the antiquated vehicle. He sat opposite Taelia. The captain slammed the door, and the carriage lurched into motion. "Well, isn't this pleasant? A dark and dingy carriage carrying us off into distant parts," Jerrol said as he leaned back.

"And such nice cushions to sit on." Taelia smiled as she prodded the hard seat.

The carriage lurched again as it turned onto the easterly road towards the city of Retarfu. Taelia flailed at the unexpected movement, losing her balance, and Jerrol caught her in his arms before twisting to sit beside her, wrapping his arm around her waist and holding her steady against him. He braced his arm and a foot against the side of the carriage.

"Well, a timely bump," she exclaimed, shoving her hair out of her face. "I am glad you came, Commander Haven."

The carriage wended its torturous way through the Elothian countryside; bleak and open for the most part. The wind howling across the plains buffeted the carriage making it sway and creak alarmingly. The snow-covered plains extended as far as the eye could see. Small destitute villages clung to the edges of the road or near an icy river crossing; all looking grey and dejected.

Zin'talia's running commentary interspersed with complaints and observations kept Jerrol amused as he tried to protect Taelia from the worst effects of the journey.

They had been travelling for at least three hours when the carriage finally came to a stop. Jerrol had to shove the door to open it, ice cracking as he gingerly climbed down. He stretched out his aching back and thighs. Captain Ragthern stopped beside him, a brief flash of sympathy in his eyes. "We stop to water the horses. The scholar can freshen up in the inn. We have a room for you."

"Thank you," Jerrol said as he turned to assist Taelia out of the carriage. He shivered as the icy air worked its way into his clothes.

Taelia staggered as she reached the ground, her legs trembling. "I'm glad he didn't suggest I be watered to," she said with a wry twist of her lips as she grabbed his arm. "Please don't make me get back in there."

"Come, there is an inn. Maybe we can find some hot tea inside," Jerrol led her towards the grey brick building standing back off the road. A large cartwheel leaned against the wall and someone had tried to decorate it with dried flowers, but the tied bunches sagged in dreary defeat, faded and weather-worn. "Mind the ground; it is uneven and a bit icy," he murmured, and she lifted her feet a little higher.

The innkeeper met them inside, offering refreshments. The ceilings were low, pressing down on the occupants of the dim taproom. The furniture was made of dark wood and sturdy, adding to the repressive atmosphere. Taelia gripped Jerrol's arm as they paused, and she raised her face, breathing in the stale air.

"Marianille, assist the scholar," Jerrol said as Marianille appeared behind them. He followed the innkeeper into the bar.

"Whereabouts are we?" he asked, as he continued to stretch, disguising it by removing his cloak.

"Pul." The innkeeper slapped an empty mug on the bar.

"Pul?"

"Yes, Pul. Last village before the ruins of Cerne and the road to Retarfu."

"Ruins of Cerne?"

The barkeeper pursed his lips and gave Jerrol a searching glance. "Yeah, miles of ruined buildings. Ghosts up there. Never travel at night, you won't come out again. Many a man's been lost in there. Confusing they are."

"What is so dangerous about the ruins?"

"Well, legend says," the innkeeper poured some ale in the mug and shoved it in front of Jerrol, "an ancient ancestor of the grand duke once had his palace there; amazing palace it was, spires and towers, houses and shops. A right town grew around it, and all prospered," the innkeeper expanded, warming to his theme.

Jerrol wrinkled his nose at the ale; it smelt stale. "Any chance of some hot tea? I am sure the lady would prefer it."

The innkeeper frowned at him for interrupting and yelled something out of the side of his mouth before resuming his tale. "Of course, it couldn't last."

"Why not?" Jerrol asked.

"The duke crossed the Lady Guardian, and she grew wroth with him and caused the land to heave and buck, destroying his wonderful city and burying the poor people in the rubble."

A small girl dressed in what looked like a sack entered the room and placed a small tray with a clay mug on the table. She stared at Jerrol from wide grey eyes before dashing out again.

"Surely not. The Guardian would protect her people. And anyway, I heard it was the Lady Marguerite's temple."

"She was jealous, that's what I think. A woman spurned, you know, very dangerous; she destroyed it all," the man said with a crisp nod.

Marianille was describing the inn to Taelia as they came into the bar. She sat Taelia at the table and, at her prompting, Taelia picked up the clay mug. She sniffed it with some suspicion and took a hesitant sip before placing it back on the table and pushing it away as an expression of distaste crossed her face.

"Why does the road run through the ruins if they are so dangerous?" Jerrol asked, turning his gaze back to the innkeeper.

"Quickest route," the man said.

The Elothian captain appeared in the doorway. "We need to leave. We still have at least five hours to travel, and it will be dark by the time we get to the city."

Jerrol nodded. "We'll be right with you. The scholar needs to finish her tea."

"That's fine," Taelia said, hurriedly standing.

"Of course," Jerrol offered Taelia his hand and led her

back out of the inn. He looked around them as Niallerion approached.

"They are nervous about something. The captain had to speak quite sharply to his men. If I didn't know better, I'd say some of them are on the verge of deserting," Niallerion said, keeping his voice soft. Jerrol glanced about, observing the skittish horses reflecting their riders' discomfort.

"Stay alert," he said in acknowledgement as he handed a reluctant Taelia back into the carriage.

"Did he say another five hours?" she asked as she arranged her skirts.

Jerrol's sigh matched hers. "That's what he said." He settled himself beside her, relaxing as she moved closer. Jerrol braced his foot against the other seat as the carriage lurched its way back onto the road, clasping his wife in his arms.

They were murmuring sweet nothings to each other to pass the time, Jerrol flinging an arm out sporadically as they met overly deep ruts that rocked the carriage, when they heard a shout. Jerrol looked up and eased over to the window. There wasn't much to see. A damp fog swirled around them in wisps, thinning to reveal grey stone tumbled amongst the wiry grass and then thickening to conceal them.

There was another shout, and the carriage lurched violently. A resounding crack split the air as the carriage tilted, throwing Jerrol and Taelia to the floor. They slid across the surface as the carriage careered at a precarious angle down a steep slope before shuddering to a groaning halt. The squealing of panicking horses and the sound of shattering glass were interrupted by more shouts, and then there was silence.

13

RUINS OF CERNE, ELOTHIA

Jerrol loosened his grip on Taelia. Fortunately, she was lying on top of him. He was wedged against the door, which had buckled under him, and something was sticking painfully into his back. "Are you alright?" he asked.

"Yes, I think so." Taelia's voice wavered. "Are you? What happened?"

"Looks like we won't be riding in the carriage anymore."

"Oh, good," she said, her voice firming.

Marianille's voice came from outside. "Captain, Scholar, are you alright?" Her horrified face appeared in the cracked window, taking in their awkward position she pulled the door open and leaned in to pull Taelia out.

"Scholar, are you hurt?" she asked, and not waiting for an answer she leaned in and helped unwedge Jerrol, who gratefully accepted the strong hand pulling him up and out.

"Are you alright?" he asked as he peered at the underside of the carriage.

"Yes, Niallerion is helping to calm the horses. One is trapped in its traces; the guards are trying to release it."

"What happened?"

"I'm not sure. We were about halfway through the ruins. It looked like the road continued straight, but when this mist swirled in it was quite disorientating. I think we must have veered off the road and run down the bank. I'm not sure we'll get the carriage back out, though Captain Ragthern seems determined."

"I'm sure he is," Jerrol murmured as they climbed out of the ditch. He straightened and surveyed the scene; controlled chaos he thought.

"Zin'talia, are you alright?"

"Fine, Niallerion and I were further back. The mist was so dense, it was impossible to see anything."

The captain shouted some more commands at his men and turned to Jerrol. "Commander, if you please, wait over there." He pointed at a group of rocks. "We will be on our way soon."

Jerrol thought he was overly optimistic but nodded in agreement and escorted Taelia over to a weathered slab of stone beside the road. "Your seat, my lady."

"Why thank you, sir," she sat, patting the rock beneath her, and then she stretched. "I'm not sure I want to sit. Do you think we could walk for a bit? Maybe work a few of these kinks out?"

"Good idea. Marianille, do you want to see if you can help Niallerion?"

"Don't go far, Captain. We don't know what's out there," Marianille said, looking around with caution. Jerrol glanced at her and Marianille laughed. "You should hear the tales these people tell."

He shooed her away. "We won't go far," he said as he turned to look at the ruins behind him and the fog parted to reveal a tall stone column. Jerrol pulled Taelia to her feet. "Look," he murmured, "this column is a lighter coloured stone than the blocks scattered around it. It's been shattered about half-way down, but there are much taller columns all around us." He placed her hand on the column. "Grooves run the length of it all the way round." He frowned up at it, then turned around.

The mist swirled around him; damp air caressed his face and lingered, sprinkling droplets of water on his hair and clothes. He took a step forward as the guards called to each other off to his right, their voices muffled in the eerie twilight air. "Taelia," he began, and then his foot gave beneath him and he dropped. He landed lightly on his feet, looking around as dirt pattered down on his head. Brushing himself down, he approached the wall in front of him. It was filled with engravings of scenes of people in action. He reached out to touch the semblance of a tall tree with broad pointy leaves and a deep ache flared through his chest.

"Jerrol?" Taelia called from almost on top of him.

"Tali, stop. There is a hole right in front of you," he shouted. She gave a slight shriek as her foot stepped onto empty air, and she landed in his outstretched arms before he hit the ground with a whoof! and lay winded for a moment.

"Jerrol? Are you alright?" Her fingers fluttered over him as she rolled off him. "I am so sorry, my love," she murmured, kissing his face, her hands patting him.

"Just give me a minute," he gasped, "get my breath back." She rubbed his back, slowing as she felt moisture and a jagged tear. She raised her hand to her nose.

"Jerrol, you're bleeding; you've hurt your back."

"It's nothing," he replied, sitting up.

"I'll be the judge of that. Take your jacket off."

"Here? It's much too cold. It can wait."

"No, it can't. Take it off now."

Jerrol gave a martyred sigh and took his jacket and shirt off. "Aren't you more interested in these engravings?" he suggested as he turned his back to her.

"No. They'll still be there in a minute." Her hands fluttered over his warm skin, which was chilling fast in the cold air. "Jerrol," she exclaimed as he shivered. "How can you say this is nothing? You have a great big splinter in your back."

"Then yank it out," he replied. "It's freezing down here."

Muttering under her breath, she ripped her petticoat and handed a section to him. "Tear that into strips for me and tie them together. I should just carry a stock of bandages whenever I am with you. I'm running out of petticoats."

Gently feeling his back, she poked and prodded as he winced, and she eased the splinter out. There was a spurt of blood as she finally got it out and clamped a pad over it. "I hope the grand duke has healers. We need to make sure there's no dirt in it," she said as she took the strips of cloth he passed her and tied the pad in place.

He kissed her nose. "Thank you," he said, and he donned his shirt, buttoning his jacket over the top. She wiped her hands on her skirts. "Come over here." He took her hand, his were freezing, and placed it on the wall. "This looks like a sentinal tree," he said as her hands slid over the wall, her sensitive fingertips registering the shapes that formed in her head.

"It is," she breathed as she moved down the wall. "Jerrol, this is Elothian history before us. We could find out so much about how they lived back then. These engravings are very old. I'd say it matches the same style we found in that small chamber you fell into."

"You could have just said 'discovered'," he complained, though she heard the smile in his voice. "You should ask the grand duke if you can come back and explore. We are not going to have time now," he said as he walked down a slight incline. The ceiling rose above his head and disappeared into the shadows. "This place is enormous," he said, his voice echoing as he reached to touch another column. A vibration shimmered in the air as he peered up into the vaulted ceiling. A gentle glow gave him enough light to see by, but he couldn't see where the light was coming from.

He squinted above him and froze, his hand resting on the column. Only it wasn't a column; it was a tree. A petrified tree, grey and silent. The pointy leaves were frozen in place, overlapping to create the ceiling of the cavern. He embraced the tree, reaching within; there was no response; the air was still and silent.

He persisted, pushing through compacted layers of fossilised wood. There had to be a Sentinal under all this hardened bark. He wormed his way past the outer rings and sifted through fading memories; a vision of a tall, muscular soldier, brown eyed, and with an impressive beard. He was kneeling in front of a young woman, a sword at his hip and laughter in his eyes. A luminous beauty glowed in the woman's face as she laughed with him. Jerrol recognised her vivid blue eyes and copper burnished hair. She knelt with him and shoved her hands deep into the earth, and all around her soft green grass and meadow flowers sprung up from the frozen depths.

"Marguerite," Jerrol whispered.

The woman raised her head and stared straight at him. "Save my warrior," she said clearly. "Do not allow him to give up." Her eyes, as blue as the sky, drilled into his and then softened, pleading. "Don't let any of them give up, please," she whispered as she faded from view.

Jerrol stirred and awareness flooded back. Taelia was calling him, and he realised he was trapped inside a petrified tree, somewhere under a ruined town in Elothia. What was he doing? He reached within. "Marguerite needs you; she is waiting for you." There was silence. "She needs your strength, and she needs your love. Taurillion, Marguerite needs you."

No response.

"The Ladies Leyandrii and Marguerite need you. Their Sentinals strong, defending their realm. You are derelict in your duty," Jerrol snapped, his voice hardening. "You've spent long enough nursing your sorrows. Awake now and report," he commanded.

A resounding crack split the air and the tree began to tremble. Jerrol stepped back into Taelia's outstretched arms. "Jerrol?" she said, gripping him tight as the ground began to tremble as well.

"It's a Sentinal," Jerrol murmured, clasping her hands and leading her away from the tree. He hugged her as the outer shell of the tree started to crack like spreading fissures in thin ice, forming a mosaic of tiny pieces that began shedding off the tree. Jerrol deepened his voice. "Report," he commanded, making Taelia jump. The canopy of leaves unfurled above them, reaching for the ceiling. The ceiling shimmered and was gone. The moon shone; the brilliant gleam meeting the questing leaves, which shivered and then stilled as they absorbed the light of the moon for the first time in centuries.

Jerrol stared at the man who appeared before him. He was the man from Marguerite's memory; tall and broad chested, his copper eyes a little wild. His face was pale with anger.

"Where is she? Where's Birlerion?" he demanded.

"Umm, they are not here at the moment."

"She promised, she promised me." The Sentinal paused, glaring at Jerrol. "Who are you?"

"Captain Jerrol Haven, Captain of the Lady's Guard, and this is Scholar Taelia Haven." Taelia tightened her grip on his arm.

"You're not the Captain. Where's Guerlaire?"

"With the Lady, I believe," Jerrol said, watching the Sentinal stiffen as he searched the cavern.

"What did you do? Where are we?"

"We are amongst the ruins of Cerne."

"Cerne? In ruins? What am I doing here?" Taurillion gazed around, disoriented. He rubbed his chest absently as he frowned. "She promised."

"What did she promise?" Jerrol asked.

"Not to leave me," he said, looking around him, his eyes haunted.

"Maybe she didn't have a choice. I believe it was chaotic towards the end. She had to save who she could. Many were lost."

"Of course she had a choice; she is a Guardian. All-powerful. Why did she leave us to die?"

"But you're not dead," Jerrol pointed out.

"Might as well have been. Frozen in time, stranded, helpless. That's dying, isn't it?"

"But no longer. Elothia needs you. Marguerite needs you."

"And she expects us to just fall back in line as if nothing happened? Why would we?"

"Because you made an oath to protect the Lady and Remargaren, and they need you now. The Ascendants threaten our lives as they did three thousand years ago," Jerrol said, keeping his voice calm.

"She tricked me, she promised. It's way too late," Taurillion spun around, looking about him wildly. "It's Birlerion's fault," he said, before he shimmered back into his sentinal and out of sight.

Jerrol exhaled his breath with a whoosh. "That didn't go too well," he murmured.

"He just needs time. It must be a terrible shock to be awoken just like that. It's a lot to get used to, and he has been

in a lot worse conditions than some of the others," Taelia
suggested.

"Why would he blame Birlerion? What's it to do with
him?"

"He may be confused," Taelia suggested.

Jerrol frowned as he thought of the Terolian Sentinals
who had been in a similar situation and came out reasonably
whole. He glanced at the second petrified tree. "There's
another one. What do you think? Should we try again?"

"Surely it would be better to be awake than not?"

He peered back towards the hole they had fallen through.
Muffled shouts penetrated the cavern but little else. Swirls of
mist drifted in the air. "It must be taking them longer to get
that carriage out than they anticipated. I'm surprised they
haven't missed us yet."

"I don't think we've been down here very long," Taelia
reassured him.

"We haven't? It feels like we've been down here for ages.
Very well, let's try number two." He reached out towards the
trunk. Taelia placed her hand beside his and, taking a deep
breath, he pushed against the petrified shell, trying to discern
who was within.

"*A woman,*" Taelia's thoughtful voice sounded in his head
as he received the impression of a lighter, more feminine
touch, but when he staggered back from the sentinal dragging Taelia with him, he was confronted by a stone-faced
warrior. Her eyes glinted silver, her hair of the palest blonde,
almost white, was plaited down her back. She stared at them.
Her uniform was a faded green tunic and trousers, made of
a thick material that looked like it was designed for warmth
rather than elegance.

"What do you want?" Her voice was low and scratchy.

"Your help," Jerrol replied.

The woman laughed and rolled her eyes. "Nothing new

there, then," she said, her voice cutting. She flexed her shoulders as if settling back into her body then turned back to her tree and laid a gentle hand on its bark. "We're back," she said, and the tree shook itself as the outer casing cracked and fell in a pearlescent cascade. A brief smile flitted across her face, before she turned back, stone-faced, to Jerrol.

"Yaserille, the Lady needs you, as does Marguerite. We need your help."

"Who are you?"

"Captain Jerrol Haven, Captain of the Lady's Guard."

"The Lady's Captain? Yeah, I can see it. To do what?"

"To save the grand duke and free his people."

Yaserille snorted in disgust. "The grand duke? He's a greedy bastard who cares for no one but himself; let him rot."

"Umm, I don't think the latest duke is the same man," Jerrol said with a tight grin.

Yaserille stared at him. "The latest? How many have there been?"

"Quite a few; you've been asleep for over three thousand years," Taelia said.

"What?" Yaserille took a step back, her eyes widening.

"It's the year 4124. It's been three thousand years since you last walked this land," Jerrol said.

"Surely not. Where's Marguerite?"

"She bonded with the Land. Her family were banished behind the Veil when the Lady sundered the bloodstone."

"She did what?" Yaserille hissed. "Who else is here?"

"Well, Taurillion, but he wasn't too impressed with his awakening either."

"Taurillion? Get your arse out here, now!" Yaserille's voice filled the cavern, and Taelia moved closer to Jerrol as she shivered in the chill air.

"Something's not right here," Taelia murmured. "These Sentinals don't feel like the others."

Jerrol sighed as he wrapped an arm around her shoulders. "I fear nothing in Elothia is as it should be," he whispered, watching the tall Sentinal as she strode towards the first tree.

"Taurillion! Get out here now. You rat-faced coward."

Jerrol cringed. This reunion was not happening as he had expected.

The tall, copper-eyed man appeared outside his tree. "Stop your shrieking, woman. They'll hear you all the way to Skaarsflow."

"Hrmph, fat chance. What do you make of all this?"

"She left us here for centuries. Centuries, Yas. Why should we listen to anything he says? Marguerite isn't even here."

"Because I am the Captain of the Guard, that's why," Jerrol said. "And your Lady needs your help."

Taurillion laughed. "Yeah right. What did Birlerion do this time?"

"You were with Birlerion at the end?" Jerrol asked, his chest grabbing at the thought of his friend.

"Long enough to be captured. That boy always finds trouble. I don't remember…" His voice faltered before firming again. "I shouldn't be here. I was in Vespers. What was she thinking?" Taurillion's eyes gleamed a soft coppery brown in the dim light. "She doesn't need me, nor does Grand Duke Egryll. Lady bless his rule."

"The Lady very much needs and wants you. I need your help, as does Birlerion," Jerrol said. "The final hours before the Lady sundered the stone were traumatic. The Guardian struggled to control the land as it reacted to the forces that the Ascendants drove into it. She tried to save as many people as she could. She did what she could to preserve life on Remargaren. You were encased in a sentinal to preserve you. Until now. Grand Duke Randolf the fourteenth currently rules Elothia; he has recently come to the throne."

Taurillion frowned. "What happened to Egryll?"

"He died centuries ago, from food poisoning I think," Jerrol said, racking his memory for the demise of such an ancient duke.

"Ha! Think I'll see for myself. Let's see what this world has to tell me," Taurillion said as he disappeared into his tree.

"Yaserille, much has changed. You won't recognise the landscape. Much damage was done. The people no longer remember you."

"I think I'm with Taurillion on this one. I want to see for myself."

"Be careful out there. Elothia is not as you left it," Jerrol said as she re-entered her tree.

14

RUINS OF CERNE, ELOTHIA

J errol blew out a breath as he stared at the two trees. They almost had an air of embarrassment about them before they shimmered out of sight, leaving Jerrol and Taelia still entombed underground.

As Taelia wormed her way under his arm, he turned them back towards the opening they had fallen through. Marianille was calling them. Jerrol raised his voice. "We're down here."

"What are you doing down there?"

"Well, you see, I thought it would be a really good idea to fall down a hole, and then the scholar being the adventurous type that she is, decided it was such a good idea that she joined me," Jerrol replied, an edge to his voice.

There was a slight pause. "I'll get a rope."

Taelia took the opportunity to hug him once last time. "Please be careful," she whispered as he nuzzled her neck.

"This was never going to be easy, but I'll do my best."

"I love you," she breathed as she heard Marianille return with some soldiers, and she let go of him.

"I love you," Jerrol whispered, dropping a light kiss on

her head; an action so familiar, she leaned back against him without realising it.

"Ah, here are our rescuers," Jerrol murmured catching the rope. He looped the end so she could put her foot in it. "Hold on tight."

He watched anxiously, as she was pulled up out of the hole and the rope returned for him. Once he was pulled out, he faced the scowling captain.

"I told you it wasn't safe," the captain snapped, his anger barely controlled.

"My apologies. We only wanted to stretch our legs, but as you see, we are unharmed and ready to continue."

The captain stiffened, Jerrol's unruffled response annoying him even more. "Then please return to the carriage. We have lost much time. It will be late by the time we arrive."

Jerrol bowed in agreement and escorted Taelia back to the now upright carriage. One window had a blanket tacked across it, and the woodwork was scratched and muddy, but Jerrol handed Taelia up without comment and sat beside her as the door was forced shut behind them. He snuck his arm around her waist, smiling as she snuggled into him. The air was chill without the sun to warm it, and the mist still swirled around them damply.

He sighed as the carriage lurched forward and he braced his foot back against the other bench. "Do you think you can try to sleep? Who knows what they expect us to do once we arrive?"

"Sleep? In this? You must be joking."

"I fear the captain wants to make up for lost time. Let's hope he doesn't find another ditch in his haste."

"Then I am definitely not sleeping," Taelia said, gripping him tightly as the carriage lurched. Jerrol flung his arm out to brace them.

"Let us hope all this discomfort will indeed get us there quicker," he murmured, his body rocking with Taelia's as the carriage thundered down the road.

Jerrol's arms and legs were stiff with fatigue and tension by the time they arrived in Retarfu. He feared Taelia was little better, even though he had tried to cushion her against the worst. He could see nothing outside the window. The city was in darkness. A few dim torches lined the road, guiding them to the palace, and they clattered under an echoey archway before suddenly pulling to a halt amidst crunching gravel.

Marianille appeared at the window, her pale face gleaming through the cracked glass. She pulled the door open and offered a hand to help Jerrol out. She watched with sympathy as Jerrol tried to straighten up, his breath hissing through his teeth. Taelia stepped out beside him, her hand reaching for his arm immediately.

"Why is there no one to greet you? I thought you were an ambassador of note." Zin'talia's voice had a note of grievance in it.

He smiled at her ardent defence of his honour. *"It's late. I expect they are asleep. I hope the duke's stables are as comfortable as the king's."*

"They'd better be," she replied.

He was sure she'd be telling him if they weren't.

"Jerrol?" Taelia murmured, her head tilting as she caught the sounds of people arriving.

"Just the household staff, here for our bags," he replied, trying to stretch the kinks out of his back. He eyed her in amazement. She seemed as fresh as when they had started the journey. Jerrol searched the courtyard for their welcoming party.

Captain Ragthern saluted sharply. "If you would follow me, sir, madam, the footman will show you to your rooms.

Unfortunately, it is too late to meet the grand duke. Your audience has been rearranged for tomorrow morning."

"Of course, lead the way," Jerrol said agreeably, guiding Taelia up the white, marble steps. Marianille followed with Niallerion behind them glancing around with acute interest. Jerrol observed the palace, noting the absence of staff or any formal welcome. His eyes met Marianille's and glided on as they passed through a large entrance hall and began to ascend the curving stairs. Ornate, gilt decorated railings marched upwards, leading them into the depths of the marble palace, and Jerrol grimaced as the thought of being corralled like livestock flashed through his mind.

Their rooms were suitably appointed, lavishly adorned with more gilt-edged furnishings and colourful upholstery, and positioned either side of a private sitting room. Marianille had a small cubby hole off Taelia's bedroom. Niallerion had a room off Jerrol's as befit his station.

Taelia was led off to the baths by a silent young maid, who murmured directions in a low voice, Marianille close behind. Jerrol washed in his room, Niallerion having brought him a supply of hot water.

"This palace is as bad as Leyandrii's; it's like a maze," Niallerion said in disgust.

"Do your best," Jerrol replied.

"Yes, sir."

Jerrol paced the sitting room as he waited for the woman putting away Taelia's clothes to finish. She padded into the sitting room. "Supper will be served when the scholar returns, sir."

Jerrol nodded and let the woman leave.

They were in a semblance of relaxed conversation about the voyage when Taelia returned, closely followed by a rattling trolley. She smelt of roses and jasmine, and Jerrol's shoulders relaxed as he inhaled the scent as she approached him.

"Feel better?" he inquired as he led her to a deeply cushioned seat next to the fire.

"Much; hot water is such bliss."

"And they let you loose in the perfumery as well," Jerrol noted as he sat opposite her.

Taelia chuckled. "I have something else to add to my list. I think I need some of that bathwater."

Jerrol leant forward in his chair and lowered his voice. "Unfortunately, I don't think you can get that list out here, at any time. Until we know the situation here, and I've met the grand duke, I'm not sure we should announce our joining."

Taelia stilled, the happiness fading from her face. "I see. That is a very great shame. I look forward to the day when we can."

Jerrol leaned back. "I very much hope that we will get a tour tomorrow after I have my audience with the grand duke. His palace is famous for the paintings and frescos in the long gallery. I am sure the grand duke will allow us to visit them; after all, you are here to help uncover the history of the palace for him."

Taelia tapped her lips, thoughtfully. "True. Marianille and I need to meet with the Archivist. I have an introduction from Scholar Deane Liliian. While you have your audience with the grand duke, I will search him out."

"Good," Jerrol said, holding Marianille's eye. They were interrupted by their supper arriving, and they had no further privacy until they had finished.

Jerrol sighed as the last servant left and Niallerion padded after them, checking the corridors. "I believe we should have an early night for all. We've had a trying day. Scholar, I bid you a peaceful night under the Lady's gaze."

He helped her rise and put his heart in the caress he gave her hands. Her hands convulsed around his in return.

"Lady bless you, Jerrol," she breathed, "as do I." She reluctantly released his hands and walked to her room, leaving Jerrol staring after her. He heaved a despondent sigh and retired to his room and his very empty bed.

He didn't think he would sleep, but he was disturbed by a slender woman with tresses of blond hair and brilliant green eyes who stood before him. "Jerrol," she said intently.

Jerrol blinked in surprise. Lady Leyandrii had never used his name before.

"For the sake of Remargaren, you must shed the Captain and embrace the Oath Keeper."

"What?" he frowned at her. "What does that mean?"

"Forsake me, Jerrol, to protect the Veil. It is the only way to prevent the Ascendants from using you to shred the Veil. I didn't see them. They are further ahead of us than I realised. This is the only way I can protect you. Forsake me. Marguerite will find you."

"Marguerite?" Jerrol struggled to think how the deity he had first met in Terolia would be able to help him, trapped as she was within the strata of the rock under the desert.

"Forsake me now, completely," the Lady demanded.

"I can't. You know I'm yours, now and always. The oath bound us closer. I can't forsake you." Jerrol lurched out of his bed. "Leyandrii? I can't forsake you. I don't know how."

Soft fingers caressed his face and his skin heated beneath her touch. "For Taelia and Jason. Would you do it for them? To protect them? It is the only way. To save my people. To save my Sentinals."

"I don't understand."

"Allow the one within you to rise. Birlerion shed the Sentinal. For me, he let go of all he knew and embraced what he once was. Every day he amazes me, and I honour him for it. You must help him. He will not know you when you find him. Only you can reach him and return him to us, when it's time. You are the Oath Keeper. Marguerite will find you. Promise me. You will forsake me. You must remain hidden from Ascendant eyes."

Jerrol trembled under the force of her will. His heart thrummed as he buckled under her regard. "For you, anything," he gasped. "But they already know who I am. I don't know what to do."

She soothed his distress and gently kissed his forehead. "They have no idea who you are. You know exactly what to do. Birlerion has, and he has been bound to me for much longer than you have. Do it now," she said as she faded from view.

Jerrol braced himself against the wall. He looked around him as he tried to catch his breath, his heart hammering in his chest. Swallowing, he tried not to vomit. Acid burnt his throat and he grabbed the glass of water by his bed and drained it. He gasped in a breath. Replacing the glass, he slumped on the bed and held his head in his hands, his mind spinning.

After a while he stirred. Sitting here moping would not solve anything. He squared his shoulders and breathed in deeply. Rising, he moved over to stare out of the window. The moon gleamed brilliantly above him, and he felt her farewell and an unspoken demand. He frowned up at her in dismay as uncertainty fluttered in his stomach. Gripping the windowsill, he bent his head before her, wrestling with the idea. And Birlerion? His stomach roiled at the thought of what his friend must have continued to suffer, but the Lady knew where he was, and he was still alive.

Of their own accord, his hands reached up and removed the leather cord from around his neck. The smooth green stone, pierced by the cord, glistened in his hand. He had always worn it, the stone rubbed smooth by his fingers over the years. He remembered finding it as a child when he had lost his way. He had taken it for a sign and clung to it ever since.

Jerrol stiffened as he felt the Lady accept his rejection, the emptiness within a physical pain. He gritted his teeth and ignored the ache. Turning away from the window he dressed; he wouldn't be sleeping any more tonight. Silently, he made his way through the palace, aware that Niallerion shadowed him and out towards the training grounds behind the grand duke's barracks. He started to run around the perimeter the rhythm of his feet pounding the dirt. He ran until the sound blotted out all thought and numbed his mind. He finally raised his tearing eyes from the ground as the rising sun lightened the sky.

15

DEEPWATER WATCH, VESPIRI

J ennery awoke suddenly, not sure what had disturbed him, but he lay tense and alert, waiting. When nothing disturbed the silence of the night, he rose and gently covered Alyssa with the blanket as she mewed a soft protest. He paused by the window and stared up at the crescent moon as a cloud passed over it, and he shivered. He dressed and silently left the room, making sure he hadn't disturbed his sleeping wife.

He met Denirion and Tagerill in the shadow-striped main hall. "What is it?" he asked as he inspected the Sentinals. They were both agitated and strained, unable to keep still.

"Something's happened to the Captain. He's gone," Tagerill said, clenching his jaw.

"You mean he's been killed?" Jennery asked, aghast.

"No, we're not sure. It's like Birlerion; we can no longer sense him. But it's not the same feeling as Serillion," Denirion said, his face drawn. The shadows aged him, deepening the lines engraved on his face. "It's possible that he has forsaken the Lady."

"Jerrol? Never!" Jennery gripped Denirion's arm and gave him a slight shake. "It's not possible."

Tagerill shrugged, rubbing his temple. "I would have sworn the same about Birlerion, and yet we can't find him. Maybe the Ascendants got to him. They've had him for months, now."

"The Lady would have protected them both. It makes no sense," Jennery said.

"Then I hope Jerrol knows what he is doing because he is in Elothia," Tagerill replied.

"Elothia?" Jennery frowned in confusion.

"With Taelia. My sister, Marianille is with them. They are in Retarfu."

"And you believe Jerrol no longer walks the Lady's path?" Jennery asked, his face paling.

"Yes," Tagerill said, reluctance clear in his voice.

Jennery paced across the hallway before abruptly turning towards his office. "There's got to be an explanation," he muttered under his breath as he searched through the papers on his desk. He reviewed the last set of orders which had arrived from the commander's office.

"He knew," Jennery said.

"What?" Denirion and Tagerill asked in unison.

Jennery sat at his desk and rifled through the papers stacked in front of him, pulling one out. He skimmed it. "He knew; he must have known. I thought his last communique odd. 'No matter what you hear or believe, follow orders. Many lives depend on it.' He wanted us to be ready on the borders; to be ready to position men deep into Elothia. The bastard planned this and didn't tell us."

"But what will we do without the Captain?" Tagerill asked.

Jennery stood and slapped him on the shoulder. "Would you forsake the Captain just for a feeling?" he asked with a grin. "He is made of sterner stuff and will no doubt surprise us all. Make sure Marianille keeps us informed," he ordered, belying his concern.

Jerrol returned to his room and then went to the baths to shower. He dressed in his formal clothes, adjusting the harsh cotton shirt and slipping on his jacket. He missed the subtle shimmer, the fine-textured linen, the weight of her attention. Leyandrii had withdrawn completely, and he felt bereft as if he had lost a piece of himself. He flexed his damaged hand, her loss even more visceral than losing his fingers, and that was something he never thought he would say. He pulled the skin-tight black glove over his hand to hide the damage.

He wondered how Birlerion felt. His faith was even more deep-rooted; for him to have stepped away was beyond belief. He clung to the fact that Birlerion was still alive, even if his situation may be dire.

Lifting his chin, he left his room. He joined Taelia for breakfast. Slipping his amulet into Taelia's questing hand, he whispered, "Keep it safe for me," as he took his seat next to her, his leg touching hers. He met Marianille's eyes, ignoring the questions and concern he could see in them. "I have an audience with the grand duke today. Hopefully, I will get an idea of the situation and what we are dealing with. I fear the Ascendants may be present and have more influence than we thought."

"Jerrol, what has happened?" Taelia whispered, aghast as she realised what he had given her.

"Whatever happens, stay together. The Ascendants will not deliberately harm you, Taelia; you are here at the grand duke's request. Marianille will attend you as she has done so far. There is no reason for them to suspect her." He held

Marianille's gaze until she nodded acceptance. "Be patient, all of you. Wait for me."

"Jerrol," beseeched Taelia.

"There is something I have to do." He looked at Niallerion. "Find out how the court works; see who gets into the grand duke's presence and who doesn't. And see if you can find a way out," he murmured for Niallerion's ears only, who nodded.

"Taelia, there is a reason you had to come with me. There is something here you must find. Find it for me, my love, but carefully."

Taelia stilled as she stared at him. "Jerrol, I don't feel good about this."

"I know," Jerrol sighed, "me neither. But we do what must be done," he said as he rose. He bent and kissed her on the lips. "Wait for me," he repeated. "I will come back to you."

"Forever," she breathed back, her hand rising to touch his face, but he backed away out of her reach.

He couldn't eat the food on the table. He looked across at Marianille and nodded. Marianille watched him go, concern in her eyes.

Niallerion followed him. "What is it?" he murmured. "What do you know?"

Jerrol shrugged. "The Lady has her pieces in motion; we can but follow her commands."

Jerrol waited at the side of the throne room. He clasped his hands behind his back and shifted his weight into a more comfortable position. He wasn't sure what to expect. He knew nothing about the young grand duke he was about to have an audience with, and he didn't think the wider world even knew that the old duke had died. There had been no rumours of ill health, no announcement. He wondered if it had been as much a shock to his son as it must have been to the rest of the nation.

Nikols hadn't given him much information on the son. All he knew was that the new grand duke had a sister, Princess Selvia, who had been married to King Benedict's son, Crown Prince Kharel. Kharel and Selvia had been part of a failed coup to take the throne of Vespiri. Kharel had died in the attempt and the king had sent Selvia back to her father. He wondered what she had been up to since she returned home in disgrace. He wondered where she was.

His heart sank as the grand duke entered the room with Selvia on his arm, escorted by the man he knew as the Ascendant Var'geris. Var'geris stood behind the grand duke's shoulder. A position of influence; a position of trust.

Jerrol observed the grand duke closely as he settled Selvia in her chair. He was of medium height, slightly built, blond-haired, and blue-eyed, with an open face smoothed by youth. Taller than his sister, he wore black trousers and a white shirt, over which he wore an ornate jacket bedecked in glittering gems and gold braid. He didn't look comfortable, as if he was wearing someone else's clothes and they didn't quite fit right. Stopping at the edge of the dais, he fidgeted with the tassel on his jacket, and observed Jerrol in return as Selvia scowled at him. "Welcome to Elothia, Ambassador Haven." His voice was low and smooth, 'rich in timbre', Taelia would have said. A base note vibrated gently. Jerrol liked his voice, and he took hope.

"Your Grace, thank you for agreeing to see me. May I offer sincere condolences from myself and King Benedict for the loss of your father, Grand Duke Randolf the Thirteenth. Word had not reached us as we travelled regarding your loss, or we would not have intruded at this difficult time," Jerrol said.

"I thank you for your kind words, ambassador. It was unexpected," the grand duke replied. "What brings you to Elothia?"

"If it pleases, Your Grace, Vespiri would like to extend its hand in friendship; to understand the issues that drive discord on our borders and to resolve them peacefully and without harm to our people."

"I am not aware of any discord that needs to be solved," the grand duke said, frowning.

Selvia's lips curved into a spiteful smile and she raised her chin. "It seems you are still seeking trouble where it doesn't exist. When will you learn? Still interfering where you are not wanted," she said, as Var'geris leaned forward and murmured in the grand duke's ear. Selvia smoothed a hand down her tightly fitted bodice as she spread her fan and observed Jerrol over the top of it.

The grand duke's frown deepened. "I understand Vespiri troops drive deep into Elothian territory. How is that extending a hand of friendship, I wonder?"

"Your Grace, unfortunately, it seems you may have been misinformed. It is Elothia that drives into Vespiri, and we are at a loss as to the reason."

"You are mistaken. I have approved no such action."

"May I respectfully suggest that you recall a general and ask for a report?" Jerrol suggested. He wondered how blind this youth was to his general's plans, no doubt driven by Var'geris.

Var'geris murmured in his ear, and the grand duke tensed. "You are the Commander of the King's Justice who annexed Terolia on a whim. Do you come here expecting to annex Elothia too, with whispered words and false treaties?"

"He's good at that," Selvia murmured.

"Your Grace, there is no such intent, only a desire to

procure peaceful relations for the good of all. Winter approaches, your people suffer ..."

"You dare preach to me about my people?" the grand duke rose to his feet, anger flaring unexpectedly. His face flushed, accentuating a fine, white scar on his forehead. He strode to the front of the dais and braced his fists on his hips. "They are my people, not yours."

"Tch, tch, you overstep, Commander." Selvia smiled at Var'geris, and he approached the front of the dais. The grand duke nodded, and his guards stepped forward.

"Detain this man who would threaten the peace of Elothia and mouth paltry lies to the grand duke himself," Var'geris commanded.

Jerrol froze in shock and then found his voice. It came out in a rasp. "Your Grace, please. You would throw away a chance at peace without hearing me out?" Jerrol hissed as a guard grabbed him round the neck, forcing him to the floor. "Your Grace. I am King Benedict's envoy. An ambassador of Vespiri. Don't do this." His voice was choked off as the guard tightened his grip.

"Remove him," Var'geris commanded before the grand duke could say anything further.

Jerrol found himself hustled out of the room at sword point, his arms wrenched behind his back, his neck burning. Niallerion stood mouth agape as they passed him in the empty antechamber, the only witness to Jerrol's demise.

At least he didn't have his sword on him to lose yet again, Jerrol thought grimly. He had deliberately left his sword in his room.

16

GRAND DUKE'S PALACE, RETARFU, ELOTHIA

Taelia sat in the chair by the open window. The sun was warm on her face, and a gentle breeze played with the loose tendrils of her hair that had escaped its binding. The breeze had a bite to it, reminding her that she was far from home.

It had been two days since Jerrol had been detained. Deep down, she had not been overly surprised; nothing about this journey had gone right. Jerrol had been worried that the Ascendants were already entrenched, though the speed of his downfall was daunting. He couldn't have had any time with the grand duke.

Niallerion was relentless in his search, his arguments, his demands, all to no avail. Eventually, Marianille had told him to stop. He was drawing too much attention to himself; he had to find a more discreet method to find out what was going on. Niallerion's opinion of that was still ringing in Taelia's ears, but Marianille had told her that his eyes had narrowed and his face had shuttered as alternative methods had obviously come to him. They hadn't seen him since.

A sharp rap at the door had Taelia twisting away from the window. She rose, hoping against all reason that Niallerion had returned with good news. She waited as Marianille opened the door.

There was a shocked silence.

"Marianille? Who is it? Is there news?"

"Taelia, I just heard about Jerrol. Are you alright?"

Taelia faltered as she recognised the voice. "Torsion?"

"Yes, I just arrived. I didn't think they were going to let me in. The palace guards are in a right tizzy."

"What are you doing here?" Taelia asked as disappointment flooded through her. She gripped the back of her chair to keep her upright. "I thought you were recuperating in Stoneford."

"I was, but I am fine now. When I returned to the Chapterhouse, Liliian asked me to come out and help you."

"I don't need any help."

"Of course you do. Liliian had intended on sending me to begin with. It was only because I was delayed in Stoneford, that she didn't."

"Delayed?" Taelia asked faintly.

"Tyrone wouldn't release me."

"You had a terrible experience. He would want to make sure you were alright. Tyrone is always thorough."

Torsion snorted. "Busy bodies, the lot of them."

"Torsion! You know better than that. They are only trying to help."

"Enough of Stoneford. What about you? You look quite pale. You ought to sit down. Get your maid to send for some tea; it will make you feel better."

"Marianille is not my maid." Taelia replied. She smiled towards where she thought Marianille stood. "But tea would be nice, if you could send for some for me?"

"Of course, Scholar," Marianille replied, and Taelia relaxed.

"Tell me what's happened here. I can't get it straight," Torsion demanded.

Taelia hesitated a moment. "First, are you truly alright? You sound tense."

"It was more the tussle with the guards to gain entry. Annoying."

"There has been a misunderstanding. Jerrol came here as King Benedict's envoy for peace, but for some reason the grand duke ordered him arrested. We can't find out why, and now the grand duke refuses all audiences, which has caused even more confusion. I am surprised they allowed you entry, considering everyone is on high alert."

Taelia heard Torsion's clothes rustle as he shrugged. "They couldn't refute my papers. No reason to deny me. But tell me more about Jerrol. What did he do to get arrested?"

"I don't know. He went for an audience with the grand duke two days ago, and didn't come back."

Huffing out a laugh, Torsion shifted in his seat. "Typical. That boy always seems to cause more problems that he solves."

Taelia stiffened. "You know that is not true."

"Of course, it is. Taelia, when are you going to see him for what he is? You know he is always in trouble. Even Benedict wouldn't have accused him of treason for no reason."

"Why do you keep dragging that up when you know it was the Crown Prince, not the king who accused Jerrol?" Taelia leaned back in her chair, resting her elbow on the arm. She propped her chin in her hand and scowled towards Torsion. "Why is it you are always so eager to believe ill of him?"

"Why is it you believe he is so wonderful? Considering what he did to your father. Why do you always forgive him?" was Torsion's sharp response.

"Because he was a child, as was I. It was an accident, you

know he was only protecting me and fighting for his life. Why would I blame him for my father trying to kill both of us?" She huffed out her breath and tightened her lips, attempting to keep harsher words unspoken. Why did Torsion continue to accuse Jerrol when Torsion knew better. "He has always protected me. He is my best friend, and I love him. We were joined ..."

"Your tea, scholars." Marianille interrupted, and the rattle of crockery entered the room.

Taelia breathed in deep, calming herself. Something about Torsion set her on edge. It was like he was gloating about something. She sat in silence as she listened to Marianille pour the tea.

"Your cup, scholar," Marianille murmured beside her, and guided her hand to the saucer.

"Thank you," Taelia said, inhaling the calming aroma.

"Who came with you?" Torsion asked.

"What?" Taelia asked, confused.

"You were saying someone accompanied you?"

"Jerrol and I are joined. The ceremony was held on the *Lady's Miracle* and blessed by the Lady. It was beautiful, I wish you could have been there." Taelia couldn't help the snap in her voice. She was not prepared to put up with any more of Torsion's petty accusations.

"What?" Torsion's voice cracked, and Taelia heard Marianille draw in her breath.

"Jerrol is my husband."

"He can't be. You love me." Torsion's voice was hard and unyielding.

Taelia almost choked on her tea. "Torsion! We've already been through this. I love you as a friend. No more."

"But you could. I know you could. I came as soon as I heard you were out here on your own. You know I would look after you, protect you. You need me. Where is Jerrol?

Locked up in a cell. How can he help you?" Taelia's cup rattled precariously as Torsion removed it from her grasp and then he grabbed her hands. "You know how I feel about you. Give me a chance to prove it."

"Torsion, stop. This is inappropriate and you know it. You promised you wouldn't do this again. My husband is incarcerated in some dungeon and you want to make love? You should be trying to help him."

"I think it's time that Scholar Torsion left," Marianille said from close by.

Torsion ignored her. "If I find out what happened to Jerrol, then will you listen to me?"

Taelia stilled. "What makes you think you can find out when we can't?"

"I have my methods."

Taelia shivered at the sharp tone in Torsion's voice. She didn't recognise him for the dedicated scholar she had known as she grew up. Something had changed, but she didn't know what. She would worry about that later. If Torsion could find out what had happened to Jerrol, then she might forgive his forward behaviour.

"Alright. Find out how we can help Jerrol, and I'll listen."

Torsion released her hands and stood. "Very well. I'll see myself out," he said as he crossed the room, and the door opened and then clicked shut.

"His face, Taelia," Marianille whispered into the silence. "You should have seen his face when you told him you were joined. I thought he might explode. He turned bright red."

"He can help us, Marianille."

"I don't think you should have told him you and Jerrol were joined."

"Why wouldn't I? He's our oldest friend."

"You mustn't encourage him. He thinks he can replace Jerrol."

"Don't be silly. I just told him I love Jerrol. He can't just replace him."

"I'm not sure Torsion would agree with you. Why is he here Taelia? How did he get here? There was no reason for the Scholar Deane to send another scholar, and Roberion wouldn't have had time to return to Old Vespers yet."

"There are other boats."

"I don't trust him. Didn't you say he had importuned you before?"

"He's a good friend, Marianille. He just got carried away. Let's see what he can find out about Jerrol. I'll put up with his delusions if he can help us rescue Jerrol."

Jerrol sat on the icy stone floor, his arms bound behind him. He flicked a glance under his lashes towards the barred door. The guards jeered at him as they lounged against the wall. *Let them jeer. At least some other poor soul is saved from their attentions for a brief while.*

The drab grey walls of the cell reflected his mood. He ached. It had been a while since his body had been used as a punching bag, though he was lucky the guards hadn't had their heart in it. They knew he had been unarmed, and they beat him up enough to make it look bad and no more. He had a black eye to rival Carsten's and a split lip to boot. It stung painfully. He dreamt that Taelia's warm arms soothed his pain and kissed away his tears of frustration as he lay on the unyielding stone floor.

He had failed his mission. It must be the fastest rejection in history. He was obviously not cut out for diplomacy. War was even more likely now that the grand duke had broken the protocols. He couldn't have sent a clearer signal to Benedict if he had tried. The king would not be happy.

He wondered why Randolf had even granted the audience. Why bother if he wasn't even going to listen? They hadn't even made it to the formal dinner of introduction. How would he explain that away? His stomach grumbled, a reminder that he was starving. He couldn't remember the last time he ate.

His thoughts jumped to Taelia. He was powerless to protect his own family, his wife. The agony of failure sliced through him. At least Marianille would stay with her; thank the Lady he had made those arrangements from the off. He could still hear Marianille's voice; her desperate concern as she struggled to hide her fear.

He closed his eyes. "My wife," he thought and tried to remember the warm feeling he felt when she was near. His diplomatic mission was a complete failure. How the king would laugh if the situation wasn't so dire. The Ascendants were in full control of the grand duke and Elothia. What could he do?

"*Find me,*" the words whispered in his head. "*Follow the path. I will be waiting.*"

The voice was vaguely familiar but he couldn't place it. As he groped for the name, his cell door was opened. His heart leapt as Torsion entered and stood over him, flexing his hands. "Pick him up," Torsion said as he moved out of the way to allow two of the palace guards to enter.

Rough hands dragged him upright, and he stiffened in the guard's unyielding grip. "Torsion? What are you doing here?" Jerrol frowned at him bemused. He was supposed to be recovering in Stoneford.

Torsion's eyes glittered as he stared at him. "How dare you?"

Jerrol blinked in surprise. The venom in his Torsion's voice shocked him. "What's happened?" he asked. "Have you spoken to the grand duke?"

"She is mine."

"What? Torsion? What's going on? Did Liliian send you?"

"You still don't get it, do you?"

"Get what?" Jerrol peered at him. What was Torsion talking about?

"And I thought Taelia was the one who was blind."

"Torsion? You must help me. Speak to the grand duke. Benedict will declare war when he hears about this. It doesn't have to be war."

"I was never a supporter of the Lady. My job was to infiltrate the scholars, to find out who the key players were, and look at you," Torsion said, his voice distant. "A disgraced King's Ranger, the Lady's Captain and you can't even see what is right under your nose. You can't tell when someone is deceiving you. Not much of a Captain, are you?"

Jerrol stared at him, his mind numb, still grappling with his words. Gone was the studious scholar with the bowed shoulders. Here was a man full of power and confident with it. No, this couldn't be Torsion; he was his friend, family. "Torsion?"

"The name is Tor'asion."

"No, you can't be. They've enspelled you." Jerrol's mind spun, it wasn't possible. Torsion was his friend. Dependable. He thought of him like an older brother.

"Is that your answer? Do you think I'm weak enough to be enspelled? Well, I'm not. Not everyone bows to the Lady. There are alternatives, and we are owed. Our time is coming, and we will rule Remargaren." His glittering eyes refocused on Jerrol. "Shred the Veil."

Jerrol's stomach roiled, and saliva flooded his mouth. He thought he might throw up. The betrayal sliced through him; he had trusted Torsion, like family. His chest ached as he struggled to control his horror, his despair, his loss. Torsion had always been there for him, reliable, sensible.

"But you've been my friend for years."

"Yes, best move I ever made. You've been useful. And think, Jerrol. You wouldn't have got where you are today without my help."

"Then help me now, Torsion," Jerrol whispered. His last desperate hope splintered under Torsion's vicious glare, and he struggled to make sense of what Torsion was saying. Torsion always knew the right thing to do. It was as if his whole life had been a lie; how could he know that anything he had done had been the right thing? How had Torsion hidden this for so many years? Though, in retrospect, Jerrol supposed it was easy; no one had even known about the Ascendants. No one would suspect or had suspected anything amiss. Why would they?

"I don't think you are in a position to make demands, old man."

Jerrol's stomach cramped. Only Torsion used that term. "You *were* in the tower," he whispered.

"Of course I was."

"Helping them. You took Birlerion."

"Yes, he paid for getting in our way."

"How did you get here? You were in Stoneford."

Tor'asion smiled. "Your Sentinals couldn't hold me. I told Jason I was returning to the Chapterhouse. They believed me; why wouldn't they? There was only ever one who didn't trust me, and I can tell you, he didn't survive. He cried for mercy, like a baby; not that he got it."

"Where is Birlerion?" Jerrol asked, dread weighing him down.

"I told you he's dead. I told you he wasn't to be trusted. You should have listened to me. Now, stop wasting time and shred the Veil." Tor'asion's voice hardened as he flexed his hands.

Jerrol tensed as agonising fear gripped his guts. Fear for

Birlerion and fear for himself. He was sure this wasn't going to be pleasant. "I can't." His head rocked back as Tor'asion hit him. Pain exploded through his mouth, and he spat out blood. It was nothing to the pain constricting his chest at the betrayal of his lifelong friend but it helped clear his mind and firm his resolve.

"Do it now," Tor'asion demanded, interspersing each word with a blow to Jerrol's unprotected body. The guards held him up as he staggered, tightening their grip against the force of the blows.

"You can't have her," Torsion grunted out between gritted teeth. "Shred the Veil."

Jerrol wheezed, his stomach burning. He didn't bother to try to frame an answer as the words and the punches rained down on him. The blows continued until an angry strike to his head took the pain away as he slid into unconsciousness.

Tor'asion stood over him, panting at the effort. The guards watched him nervously. He lifted Jerrol's head and stared at the blood-masked face. A tremor went through him, and his grip tightened on Jerrol's hair. One of the guards spoke up. "If you want him alive, sir, I don't think he'll take much more. He ain't a particularly strong bloke, is he?"

Tor'asion glared at him and then returned his gaze to Jerrol. Stepping back, he released Jerrol's hair and rubbed his sore fist. "He's stronger than he looks," he said, eventually. "Leave him here; tell me when he wakes up."

"Marianille?"

"Yes, Scholar?"

"Describe to me what the view is out of this window," Taelia asked. Marianille moved away from the door where she had been standing.

"We are in the East Tower. Your window faces north

towards a distant range of mountains, which fill the horizon. They are a mauve colour, and white-tipped with snow that glistens against the azure sky," Marianille began.

"Ah, a poet," Taelia murmured.

"No, that would have been Serillion; he always had a way with words." Taelia winced as Marianille continued. "I'm just describing what I see. There is a courtyard below us, surrounded by ten-foot-high walls made of grey stone."

"Whereabouts are they keeping Jerrol?"

"I don't know."

"And if I ordered you to go and find out?" she asked tentatively.

"Niallerion is already searching. There's no point both of us turning this palace upside down."

"Why? He is your Captain. Surely your prime directive is to find and save him?"

"No, Scholar. My purpose here is to protect you."

"Ordered by whom?"

"The Captain, Scholar." Marianille raised her voice at a knock on the door. "Immediately below us in the courtyard, there is a small garden with orange trees. There is a stone fountain of a rearing horse in the centre," she said as she walked over to open the door.

"Oh, is there seating? Could we go and sit in the garden?"

"You have but to ask, my dear, and your wish will be granted," Torsion said from across the room. She heard him approaching and turned her face towards him, forcing a smile in welcome.

"Torsion, where have you been? Marianille here was just describing the view for me."

"I was searching for news of Jerrol as you asked. I'm afraid it is not good."

Taelia smile faltered, and her heart fluttered. "Please have a seat. What did you find out?"

"Jerrol drew his sword on the grand duke. I am sorry, Taelia. I warned you that you couldn't depend on him. The grand duke is being diplomatic, for the sake of relations with Vespiri, but my understanding is that Jerrol tried to kill the grand duke, not save him."

"I don't believe you. Jerrol is here on a diplomatic mission. The only reason he would draw his sword would be to defend himself."

"Don't worry. The grand duke is offering clemency; he is waiting for King Benedict's response before we release him."

"Release him?" Taelia shivered as she felt a change in the air. It sharpened. And as Torsion spoke, she knew something had changed.

"Yes, he is to be sent home in disgrace."

"This is not right. Jerrol would not threaten the grand duke."

"Your confidence in him is commendable but mistaken. Taelia, you need to open your eyes and see the real Jerrol. He is dangerous. A threat to all of us. I keep telling you his reliance on the sword is …"

Taelia zoned out, ignoring his words as she grappled with the ramifications of what he was saying. If they were accusing Jerrol of attacking the grand duke, then his diplomatic protections would be nullified. They could do what they wanted with him.

Frustration rushed through her. Where was Niallerion? Hadn't he any news? They needed to be planning to rescue Jerrol not leaving him in the hands of the grand duke. Her attention sharpened as she realised Torsion had stopped speaking.

"I-I am sorry. This is all a bit of a shock. Could you get

me a glass a water?" she said, as she raised a hand to her head.

Taelia heard Torsion snap his fingers and cringed. Marianille would not appreciate that, and then, Marianille was beside her, calm and solid, placing a glass in her hand. "Here you are, Scholar. Maybe Scholar Torsion could return to tomorrow, once he has found out the grand duke's intentions?" Marianille suggested, her voice firm and comforting.

"Yes. Thank you, Torsion. I have a headache; this has all been quite distressing. I think I might rest."

"Of course, my dear. My apologies for being the bearer of bad news." Torsion leaned forward and squeezed her free hand and then rose. "I'll return tomorrow, hopefully with better news."

Taelia waited until he left and then straightened. "Where is Niallerion? He needs to tell us what is really going on. I need a report."

"I'll go and find him, Taelia."

"Thank you." Taelia stared across the room towards Marianille. She thought she might throw up. "He said 'we' didn't he?"

"Yes, he did," Marianille replied, and then closed the door behind her.

It was dark when Jerrol came too, gagging as someone tried to force a liquid down his throat. Everything hurt, especially breathing. His face felt like it was twice its usual size, and his muscles spasmed as he tried to move.

Voices whispered above him.

"Clean him up a bit. He can't go looking like that."

"It won't be an improvement; this man's been badly beaten. Did the grand duke order this?"

"No," the soft voice sighed.

"I'd say his nose is broken from the sound of his breathing, maybe cracked ribs. You sure he wants to see him?" the healer asked.

"Yes, and it's got to be now."

"That draught won't take away the pain of moving him."

"Do what you can. We don't have much time."

Jerrol hissed in pain as the healer tried to clean his face. "Sorry, got to straighten your nose now as much as we can," the voice said as a tight strap was stuck across his very sore face. "Not much I can do, but it will help you breathe."

The healer helped Jerrol sit up, cutting his bindings, muttering curses under his breath the whole time.

"Enough!" the other voice whispered. "Let's get him up."

Jerrol groaned as he leaned heavily against the healer.

"I know, lad, I know. The draught will take the edge off, but I can't give you any more now."

The two men steered him out of the cell and helped him up the stairs.

Jerrol's eyes were swollen shut. He could barely see where they were going. Each step awoke more aches and pains. He wondered what had happened to the guards and where they were taking him now.

He was shaking with the effort by the time they deposited him in a chair. His breath wheezed out in a weird groan, and he hugged his arms around himself, leaning to one side.

"The ambassador, Your Grace,"

There was a fraught silence. "What happened to him?"

"I understand one of your advisors paid him a visit, Your Grace. And intends to return tomorrow."

"We can't send him back like that."

"To be honest, Your Grace, I don't think they intend on sending him back."

"I wonder why?" The grand duke stared at Jerrol intently. "Is he aware?"

"Some, Your Grace, though how much it is difficult to tell."

Jerrol rolled his head to look at the grand duke. He squinted at him blearily.

"Ambassador, I apologise for your situation, though I'm sure King Benedict will not believe me. I was hoping you … well it doesn't matter what I was hoping. It seems I am in even less control of my palace than I thought."

Jerrol wheezed. He hurt. His brain wouldn't work. He tried to concentrate, but his head ached terribly. He couldn't form a sentence to push out of his battered lips. He couldn't remember where he was or what he was supposed to be doing. Waves of pain engulfed him, and he groaned as he sagged against the man supporting him.

"Ulfr, I will distract my advisors; you need to get him out of here. Tonight, if you can."

"Yes, Your Grace," the soft voice replied.

"He is in no fit state to go anywhere, Your Grace," the healer spoke up.

"He'll be dead if he stays here. Hide him until he is fit. We'll say he's gone missing or something."

"Yes, Your Grace," Ulfr replied, helping the healer lever Jerrol out of the chair. Jerrol swayed as their grip tightened. He didn't remember leaving the chamber, or anything else for that matter.

17

KING'S PALACE, OLD VESPERS, VESPIRI

King Benedict sat on his throne, acknowledging the delegation from Terolia, his new territory, but he was more interested in an update from the neighbouring Elothia. He regretted sending Jerrol off to Elothia as he was now without his Commander, as well as his Oath Keeper. He feared he had lost his gamble. They would have received word by now if all was well.

As he called an Arifel, impatient for an update, a surprised murmur rippled around the room and Fonorion leant forward. "Sire," he said in his soft voice, "the Oath is glowing."

The king rose and stared at the Oath. It was indeed flushed an angry red. He had never seen it glow such a colour; in fact, the only time he had seen it glow, was when Jerrol, his Oath Keeper, was present, and it was usually a golden yellow.

"Does the Oath usually glow red?" Medera Maraine, the Leader of the Atolean Family said from below him.

Benedict turned to her and smiled. "Not often, though I am sure it's nothing to worry about."

Maraine pursed her lips. "I understand Commander Haven travelled to Elothia. I hope they listen and his venture is successful," Maraine said, staring at the glowing words carved in the wall.

"As do I," the king replied. He paused as Fonorion hissed and stiffened. The glowing Oath abruptly flared a brilliant white and went out.

"Fonorion?" The king watched Fonorion gulp, his face paling. The king smiled at his guests. "Please enjoy the refreshments. I will return momentarily. Fonorion, Lieutenant-Commander Bryce, attend," he said abruptly, leaving the dais and walking to a side chamber.

"What is it?" he asked as the door was shut behind them.

Fonorion stared at the king. "The Captain," he whispered, "he's gone. I can't feel him."

"You've said that before and were wrong. I need proof this time," the king said.

"He would not be easy to kill. Not with the Lady watching over his shoulder," Bryce said uneasily.

"It was a diplomatic mission. He should have been protected by immunity. If they have killed my envoy, then it will mean war, and I do not see how Elothia can gain from that." The king paced. "What about Marianille or Niallerion, can you still feel them?"

"Yes, they seem fine."

They were interrupted by a hysterical Arifel erupting into the air above them. Fonorion coaxed him down onto his arm, and the Arifel delivered a small tube holding a note, alongside frantic images of a distressed Taelia, and a severe-looking dark-haired man who was comforting her. Fonorion eased off the tube on his leg, he unrolled the paper and passed it to the king. Sometimes, it was easier to have the Arifel to carry written messages than decipher their haphazard images.

The king's eyes ran down the tiny writing before he handed it off to Bryce. His face paled. "This can't be true!" he exclaimed. "It doesn't make sense; why would Jerrol attack the grand duke? I don't believe it."

"Even if he did draw his sword on the grand duke, and I'm not saying he did," Bryce said quickly as Fonorion tensed. "Jerrol would still have diplomatic immunity. They would have to treat with us, not just execute him summarily."

"So we have some time to discover what really happened," Benedict said.

"Wasn't that an image of Torsion just then?" Fonorion asked.

"Torsion at the palace? Isn't he supposed to be at Stoneford? How did he end up in Retarfu?" Bryce asked.

Fonorion scowled. "I don't know. Tianerille reported that she thought there was something off about Torsion, and I know Birlerion never trusted him. What if he is enspelled? What if he is working for the Ascendants?"

"Tyrone's report said he wasn't enspelled," Bryce said.

"He must be. There is no reason for him to be in Retarfu, unless Liliian sent him. But she would have said. Bryce, find out if Liliian sent him." Benedict paced. "It doesn't make any sense. None of it."

"It does if this is all driven by the Ascendants," Bryce said. "The Ascendants disrupt; they want to rule the world, and Randolf has something they want." He paused. "An army."

"That would mean the Ascendants must control Randolf, then," the king said, "and we walked straight into their trap and handed them the Lady's Captain."

"It looks like they didn't get what they wanted, though. The Veil is still sealed," Fonorion said.

"Jerrol would not assassinate a head of state," the king said. The furrows on his brow deepened. "I don't believe it.

Something obviously went wrong, and they are using it as an excuse. Do you think he is dead? Do you think they killed him for not shredding the Veil?"

Bryce and Fonorion stared at him, horrified. "They wouldn't. That would be a declaration of war, and Randolf can't want to show his hand yet. We should go to our contingency plan, though," Bryce said as he strode towards the door.

Benedict stared at him. "Contingency plan?" he repeated.

Bryce nodded, pausing in the doorway to glance back at the king. "We discussed the possibility of things not going to plan. We've been implementing his orders, just in case."

"What orders?" the king growled.

Bryce hesitated. "The strengthening of our defences along the Elothian border and scouting runs to test the strength of their forces and their positions, Your Majesty."

There was a pregnant silence, before the king covered his eyes with his hand and started muttering under his breath.

"Your Majesty?" Bryce wasn't sure he wanted to hear what the king was muttering, though Fonorion grinned in appreciation.

"The commander has over-stepped his authority," the king bit out.

Bryce shrugged. "His logic is sound. He said we would be suffering attacks from Elothia and to guard our borders. We have had incursions in both Stoneford and Deepwater. Men have been taken from both Watches by the Elothians. The generals are co-ordinating their attacks, splitting our defences."

"I have a throne room full of Terolians, a result of the commanders last expedition, expecting to be feted. When it finishes, you will provide me with every detail of this contingency plan," the king ordered, glaring at them. "In the meantime, get Taelia, Marianille and Niallerion back here."

"Yes, Your Majesty," Bryce replied, bowing before he left the antechamber.

18

TAELIA'S ROOMS, RETARFU, ELOTHIA

Marianille paced. An agitated stalk back and forth across the private parlour they shared with Taelia, and Niallerion eyed her in concern. The air positively crackled around her, a hint of blue sparks trailing in her wake. She was beautiful. Glossy brown hair cascaded in waves down her back, the longest he had ever seen her grow them. Her deep blue gown complemented her creamy complexion and the slight blush to her cheeks.

She looked toned and fit having found somewhere to train, just as he had but obviously not enough. Maybe, he could use her excess energy to his benefit, and keep her occupied while he went snooping. He knew she would not approve of his plan, so he had no intention of telling her.

"Why don't you go and train?" he asked.

"And break our cover?" Her glance of disdain cut him, and he tried to quell his flinch. She had such expressive eyes, currently molten silver, or maybe molten silver that had been worked into arrow tips because they pierced his skin and he had no defence against them.

Taking a slightly deeper breath, he said, "Don't you think

that is already blown? The Ascendants know what we are. I'm surprised they haven't outed us already."

"I expect they have," Marianille replied with a toss of glossy hair. More sparks flashing at the tips as they whipped passed.

"You are brimming with energy. It is noticeable, you need to go and work some of it off. Go show those palace guards how it is done.

"Aren't you offering?"

Niallerion huffed. He would love to, just not when she was ready to pounce like some vengeful mountain creature and slice him up into little pieces. "I'll let them take the edge off first."

"Coward." Marianille's severe expression softened as she stopped pacing and stared at him. "How are we going to find Birlerion, Niallerion? With the Captain under arrest," she gulped as she said the words, their failure still raw enough to bite, "he is our next best hope. We have to find him."

"What do you know about Birlerion that the rest of us don't, Marianille?"

Marianille started pacing again. "I don't know anything for sure. I just have this feeling, this need, that we have to find him."

"Then, for Lady's sake, go work some of that energy off so you can concentrate. We need to plan what to do next. We can't kick our heels here forever." Niallerion hesitated and then, casting her a calculated glance, said, "I heard that chevron lieutenant claiming women can't fight. That they shouldn't be allowed in the army."

"There *are* no women in the grand duke's army, nor the king's come to that," Marianille replied, halting as the realisation struck her. "Leyandrii was really open-minded, wasn't she? I wonder when they lost that trait?"

"Who knows? Why don't you go and remind them why

they are being so short-sighted? I saw the lieutenant on the way to the training grounds."

A grim smile on her face and a martial light in her eye, Marianille strode out of the room, her skirts swirling. Niallerion sighed out a breath, and shook out his hands. He had tensed up as a direct result of her anguish and his inability to take it away.

Ignoring his own desperate fears for their future, he concentrated on his plan. Tugging out a bundle of cloth from behind one of the chairs, he struggled into a simple embroidered blouse and the layered skirts of a lady in waiting, thanking the Lady he didn't need to try and get into a gown on his own. Wrapping the blue silk shawl around his shoulders and pinning it with a silver dagger broach, he walked back and forth across the room a few times, adjusting his stride to avoid tangling with the skirts.

Catching sight of himself in the mirror, he grimaced at the reflection. The things he did for Lady, king and country! Marianille would never let him live it down if she caught him. He concentrated on positioning a wig made of deep brown human hair rolled up into an elaborate style currently popular with many of the young ladies, on his head, and pinning it in place. A quick dusting of the white powder they used on their faces and he didn't recognise himself. Even his eyes had a blue tinge to them, softening the silver. All to the good then.

He stuffed his clothes out of sight behind the chair, swung a warm woollen cloak around his shoulders and left. Having tripped on his skirts for the third time, Niallerion took a deep breath, shortened his stride again and calmed his racing heart. Deciding to dress up and actually doing it were two different things. Every time someone approached him, his heart skipped a beat as he held his breath, exhaling in a rush once they had passed.

He had only traversed two corridors and he was a nervous wreck.

Taking courage from the fact no one had commented on his appearance, in fact, no one had even looked at his face, he continued on his way. Finding his rhythm, he swayed his hips, enjoying the swirl of material around his legs. *Actually,* he mused as he sashayed down the hall, *this was not too bad.*

The corridor led out into the inner courtyard, a square open space decorated with a fountain in the centre, an centrepiece for all the surrounding windows to observe. Skirting the frozen fountain, the tang of damp stone in his nose, he continued through the archway that led to the outer courtyard.

Inhaling frigid air made his chest ache and then he coughed it out as the cold air struck the back of his throat. The relatively sheltered courtyard had deceived him into thinking it was warmer than it was. The outer courtyard was the centre of a fan that led out from the palace into the palace grounds. To the left the stables and barracks, straight ahead the formal gardens which led to glasshouses and work-shops peeping behind tall hedges and plant covered arch-ways, supplying the palace with produce and wares. To the right behind more tall hedges an open parade ground leading to the large gilt gates separating the duke from his people.

Gritting his teeth against the cold, Niallerion tugged his woollen cloak tighter and hurried across the open parade ground and through the hedges on the other side towards the training grounds which extended down a sloping field, out of sight of the palace.

Plumes of steam rose from sweating bodies, not engaged in strenuous activity as you would expect, but crowded around the sparring ring where Marianille taunted her oppo-nents. She had changed into leather pants and jerkin, *they look good on her*, Niallerion thought as he watched her parry a strike and drive the stocky young man across the ring. The other guards jeered and taunted as the man struggled to defend against her attack.

Grinning, he scuttled along the edge of the grounds towards the side entrance to the east wing, which was called the Flower Palace, so named for the colourful designs painted on the interior walls, and the residence of Princess Selvia, the grand duke's sister.

Niallerion froze as he approached the entrance, intending to search out the ladies in waiting. He had heard Selvia had thrown a tray of sweetmeats at her lady in waiting the previous day, and the woman was still griping about her. Niallerion was hoping he could get her to tell him what Selvia was up to. The servants loved to gossip about their employers.

But here was Selvia, wrapped up in a thick fur coat, coming towards him. He shrank back against the wall with his eyes downcast.

Selvia snapped her fingers towards Niallerion as she approached him. "You! Come with me."

Niallerion bobbed his knees. "Yes, your highness." He swallowed against the shocked breathiness of his voice as he followed her back the way he had come.

"You'll do as well as any others," she muttered as she continued walking across the open parade ground towards the gilt gates and the city of Retarfu. She ignored the biting wind swirling around the open space. The once majestic fox tails trimming her coat trailed behind her like a pack of frolicking puppies.

Niallerion followed, straining to hear what the woman was muttering under her breath. Someone had upset her, that was obvious. He stiffened as four guards flanked them, two either side and he concentrated on swaying his hips in a parody of Selvia's glide across the ground.

As they passed out of the gates, Niallerion flipped his hood up, providing some protection for his freezing ears, tucked his hands in his sleeves, and carefully watched where he put his feet, trying to avoid dragging his skirts in the slushy snow.

Picking their way through the piles of grubby snow lining the street, Niallerion followed Selvia towards the White Stag, a tavern off the main square, and more usually frequented by passing travellers, it being the only one on the main road with room for carriages.

Selvia stamped her feet on the mat in the entrance and then gestured imperiously to one of her guards. The man bobbed his head and entered the tavern. Niallerion inspected the taproom, which at this time of day was mainly empty, the lunchtime clientele having wandered off and the evening customers not yet arrived.

The aroma of stale hops and polish mingled with the mouth-watering scent of roasting meats and Niallerion's stomach growled. Selvia tutted. "We are not eating here, control yourself." She shifted from one foot to the other, her fox tails wiggling on the floor. Niallerion averted his eyes from the sight and inspected the man approaching. The inn keeper, he assumed.

He bowed. "Your highness. You honour our humble inn. Welcome. The private parlour is reserved for your use."

"Lead on, then. I do not wish to be ogled by every man in the street."

"Of course, your highness. This way, if you please."

Niallerion trailed behind, trying to keep the shadows. He wasn't sure he could maintain his disguise for an extended period in front of so many people. Marianille would kill him if she found out. That was, if he lived to tell the tale. Maybe this would be one story he would keep to himself.

The guards herded him before them, and he entered the parlour, and found a shadowy nook behind the seat Selvia chose. And then one of the guards began lighting all the lamps in the room, revealing every corner. Niallerion began to sweat.

Selvia stripped off her gloves and coat and held them out. Niallerion started and moved to take them. Casting him a sharp glance, Selvia sat. "You will stand behind me and remain silent. Not a word of this meeting will leave this room."

Niallerion bobbed his head. "Of course, your highness."

"Good." Selvia folded her hands, and sat straight backed, waiting.

Niallerion eased open his cloak, but didn't remove it, at least it disguised the fact he didn't have the requisite curves. The room warmed as they waited, and he wondered who dared to keep a princess waiting.

By the time a commotion occurred outside the parlour door, the princess' foot was tapping an irritable staccato on the floor, and Niallerion was glad of the hours of sentry duty he had stood, else he would have collapsed by now. A deep voice, sharp and also irritated, heralded the arrival of a broad-chested man, dressed in a navy blue uniform, with many ribbons on his chest. His face was reddened by the icy blast rattling the windows. Niallerion was not looking forward to the walk back to the palace.

Selvia rose to greet him, an eager smile on her face. "Uncle Samuel! Finally! What took you so long?"

"Sorry dearie, it's the roads, y'know. New snow fall always causes issues. I'll have even more trouble returning to the front, no doubt."

A general then, Niallerion thought, *but which one?*

"What news?"

"Apart from a lack of decent inns, you mean? They have us sleeping on the floor in tents! I don't know what the world is coming to."

"Stop teasing. I know perfectly well you are not sleeping on the floor. Your aide wouldn't allow the Grand Duke's Chief of Staff to be so inconvenienced. Now sit and tell me the latest situation. How many Vespirians have you killed?"

Shit! Niallerion thought trying to efface himself, but there was nowhere to hide. If he got out of this room alive it would be a miracle. Her uncle was General Kabil, the supreme commander of the Elothian Army.

"You are such a blood-thirsty wench," the general said, as he thrust his gloves and cloak at one of the guards. He sat in the chair opposite Selvia, his bulk making the chair creak in protest. "Isn't there something to drink?" he snapped his fingers at Niallerion. "You, girl. Go get some wine. The good stuff, tell them." He turned back to Selvia as Niallerion hesitated.

"Stay. You go." Selvia said and nodded to one of the guards.

The general's eyes narrowed as he inspected Niallerion. "Who is she? Do you trust her?"

"Of course. I promise, not a word of this meeting will pass her lips. Uncle, the time is ripe. We should strike now. Randolf is off balance, he didn't expect to ascend to the throne. We should remove him before he finds his stride."

Oh dear Lady. Niallerion breathed shallowly. His mind spinning. *Selvia was scheming with General Kabil, the five-star general himself.*

"Now, now, there is no reason to rush into things. The boy isn't going anywhere. We have to time it right. I've got my hands full with moving the army south. We are not ready to strike at Stoneford. That Jason is a wily old fox. He will not be so easy to defeat. I need to double my numbers first, and it takes time to move that many men."

"When *will* you be ready?"

"Not till the summer. We need the warmer weather to dry out the plains. Trying to slog through all that ice and mud will just tire out the troops. Inefficient."

"The summer!" Selvia hissed. "That will be too late."

Kabil patted her hand. "Child, leave the war to me. You make sure you are ready to unseat your brother."

"Uncle, we are ready now."

They were interrupted by the arrival of the wine. A young serving girl poured the drinks with shaking hands.

"Leave the jug," Kabil said, taking a gulp.

Selvia sipped her wine more delicately. "Randolf will be suspicious of you being here."

"Don't tell him, then."

"What? You aren't coming up to the palace?"

"Why would I? Those bloody idiots would try and tell me how to run my war."

"Those idiots as you call them, are the ones making your subordinates amenable to your suggestions. Be careful how you speak of them."

Kabil leaned forward. "Are you sure we need them? They are arrogant bastards. What are they really after? Those Watch Towers won't give them power, nor money; they are just empty stone towers."

"The towers are the path to their salvation. They will open the door and their ancestors will step through."

"And do what? Challenge us for power or shrivel up and die?"

Selvia snorted. "They will support my claim of course. We help them get the Watch Towers so they can save their people, and they help us get the Grand Duchy. I am the eldest. I should be the Duchess."

"And a lovely duchess you'll make, my sweet."

Selvia preened and then grew more serious. "Uncle, there is a wrinkle. King Benedict sent an envoy. Ambassador Haven. He came to negotiate peace. But there was a situation and Randolf overreacted and killed him."

"What?"

Niallerion silently echoed the general's exclamation.

"There hasn't been time to receive King Benedict's response, but you may not have until the summer to prepare."

"How did that happen? There are *rules* around diplomacy."

"I'm not sure of all the details, suffice to say he is dead and the king may retaliate."

'Damn and blast it. We only have one chance at this, Selvia. Everything needs to be perfect."

Selvia shrugged. "It's done. I told you Randolf wasn't fit to rule. More reason to replace him."

Kabil rubbed his face. "You tell those Ascendants we will march when the plains dry out and not before, otherwise we will not have an army when we arrive."

"Uncle, darling, please don't be difficult."

The man snorted. "Difficult? You don't know the meaning of the word. You try slogging through five feet of snow for miles on end." He poured some more wine into his glass and swirled the red liquid. He sighed. "It would help to know why they need us to move now. Find out! I'll be here until the weather calms down, a few days at least. Bring me word here, and I'll see."

Selvia leaned forward and patted his arm. "Thank you, uncle."

"No promises mind."

Rising, Selvia held her hand out towards Niallerion and he gave the gloves to her, and then raised her coat to place over shoulders. Her nails caught his skin as she pulled it closer around her. A sharp sting, sudden and unexpected. He drew his breath in and shook his hand out.

Selvia turned at the door. "I will send word tomorrow, but be prepared, uncle. I do not intend to let Randolf rule for a day longer than necessary." Her eyes glittered like sparkling ice crystals in the lamplight as she stood framed by the dark wood timbers. A snow fox in her winter coat, preparing to kill whatever stood in her way. Her icy eyes passed over Niallerion and he wondered what she saw.

He shivered as the guard opened the door a chill gust blew in. Selvia ignored it and strode out. "Call my carriage," she instructed and Niallerion raised an eyebrow. At least they wouldn't freeze to death walking back to the palace, though sitting in such close proximity to Selvia could be a problem. He couldn't decide which was worse.

One of the guards trotted off, and Selvia led the way out of the tavern. It was nearly dark. The luminous grey-white clouds heavy with more snow closed around them. Shadowy people hurried through the freezing slush, the crack of breaking ice under foot echoing in the dim twilight. Niallerion shivered in his cloak; the temperature was dropping rapidly.

The arrival of Selvia's carriage couldn't come soon enough, and when it did, one of the guards jumped forward to open the door and lower the step. Selvia climbed in without delay but then twisted around in the doorway, and stared down at her maid. "I promised General Kabil that not a word about today would pass your lips." She glanced at one of the guards. "See that it doesn't. Cut out her tongue." The door slamming shut punctuated her command, and strong arms grabbed Niallerion before he had time to absorb the meaning of her words.

19

BACK ALLEY, RETARFU, ELOTHIA

The guards didn't hesitate and dragged Niallerion into a side alley before the carriage had even moved.

"Hang on, wait a minute," Niallerion gasped, trying to dig his heels in, but his boots slid on the ice.

"Shut it," the stocky guard with the bristly brown beard said. "It's too cold out here. Beren, try the shed."

As Beren, the skinnier guard of the two, released Niallerion to check the door, Niallerion thrust his hand up under the stocky guard's chin, snapping his head back. He began twisting out of the guard's grip but Beren was back, and he kicked Niallerion's feet out from under him.

"Bitch," the stocky guard hissed, following him down to the ground. He pressed a knee in Niallerion's back. Freezing water seeped into his bodice and through the material of his skirts as Niallerion struggled to free himself. His skin cooled fast. A fist grabbed him by the hair and the man cursed as the wig came away in his hand. Niallerion yelped as the pins ripped out tufts of his hair with it. Instead, the guard grabbed Niallerion by his ears and rammed his head against the icy ground until Niallerion was on the verge of losing consciousness. Niallerion gasped a ragged breath, his face smarting, his head aching and unable to stop the guards from tying his hands behind his back, and hauling him back to his feet. He swayed woosily, trying to blink away the double vision.

As the guard tightened his grip on Niallerion's arm, Niallerion staggered into the stockier guard, off balance and desperate. The guard back-handed Niallerion, splitting his lip, and pushed him against the wooden planks of the shed wall. Niallerion scraped his face, hissing as he collected a few splinters. Hot breath caressed his cheek as the guard spat in his ear. "You'll pay for that, slut. We were going to play nice, but now …"

Niallerion squirmed and then froze as a knife pierced his skin under his ribs. "Enough," the guard growled and shoved him into the dim shed. Forced to the ground, Niallerion knelt, his head hanging as he felt his split lip with his tongue. It was beginning to swell, much like his chin. As the door shut behind them, his mind spun, trying to think of ways to escape and coming up blank.

The sound of a flint striking preceded the sudden flare of light and the guards stood over him, holding a lantern.

"Let's see what we have 'ere then," the stocky guard said, and tilted Niallerion's face towards the light.

The guards peered at him. "Stev, is it a woman?" Beren asked, scowling in confusion. "She's a bit stronger than I expected."

"Don't be daft, he's no woman." Stev waved the wig. "Now why would a bloke be disguisin' himself as a woman? I am sure the princess would be interested in your answer, before we remove your tongue."

Niallerion was silent.

Cold steel pressed against his throat. "Or we can cut you

up piece by piece until we reach your tongue," Stev said as he pushed the blade in, piercing the skin.

Niallerion hissed his breath out, keeping as still as possible. The bite of the metal faded as warmth spread down his neck.

"Search him," Stev said.

Beren began patting him down. "There's too much material to feel anything," he complained. Niallerion was suddenly glad of the underskirts until he was wrenched upright and the guards began cutting the clothes off him. They weren't particularly careful and the knives sliced his skin, leaving him slick with blood and only wearing his underclothes. He shivered as his skin turned blue, and his teeth began to chatter. He was forced back onto his knees as he wondered how he had managed to get himself on such a mess. *Leyandrii, I am so sorry. I never meant to fail you like this, please forgive me.*

Niallerion shuddered as a gust of icy air cut through him. The lamplight flickered for a moment, casting long shadows across the shed. He twisted his wrists, but the ropes just burned his skin.

Cold steel pressed under Niallerion's right eye and his breath stuttered.

"Now I'll ask one more time. Who are you and what are you doing spying on the princess?" Stev asked.

Niallerion's teeth chattered as he gasped out a nonsensical reply.

"What was that?" Beren leaned closer.

"I-I …" Niallerion's reply was cut off as Beren was jerked away from him. Stev released him with a sharp exclamation that morphed into a gurgling grunt as he staggered back, holding his chest. Blood pooled in his fingers and spurted out as he collapsed.

A tall shape hovered over Niallerion and then sliced the

ropes binding him. Niallerion slowly folded over and his rescuer caught him. A sharp exclamation and he was bundled in a blanket that smelt of horses. "Niallerion? Are you alright?"

Niallerion groped for the name that went with the voice. Taurillion. Marguerite's companion. The only Sentinal claimed by Marguerite and not Leyandrii. The only Sentinal with copper-coloured eyes. He was glad that Taurillion hadn't found him dressed as a woman was his last thought as he collapsed into Taurillion's strong arms.

Niallerion awoke in his own bed in his room in the palace. A shaded light cast a dim glow and as he stirred Marianille rose from the chair beside him and leaned over him.

"At last," she murmured. "Drink this." She raised his shoulders and tipped a sweet liquid in his mouth, cider laced with something. He swallowed with difficulty. His lip stung. His cheek smarted. Various other aches and pains made themselves known as he lay back with a groan.

"Marianille," he croaked.

"Not now, rest. Taurillion found you. Footpads he said."

Niallerion heard the disbelief in her voice, but his eye lids drooped. The room went blurry but he thought he heard her whisper. "Sleep, my dear, you are safe now." And all his aches faded.

The next time he opened his eyes, both Taelia and Marianille were seated beside his bed. Daylight lit the room and the grey light revealed their careworn faces and he felt a spike of guilt for causing them even more concern, on top of all their other worries.

Taelia tilted her head. "Niallerion? Are you awake?"

Marianille exclaimed and leaned forward her grip convulsing around his hand, which she had been holding.

"Niall! We've been so worried. When Taurillion brought you here you were a lump of blood-streaked ice. I thought you were dead."

Wincing, Niallerion gripped her hand back at the tremor in her voice. "It was a close call," he admitted. "How long have I been out?"

"Two days. You've been fortunate, I suppose. You slept through forty stitches, and the removal of too many splinters to count."

Ah, that explained his sore face, throat and torso.

"What happened? Do you remember?" Marianille asked.

Niallerion shifted and realised he was naked under the covers. Soft furs slid against his skin, trapping the heat. His wrists were bandaged, as were many other places by the tight pull of bandages against his skin.

"I accompanied Selvia to a meeting with her uncle, General Kabil."

"What do you mean you accompanied?" Marianille demanded, suspicion colouring her voice.

Niallerion's shrug was cut short by a wince. "I had intended on speaking with some of her ladies in waiting. I heard she wasn't a very nice employer, so I thought they would be more likely to gossip, but before I got there, I met Selvia and she dragged me with her to her meeting."

"Why would she take you?"

Niallerion scrunched up his face, trying to think of a way out of telling her. "Selvia is scheming with Kabil to over-throw Randolf. She wants to be the new duchess."

"That doesn't explain why she would take you."

Exhaling a deep breath, Niallerion gave in. "I disguised myself as one of her ladies in waiting," he said.

"You did what?" Marianille was horrified.

Niallerion flushed. "It seemed a good idea at the time."

"A good idea …" Words failed her.

"What gave you away?" Taelia asked shrewdly.

"Nothing, which surprised me. I didn't realise I looked so feminine. It wasn't until we were leaving that Selvia instructed the guards to cut out my tongue so I couldn't tell anyone about the meeting. It went pear-shaped from then on."

"She did what?" Marianille asked, the blood draining from her face.

"Fortunately, Taurillion arrived in time to prevent them. I have no idea where he came from." *Thank the Lady,* he thought. "The Ascendants are trying to get Kabil to move his army on Stoneford. She said ..." he trailed off, staring at Taelia.

"What did she say?" Taelia asked.

"I'm sorry, Taelia. Selvia said that Randolf killed Jerrol. She didn't know the details but it sounded like they have informed Benedict."

Taelia stilled, and then shook her head. "I don't believe it. Randolf wouldn't kill Benedict's peace envoy."

"He's lost, Taelia. We can't sense him. There is no Captain." Niallerion gentled his voice, even though the words cut him deep.

"No, I don't believe it."

"Never again," Marianille said, her voice sharp. "Promise me. You won't do anything so stupid again. You were reckless going in without support. It is not worth losing your life."

Niallerion observed her pale face. The sheen of tears in her silver eyes. She meant it.

"Promise me," she hissed.

"I promise," he replied, holding her eyes.

Marianille nodded, once, and released his hand. "Tell us what you heard. Every single word." She produced a notebook and rested it on her lap, all business. The concern for him absent.

The next day they let him get out of bed, and Marianille had helped him dress with a curt "I have four brothers. I've seen it all before." Which didn't ease his embarrassment, but his cheeks cooled as he sat in the armchair in the parlour.

Marianille handed him a mug of chamomile and aniseed tea. "Healer's advice, it will help calm the bruising," she said as she sat beside him.

He reached across and gripped her hand. "I am sorry for scaring you," he murmured.

Marianille sat with her head bent for a moment, and then cleared her throat. "We have enough family lost without you as well," she said at last, and his heart warmed as she raised her face and gave him a searing glance that made him hold his breath. And then it was gone.

"We sent off a message to Benedict this morning. We should get a reply tomorrow."

"You didn't tell him about me, did you?"

Marianille shook her head. "We didn't want to give him more reasons to demand our return. Taelia is adamant the Captain is alive and we must wait for him."

"Where is Taelia?"

Marianille's face tightened. "She is with Torsion. She says he is finding out where Jerrol is for her, but I don't trust him, Niall. He is not just a Scholar. There is something, I don't know, something off about him."

Sipping his tea, Niallerion watched her. Lines traced her brow, and creased around her mouth. The stress of Birlerion's absence was beginning to show, more so because there was nothing she could do to help him. There was nothing any of them could do. He cursed himself for his foolishness. He had lost days, when he should have been spying on Var'geris and the other one, Sul'enne.

Marianille couldn't leave the scholar unattended, though it seemed the scholar had no compunction abandoning Marianille. "I'll set up a listening device in the Ascendants quarters. They won't know it's there, and they won't know we are listening." He held up his hands as she tensed. "I promise."

Sharp silver eyes inspected him for a moment and then she nodded, and he breathed out a sigh of relief.

20

SOMEWHERE IN ELOTHIA

Owen Kerisk awoke in chains. His head felt thick and heavy as if he was fighting his way up through dark treacle to reach the air. He inhaled sharply as a boot connected to his ribs and pain exploded through his chest, but it got some air into his lungs. He deeply regretted drinking that gut rot at the inn last night. He shouldn't have stayed there. They had caught him unawares.

"Wake up, sunshine, time to move," a rough voice said from above him.

Owen rolled onto his side and levered himself to his knees, swaying as he looked around him. His body ached. His eyes were crusty and sore, and his head thumped painfully.

"Water," he croaked.

A bucket and a dirty rag were dumped beside Owen before the soldier prodded the sleeping man lying next to him with his foot. The man already looked pretty beat up, and he stirred, obviously in pain, at the rough awakening.

Owen gulped a couple of handfuls of water and dabbed at his face and eyes before they took the bucket away. The bucket was rimmed with ice, and the water was so cold, it hurt. His head ached, oh how his head ached. He looked down at the next man in the chains; a bundle of misery that they had dragged out of the inn last night. It looked like the slightest breeze would knock him over. The innkeeper had tried to stop them, saying he was a paying guest, but the soldiers had ignored him.

His gaze wandered around the barn in the lightening gloom as more soldiers entered with torches held aloft. Dejected men lay huddled together for warmth, each chained to another. His gaze dwelt on the man that had been dragged out of the inn with him. He wasn't very big; maybe he'd reach Owen's shoulder once he was standing. His stubbled chin failed to hide the faded bruises of a recent beating, and he looked drawn and frail. Straggly brown hair flopped over his face, which he moved out of his eyes with a hand that was missing two of its fingers. A dejected and battered sight. Owen rubbed his bearded chin and sighed. He hoped he could walk; he wasn't carrying him that was for sure.

The soldiers eventually got everyone on their feet and back in a double file. Owen's companion huddled in on himself and visibly shivered. They marched them off down the frozen road, boots slipping on the ice. A blanket of snow softened the landscape, blurring its edges and hiding its features.

Owen lurched through the ice-rimmed puddles, his boots getting soaked. The chains wrenched him forward as the men in front of him slipped on the ice. A trickle of icy water penetrated the leather, and he shivered. Even wrapped in his tattered cloak, the cold penetrated and invaded his bones, and he knew the cold would only get worse.

The brown-haired man barged into him as he slid on the ice, taking them both down onto the slushy street. The man's breath was hot on his face, and although his breath hissed out in pain, his grey eyes were surprisingly alert. The guards shouted at them and struck out with their sticks, hauling them back to their feet and pushing them on.

They were made to march in place as they waited for the soldiers to sweep through a brightly lit tavern. "Keeps you warm," one of the soldiers shouted, rapping their legs with a stick. "The only thing you get for free in the grand duke's army," he laughed, sharing the joke with one of his companions.

The lieutenant returned with a scowl on his face. "Waste of time," he complained. "Let's get this sorry lot back." He remounted and set a smart pace down the road, leading the way out of what Owen had heard them calling Tortval, which he knew was a small town on the outskirts of Daarl, not big enough to rate a mark on a map.

Owen tried to picture the map in his head. The only town of any importance north of Tortval was Meerange, a centre of commerce and textiles, feeding the ports of Daarl and Hjull on the coast, neither of which were very large, but busy all the same. There was no army training facility there that he was aware of.

The air was full of plumes of breath as the chained men were hustled down the road. The men slid into each other as they tried to keep their feet at the fast pace the lieutenant set. Owen reined in his wandering mind and took note of their surroundings. Pinpoints of light indicated where sparse dwellings crouched in their snowy disguise.

Apart from the echoes of the horse's hooves and the crack of crunching ice, the night was silent. No animals shifted in the frozen fields. No wind stirred the sparsely-leaved trees. The dark sky was swathed in thick clouds; only the soldier's torches lit the way.

He frowned. Where were they going? He thought the

river was ahead, but apart from Meerange, there were no other cities in the central plains, only snow and more snow.

One of the men in front of Owen collapsed, groaning in the slush. Owen and his companion were forced to help him up, blows raining across their shoulders to hurry them up. As they dragged him to his feet, Owen realised that he was just a youth, slender and ill-clothed for such a venture as this. A surge of irritation rushed through him. This whole situation could have been avoided if he had paid closer attention; he shouldn't even be here.

"Get up," Owen growled.

"I-I can't," the boy stuttered through chattering teeth.

Owen jerked in surprise as the slight man next to him hissed at the boy through clenched teeth. "Yes, you can," he said in a hard voice as he awkwardly wrapped an arm around the boy's waist. The boy cringed closer to the man's meagre body heat in desperation. Owen flipped his cloak over the boy's shoulders and helped to half-carry half-drag him as they were herded down the slushy street and onto a wooden pier, which trembled under their weight.

They were shanghaied down the jetty and forced into the hold of the boat tied to it, then shackled to iron rings hammered into the thick wooden beams. They huddled together for warmth, cowed by the boat hand's ready fists. Shivering men were already restrained, turning blue as they crouched in the hold.

Shouts from above warned Owen that they were about to cast off and he braced himself as the boat rocked haphazardly and the sailors pushed them out into the river. The boat drifted on, picking up speed as the oars began to pull through the water. He almost wished he was doing their job. At least he would be warm.

Shivering uncontrollably, the interminable night wore on. Cold seeped into his limbs, but he couldn't stretch in the confined space. He couldn't see the battered man next to him, but he knew he fared no better; he could feel his constant trembling. Owen could just make out the gleam of his eyes; he wasn't sleeping either.

It was still dark when dim torchlight seeped through the decking onto the misery stashed in the hold. Owen reluctantly pried his eyes open. Was he still alive? He couldn't feel his body.

Owen stiffened as the guards rattled down the wooden stairs. "Alright you miserable lot, get up!" they yelled as they started wielding their sticks in an effort to get the frozen men moving.

It took far too long and much brutality to get the ice-ridden men onto their feet and marching in place. There was one who didn't move, no matter how much the soldiers beat him. After much cursing, they dragged him out of the hold and tossed him overboard.

As they climbed out of the hold onto the deck, Owen scanned the surroundings. The pier they were tied up to led to nothing. There was no town, no warehousing, no mercantile of any form. Owen frowned. Where were they?

The guards led their horses up onto the pier and remounted their horses once they had reached dry land. They looked much happier on land, though they still didn't look eager to be returning. Owen peered around him as the shackled men stumbled down the icy road.

The air around the lead soldiers undulated, and then they disappeared, and the men at the front baulked, causing the rest to stumble to a fearful halt. A delayed ripple of confusion sped down the line before the soldier's sticks were back out and the men were forced ahead.

As Owen approached, the texture of the air changed. It shimmered, blurring the surroundings and consuming the men as they passed through. The barrier caressed his skin, and the column of weary men appeared before him. A creaking chain warned him that they were approaching an entry point. Faint shouts ahead were muffled by thick wooden gates, which became clearer as flickering torches revealed a gaping maw as the portcullis was raised, jerking spasmodically as slaves pulled on the ropes.

Owen noticed the man next to him, peering around the opening courtyard as they shuffled under the suspended gate. The courtyard was bleak and empty. The ground hardened by many stamping feet. It had been bedded down like stone. No puddles littered this courtyard; it was clear of all impediments.

A giant of a man loomed ahead of them. "What's all this, then?" he barked as the soldiers herded their meagre haul into the courtyard.

"Latest recruits, sir," the lieutenant reported, saluting.

"Really?" the giant said, scowling at the lieutenant. His bald head shone in the light of the torches extending from the walls.

The lieutenant cringed and took a step back. The overseer strode forward and inspected the dregs before him. "And these recruits are for the Third Chevron?" He turned on the lieutenant. "You bring me this to work with? Are you sure you're recruiting for the grand duke?"

The lieutenant swallowed, his eyes darting towards his men. "There isn't much left, sir. The area has been stripped already."

"Then travel further. This is not acceptable. The grand duke expects better," the overseer hissed.

The lieutenant cowered before him, and at his signal, his men remounted and headed back under the portcullis with alacrity.

The overseer glared at the rabble before him. His heavily muscled arms gleamed in the torchlight, and he slapped the baton he held in his hand against his leg. The thwack of the stick against his trousers echoed in the silence, and the prisoners stirred uneasily. "Well, well," he said surveying them critically. "Welcome to *the* elite chevron training compound. Here we train the best soldiers in the grand duke's army. This is your new home until you can satisfy us that you are one of the best," he said as he continued inspect them. "We do not accept failure. We do not accept excuses. You are now a volunteer in the grand duke's army, behave like one or pay the consequences. Let's see what you're made of." He snapped his fingers, and the recruits were herded into a sawdust-covered training ground which muffled the sound of their shuffling feet.

A man with hammer and chisel struck the shackles off their wrists and feet. Owen rubbed his arms as he surveyed the grounds. A high ceiling enclosed the area and kept the inclement weather out. Tiered seating rose up the walls, circling the arena. The men training in the arena looked lean and fit. They paused their sparring and moved to the edges of the grounds, expectant smirks on their faces.

Owen considered his strategy; he didn't want to overplay his hand, but he had to show potential. He had some training, and he was used to hard labour having worked many years on his family's farm. Surreptitiously, he looked at the man who had been chained to him. In the light of the arena, he looked even worse. Blue tinged skin, mottled with bruising, sunken grey eyes glazed with pain, and a constant shiver. The arena was freezing. The grey-eyed man was one of the smallest men conscripted; the young boy was the only other similar in size. The rest were all bull-necked or taller, though in their stiff and frozen state, maybe he would have a chance.

Shaking his hands out, he flexed his shoulders as he scanned the area. His gaze paused briefly on a quiet spot and then kept moving. He assessed the other men, awaiting the travesty that was no doubt about to happen, noting his companion doing the same. What a waste of resources, he thought. Had they such a large army that they could waste the few men they had culled with senseless violence?

The overseer's voice barked out a series of orders and the guards shoved the men into two lines. Owen sighed as he looked at his opponent; he was huge. His neck was so thick he had no hope of throttling him.

At the overseer's command, the men began to spread out and circle each other. Owen tried to keep an eye on his travelling companion. He wasn't sure why, but he felt concerned for him. The poor man was facing an opponent twice his size. He didn't have a chance. Owen shook his arms out and focused on his own opponent. The man was stiff and awkward, and Owen soon had him immobilised in an arm lock.

The overseer ordered his men to separate them into smaller groups. The grey-eyed man grimaced at Owen and grabbed the young lad they had helped before saying: "Dive for their ankles," as they circled around the equally exhausted men facing them. The boy panicked, staring wild-eyed at him. "I-I can't," he whimpered. The man grabbed him by the throat and growled, "You will because you have to," before shoving him away and turning back to his looming adversary. The boy stiffened as Owen glared across at him.

As their opposition lunged, Owen and his companions dived taking their opponents' feet out from under them, letting them fall with leaden thumps. Owen and the grey-eyed man spun and wrenched their opponents' necks back in vice like grips. The young lad flailed as his man rolled him over and clipped him around the ear. The boy dropped like a stone. The grey-eyed man rolled his eyes and tweaked the nerve in his opponent's neck, feigning a twist he slipped between the remaining large man and the unconscious boy.

The boy's opponent roared with anger and his hands extended to grab his neck.

"Halt," a cold voice echoed around the arena, and they all froze. The overseer walked through the chaos allocating men to units until only Owen and the grey-eyed stranger waited in the middle of the arena.

"Managing untrained brute force is a definite skill. Let's see what you can do with a weapon," the overseer said as two of the grinning guards threw swords at their feet. Owen eyed the other man warily as he ducked to grab a sword, rolling away out of reach as he regained his feet. They slowly circled each other, ignoring the heckling and jeers from the side lines.

The grey-eyed man gave way under Owen's ferocious attack. Owen was heavier and stronger and easily forced his opponent to give ground. The grey-eyed man managed to parry each blow as he gave way, until he suddenly side-stepped and retaliated. Owen found himself hard pressed to block the blows. The man feinted under the overhead strike that Owen attempted. They thrust and parried, evenly matched, though Owen's energy levels began to flag, sapped by the cold. The man took advantage of Owen's inattention and spun within his guard, thrusting his right hand upwards. Owen's head snapped back painfully. He snarled with anger and counterattacked, forcing his opponent back across the arena. The man feinted again, allowing Owen within his guard, but Owen knew, he just knew, that the man had deliberately stepped into the stunning blow he delivered.

Owen leant on his sword, breathing deeply. He looked down at the man lying in a heap on the ground. He knew that this man had thrown the fight. Why? He took a deep breath and raised his eyes to the stands as a slim man walked out of the shadows clapping slowly. He wore a full-length black coat that absorbed what little light there was around him. He wore it open and seemed impervious to the cold.

"A worthy foe. I suggest you escort him to the barracks and wake him up. You have much to learn." His voice was silky smooth and very much in command. Owen bent to grab heave the unconscious man into his arms.

"You'll need your weapons in the Third Chevron," the shadowy man's voice rebuked him. Owen hesitated before gripping the swords, then he heaved the limp body over his shoulder, and staggered under its unexpected weight. He followed the private who had led him to the barracks of the Third Chevron.

Owen dropped his opponent's limp body onto a cot indicated and propped the swords against the wall between them, before sitting down on his cot, panting heavily. As his breathing eased, he stared at the man. He may be smaller than Owen, but he knew how to fight. Owen knew he would have been bested, maybe even been killed, if this man had tried. But for some reason, the grey-eyed man had wanted them both to live. Owen's gaze flicked around the barracks. Ten empty beds lined the walls, the rest of the unit; he wondered when they would return.

With a soft sigh he leaned over and gently slapped the unconscious man's face. He lay unresponsive. Owen stood up and, searching the room, found a bucket to fill with water, and went to search for the shower room. Returning, he stood over the dark-haired man briefly before emptying the bucket of icy water over his head.

The man came to, gasping for breath, barrelling up out of the cot before stopping with a groan as he held his head in his hands. Water dripped down his sleeves. Concussion, Owen thought, as he watched the man swallow. His face was pale under the bruising. The man slowly raised his head and met Owen's eyes.

"How do you feel?" Owen asked, as he placed the bucket beside him.

"Never better," the man replied, heaving. He lurched for the bucket and vomited.

"Welcome to the barracks of Chevron Three, Unit Four. I bet they are just going to be pleased to see us," Owen said with a wry smile.

"Yeah, I bet." The man rested his head in his hands, leaning over the bucket. Owen was sure his face must be sore as he prodded his cheek and jaw. "What did you hit me with? A sledge-hammer?" the man asked as he winced.

Owen chuckled. "Just my sword; you walked straight into it for some reason."

"Yeah." He sighed as he closed his eyes.

"Why?"

"Why what?" The man retched, struggling not to throw up again.

Owen watched him before he took a breath and said, "You could've taken me easily."

The man swallowed. "I was thinking of the waste."

"The waste?"

"Of your death," the man admitted, "or mine."

"You don't even know me."

"Doesn't make it any less of a waste," he said. "Anyway, I knew I wouldn't be able to carry you out of that arena."

"True," Owen agreed with a grin. He sat on his bed. Hesitantly, he extended his hand. "Owen Kerisk of Tierne," he said.

The man opened his eyes and, seeing the hand in front of him, extended his. "Finn," he said, after a slight hesitation.

"Finn of?"

Finn shrugged and then vomited in the bucket again. "I don't know. Finn is all I remember," he said, wiping his mouth. His skin was a sickly greyish green under his bruises.

"I'd say it was a pleasure," Owen's lips quirked, "but I'd be lying." His fingers absently twirled his beard as he looked morosely around the barracks before returning his gaze to Finn. "But I'm thinking you're the closest I have to an ally in this place. Especially when the others turn up."

Finn sighed in agreement as he took in the empty beds, all smartly made up and identical. He lay back down with a groan and closed his eyes. "Better make the most of it, then."

Owen emptied the foul-smelling bucket, placing it next to Finn's bed, and then he watched him doze until the clatter of boots stopping at the end of his bed drew his gaze away.

21

GRAND DUKE'S PALACE, RETARFU, ELOTHIA

Niallerion skulked down the corridor, keeping the Ascendant in sight. He had a bag of tools and cloths ready to duck into a room and begin cleaning if anyone questioned his presence. After his close call with Selvia, he had spent a week recovering and the last week exploring every inch of the palace and ingratiating himself with the staff. Observing from a distance seemed the more sensible bet. He was sure Marianille would be proud of him, if she knew.

The housekeeper was now his best friend and let him have the run of the palace after he had fixed a frozen pipe for her and created a more efficient rack to hold her pans. She had been mesmerised by the pulley system he had built, which doubled her storage space.

Niallerion knew where every corridor went, even those he wasn't supposed to know about. He also knew the wing where the Ascendants were located, which was where he was currently headed as he followed the Ascendant called Tor'asion. Niallerion was not impressed with what he had seen of him so far. He was arrogant and cavalier; he walked down the corridors as if he owned the palace, and ordered the staff about in much the same manner.

Taelia had nearly fainted when he reported that Torsion was also known as the Ascendant, Tor'asion. Marianille had to talk fast as the blood drained from Taelia's face and she had gone deathly still. Torsion had been a friend of hers and Jerrol's for a long time. When you discover the dark truths about a person, it can shake the very foundations of your beliefs, and Torsion had betrayed them both.

Watching Taelia's face stiffen with cold calculation had chilled Niallerion to the bone; it was an expression he had never expected to see on her face. Once Taelia had recovered from the initial shock, her eyes had narrowed; making plans, Niallerion was sure. She had been determined to find out everything they could about what the Ascendants were planning, even to extent of pretending to like Torsion, and Torsion was lapping it up. She had ordered Marianille to call an Arifel and while they waited for one to turn up, she had dictated a report to her. Then Marianille rolled the paper up and gave it to the Arifel to take to the king.

Since then, Benedict had demanded that they return in every message he sent. Taelia refused to leave, with Marianille a close second. Niallerion didn't think twice about agreeing with them. They were finding out information that could be crucial in helping to win the war. At least Stoneford and Deepwater would be as prepared as they could make them.

The Ascendant cut across another courtyard, of which there were many, and Niallerion waited for him to exit the other side before he followed, skirting the ornate statuary of a tumbling waterfall in the centre.

There were three Ascendants at court: Var'geris, who Niallerion recognised from the Terolian deserts; Tor'asion, who looked just like Var'geris, if a little broader across the chest; and Sul'enne who liked to spar. He thought himself quite the swordsman, though Niallerion curled his lip as he imagined what the Captain or Birlerion would do to him if they got the chance.

Niallerion's chest constricted at the thought that both the Captain and Birlerion were reported dead. He hung on to the belief they lived; he was sure he could still sense them, though they were both so muted, sometimes he wondered if it was just wishful thinking. Breathing deeply, he calmed himself. He crossed the courtyard and entered the building opposite and flattened himself against the wall as Tor'asion stopped outside a door and flexed his hands before opening it.

Tor'asion flicked a glance down the hallway and entered the room. Niallerion ran past on silent feet and climbed the servant staircase at the end of the hall. He opened the small panel in the casement wall and reached into the gap, pulling the listening cup towards him. He uncoiled enough of the wire to reach the deep window seat and slid the panel shut.

Installing the contraption had taken but a matter of moments the previous week, once he had had discovered the room the Ascendants tended to meet in. It was a simple cone-shaped collecting bowl placed over the communications crystal he had repurposed to become an amplifier and connected to a wire, which transmitted the voices.

Settling himself on the window seat, drawing the curtain enough to shield him, he tucked the listening cup into his ear and leaned back, staring out the window. The ranks of grey stone ridges and spires rising from palace roofs blurred before him as he concentrated on the voices rising from the Ascendants chambers. His hand slipped into his pocket and caressed the onoff that Birlerion had created for him. The smooth ball of acquiescent energy, a reminder of the Lady's magic, which they had used to provide light instead of candles, was a comfort in this strange new world they lived in.

Tor'asion's voice floated up through the crystal, as clear as if he was sat in the same room. Niallerion wriggled his shoulders against the hard wall to get more comfortable and listened.

"Kabil should be in position now, with the Second Chevron. I just need him to get moving across the plain. He is reluctant; too exposed he says. He's dug in just south of the Summer Palace."

"I thought you had him enspelled?" Var'geris' voice was hard and clipped.

"His military knowledge is interfering. He knows it's suicide for about half his men, so he's baulking," Tor'asion replied. Niallerion smiled at the edge of frustration in his voice.

"Then you'd better get down there and get him moving."

"I thought maybe you should go. I need to stay here with Sul'enne. He's struggling to keep Randolf under control. I need to reinforce his suggestions."

"That is my strength, you know that. Don't put our plans in jeopardy because of a woman, Tor'asion. She'll still be here when you come back. They are showing no intentions of leaving; she hopes that Haven will come back."

"I'm not. Taelia was a way to get to Jerrol; he always liked her. I can use her. She is weak and timid, and bereft, of course. She is vulnerable, willing to depend on Torsion. If she hears anything about Jerrol, she'll tell me. I wouldn't bother with her. But we do need to find him."

Var'geris snorted. Niallerion recognised the huff of breath he made when he laughed, or pretended to. Var'geris never laughed, not like he meant it. "Randolf said he died. So he must be dead. I thought he came up with quite a good story for Vespiri; gives us a little more time to get ready."

"If we can get Kabil moving."

"Then you'd better go make sure he does move. You can check in on our dear chancellor while you're at it; ensure he hasn't fouled that job up."

"Pev'eril will have them under control, but I'll make sure," Tor'asion said.

"Good. I will assist Sul'enne with Randolf. We just need to make sure we have the Watch Towers. Without the Captain, they are our best chance." There was a slight pause. "I might see if I can find where they are holding Mer'iteras; we need him. If we'd had him at Adeeron, we might have got something out of that Sentinal before you beat him senseless."

"He was stubborn. But he's lost now. I didn't expect to beat it out of him; my intent was to soften him up."

Icy shivers ran down Niallerion's spine. Beat what out of Birlerion? Lost? What did they mean he was lost? He fumbled for the essence of his friend, but he couldn't find it. No vibrant spark hung like a bright star in his awareness. The voices continued in his ear and he bit his lip. Concentrate, you fool.

"You get carried away, Tor'asion. You need to learn restraint. We lose too many informants through your anger."

"What about you?" Tor'asion asked, an edge to his voice. "Is it worth the risk to find Mer'iteras? We can't afford to lose you, too."

"You concentrate on Kabil. Remember, he must be marching by Maru; you've got two months to get his army in position."

Tor'asion heaved a deep sigh, and the crystal vibrated. The floor creaked as the Ascendant stood. "This is not the time of year for manoeuvres, you know. The snow is a good four to five feet thick around here."

Var'geris gave his huffing snort again. "Tell Kabil it'll be warmer down south. He'll soon get them moving."

Niallerion removed the ear cup and listened intently. He dropped to the floor, coiling the wire. He knelt to slide the panel open, returning his device to its hiding place. Footsteps started up the stairs and he darted down the gallery to the stairs at the other end and descended. He made his way back to Taelia's rooms, and silently entered.

Leaning against the door, his lips twitched as Taelia stared right at him.

"Don't just stand there, come and tell us what you found out. Marianille make notes," she said.

Niallerion summarised what he heard, pausing to let Marianille catch up.

"And you're sure they didn't know what happened to Jerrol?" Taelia asked, a little breathlessly.

Niallerion nodded, even though she couldn't see him; he kept forgetting. "They were annoyed. They need him for something, and without him to do it for them, they have to get the Watch Towers back."

"They are after the Veil," Marianille said, looking up from the report she was writing. "They are moving on Stoneford. It's the only way they'll get the towers."

"But if they don't have Jerrol, who does?" Taelia asked.

Marianille wrinkled her brow and sighed. "I don't know."

Niallerion hesitated, staring at Birlerion's sister. Even with her face shadowed with sorrow, she was beautiful. She had such smooth, creamy skin; so pale, it reminded him of the delicate shells found on the beaches in Birtoli.

Marianille lifted her head and smiled at him, her complexion smoothing as it lightened. "Tell me. We said we would report everything, no matter what we heard. We both know the Captain and Birlerion are still alive, even if they are in trouble. The more we know the better chance we have to find them. What did they say?"

"Var'geris said Tor'asion beat Birlerion senseless. Var'geris wants to go and get Mer'iteras; he said they could have got what they wanted to know out of Birlerion if they'd had him there." Niallerion hesitated. "They said he was lost, Marianille. I am so sorry."

"At least we know Birlerion didn't tell them what they wanted, not that I ever thought he would," Marianille said, her eyes glittering with tears. "But now I know who is responsible, and he will pay for what he has done to my brother."

Taelia reached over and squeezed her hand. "Then it's a good job he's leaving for a while, much as I'd like you to kill him. I doubt the duke would appreciate dead bodies in his palace."

Marianille wiped her tears away and looked down at their next report in her hands. "Then he shouldn't consort with Ascendants. Anything else before I call Ari to take this to Alyssa?"

"They said Birlerion was taken to Adeeron," Niallerion said with some reluctance.

Marianille stilled and closed her eyes. "The one place we can't go," she whispered. She opened her eyes. "It's the home of the Third Chevron, and no one knows where it is."

22

ADEERON, ELOTHIA

F inn blearily opened his eyes and stared up at the men gathered around him. He grimaced as he sat up, stretching his jaw. His face felt stiff and tender. He was sure it was bruising spectacularly, yet again. He observed the men as he moved to stand by Owen's shoulder. They looked lean and mean. They'd need to be to survive here, he thought.

"Well?" Owen asked, his voice cold.

"Think you could take us, do you?" A broad-chested man with a crooked nose and a full beard spat. His beady eyes inspected them and found them lacking.

"Preferably not all at once," Finn said from behind Owen. He really wasn't in condition for a fight. He rubbed his temple. He wasn't in condition for anything. He had no idea who he was or how he had ended up here. His head hurt; a deep dull ache that made it difficult to think.

"Ah, a scholar, eh? A scholar who can fight," the man sneered.

A scholar? Am I? Finn wondered. He had been travelling through Elothia, according to that innkeeper, so maybe he was. "Only if necessary. I prefer not to," he replied, keeping his voice calm.

The blonde-haired man at the recruit's shoulder laughed. He too wore a thick beard. "A man in the Third Chevron who prefers not to fight?" he said in disbelief.

"Well, not by choice," Finn said. "I guess we'll see if any of you are worth fighting for."

"There are few worth fighting for," a soft voice said from the doorway, and the men parted to reveal a gaunt man, taller than the rest, but more battered. His left arm was splinted, the bandage grubby and ragged. He sported a nasty wound bisecting his eyebrow, though his dark blue eyes were sharp. His chin was covered by a neatly trimmed black beard, but it didn't conceal the unnaturally pale skin or the bruises beneath. Finn's memory stirred just out of reach at the sound of his calm voice. The man walked through the others and lay down with a grunt on the bed at the end of the room.

The dark-haired man with the broken nose brushed past Owen and poked Finn in the chest. "I think you'll find you are the one under scrutiny, grunt," he said as he pushed Finn up against the wall. Swords clattered to the floor around them.

Finn smiled. "As you wish."

"'Ware Tasker," a voice hissed from the doorway, and they all fell back to their beds and stood to attention. Finn slipped into place and watched with interest. This environment felt familiar; he had been in a barracks before and enjoyed the camaraderie of fellow soldiers and good friends. He didn't remember being conscripted, though.

"Good, getting to know each other, eh? No broken bones, understood?" the Tasker rapped, looking intently at the apparent leader of the group. The dark-haired man swallowed and responded. "Yes, sir."

"Good," he repeated, his long black coat swirling as he turned and stared at Owen and Finn. "Our new recruits." He pointed at Owen, "You will be called Centa OneOne, and you," his gaze inspected Finn, "Centa OneTwo. Welcome to the Third Chevron. You will be tested, but then," he smiled coldly, "the grand duke only expects the best. Get them some uniforms. I expect you all out on the track in thirty minutes." His eyes drilled into the dark-haired man's eyes. "Understood, Centa One?"

"Yes, sir."

The Tasker's eyes narrowed as his gaze paused on the battered man at the end of the room. "I will be watching." His harsh voice echoed in the room long after he had left.

"You heard him, take them to the storage room." Centa One's lips twisted as he watched them leave. "Like lambs to the slaughter," he murmured under his breath.

"Are you so sure about that?" Centa Two asked.

Centa One curled his lip. "Oh yes," he replied.

They were out on the parade ground within half a chime, dressed in rough spun cotton trousers and a loose shirt. The arms master, Krell, strode down the line of men, pausing as he reached Owen and Finn.

"So," he snapped. "Looks like you came off worse." He lifted Finn's face with his stock.

"Yes, sir," Finn mumbled. His face had stiffened painfully.

The master leaned in. "What was that?" he asked. "I can't hear you."

"Yes, sir," Finn barked, wincing as his head throbbed in time.

"Ah, sir?" Owen interrupted him. "Centa OneTwo was

knocked unconscious earlier today. If you want to get any use out of him, it would be wise not to hit around the head."

Krell turned his head in disbelief. "And who might you be?"

"Centa OneOne," Owen replied.

"Really? And what makes you the expert on Centa OneTwo's health?"

"Well, I knocked him out, and I think he's suffering from a slight concussion."

"A healer, are you?"

"No, sir."

"Well then, I suggest you get on the floor and give me fifty, now," Krell snarled in his face. He turned back to Finn as Owen dropped to the dirt and began counting.

The arms master circled Finn before returning to stare intently at his face. His face tightened, obviously not liking what he saw. He pursed his lips. "Stand there and don't move," he said, turning back to the others, who were watching with interest. They snapped their eyes forward.

He started counting them off and sent them on circuits of the training field that Finn wished he could join. He missed running.

Owen was now gasping out numbers. The master stood over him as Owen's arms trembled and wavered. "Twenty-eight," he gasped before collapsing in the dust.

"Don't leave until you reach fifty." The master hissed in Finn's ear, "You, hit the dirt and help him."

Finn dropped to the ground and started pumping. Counting out loud, he closed his eyes as his head began to thump in time. He kept pumping. "Six, seven."

Owen gasped beside him.

"Nine, ten." Finn thought he might throw up, and he concentrated on swallowing between counts. "Twelve." His arms were shaking; he'd never felt so weak. He gasped out, "Fifteen."

"Enough," Krell said. Finn wavered as his arms trembled.

Owen collapsed to the ground beside him, chest heaving. "Centa OneOne, join your colleagues on the circuit. Centa Six take Centa OneTwo and report to the infirmary to get him checked out; get your splint taken off as well while you're there."

Finn levered himself to his feet, sweat running down his face. He swayed in front of the Arms master.

"Now," barked Krell. Finn winced as the command reverberated through his skull. He managed to make it to the exit of the training ground before his stomach betrayed him, and he threw his guts up. He retched painfully as his head thumped.

Centa Six stood next to him, patiently waiting as Finn wiped his mouth. He took a deep breath and turned to the man next to him. It was the battered, soft spoken man from the barracks. Sharp blue eyes observed him from under straight black eyebrows, one of which was bisected by an angry scar.

"Lead on," Finn said. He staggered out of the training ground, following Centa Six, and peered at the walls rising all around him. The basalt stone of the central square structure was oppressive and the narrow corridors leading into its depths, confusing. The walls wavered, and Centa Six offered an unexpectedly strong arm. He held most of Finn's weight by the time they came to a halt in the doorway of a brightly lit room.

Finn thought he heard an exclamation before strong arms took hold of him and forced him down on a bed. The blinding lights were shaded as his chalk-white face, glazed eyes, and trembling limbs were assessed. He flinched as a bright light passed over his eyes before a cold compress was placed over them. He sighed with relief until a vile draught was forced down his throat and the room faded away.

When he awoke, he lay still, trying to remember where he was. His head no longer felt like it would explode, and he gingerly opened his eyes to a dimly lit room. He sensed it was evening. The room had a muted feel about it as if everyone went about with hushed voices so as not to wake the sleeping. Somehow, he had found the infirmary, though he didn't remember getting there. There was a lot he didn't remember, including getting changed into the loose gown he was now wearing.

A severe-looking man paused at the end of his bed. "How are you feeling?" he asked, his deep voice at odds with his fierce appearance.

"My head has stopped thumping."

"You should have come here immediately. Leaving a concussion will only make it worse," he said, irritation colouring his voice.

"I don't think the choice was mine to make," Finn replied.

"Name," the man asked bluntly, watching him closely.

"Centa OneTwo."

The man grunted, making a note on his pad. "Well, you've been in the wars, so I guess you know what your body can or can't take. What happened to your hand?"

Finn looked down at his right hand and flexed it thoughtfully. He was missing two fingers. "I don't remember."

"What do you mean you don't remember?"

Finn looked up and shrugged. "I had an accident. They

were gone when I woke up. I don't remember what happened."

"Very well, Centa OneTwo. Get dressed. Return to your barracks. Light duty for two days and no sparring, understood?"

"Yes sir," Finn said, doubting that would be his decision.

The man looked at him from under his thick black eyebrows and grunted again making another note on his pad.

"Off you go, then," he said, turning away, his sudden movement betraying his impatience more than his voice.

Finn rolled off the bed, feeling clear-headed as he stood. Grabbing the clothes on the chair beside the bed, he dressed.

"Thank you for your care," he said as he left the room. The healer watched him leave.

Finn hurried down the corridor, not sure if he had lost a day. He followed the stairs down to ground level, not remembering climbing any stairs. Frowning, he entered the central courtyard, which he recognised with relief. As he crossed it, he wondered what the healer had given him to make him feel better so quickly. He hurried across the courtyard and into the training grounds, where he could see the rest of his unit being put through their paces.

"So kind of you to join us," Krell said, glaring at him. "Five circuits, now," he barked and turned back to the other men. "No slacking or I'll add another ten on each set," he shouted, striding down the row of grunting men. "Once you finish, obstacle course," he said as the men slowly stood, shaking out sore arms.

Finn completed his circuits and then ran up to join the men and dropped. He started his set of pushups, focused on the alignment of his body and the smooth motion, soothing in its way, as his body remembered the exercise. His heart rate increased as he reached his rhythm, and he continued counting, enjoying the activity.

He was aware of Krell, who had paused beside him, until he moved off to the obstacle course, keeping an eye on Finn, making sure he didn't stop. He kept the men working until he released them to eat and wash. Finn forced himself to eat the disgusting bowl of fish soup that they were offered and chewed the hard bread before collapsing into his narrow bed. He was asleep as soon as his head hit the pillow.

The next day, apart from a brief pause for more tepid fish soup for lunch, they trained and sparred. Krell paired the men off and had them spar one pair at a time. The first four were acceptable, and he sent them off to practice. The second four were dismal, hadn't a clue, so he sent them off with his parade sergeant for basic training.

The last two were interesting; the latest recruits from the press gangs. Centa OneOne and Centa OneTwo knew how to fight. They were well matched, Centa OneOne's strength versus the Centa OneTwo's speed.

"Where did you learn to fight?" Krell asked.

Owen and Finn flicked a glance at each other before Owen spoke up. "I spent two years in the customs guards. Got basic training there."

"And you?"

Finn shrugged. "I must have been taught the disciplines when I was younger. I don't remember who taught me."

Krell inspected him, and slowly nodded. "Well, that's fortunate then, isn't it?" he grinned wickedly in anticipation. "Did you complete all the disciplines?"

"I believe so, sir."

"Right," he looked over at the group who were desultorily sparring, throwing annoyed glances over at Finn and Owen. "Centa One to six over here," he shouted. The Centas trotted over immediately. "One versus OneTwo," he instructed, "the rest of you circle."

Finn sighed. Centa One was twice his weight and pleased to have the opportunity to show off his skills. Flattening Finn looked to be high on his list. Centa One beckoned Finn forward, grinning with anticipation.

Finn circled slowly, his sword raised in front of him. Centa One flicked his blade at Finn's sword, teasing a response. Finn ignored him and continued to circle. He waited until Centa One lost patience and struck. In response to the man's minute shift in balance, Finn spun, and when Centa One's sword came down, he was no longer there. Centa One staggered cursing, and they went through the same motion over and over. Centa One began to taunt him. "Too afraid to fight?" His swings were getting wilder and less controlled as his anger took over until Finn finally engaged and disarmed his opponent in one smooth move.

Centa One gasped, furious, but dropped his eyes as Krell strode forward. "What does that tell you?" he asked, handing Centa One his sword. Centa One was silent, and Krell looked around the equally silent men. "Never underestimate your opponent," he said. "Centa Six, step up."

The man who had silently escorted him to the infirmary the previous day stepped forward. He no longer wore a splint. The men jeered as he stepped into the ring.

He stood in front of Finn and waited.

"Commence," Krell commanded. Centa Six dropped into a familiar stance, and Finn responded. Centa Six smiled in acknowledgement, and the two men smoothly went through the movements, each a mirror of the other.

"Halt," Krell snapped. He stood in front of Centa Six. "Since when did you have the disciplines?" he snarled.

Centa Six shrugged. "It's amazing what you can learn on the streets," he replied in his soft voice. Krell struck him across the face, and Centa Six rocked back but held his position. "Be very careful, Centa Six. You could be back in that cell with one word."

"Yes, sir," Centa Six said, his voice emotionless as the men laughed at him. Finn observed him. There was no reaction on his face, just acceptance.

"Right, pair off." Krell crossed his arms. "You all just saw the disarm, now you try it," he said. "I hope you were watching."

Finn circled Centa Two.

"How did you do it?" Centa Two asked in an undertone.

Finn looked across at him. He seemed in earnest. "It's about doing the unexpected," he said as he continued to circle, "and patience," he added with a slight smile.

He moved suddenly, forcing his blade down the side of his opponents, and with a twist, the blade went flying.

Centa Two stood frowning at him. "How did you do that? Show me."

"Pick up your sword, then," Finn said, raising his blade again. He looked across as Centa OneOne disarmed his opponent in a more traditional manner, using brute force.

Finn demonstrated the disarm, aware of the others watching, and allowed Centa Two to disarm him. Finn saw Centa Six allow himself to be defeated, his partner oblivious to the fact that the man could have killed him where he stood. Finn wondered where he was from.

Centa Two grinned. "Again," he said. And so it continued, sparring and swapping partners until Krell called time. "One chime:, wash and eat, then report to the ring," he rapped, glaring at Centa Six, and then strode out of the arena without looking back.

After lunch, they trained all afternoon until they were

told to gather around the ring, where they nervously looked at each other, though Finn thought Centa Six looked resigned. He soon saw why. Centa Six was called forward. He stood still as his left arm was strapped to his side, and then he was giving a training sword. Centa Six stood waiting, his face expressionless.

"Why did they strap his arm?" Finn asked the man next to him.

"Just watch," the man chuckled.

Krell pushed two men into the ring, and Centa Six flicked his sword up immediately, dropping into a defensive stance. Krell barked at the men, and they reluctantly approached Centa Six. He dealt with them without changing his expression, and they lay groaning on the ground.

"See, even with one arm, he's a beast. Unbeatable one on one. They make him fight with one arm, so he doesn't kill them. They've lost too many men to him."

Krell pushed more men into the ring, and Centa Six stiffened as he caught the shine of steel. Finn hissed; these were no training swords. Centa Six had no chance. He put up a resistance for longer than Finn would have thought possible, but the men finally co-ordinated themselves in a rush and he went down beneath them. Krell called a halt, and the men stood.

Centa Six lay bleeding into the sawdust. He was silent and grey with pain, a sword still impaled his stomach. His hand gripped the blade, keeping it still, which explained why his opponent hadn't yanked it back out again. Finn noticed the other blades were lined with red, and the men were congratulating each other.

Krell approached and gripped the sword. "Maybe you will be more careful in future," he said, drawing the blade out. Centa Six paled even further and clamped his hand over the wound; ruby red blood welled, rich and vibrant against his shaking fingers. Krell snapped an order, and he was dragged away. Krell stared after him, and then seeing the men watching, dismissed them to the stables for evening duties.

23

DEEPWATER WATCH, VESPIRI

Alyssa scowled at the papers on her desk. The amount of paperwork it took to run a Watch was astonishing. The previous lord had left it in chaos, with poorly trained militia and badly organised defences. They had spent the last four months changing that.

Denirion, her Watch Sentinal, said it was much improved. At least that was something. She twisted in her seat and stared out the window down towards the lake and the two graceful sentinal trees standing beside it. She smiled as a gentle hum buzzed in the back of her mind. The sentinals were watching.

Ari popped into view above her, squawking as he flapped his wings and landed with a thud on top of the papers on her desk. Alyssa huffed and stroked his furry head. "Aren't you fortunate those papers were not important?" she murmured, sliding her hand down his fur, and pulling the message out of the tube on his back.

She scanned the note and wrinkled her nose. "Go find Lea and Tagerill for me, and then return. You need to take this message on to Jason and the king."

Ari chittered and then popped out of sight as Alyssa

copied the message into her journal. She ran her finger down the page, then sighed. Rising, she strode over to the large painting hanging on the wall, depicting a scenic view of the lakes that gave her Watch its name.

Releasing the catch at the bottom of the painting and pulling a cord at the side, she stood back as the canvas rolled up, revealing a map beneath it. Niallerion's gadgets were useful, she mused, as she scanned the detailed map of the Elothian borders. Checking the note in her hand, she moved a pin in the map marking the chevron's locations according to Taelia.

Taelia, Niallerion and Marianille were a potent team. Troop updates arrived almost everyday. She wondered how they were finding everything out and what risks they were taking. The news they had sent today was concerning. Even she could see that the forces were massing on the plains below the Summer palace, across the borders from Stoneford.

Her husband, Lea, had said that they would be after the Watch Towers, and it seemed he was correct. The Elothians had their sights on the passes. Even though the Deepwater river valley was the easier egress into Vespiri, it was a longer journey, and from their actions it seemed they had a healthy respect for Deepwater's defences. Alyssa felt a glow of pride. They had worked hard to restore her Watch. Especially since Lea and Tagerill had bloodied the noses of a few Elothian scouting patrols.

Her face relaxed as the sound of her husband's heavy footsteps preceded his arrival into her office, closely followed by the tall red-haired Sentinal who was now his trusted lieutenant. Alyssa was thankful the day Tagerill had relocated to Deepwater, even if it was only because he had been seriously injured when they had retrieved the Watch from the previous lord, Aaron. She was quite sure they would not have been so prepared without him.

"Taelia's message arrived," Alyssa said without preamble, indicating to the map and stepping back. "They are swinging towards Stoneford."

The two men filled her office. Broad shouldered and muscular, they made her feel dainty in comparison, especially as they both towered over her. Tagerill wore the silvery green uniform of the Lady's guards, the trim ensemble moulding to his body and casting him as 'other'; a reminder of his ancient past. The huge broadsword on his back was proof enough of his strength. Alyssa couldn't lift it. Even the air sharpened when he was present; a sign of his excessive energy, according to his brother, Birlerion.

Tagerill traced the front line on the map. "They are foolish," he muttered. "They will be exposed all the way across the plains to Stoneford."

"They must be desperate," Jennery replied, peering over his shoulder.

"At least it gives us time to reinforce the trenches before they realise they won't get far," Tagerill said, his hand sweeping down to their own border. "They'll have no choice once they've battered themselves against the mountains for a while."

Jennery chuckled. "Let them. Stoneford will contain them."

"As long as we prevent them from sweeping in from behind," Tagerill said, his deep voice determined.

Alyssa leaned against her desk as her husband's face fell. His eyes narrowed as she watched and then he straightened and looked at her. "Anything else in the report?" he asked.

Alyssa nodded, suddenly reluctant to share the rest. "They have word of Birlerion." She hesitated as Tagerill stiffened, and she patted his arm. "I'm sorry Tagerill, it's not good. The Ascendants have him at Adeeron, and he has been severely tortured by all accounts."

Tagerill hissed. "At least we know he does live," he said, squaring his jaw.

Alyssa frowned. "But you've always said he lived. You said you could feel him."

"The feeling has been muted, barely recognisable; more of a hope. At least we know he's alive and where he is. We can go and get him."

Alyssa shook her head. "Adeeron is deep in the heart-lands. No one knows its actual location, only that it is in the very north of the country."

"We are not leaving him in their hands any longer than we have to," Tagerill said, his expression hardening.

"We won't," Jennery said, gripping his arm. "Believe me, we won't. But we need to co-ordinate with the king first. We can't leave our borders exposed."

A gamut of emotions chased across Tagerill's face as he swayed, as if buffeted by the need to move. Alyssa winced at his expression; she knew how close Tagerill was to his youngest brother. Tagerill had been hanging onto the belief that they would be able to rescue Birlerion. It was the only thing keeping him sane as he threw himself into preparing the Watch for war.

"Please Tage, don't undo all our hard work. We need you here," Jennery said, his voice carefully neutral.

Exhaling, Tagerill stared at the map and then at Jennery. He nodded once. "In that case, I need to speak to Landis. He needs to reposition his men; our east flank is going to take the brunt of any force the Elothians send our way."

Alyssa's office felt suddenly empty as Tagerill left. Jennery stared after him for a moment and then rubbed a hand over his face as he sagged. "Was there anything else?" he asked, and Alyssa cupped his worn face. He looked tired. They hadn't once stopped with their training, reorganisation, or planning. It was endless, and it was taking its toll.

"You and Tagerill will join us for dinner tonight," Alyssa said. "Don't argue," she added as he opened his mouth. "We haven't sat down together all week. Landis can cope for one evening. My mother is complaining that she's forgotten what Tagerill looks like."

A puff of laughter escaped Jennery's mouth.

Alyssa smoothed her fingers over his cheeks. "Hugh misses you, as do I. We need to take the time while we can. Once the fighting starts …" Alyssa ended on a sigh and tugged his rugged face towards her so she could kiss him.

24

ADEERON, ELOTHIA

The following day, Finn was horrified to see Centa Six returned to the barracks. His movements were slow and careful, pain etched on his haggard face. He eased on to his bed, tense and stiff and holding his side as he lay down.

Finn approached him with a glass of water.

"Try it," Centa Six murmured, his eyes still closed.

Finn exhaled. Was Centa Six that suspicious of everyone? Had others tried to attack him? He had enough faded bruising for it to be plausible. "It's water."

Centa Six opened his eyes.

"Why aren't you in the infirmary?"

"I'm not worth the price of a bed," Centa Six replied, closing his eyes again. Finn observed the rents in his uniform, red-rimmed with blood; proof that he had taken more than one wound. He placed the water next to the man and left him alone.

The next morning, Finn watched Centa Six struggle to rise. He strode across the room and offered a supporting hand. "They are not expecting you to return to training, are they?"

"If I don't, they will just repeat it until I'm dead. Maybe it's time." Centa Six swayed, and Finn tightened his grip. He helped him change out of his bloody clothes, his horror growing at the sight of the blood-soaked bandages.

"They did stitch them, didn't they?"

"Yeah."

"Lay back down. I'll bring you some food."

"Don't bother; not hungry. Just some more water if you wouldn't mind." Centa Six closed his eyes, but by the crease on his brow, Finn could see he wasn't comfortable. His face was tinged with grey and strained.

"You'd think you'd get used to pain, but you never do," the man said, his voice so low Finn had to strain to hear it. "I suppose it's a sign you are still alive."

Finn was relieved to see that Krell had, for once, realised that the man was barely standing and sent him back to the barracks. He worked the rest of the unit harder to compensate for his moment of compassion. The men returned to the barracks groaning and bruised, more interested in their own woes than the silent man in the bed at the end of the room.

Finn paused beside Centa Six. It looked like he had only just made it to the bed; he was laying on top and not tucked in as he should have been if someone had been caring for him. His usually pale face was flushed, and he didn't stir when Finn felt his skin. He was burning up.

Finn cursed under his breath. Couldn't they see they were throwing away the best fighter they had? He found his way back to the infirmary and reported Centa Six's condition.

The Healer shrugged. "I warned them, but they wouldn't listen."

"He's our best fighter; we can't afford to lose him," Finn argued.

"Some would prefer it," the healer replied. "Give him

this, diluted in a glass of water. One sachet per night. It will knock him out. You'll have to keep an eye on him. It's all I can offer, and you'd better not let anyone catch you."

"Can I take some fresh bandages?"

The healer stared at him and wordlessly handed him the bandages and another sachet. "Treat the wounds with the powder before you rewrap them."

That night, after everyone had fallen asleep, Finn woke Owen. "Hush, don't wake the others. I need your help."

Owen complained under his breath. "Do you know what time it is? Krell is going to work us just as hard tomorrow until we're back to full strength."

"Then help me help him," Finn said, stopping beside Centa Six.

Owen stood the other side. "Are you mad? He'll knife us if we touch him."

"No he won't, he's ill. He needs help, and he's too heavy for me to manage on my own. Help me give him this." Finn waved the glass and leaned over Centa Six. Owen cautiously slipped his arm under the man's shoulders; the heat radiating off him made Owen clamp his lips tight. Finn dribbled the liquid into his mouth, and the man gulped desperately. "Hold him," Finn said before dashing away to get more water. Unsurprisingly, the man was dehydrated. He returned and helped him drink.

"We need to change his bandages."

"What? You've got to be kidding me," Owen protested, dropping his voice at Finn's glare.

"No. Help me unwrap them." It took them all night. Owen's grumbles were silenced at the sight of the angry-looking wounds. Finn gently bathed them, patted them dry, and sprinkled the white powder over them, and between them, they carefully rewrapped his torso in bandages. The man slept through it all. The healer had been right. His face was smooth, the creases of pain soothed by whatever had been in the sachet. They tucked him in tight and thankfully found their beds.

The next morning, Krell stood looking down at the feverish man, his lips clamped tight, and left him there. The cadets groaned as he put them through their paces. Finn returned to the barracks at every opportunity, trying to cool Centa Six down, forcing water down his throat.

"Don't." Finn froze as Centa Six spoke. "Captain, don't. You shouldn't be … I'm so sorry. I failed you. They were too many; I couldn't hold them."

"Hush," Finn replied, realising the feverish man was rambling.

"They were after you. I had to stop them."

"I know, and you did, you did fine, now sleep."

"I couldn't stop them. They kept coming …" his anguished voice faded away.

Finn stood over him. The creases of pain were back, his cheeks sunken and grey. The man before him was suffering, but there was nothing else he could do. He didn't question why he felt the need to do anything.

"Sleep," he soothed and returned to his duties.

The days blended into weeks. Centa Six made an unexpected recovery and resumed his place in the unit. One of silent resignation as he was consistently belittled or ignored. The unit coalesced into a team of competent soldiers. Finn enjoyed the evening chores in the stables but never grew to like the staple diet of fish soup. The glutinous bowl of fish bones was just unappetising. He ignored the taunts from Owen, who couldn't believe an Elothian could dislike fish, though Finn wondered some days whether he was truly an Elothian. It didn't feel quite right, nor did his beard, but then he had no memory of who he was, so he couldn't say why.

Centa Six remained remote; an outsider even within the team, though by far and away, the most skilled swordsman. The day they were given a bow and arrow and stood in front of a target, Centa Six blew everyone away. Even his most ardent tormentors were silenced. The instructor had immediately drafted him as an assistant; he didn't need the practice.

Finn followed Centa Six's soft instructions, advising how to compensate for his lack of fingers without pause. His calm voice was soothing, and Finn relaxed for the first time in weeks, comforted by his voice behind his shoulder. His arrows hit the target, and Centa Six sent him off to collect them, moving on to the next man.

Finn watched Centa Six discreetly, unable to ignore him. He searched him out wherever he was. He was far too young to be conscripted or to have suffered all that he had gone through. Old scars marked his skin; his recent stomach wound had not been his first.

He had a quiet strength about him, and men deferred to him, not only because of his deadly skills but because of his inherent authority. Finn couldn't understand why those in power were the only ones who couldn't see it. Then he realised Centa Six was a different person, docile and submissive when any person of authority was present.

He listened with interest and growing horror as the other men gossiped about him; about how he had been dragged in severely beaten and repeatedly tortured until he had submitted. Submitted to what they weren't quite sure, but whatever it was it hadn't affected his fighting ability. He obeyed every command without protest, seemingly docile, but threaten him and you'd better be ready to back it up. Everyone walked very carefully around Centa Six.

Finn felt some affinity with him. Owen had been clear that Finn had been recovering from a beating when he had been dragged out of the inn in central Elothia. Finn had no idea why, or how he had got there or where he was going. Maybe the memory loss was a side effect from that? All he knew was that he felt an aching loss in his chest, only he didn't know why. Maybe all he needed was time. His bruises had faded like Centa Six's, after all.

25

CELLS, GRAND DUKE'S PALACE, RETARFU, ELOTHIA

Taelia sat on the floor and ran her fingers down the stone wall. She had gradually worked her way through all the dank cells in the lower level, struggling to concentrate as she imagined the pain and fear that must have seeped into the stone floors.

She wondered which one Jerrol had been incarcerated in and what had happened to him. After her initial shock, she had realised that he wasn't dead. She knew it deep inside, and nothing anyone could say would make her change her mind. She had stopped protesting. As Marianille said, it was probably better that they believed he *was* dead.

Jerrol had asked her to wait, so she would wait. While she was waiting, she would complete the work that the grand duke had requested, though she now knew that the grand duke hadn't asked for her presence. He knew nothing about her or her work and had shown no interest in her findings. But it was a good excuse to delay her departure. King Benedict could send demands for her to return, but until she had finished her search, she had a legitimate reason to stay.

"Marianille," she said, drawing the Sentinal's attention to the lower portion of the wall. "Can you see what this is?"

Marianille knelt beside her and placed a piece of paper over the area, rubbing a charcoal stick over it. She frowned. "It's a tree."

"Like the Lady's symbol in the Chapterhouse or the Watch Towers?"

"Not the same, though very similar. The roots reach deep into the ground and spread far wider than the branches."

Taelia's sensitive fingers fluttered over the symbol. "Finally! I was beginning to think there would be nothing here."

"We need to stop. It's getting dark, and you are supposed to be attending the dinner tonight with Torsion."

Taelia sighed as she heard the bitter undertone in Marianille's voice. "I know you don't like it, but it's the only way for us to keep an eye on them all. It's surprising how people who know you are blind tend to forget that you can still hear perfectly well."

"He thinks you are his intended. You need to be careful, Taelia. He won't take rejection well."

"When Jerrol returns, he will deal with him. Don't worry so."

"The Captain asked me to protect you. Taelia, each time you are with him, you are at risk. You don't see his face; you don't realise how manipulative he is."

"I trust the Lady. She will protect me."

"She didn't protect Jerrol or Birlerion," Marianille said, her voice sharp enough to cut.

"Marianille!" Taelia was shocked. Was she criticising the Lady?

"She is not all-powerful anymore, Taelia. She cannot intervene in this world as She once could. She can only work through us, and if I am not with you, then there is nothing She can do."

"Marianille," Taelia gripped her arm. "Jerrol is alive. I promise you. He will return soon, you'll see."

She heard Marianille rub a hand over her face and tightened her grip. "I swear, Jerrol and Birlerion are alive. I know it is hard to believe. To suffer the constant scrutiny. Pretending to be something you are not is exhausting." Taelia twisted her lips. "And I'm not making it any easier, but we need to know what the Ascendants are planning and Torsion is our best option."

Marianille hissed her breath out. "If it's not you, it's Niallerion. Overnight he seems to think he had become some super spy. After his run in with Selvia, I thought he would be more careful, but instead, I expect him to get caught red-handed any day now."

"We are under siege, but not for much longer," Taelia promised. "I know you are worried about Birlerion. I worry for Jerrol." Taelia blushed, but said it anyway, Marianille needed to hear it. "He leaves an aching gap my heart, as does Birlerion. But they will return to us."

Marianille stirred. "It's getting dark. We should return to your rooms. You won't have time to change," she said.

"Very well. Let me gather my papers," Taelia said, accepting the conversation was over. She followed Marianille up the stone stairs and out into the frigid evening air. Raising her face, soft snowflakes kissed her skin. "More snow," Taelia breathed, her breath pluming in the frosty air. It had snowed every day since Jerrol had disappeared. Somehow, she doubted it would stop until he returned.

Adeeron, Elothia

As the weeks turned into months, the recruits were regrouped into units and given their names back as they were promoted out of the grunts to corporals and then lieutenants, and for some, rushed through the officer's program. Those who preferred to shave were given razors, though Finn had gotten used to his beard now. They began preparing to relieve the unit of the Third Chevron currently on duty at Retarfu. They went on sorties into the surrounding areas, commanding units and getting to know the men and their strengths. Finn mapped the terrain instinctively as he covered it.

Finn was out with Owen and his unit on patrol, cursing the biting wind that cut across the plains to the west of Adeeron, and trying to muffle his face against the sharp pieces of ice trying to burrow into his skin. Surviving the weather looked to be more of an issue than surviving the training.

Barking a command, Finn led his men towards what looked like a cave in the limestone ridge that rose along the western edge of the plains. He gasped out orders as the howling wind dropped and they could finally hear themselves speak. "Set up camp, two-hour rotation. Make sure you have full gear on whilst on watch," he ordered as they entered the cave. His men jumped to and soon had a fire burning and snow melting in a bucket.

He was straining to study his map in the dim light when he was interrupted. "Lieutenant." Corporal Denning offered a battered tin mug. It was steaming in the cold air. Finn smiled briefly at the broad-shouldered soldier as he took it. "Thank you," he said, taking a sip. It was a bitter chicory drink that the troops relied on. Rumour said it made them more virile, but the wit in the army said they needed it to *escape* the hot-blooded Elothian girls.

Finn sighed as he leaned back against the rock wall. He couldn't understand why the grand duke was attacking Vespiri when his troops were understrength and ill-equipped. He was throwing away the lifeblood of his country. His current unit wouldn't last an hour against the rangers or Jennery's men. He stilled and turned the name over in his head. Jennery. Who was he and how did he know him?

"*Come to me, and I will tell you,*" a soft voice murmured. "*You are late again, Captain. It seems to be a trait, though my sister did warn me,*" the voice chuckled.

Finn looked around the cave. Owen had gone to relieve the watchman and his men were in various stages of relaxation, making the most of the opportunity to sleep, all except Centa Six or Private Birler as he was now called, who had sat up abruptly and was searching the cavern. Finn did not understand why the man was never promoted above a private. If there was ever officer material, he was it.

He glanced around again. No one was else paying him any attention. Was this a side effect of his memory loss?

"*I'm not a captain. Who are you?*"

"*Come to me at Leyarne and I will tell you all,*" the voice breathed in his ear. She was young, that much he could tell.

"*Leyarne?*"

He frowned down at his map. He couldn't see anywhere marked with the name Leyarne. Well, all he had to do was survive this patrol and he would be going to Retarfu. Finally returning to civilisation. He felt a tremble under his feet and looked around him. Birler had reached out to steady himself against the wall and met Finn's eyes across the cavern. No one else had noticed anything amiss.

He closed his eyes. Maybe he was just going mad. He sensed a presence next to him and opened them again.

"Lieutenant Finn, is everything alright?" Birler was crouched beside him.

"Of course, why wouldn't it be?"

Birler shrugged. "Just a feeling." He hesitated a moment and then stood and buttoned up his jacket, pulled on his gloves and left to take the next watch.

Folding his map, Finn moved over to sit by the fire, absently watching as one of his men stirred a pan of liquid. More fish soup. "So, who knows this area well?" he asked as he stretched his legs out.

"Erik, maybe, but there's not much around here, to be honest, sir," the soup stirrer said.

"There's a bloody great ridge stretching across the horizon. I would have said that's something," Finn said with a grin.

"That's why there's not much here, sir. You can't climb it. It's not called the Unworthy Man's Drop for nothin', you know. You have to go around it, and that's miles in either direction. These plains are empty."

"The Unworthy Man's Drop? Sounds like there should be a story to go with that," Finn said comfortably. His nose twitched. That was not fish soup. "What are you cooking?" he asked, sitting upright.

Corporal Denning grinned as he ran his hands through his straggly blond hair. "Knowing your dislike of fish, sir, we managed to scrounge a scrag of goat; so it's goat soup, sir. More soup than goat, but it sure smells good." He sighed and rubbed his pointed nose.

"Where did you get it from?" Finn asked as he leaned forward, inhaling deeply. He was touched that they had made such an effort for him.

"Best you don't know, sir," Denning said with a grin.

"Don't you go getting into trouble for me," Finn said, shifting to get more comfortable on the rocky floor.

"No, sir, we won't. It's a treat for all of us." Denning started pouring the soup into tin mugs; as he'd said, it was more liquid than lumps. He handed the first mug to Finn.

Finn communed with his mug, inhaling the fragrance as his mouth watered in anticipation. He sipped the steaming liquid with caution and relaxed as the warmth spread through his body. His men changed watch around him and he shuffled over to make room for a private relieved from standing duty. The cold air rolled off him as he spread his hands towards the fire. "It seems even more bitter out there than usual," the private said as he took a mug and cupped his hands around it.

Finn grunted in agreement. "Only fools like us come out here."

"Didn't used to be like this; it never used to freeze south of the ridge. The ridge protected us, and this was all grass-lands when I was a kid. Herds of cattle grazed these plains; rich grass. Now, everything perishes."

Finn watched him as he loosened his fur-lined hood. His short brown hair was plastered to his temples, the frost melting slowly in the meagre heat of the cave. The private was one of his youngest men. "When you were a kid? That wasn't that long ago."

The men laughed, and Denning stretched his hand out to ruffle the youngster's hair.

"Gerroff! I ain't no kid."

"No, *that* you are not," Finn soothed. "So tell us why the ridge is called the 'Unworthy Man's Drop'. You must know the story."

The boy shrugged. "It's just tall tales; it's not true." He pushed his damp hair off his face, leaving it sticking up in tufts.

"Well, we haven't got anything better to do, so why don't you tell us anyway?"

"Go on, Erik, tell us. I'll give you another mug of soup," Denning offered.

Erik grinned acceptance and wrinkled his nose. His cheeks were red from the cold, and he rubbed his face vigor-ously after he handed his empty mug to Denning. "Well, it dates back to the Lady and her guardians. It's said that one of the Lady's sisters became the Guardian of Land. No one's quite sure how or why, but it happened around the time when they all left."

"When she broke, what was it called? The Bloodstone?" Finn asked.

Erik shrugged. "No one knows. No Bloodstone in this story. They all suddenly upped and left; never came back. Left Elothia under the rule of the first Grand Duke. That was thousands of years ago. But the Lady of the Land stayed. Well, she didn't have much choice; she was the land, after all." He paused to take the mug back from Denning and breathed in the steam before continuing. "She was young and beautiful with long auburn hair the colour of rich copper, and brilliant blue eyes the colour of the sky. She had a tinkling laugh that lifted your spirits."

"And she was called Marguerite," Finn said slowly as her face crystallised before him. The name rolled off his tongue even though moments before he would have said he didn't know who she was.

"That's right, sir," Erik nodded. "They say she used to dance across these plains barefoot, encouraging the ground to thaw and the crops to grow."

"I doubt she's done that for a long time," Denning grunted morosely.

Erik laughed. "She'd lose her toes if she tried to do it now, but you're right, she used to banish winter and welcome spring. But no one's seen her for centuries, and our winters are getting worse, and spring never seems to arrive anymore."

"People saw her?"

"So it's said. Marguerite used to live above the ridge, waiting for her guardians to arrive."

"But they didn't arrive?" Finn asked.]\

"A few did in the beginning, but there was a period of

upheaval; a backlash or something. No one's sure, but the land was torn. It rose on one side and dropped on the other. I think back then it would have been easier to reach her, but that ridge out there is what is left of it after centuries of freezing weather and snow. Only the worthy could climb to her tower, and no one can climb that ridge today."

"Her tower?"

"Yeah, she had a tower; the Tower of Larne. That's what she named it."

"Leyarne," Marguerite corrected.

Finn glanced around, but no one else seemed to have heard the voice.

"There's nowhere on the map called that," Finn said.

"It's not on any map. No one's found it," Erik said. "No one's stupid enough to try and climb that ridge. That's why it's called the Unworthy Man's Drop. Everyone who has tried has fallen to their death. They weren't worthy enough to reach her tower."

There was a short silence as Erik sipped his soup.

Finn frowned at the fire. "Is that it?"

"Well, others can tell it better. They add all the flowery descriptions and stuff, and the tale takes a couple of hours when it's told in full story-telling mode, but that's the basic story."

"Thank the Lady," Denning said, rolling his eyes, "Who'd want to sit and listen to that for two hours?"

"You'd be surprised." Finn laughed. "What about the Guardians that did reach her; what happened to them?"

Erik shrugged. "Died, probably."

"Maybe that's why spring don't come no more?" Denning said as he poked the fire, causing a shower of sparks to light up their tired faces in the damp gloom. On that sombre note, the men broke into smaller groups settling down for some much-needed sleep.

"Denning, make sure the watches are no more than two hours. Wake me at third chime, and I'll take over. You can get some shut-eye then." Jerrol wrapped himself in his bedroll and settled down to sleep.

"Yes, sir," Denning replied.

Owen woke him at third chime. "I don't know how you do it," he murmured.

Finn yawned and reluctantly rose. "Do what?"

"Goat soup? They wouldn't have made it for me."

"Of course they would, if you made an effort to get to know them," he said, watching Owen wrap himself in the warm blankets he had just left.

"What's the point? I don't want to be a captain. Too much like hard work."

Finn snorted. "You already do the work. May as well get paid for it."

Owen propped himself up on an elbow. "Conscripted remember? We don't get paid." His blond eyebrows rose into his hairline. "Don't make me laugh."

"Well, apparently you do if you make officer rank. Not that there's anywhere to spend it."

"Now he tells me. Just wait till you get to Retarfu, plenty of shops there. You'll have a ball there."

"And you won't?"

"Nah. I'm just a peasant."

Shaking his head, Finn tugged on his fleece lined jacket. "Why do you always pretend you don't care?"

Owen hunched his shoulder. "Doesn't pay to care," he replied and rolled over leaving Finn staring at his back.

26

BALL ROOM, GRAND DUKE'S PALACE, RETARFU

Taelia sipped her glass of wine and concentrated on identifying the voices around her. Over the past few months she had made sure that Torsion had introduced her to everyone in the grand duke's court. She always spent a few moments in conversation each time, giving her time to learn their typical cadences of speech, their perfume, and, for some, tobacco smoke or alcoholic fumes to catalogue who socialised with whom. She soon found it easy to identify the groups of people around her. The swish of cloth or the staccato of heels narrowed the possibilities by half, and often, it was Torsion's reaction that gave her warning.

Tonight, the ball was in honour of the grand duke's sister, Princess Selvia. She was celebrating her borning day, though she was being coy about how old she was. As Torsion had led her down the reception line, the waft of musky perfume had made Taelia choke as it caught the back of her throat. The princess had inquired if she was alright, her voice filled with bored condescension as Torsion had hurried Taelia away to get a glass of water. He had been mortified and had been quick to berate her.

Fortunately, he had been called away from Taelia's side

and left her to her own devices, so she began drifting around the edges of the dance floor, trying to track down the princess. Short bursts of conversation flitted past as dancers twirled on the dance floor.

"… time to take the next step …"

"... doesn't she look exquisite? Though don't you think that necklace is gaudy?"

"… I hope we don't have fish again tonight …"

Heavy footsteps approached and she turned, smiling in welcome. The slight irregularity in the steps identified the man approaching as the grand duke's steward, Ulfr.

"Scholar Taelia," Ulfr said, clearing his throat.

"Ulfr, how are you?"

"Fine, fine. Princess Selvia was asking if you had recovered? If you are at liberty, she would like to speak to you."

"Of course. I'd be honoured," Taelia replied, extending her hand.

Ulf tucked her hand under his arm and patted it. "Just a note of warning, I would avoid mentioning Ambassador Haven, if possible."

Taelia stiffened. "May I ask why?"

"She blames him for her fall from grace in Vespiri. Sore subject," he replied, and Taelia heard the amusement lacing his voice.

"I would not wish to spoil her party," Taelia said, a small smile hovering over her mouth. Ulfr repressed a snort, and Taelia waved a hand. "Everyone seems to be enjoying themselves. The grand duke does like lavish events."

"He doesn't. He just puts up with them. Easier to cope with than Selvia's tantrums," he replied in a low mutter.

Taelia choked in surprise.

"Sorry, that slipped out. The woman is a nightmare. I'm not surprised King Benedict got rid of her."

A delighted chuckle escaped her, but she straightened her

face as Ulfr squeezed her arm in warning. His arm rose beside her and she fumbled for the step that she knew must be before her. "My apologies, scholar," Ulfr said, tightening his grip as she tripped. "There are three steps to the platform and the princess is seated in the middle. Her ladies are behind her."

Taelia's face heated as the ladies tittered as she approached, but she lifted her chin and glared at them. Silence fell. When Ulfr stopped walking, she dropped into a curtsey, saying as she rose, "Princess Selvia, Lady's blessings on your borning day."

"Thank you, m'dear. Ulfr, you may leave us." The Princess sounded bored. Taelia heard the snap of a fan being opened and then the slight puff of air it generated as it wafted past her. She thankfully sat in the seat Ulfr guided her to, and after another gentle squeeze of her arm, he left.

"How did a blind girl ever become a scholar?" the princess asked. Taelia heard the hiss of breath as the princess yawned behind her fan. Her ladies tittered again behind her, like a chorus of empty-headed chimes clacking in the breeze.

Taelia smiled, turning towards them. "I was fortunate to meet Scholar Torsion when I was a young girl, and he sponsored me into the Chapterhouse."

"I'm sure he did; he likes you, doesn't he?"

Taelia blushed. "We are good friends. We've known each other a long time."

"Oh, more than good friends, I think. He is looking for you." A trace of amusement threaded her voice. "He doesn't like you out of his sight for long, does he?"

Taelia shifted in her seat. "He is attentive," she admitted.

"I wonder what he sees in you?" the princess mused. "He is no longer a scholar, you know. He uses his Ascendant name now, Tor'asion. You should use it too."

"I only know Scholar Torsion," Taelia said.

"Really? It's the same man. How can you not know Tor'asion?"

"He will always be Torsion to me. We share a love of antiquities and language. That is the man I know."

"Antiquities? What use are they?"

"Understanding our history and where we come from, helps us understand where we are going," Taelia replied.

The air sharpened. "And you know where we are going?" the princess asked.

Taelia had the impression that the princess was staring at her and tried to keep her expression smooth. Jerrol was always telling her that she expressed all her thoughts on her face. "I have no idea. Do you?" she asked with a laugh.

"A new path," the princess breathed. "A new leader to raise us."

Taelia tilted her head at the reverence in the princess' voice. "Who?" she asked.

The air changed again, and the aroma of oak moss and green leaves replaced the musky perfume. The princess tapped her fan against the arm of her chair. "Randolf! Where have you been?"

"Selvia, my dear. Are you enjoying your ball?"

"You promised me entertainment. Where is it?"

"They are just setting up. They were delayed by the snow."

"It's snowing? Again?" Selvia tutted, diverted from her complaint. "The generals won't like that."

"No, their progress south is delayed. More expense," the grand duke said. "Var'geris promised …" he caught himself. "But enough of that. Have you been dancing?"

"There is no one to dance with," Selvia replied, her voice cutting.

"What of your new friends? Aren't they paying you enough attention?"

"They are our friends, Randolf. They have our interests at heart."

"Yeah, right," the duke breathed, too quiet for Selvia to hear, but Taelia's lips twitched. She felt his regard on her. "Scholar Taelia, how is your research going?"

Taelia blinked in surprise. "Slowly, Your Grace. I have not been granted access to all the lower levels. That is where the history will be found, in the older sections of your palace."

"Has your man not reported? He seems to find access wherever he chooses."

Taelia grimaced. "Niall does tend to be a bit enthusiastic. I hope he has not offended, Your Grace?"

"No, not really. I am only hearing good reports from my staff. I believe you may find it difficult to tear him away when you leave us."

"Are you leaving us, Scholar Taelia?" Selvia asked, her voice sharp.

"I have not completed the work the grand duke requested of me," Taelia replied.

The grand duke shifted, and Taelia knew with certainty that he hadn't requested anything, but he was polite, and said, "Well, there is no reason for you to be refused access. I will let it be known that you have my permission, so you can complete your work," he said.

"Thank you, Your Grace."

"Ah, here comes Tor'asion, at last," Selvia said, a coquettish note to her voice.

"If your highness wishes to dance, you should ask Tor'asion," Taelia said. "He is an accomplished dancer." *Among other things*, she thought as Torsion stomped up the steps. He was not happy.

The grand duke sighed beside her, and she tilted her head towards him.

"Do you dance, scholar?" he asked.

"I would love to, Your Grace."

Warm fingers grasped her hand. "Then maybe I should lead by example and Selvia can snare her partner," he said, his voice serious, though Taelia knew he was silently laughing at his sister.

"It would be my honour, Your Grace," she said as she rose, and the grand duke guided her down the steps and away from Tor'asion for a little while longer.

"You dance very well," the duke said into her hair.

Taelia smiled. "I learned to dance from an excellent teacher," she said, remembering the endless lessons Jerrol had insisted upon. He had said that dancing should be instinctive, and only practice would help her anticipate what her partner's body was going to do. As she twirled around the dance floor, she recognised the tension in the grand duke's body.

"Is something amiss?" she asked.

"Not at all," the grand duke replied, gallantly.

"Did your sister manage to convince Tors-Tor'asion to dance?"

The grand duke chuckled. "Oh, yes."

"Will she enjoy your surprise, do you think?"

"She'd better," the grand duke said, a note of grimness entering his voice. "Var'geris was insistent."

Taelia shivered. "Your Grace, I hope you don't mind me asking, but do you hold the Lady close?"

The grand duke stiffened. "What?"

"The Lady. She will always help, if you ask her."

Before the duke could respond, they were accosted by Selvia, and Randolf was forced to relinquish her to Tor'asion. And it *was* Tor'asion, not Torsion.

"What were you talking about with the grand duke?" he demanded.

"We talked about dancing," Taelia murmured, refusing to enlighten him further.

The following morning, Marianille watched Taelia paced the parlour as she finished dictating her report. "The grand duke mentioned his generals were delayed by snow, but they continued south towards the borders. Princess Selvia continues to court the Ascendants, though the duke does not seem so enamoured. It seems the Duke may not be such a willing participant after all. I wonder if he has discovered Selvia's allegiances."

Marianille sat back and stared at what she had written. "Maybe it's just common sense prevailing!" she said, unable to keep the frustration out of her voice.

Taelia grimaced. "Maybe. It confirms what Niallerion heard."

Marianille sighed and rolled the paper up, calling the Arifel.

"Send him to Jennery and Jason. They are going to take the brunt of any action on the borders. They need to be warned the troops are massing."

"They ought to know by now. We've been saying this for months," Marianille said.

"I know. It just feels more definite. Niallerion is observant; he's quite good at spying."

"When he doesn't get caught!" Marianille said, rolling her eyes. "He is going to get us into trouble if he's not careful."

Taelia smiled. "No, he won't," she whispered, as the little mackerel-striped Arifel flickered into the room and perched on Marianille's hand.

"Ari," Marianille crooned as she slid the message to tube on his back. "Find Alyssa and tell her to pass on the word."

The Arifel chirruped and flickered out of sight.

Marianille rose and placed another log on the fire, using the poker to wedge it in place. She watched the golden firelight flicker over Taelia's face as she stared blindly at the flames, a silver hair clip rotating between her fingers, brooding again. There was a tightening around her jaw and her shoulders had slowly stiffened. The high-backed chair dwarfed her; it made her seem small and vulnerable.

She considered mentioning that she thought she had seen Taurillion in the square earlier this morning. She had been so surprised that he had slipped away before she could accost him. They hadn't seen him since he had stepped in to rescue Niallerion all those weeks ago, but he and Yaserille were still in the city somewhere. Niallerion was out searching for them. They could use the back up if he could find them.

The floor creaked as she moved, and Taelia turned her head. Marianille caught her breath at the sight of her face. Taelia's eyes were luminous, filling her face, and they stared straight through her.

"They come. We must wait."

Marianille froze. "What?"

"The sword and the shield; they will return soon," Taelia said, her voice soft. The fire crackled loudly, and she turned her head back towards the flames. She seemed to shake herself, and then she relaxed back into her chair.

"How do you know?"

Taelia shrugged, and then smiled impishly, her eyes twinkling. "The Lady moves in mysterious ways." She laughed. "I've always wanted to say that."

"The Lady told you that Jerrol and Birlerion will come here?"

"Not in so many words, but yes, she did."

Marianille rubbed a hand over face as her heart thudded

in her chest. Her brother was coming here? He was well enough to travel? "When? Are they alright?"

"I don't know. We have to wait."

"We have been waiting," Marianille said, bitterness and hope warring in her voice. Could it be true? She didn't want to get her hopes up, but they could do with some good news. "How long are you going to continue with this, Taelia? We can't wait here forever. You can't keep leading Torsion, well, Tor'asion on. I still can't believe he is openly flaunting himself as an Ascendant. Jerrol swore by him. He was his friend, and he's been an Ascendant the whole time."

"You know, I don't care. He betrayed Jerrol." Taelia's lip trembled. "He betrayed me." She lifted her chin. "He has no right to anything. It's like he's two different people. I can feel the change in the air when Torsion leaves and Tor'asion ascends. I'm cautious around Tor'asion; he is not so considerate. But most of the time, he is oblivious to me being there. He is arrogant, rude, forgets to guard his tongue. Which is all to the good as he says things he wouldn't normally."

"In a way I wish he hadn't come back from the front, but at least we know where he is. Combined with the information Niallerion is picking up, Vespiri is warned, at least." Taelia shivered. "Let's not talk about him anymore. Come sit with me, Marianille, talk to me. You promised to tell me about yourself. How did you become a Sentinal?" She pointed with the slender hair clip at the chair positioned opposite her. "Sit."

Marianille sighed. She had managed to avoid this conversation on many occasions. She could see that, tonight Taelia was determined, but she had to admit, her thoughts returned to Birlerion often; it would be comforting to talk about him. "There's nothing much to tell," she said as she sat. She leaned forward and stared at the flames, her expression serious.

Taelia tilted her head. "Of course there is." She smiled, her eyes bright. "Tell me about your family and where you come from." She reached forward and gripped her hand. "Tell me about Birlerion."

Marianille looked down at Taelia's hands. They were so small and delicate. They were like her mother's, and just as strong. Taelia may be mourning the absence of her husband, but she was unwavering in her belief that he would return. She squeezed Taelia's hand before releasing her and leaning back in her chair. "I was born in Greens," she began slowly as the warmth of the fire caressed her face. Taelia smiled as if she could see her.

"I was born in the month of Julu in the year 1100 in Greens. I had two older brothers and two younger brothers. So, I suppose, it's not surprising that I turned out a bit of a tomboy. My mother thought she finally had a princess to dress, but it was not to be. I preferred fighting with my brothers, usually coming home covered in scrapes and mud.

"I became a Sentinal in 1123 when the Lady called. I had been a ranger for two years. Tagerill and Birler had graduated the year before." Her laugh was soft. "There were moments when we thought they wouldn't make it, but Serill kept them on the straight and narrow."

"Serillion? I always thought Birlerion was the calming influence?"

Marianille smiled. "Birler calmed Tagerill down, that is true, but Birler came from the streets. He had to fight his way up through the ranks the hard way. Many wanted him expelled due to his lack of family bloodlines. He wasn't always calm; certainly not as self-contained as he is today. He was a joy to be with. He had a gift for life and embraced it."

"I think I saw a glimpse of it once," Taelia said. "In Old Vespers, he introduced me to his sentinal. It was the first time I truly saw him relax; he was like a different person. I could hear the warmth in his voice, and he looked much younger; his sentinal had eased the strain of living in this new world." She swallowed. "I didn't realise how much it affected him until then. I was glad he had his sentinal to help."

"They are a gift from the Lady," Marianille agreed. "You were honoured. We don't tend to open our sentinals to others; they are part of us you see. What you see on the outside is very different from the inside." She paused for a moment and then continued describing her brother. "I first met Birlerion when he came home from the academy with Tagerill. He was recuperating from an injury. My parents decided, that first time he came to stay, that he should be part of our family. It took them months to persuade him."

"Persuade him?" Taelia asked.

"Yes, he thought he would only bring trouble to our family. He didn't realise how much we loved him. We got there in the end, and we adopted him." Marianille's voice wavered. "My brother had a keen eye. Arrows were a natural progression from the slingshot, and he was deadly, I can tell you. He was rather undergrown, to begin with, and we all wondered what Tagerill saw in him. He had to build up strength to manage a broadsword. It didn't come easily, but we all learnt not to underestimate him in the end." She stared into the fire. "That's what makes me believe he will return; he won't give up on the Lady or the Captain." Marianille heaved a deep sigh. "He travelled far and wide, across Terolia, even up here into the wastes of Elothia. I don't know what he did here, but Lady Marguerite had to come and rescue him. He was searching for something for her, and I guess he found it, because they returned home after that, and not long after, Marguerite bonded with the Land." She shook off whatever image she was seeing and smiled. "Tagerill now —you couldn't keep him down for long. He was irrepressible."

"What was he like as a child?"

"Tagerill?"

Taelia nodded.

"Much like he is now, only less disciplined. He always got us into trouble. He couldn't resist a prank once he'd got it into his head, though he always owned up to it when it was discovered. At least he's grown out of that, at last.

"And Serillion, well." Marianille sighed. "He was a book-worm at heart, quiet and studious, but he was always at their backs and invariably got dragged into trouble, too. I think he saw himself as the responsible one, trying to curtail Tagerill's more outlandish ideas. It was always the three of them. She fell silent at the thought that they would never be together again. She wondered how Tagerill was coping with the loss of both his best friends.

"You were at the palace with the Lady Leyandrii?"

Marianille smiled. "Yes, towards the end. She was the most beautiful woman; not tall or imposing, but you couldn't miss her. She was soft-spoken and youthful, yet wise beyond her years, and very determined. How she got all the palace staff out before the end, I'll never know, but she did. They all left under protest, as I did, but only because she said that if we stayed, it would make it more difficult for her. I still can't believe that she did it. She destroyed everything to save us.

"You're going to ask me what happened at the end, but I don't remember. I was swept away into darkness, and I don't remember anything until the Captain woke me. I think the only one who truly knows is Birlerion; he was with them at the end, but he won't speak of it."

"What about Marguerite?" Taelia asked.

Marianille's voice lightened. "She was a free spirit, always disappearing. I'm not surprised she bonded with the land; she was always running free somewhere. Taurillion was the only one who could slow her down long enough for us to appreciate her. She was young, with long tresses of auburn hair and brilliant blue eyes, like yours, though hers were more the colour of the sky, while yours are more like the sea around Birtoli."

"The Lady had green eyes, didn't she?"

"Yes, emerald green. Guerlaire's eyes changed to match hers over time. His were green in the end; he loved her so much." Marianille paused, remembering.

Taelia smiled. "I'm sure she knew," she said. "Tell me about Guerlaire. Where did he come from?"

"I think the story of Guerlaire is for another night. It's late. You need to sleep."

Taelia scrunched up her face in protest, but rose all the same. She paused in the doorway and smiled at Marianille. "Thank you for sharing your story."

"Your turn tomorrow. You can tell me when you first met Jerrol," Marianille teased and was relieved when a gentle blush touched Taelia's cheeks.

"I think I loved him from the moment I fell into his arms," she said with a soft laugh. She displayed the silver hair clip still in her hand. "He gave me this. A gift. It reminds me of him. Exposed at all times it is not all that it seems. Concealed within it is a tool." She eased it open and Marianille saw a serrated edge. Taelia smiled a gleam in her eyes. "He taught me to pick locks, cut ropes, ways to escape. Just like my husband, this clip has hidden depths." She snapped it shut. "Tomorrow, then."

Marianille watched her turn away and close the bedroom door. She sighed as she returned to her post by the door.

27

ADEERON, ELOTHIA

O ne evening, when they were finally allowed to stay long enough at Adeeron to sleep in their beds, Finn was shocked to see an infantry troop return ragged and battered, hauling a line of even more ragtag prisoners behind them. Finn frowned as he watched, staring more intently as the prisoners filed passed. His stomach tightened as he recognised the uniform. What were Stoneford troops doing this far north? And how did he know them?

He barked an order and a corporal trotted over and saluted. "Report," Finn growled, his eyes like flint.

The corporal gulped nervously, flicking a glance at the stern-faced lieutenant before him. He turned his gaze toward the men trudging by. "Sir, we engaged just north of Arla. We held the line, but they flanked us and took out the second unit, so we had to retrench. These were the only men we managed to cut off."

"What unit are they?"

"Stoneford, sir, 2nd Unit, First Division."

Bryce's old unit, Finn thought, and then, *Who is Bryce?*

"Why do we have prisoners to feed?"

"The Tasker wanted some labour, sir, for the mines."

"Well, you'd better patch them up if you expect them to work. They'll be dropping like flies the state they're in."

"Yes, sir," the Corporal replied, thankfully retreating and herding his prisoners before him.

Finn watched, frowning as he considered various plans to rescue them. He shook the thought away as he strode to the officer's mess. Why was he thinking of rescuing the enemy? He joined Owen at a table and accepted a mug of coffee. "Owen, how long have we been here?" he asked.

Owen gazed at him, his blue eyes questioning. "Coming up for three months, why?"

"I just saw a unit returning from a skirmish on the Vespiri borders. What do you make of these sporadic engagements? What is the point if we don't advance? They don't retreat, and we all end up in the same place."

"I think the general are just testing their defences. I expect we'll hear of some major engagement soon."

"What makes you say that?"

"Typical infantry manoeuvres; test and then strike."

"No." Finn shook his head. "We have shown our hand. Why give them time to prepare when we know they outnumber us? And anyway, what is in Stoneford that would be of any use to us? Why risk the army over a non-strategic piece of land. Surely, Old Vespers should be the target, if anywhere?"

"Let the generals worry about that; that's what they are paid for," Owen said. "I heard a rumour we'll be shipping out soon."

"Do you think we're ready to replace the first unit in Retarfu? They say the grand duke is picky with whom he allows to be his guards," Finn asked, allowing the change of subject.

Owen laughed. "He has no choice. You know we're the only unit Adeeron has turned out that has any chance of pleasing the grand duke. You're a natural. I wouldn't be surprised if you make captain before we leave, or Birler, but he won't be made an officer. You are the only one with the diplomatic skills to manage the grand duke; the rest of us are too heathen."

Finn flinched. Captain? He felt a thrill rush through his body. Had he been a captain before? He leaned back in his chair, sipping his coffee, trying to hide his discomfort. "And you, surely?" He was surprised that Owen was still here. He had half expected him to desert at the first opportunity, back to his family in Tierne.

"Nah, you have a way with the men; they respect you. They couldn't give a toss about me."

"You mean *you* couldn't give a toss; if you did, you would make a good captain."

Owen shrugged. "That's alright. I'll let you make all the decisions."

"When do we get leave? Aren't we supposed to get a week's respite before we are posted?"

"Not us. We might not come back; we were forcibly conscripted, remember?"

"Yet they're going to trust us with the safety of the grand duke?"

"I never said it made any sense. Anyway, where would you go? You still don't remember anything, do you?"

Finn sighed into his coffee mug. "No, nothing. I only think I must have been in the military. As you say, it all seems so natural. Yet no one knows me, or where I came from."

"Well, Lieutenant Finn, a blank page awaits you, and I look forward to finding out what you write on it," Owen grinned.

"Thanks so much," Finn said wryly. "But what about your family? Didn't you say you were from Tierne?"

"They probably think I'm dead by now. No point disappointing them by turning up," Owen said, staring into his coffee.

Finn frowned at him. "It can't be that bad. Why can't you go home?"

Shrugging Owen leaned back in chair. "You know, typical story. Youngest son, no one notices if you're there or not, no one needs you."

"I'm sure that's not true."

"They couldn't wait to send me away. Only m'sister got upset; the rest couldn't wait to grab the sign on fee." Owen scowled. "Money-grabbing penny-pinchers signed me up to an apprenticeship in the custom guards when I was fifteen. One less mouth to feed."

"You didn't like the guards?"

"That was so boring. More likely to freeze your balls off than meet a smuggler. Who's going to smuggle ice for Lady's sake? It will just melt."

Finn laughed. "Not unless you go a lot further south, then it would be worth something."

Owen huffed. "I'm worth more to them dead than alive. My father has been preparing my eldest brother to step into his shoes for years. He will lord it over those lands fine. Without me, my brothers will only have to split everything two ways instead of three, and I was never much of a farmer; never much of anything, really." He sighed, his shoulders slumping. "And then my sister went off to get joined, but that went wrong. The atmosphere at home was pretty dire. No. No reason to go home."

Retarfu

Niallerion rubbed his numb hands together and then tucked them under his armpits as he stamped his feet on the frozen ground. The cold was vicious, making his bones ache. He was about to give up his search of the market square when he felt the tingle of another Sentinal's presence.

At last. He scanned the milling crowd, and met a searing copper gaze. Taurillion! It really was Taurillion. He was bundled up in a fur cape, his head and ears muffled in a fur lined cap. He would never have recognised him without the warning sensation.

Taurillion cut his way through the market, and Niallerion left the shelter of the doorway to meet him. He had stayed in one place too long and had stiffened in the freezing air. Shuffling across the icy cobble stones, he tried to ease his protesting muscles.

Slipping on a patch of ice, he fell into the strong arms of the other Sentinal. Taurillion huffed, his breath a plume of steam, and after a searching inspection of Niallerion's face, he hauled him into the relative warmth of a nearby inn.

"You are frozen solid, you fool," Taurillion muttered as he pushed Niallerion into a chair next to the fire. "Stay there," he ordered and went to the bar. He came back with a fur rug which he tucked around Niallerion's lap. "Your lips are blue. How long have you been standing out there?"

"T-too long," Niallerion stuttered as shivers began to shake him.

Taurillion knelt in front of him and stripped off his gloves. He massaged Niallerion's chill skin. "You should only wear fur-lined clothes; it helps trap the heat against your skin," he said as he continued to massage some life back into Niallerion's hands.

"I've been s-searching for you. Why didn't you keep in touch?"

"Drink this." Taurillion handed him a steaming mug and helped him hold it steady as he drank. Niallerion shuddered as the warmth slid down his throat. Taurillion had spiked it with a strong liquor that started a fire in his belly and as the heat spread he relaxed back in his chair. Observing him for a moment, Taurillion sighed and sat in the chair opposite, loosening his cloak.

Niallerion inspected him in silence. Taurillion's grave face was framed by dark blond hair, plaited in thin tails at the front, and pulled back into a loose queue and out of his copper eyes. His cheeks were currently flushed with the heat from the fire. His chin was camouflaged under the thick beard he wore, but Niallerion was sure he was just as stubborn as he used to be. "Where have you been?" he asked after a short pause. "I wanted to thank you for your help."

Taurillion shrugged, twisting his lips in distaste. "Realising the world is much changed and not necessarily for the better."

"Where's Yaserille?"

"Around."

"Taurillion, we need your help. Both the Captain and Birlerion are missing. We know Birlerion is in Adeeron, captured by the Ascendants. The Captain is missing, presumed dead."

Taurillion scowled. "He is not dead."

"They are not well. I can't feel the Captain, and Birlerion is so muted I'm not sure if it really is him or not. I sometimes wonder if it's my imagination."

"Birlerion could fall into a manure heap and turn up smelling of Leyandrii's roses," Taurillion growled.

Niallerion scowled. "Not this time," he said, his face strained. "It's been months."

"Why are you still here, then?"

"Taelia, uh, Scholar Haven, insists the Captain will return. We're waiting for him."

"To do what?" Taurillion asked, his copper eyes glittering in the candlelight.

"To save the grand duke and Elothia from the Ascendants."

Taurillion snorted. "No change there, then."

"Where is Marguerite, Taurillion? We need her help."

Taurillion stiffened, his face losing all expression. "She's not here."

"She must be. Marguerite is the Land; where else would she go?"

Shrugging, Taurillion's cold gaze flicked around the room. "She abandoned us, abandoned me. She's not here."

"She wouldn't. You know better than that. Marianille is here with me, guarding the scholar. The Elothians are preparing to attack Vespiri. They want to destroy the Veil. They are after the Captain and the Watch Towers."

Taurillion quirked an eyebrow. "Why? They already have Birlerion."

Niallerion froze. Birlerion? He knew Birlerion was different, that Leyandrii had depended on him, but an equal to the Captain? "What can Birlèrion do?" he asked, his voice hushed.

"What can't he do?" Taurillion asked, his expression bland.

"They don't know what they have," Niallerion whispered, his gaze darting around the tavern as his memories of Birlerion, always in the midst of trouble flitted through his mind. His busy mind catalogued events, parsing the details he had accepted without question, because Leyandrii had managed it so.

"Are you sure about that?" Taurillion asked. "Their

posturing could all be camouflage. If they've had him for months, they would have broken him by now. We can't trust him even if he does return."

"No," Niallerion shook his head. "No." His voice strengthened. "They got nothing from Birlerion. I heard them talking. They don't know who he is." He paused, and stared at Taurillion. "Who is he?"

Taurillion smiled. "A pain in my arse," he said.

28

RETARFU, ELOTHIA

Taelia and Marianille were walking down the main street, back towards the palace when Taelia halted. "Marianille." Taelia's voice was sharp. "That's Jerrol over there."

Marianille looked where her gloved finger pointed. There was a unit of the Elothian Third Chevron marching up to the palace, resplendent in their red and blue uniform.

"Where?"

"There!"

"I can't see him. There's just a unit of the Duke's Third Chevron changing guard. Are you sure? You know, every other time you've said this, it hasn't been him. You can't bring back the dead. We can't feel the Captain; he's lost. We've been over this Taelia; why torture yourself?"

"He might be in disguise. We need to be careful if it is indeed him. It's been three months. He wouldn't just appear out of nowhere. There must be a reason. That was the Third Chevron you said? Wasn't that his back-up plan? To infiltrate the Third Chevron?" Her voice was rising with excitement.

"Hush; mind we're not overheard. If it *is* him, and I'm

not saying it is, then we need to be very careful. We don't want to betray his cover."

Taelia looked at her, tears in her eyes. She grabbed Marianille's arm and shook it. "I'm telling you, it's him; I can feel him." She dashed the tears away from her flushed cheeks before they could freeze on her skin.

"Well tone it down. Torsion will be suspicious, and Tor'asion even more so."

"Call Ari. We should send a message to the king," Taelia whispered.

"Not until we confirm. We need to know what the plan is, if there even is a plan," Marianille muttered to herself.

"Come on, let's get back to the palace. You can find out who's who in the new unit. I'll just listen. I'm telling you, it's Jerrol. I can't believe it, after all this time, finally! He said, be patient, to wait for him."

"When did he say that?"

"Before he was taken away, he said be patient; you were there."

"If I was, I don't remember it. Is that what you've been doing? Stalling Torsion, so you could wait?"

"Yes, it's worked quite well, hasn't it?" she said impishly as she dragged Marianille along the street.

"Taelia, slow down, people are staring."

"Sorry," she said, contritely slowing to a more decorous pace. "Won't we meet the new guards at dinner tonight?"

"Only the officers."

Taelia beamed at her. "Well, of course, he'll be an officer; he's the Captain after all!"

Finn inspected the grand duke's palace as they marched up the approach road. This road was in much better condition than those around Adeeron and carved through the centre of the sprawling town before curving up towards the palace. He had a dim memory of riding in a carriage up to the palace. He shook it off. Impossible.

The building was built out of soft golden stone and glowed in the brilliant sunlight. The grand entrance was graced by tall columns that curved away on either side, opening into vaulted arches that led into the depths of the palace. He approached the Third Chevron's First unit, who were on guard. They were smartly turned out and alert, saluting as he strode through the tall iron gates at the head of the column.

His men were soon dispersed to the barracks to freshen up. Finn instructed Birler to settle the men whilst he and Owen were escorted to the office of the Captain of the First unit. Captain Vinnsen rose from his chair and grinned at them broadly as he perused the orders that Finn handed over to him. Vinnsen was tall and muscular and filled the room. "Am I glad you are here. I hate to say it, but this is one of the most boring posts going. Your challenge will be to keep your men alert." His voice was loud and strident and grated against Finn's ears.

"It seems you have managed well enough," Finn said, his voice soft and cultured in comparison. He sipped the glass of whisky that Vinnsen had placed in his hands as soon as they had arrived and rubbed the soft beard that covered the lower half of his face.

"Oh, it's much improved this last week. I threatened to extend the posting of any man I caught slacking," he grinned evilly over the rim of his glass.

"What is the grand duke like?" Owen asked.

"If I am being diplomatic, he is a great man, who will change Elothia for the better; he will be good for our people and the Land. If I am being honest …" He blew his breath out and looked at them blandly. "Too young to be in command. He is too pliable. The general's run all over him and now he has these advisors he is always referring to."

"Advisors?" Finn asked.

"Yeah, councillors of some sort. They are warmongers so the general's love 'em."

"But you don't?" Finn suggested.

"I don't like any outsiders telling us what to do. First question the grand duke should be asking: What's in it for them?"

"Have you asked him?"

Vinnsen laughed. "Who do you think we are? We're just the help around here. We're given orders and not expected to question them."

Finn glanced at Owen. "Really?"

Owen grinned. "Our captain tends to get more involved."

"Well, I recommend you don't. Quickest way to get in trouble around here." Vinnsen snorted. He rose and placed his glass on his desk. "Come, I'll give you a quick tour so you can get your bearings before freshening up. The grand duke will expect to meet you tonight at the reception."

Finn raised his eyebrows. "And not before?"

"I told you, you just receive orders; don't expect more."

"Who else is here?"

"You'll meet most of the Administration and their families; they make up most of the court. General Kabil is visiting from the front, so I suggest you listen carefully to him. He's the only one with anything interesting to say. The grand duke will be there, of course, and his advisors. Oh, and some Vespirian woman who is with one of the Advisors. She stayed after an emissary visit went wrong. The grand duke took offence, apparently, which must be a first," he said with a twist of his lips as he led the way out of his office.

. . .

It was much later when Finn sat at the table in his room, poring over the map of the palace that Vinnsen had given him. His room was as far from the grand duke as possible, which he found strange. Surely, the grand duke would want easy access to his guards? He wondered if he would be able to suggest a change. The location of the guards was impractical. Were they here to protect the grand duke or just for show? After spending an hour reorganising the positions of his sentries, he folded the map and tucked it into his tunic, though he was sure he had it memorised. He had a few hours before he had to attend the reception, leaving him enough time to explore. He would begin with meeting the steward; the man behind the organisation of the palace.

Finn was relieved that his sense of direction and recent memory seemed to be working, even though he still didn't know who he was or where he came from. He arrived at the Steward's office at the first attempt and tapped on the door. Waiting, he glanced down the silent corridor until he heard the command to 'come'.

Closing the door behind him, he walked across the room, his hand outstretched. "Steward Ulfr, my name is Captain Finn of the Third Chevron. I am here to relieve Captain Vinnsen and his men."

"Captain Finn." The stocky man who rose from behind the desk seemed surprised. He was broad-shouldered, red-faced and looked ex-military. His elegant moustache was still a vibrant brown, like his hair. "I wasn't expecting to meet you until tonight."

"I thought we would be able to talk more easily here than in a reception line, especially as I am sure you are the one who really runs this place," Finn said.

Ulfr straightened slightly at the compliment and smoothed his moustache. "Of course, please have a seat."

"You must have your hands full with the Administrators staying here as well."

"Yes, they seem to have made themselves comfortable. I keep trying to advise the grand duke that it is time they returned home, but he just waves his hand, and they get to stay."

"Must be costing him a pretty penny," Finn said thoughtfully.

"Yes," Ulfr said on a melancholy sigh.

"Between us, we are responsible for the safety and comfort of the grand duke; is there anything you think I should be aware of?"

"Well," Ulfr smoothed his moustache again, preening slightly at being asked for his opinion. "I appreciate you asking. Your predecessor, Captain Vinnsen, wanted nothing to do with the household staff."

Finn smiled. "We all work differently. That's why I wanted to meet you. I like to work closely with the staff; we are all one team, and we all want what is best for the grand duke and Elothia."

"I am so glad to hear you say that," Ulfr said. "I had begun to wonder ..." He caught himself and cleared his throat. "The staff rise at five am and begin to prepare the grand duke's rooms, clear and restack the fires, perform general duties, and lay out breakfast in the main hall and the grand duke's private room should he choose not to join his guests."

"Does he often choose not to join his guests often?"

"More often of late. He has broken his fast in the company of his advisors for the last three days."

"And you are concerned?"

Ulfr stared at him. "Do I know you? You look familiar."

Finn shrugged. "I don't believe so; this is the first time I've been to Retarfu."

"I'm not sure I should be discussing the grand duke's habits with you."

"I am the captain of his guard, responsible for his safety. I need to know everything about him, so that I know if something out of the ordinary happens. We should be one team working together, but if it comes down to it, the safety of the grand duke is most important to me, and I will work around you if necessary. But I would prefer to work *with* you."

Ulfr relaxed in his chair and smiled. "I believe you, Captain Finn." He stroked his moustache. "These advisors turned up about three months ago, maybe a bit longer, wheedled their way into the generals' confidence, and got them all riled up. They took the advisors to see the grand duke, and they never left."

"What do they want?"

"For the grand duke to attack Vespiri. Why, I don't know. There is no reason for Elothia to go to war with Vespiri; there is more reason for King Benedict to attack us. One of his envoys met with an accident a few months ago; he was on a peace mission, too. You would've thought they would be attacking us. Gave the generals more ammunition to beef up defences, of course."

"And you think this has all been driven by these advisors?"

"Has to be. The grand duke had no notion of attacking anyone. He was preparing to be joined before she walked out on him. Never seen him so happy."

"Really? I hadn't heard."

"It was all hushed up. An embarrassment for the grand duke, you know? Lovely girl would have made a beautiful duchess." Ulfr sighed his hand straying to his face again.

"Who was she?"

"Lady Guin'yyfer from Tierne. Beautiful, she was, and not just in looks. Always knew what was right; had time for people, you know?" Ulfr looked up sharply. "Whatever you do, don't mention her in the grand duke's hearing."

"Good to know," Jerrol said. "What happened to her?"

"No one knows. Went back home and hid her face in shame, I expect."

"Well, first things first. To begin with, let's see if we can free up the grand duke from all these pressures; help him think more clearly. If I recommend to the grand duke that he should send his courtiers home, will you support me?"

Ulfr sat up. "Of course I would."

"Right, once we've changed the guard tomorrow, that's the first job, then. Oh, and Ulfr, any chance you can move my room closer to the grand duke's? I am too far away should he need me."

"Of course, consider it done." Ulfr stood and moved over to a map on the wall. "The Captain of the Chevron used to be billeted here in this small complex off the grand duke's wing. I'll move you there tomorrow. Back where you belong." Ulfr nodded sharply. He held out his hand. "Captain, I look forward to working with you."

Finn grinned. "As do I." They shook on it.

Finn returned to his room to dress for the reception. His clean uniform would have to do; it was all he had. He met a grim-faced Owen in the corridor leading out of the wing, similarly dressed. "What's wrong?" he asked.

"Nothing."

"Then you'd better get that look off your face or you'll have everyone panicking. You look like a storm is about to break. Come on, let's meet the grand duke," Finn said as he led the way. Owen dragged his feet as he followed.

They were met by Vinnsen and escorted to the reception line. They threaded their way along the line, shaking and bowing over hands until they reached the golden throne on the dais.

"His Royal Highness the Grand Duke of Elothia, Randolf the fourteenth," Vinnsen intoned. "Your highness, Captain Finn, Third Chevron, fourth unit, Captain of your Guard."

Finn knelt on the lower step, flicking a glance to his right as he heard a gasp. A young woman standing with a tall dark-haired man stared at him in shock; the dark-haired man looked horrified. He smoothly turned back to the grand duke. "Your Grace," he said, holding his left hand over his heart.

"Rise." The grand duke's voice was bored.

Finn rose and smiled at the grand duke. "I look forward to the honour of guarding you, Your Grace."

The grand duke looked at him and frowned. He rose and approached Finn, stopping a step above him. "What did you say your name was?"

"Finn, Your Grace, from Arla."

"You look familiar."

"I expect you meet many people, your highness," Finn said with a soft smile.

"True. Still, come see me tomorrow first thing. I like to know who is guarding me."

"Of course, Your Grace."

"Enjoy the evening. There's a singer or something tonight; supposed to be very good."

Finn moved on down the line, dismissed. He approached the young woman with the brown curls who had caught his attention. Her brilliant blue eyes were sparkling as she reached out. He took her hand and bowed. He tensed as a spark of energy sped between them. He tried to relax as he rose and looked her in the eyes. "Scholar Taelia Haven of Vespiri," she said, and her voice curled around his ears. "A pleasure to meet you, Captain."

"The pleasure is mine," he replied, mesmerised by her

shining eyes. He dragged his gaze away and glanced at the tall woman behind her. She had a broad grin on her face. Her silver eyes shone, but Finn kept his eyes moving. He shook hands with the tall man next to her. "Tor'asion," he repeated, before moving on. His heart fluttered, making him catch his breath. Who was she, to cause such a reaction in him?

As the evening progressed, he spoke to various government officials, all trying to ingratiate themselves with the new captain. Finn watched and smiled and said little. His eyes brightened when he was introduced to General Kabil.

"General, a pleasure to meet you," he said, inspecting the large man before him. He looked like he had been behind a desk for far too long, the drink in his hand no doubt the cause of his red complexion.

"Ah yes, what? Finn is it? Third Chevron? About time. Vinnsen has been complaining for weeks; about time he had some leave."

"Will he be joining you on the front?" Finn asked.

"Yes, yes about time too. We need men like him to protect the approaches, and the palace, of course."

"From what?"

"Those Vespirians, of course. Those blighters keep crossing the border."

"In retaliation to our incursions, or so I understand."

"Don't you believe in protecting Elothia, Captain Finn?" he said, catching the attention of nearby dancers.

"Only if we are defending against what *needs* defending, General," he replied. "This, of course, is very nice," he said with a grin, indicating the room, "But hosting all these people and putting on these grand events must be costly, all money being taken away from your war coffers, of course."

The general blinked. "Right, well said," he said nodding with approval as he moved on frowning. Finn overheard him later, expounding his virtues. "Good chap that Finn. Third Chevron turn out good people."

It was much later when he came face to face with the pretty young scholar again. "Captain, do you have time for a dance? I know officers are usually kept busy."

"Of course, my lady."

"Call me Taelia, please."

"As you wish. I am called Finn." He swept her out onto the dance floor, his fingertips tingling.

She raised her face to his, smiling with pleasure. "You dance very well for a military man," she said.

"A misspent youth no doubt," he murmured breathing in the scent of her hair. He relaxed at the familiar scent, the tension dissipating from his shoulders.

"We've missed you," she said. "We have been patient, waiting as we promised."

Her words ran like wildfire through his veins, and he raised his head. Where had he heard those words before? There was so much he didn't remember.

"Who do you believe me to be?" he asked as he twirled her around the room. Envious eyes followed their easy partnership; they seemed to know exactly what the other was going to do.

"Commander Jerrol Haven of the King's Justice, Captain of the Lady's Guard and the Keeper of the King's Oath. My husband. King Benedict misses you, as do we all," she said quietly, covering as Finn missed a step.

"I think you may be mistaken," he murmured.

"No." Her blinding smile faltered. "I'm not. I know you, and you know me, as we always have."

"My lady. I am Captain Finn of the Third Chevron. This is my first visit to Retarfu, so we can't have met."

"Jerrol," she whispered, her grip convulsing in his hand. "You must remember me, and why we came here."

Finn searched her face, observing the shine of tears in her brilliant eyes, a hint of fear clouding her expression, and his gut tightened at the thought of upsetting her.

"I am sorry, my lady. I-I suffered an injury, and have lost some of my memories." He smiled at her. "Though I am sure I could never have forgotten anyone as beautiful as you."

Taelia stared up at him, her eyes wide with fear, and she bit her lip. "You were hurt? What happened? Are you recovered? Did they look after you?"

Jerrol twirled her around the dance floor, and his gaze flicked around the room, avoiding her anxious face, though he felt warmed by her obvious concern for him. "I would not be on duty if I was not fit," he reassured her, and she exhaled a shaky breath.

Deep down, he knew the truth of her words, and yet, how could they be true? She belonged in his arms. He hadn't felt this relaxed in months and he knew her soul to soul and yet he didn't. He caught sight of the tall, dark-haired man who had been escorting her, a brooding scowl on his face. "Umm, your escort doesn't seem too happy."

"Torsion? Jerrol, do you not remember him, either?" Her face paled. "He was your friend and mentor, but no longer! He is your enemy, Jerrol. We knew him as a scholar called Torsion, but now he is openly calling himself an Ascendant called Tor'asion. Be very careful around him and Var'geris. They are trying to enspell the grand duke. They were the ones who caused you to be cast out; they said you had been killed." She clutched him a little tighter. "I knew it was a lie. But you've been gone for so long. It's been over three months."

The music came to an end, and as they came to a halt, she asked urgently, "Did you find Birlerion? Tell him Marianille is here."

As Finn bowed over her hand, he realised he couldn't remember what they had danced to. He cleared his throat. "Thank you for the dance," he said as he escorted her back to her glowering companion. Turning away, he found a bevy of young ladies clamouring to dance with him. Laughing, he accepted a hand and led one of them back into the fray. None of them danced as well as Scholar Taelia, and he found his eyes drawn to her repeatedly over the evening, though he kept his distance, not wanting to upset her companion any further.

"It seems you are a hit, Captain," Vinnsen said with a laugh, breathing fumes over Finn. "You know, you will have to dance at every shindig now. You won't be able to make excuses, y'know."

Finn smiled. "Fortunate that I enjoy dancing, then."

"A word of warning. I wouldn't dance with that blind lass again; her fiancé gets upset. And y'know, he has influence with the grand duke. So tread careful there," Vinnsen said in a loud whisper.

"Blind lass? I haven't danced with any blind girl," Finn said, looking around the room.

"First one you danced with; the one in the green dress from Vespiri."

"Scholar Taelia? Is she blind? I never realised." Finn watched her with new eyes, seeing her questing hand. She had seemed so natural with him. "She has a fiancé?"

"Yeah, possessive one at that," Vinnsen said as he finally moved away.

Finn stood quietly to the side of the throne, hands clasped behind his back, observing the room. The general was holding court with some of the senior government members. Finn's lips twitched as he saw that he was talking to the minister of the treasury. The evening finally came to an end as the musicians played the end of the song with a flourish and began to pack away their instruments.

Tor'asion stood to escort Taelia and her tall protector, Marianille, he assumed, from the room. Taelia flashed Finn a smile as she left, unerringly picking out where he stood. She smoothly diverted Tor'asion, who didn't notice him. And she was blind? She could see *him*.

Ulfr joined him by the dais. "Well, you don't waste time, do you?" he grinned, rotating his shoulders.

Finn looked at him. "What do you mean?"

"Heard the general bending the minister's ear, asking how much these evenings cost and if we could afford them."

"Ah," Finn grunted.

"Clever. Well, see you later. We've got to clear this little lot up now."

Finn watched the staff efficiently clear the room, waiting to give Tor'asion and Taelia time to travel the corridors before he too left to find his room.

Sleep was long coming; it all fit rather too well. He had been at Adeeron for at least three months. He *could* be this Jerrol Haven, but what could he do about it? And how would he get his memory back? He considered for a moment; if he was Jerrol, how had no one recognised him except for Taelia? Had he changed that much?

And Birlerion; could that be Birler? He would manoeuvre him into the vicinity of the tall woman, Marianille, and see what happened. Maybe that would trigger something?

His objective was unchanged; he was here to protect the grand duke and his people. He felt a sense of relief that he was, at least, still fulfilling his duty. Then that was what he would continue to do. The rest would no doubt solve itself. He closed his eyes and finally slept.

29

RETARFU, ELOTHIA

Finn was up at five the next morning with the household staff, roaming the halls, making himself known, though most had already seen him from the previous evening. The maids followed him with wistful eyes. The footmen recognised a kindred spirit. He had won them all over by the time he had finished his tour.

By seventh chime, the guards had changed. Vinnsen and his men left promptly, and Finn's men were in their new positions, eager to prove to the captain that they were ready. The off-duty guards were busy poring over maps and memorising routes. The more alert were taking their cues from their captain and making efforts to get to know the palace staff, especially those in the kitchen.

Finn met Owen on the way to the grand duke's chambers.

"You certainly know how to make an impression," Owen said as a rare grin flashed over his face before taking position outside the double doors that led to the grand duke's chamber.

"Remember, no one enters unless they are on that list." Finn tapped the board in Owen's hand.

Owen rolled his eyes. "I know how to do my job, sir."

Finn grinned, opened the outer doors and knocked on the inner door. He entered at the soft command. He closed the doors behind him, saluted the man standing in front of the window and waited.

The grand duke turned around. "Captain Finn." He stared at Finn, his pale blue eyes sharp as he observed him. "What are you going to tell me I need to do?" he asked, his voice tinged with weariness. Wearing just a white shirt and black trousers, he looked very young and strained. His fair hair was swept back off his face and tied in a queue with a thin black ribbon. His ornate jacket was slung over the back of a chair.

"I'm not here to tell you to do anything, sir. I can report that your guards are now stationed more appropriately to ensure your safety. There will always be a guard outside your door should you need him, and they will only admit personnel whom you have approved. If they are not on the list that you agree with Steward Ulfr every evening, then they will not be granted entry."

"How do you expect to manage that?" the grand duke asked with interest.

Finn looked at the grand duke blandly. "Sir, you are the Grand Duke of Elothia. What you order will be."

"And if I say I would like to have a solitary breakfast for once?"

"Then that is what you shall have. Your word is my command, sir," Finn replied.

"Very well, I desire breakfast for one this morning. Var'geris can wait until the morning session for his audience."

"As you command. Anything else you require, sir?"

Randolf looked at him. "Not at this moment. The novelty has yet to kick in."

Finn's lips twitched. "Of course, sir. When would Your Grace prefer I report? What time would suit you?"

The grand duke raised an eyebrow. "You think you will have something to report every day?"

"Of course, sir, even if it is just to say that all is well."

"Good. I expect you to report at seven every morning at these chambers without fail," the grand duke ordered firmly.

Finn bowed. "As you command, sir. Your duty guard is Lieutenant Kerisk."

The grand duke nodded dismissal and was pleasantly surprised when the captain smartly turned and left. He was even more surprised when breakfast for one arrived, and he enjoyed a quiet meal for the first time in weeks without interruption.

Finn spent the day instilling in the grand duke's household that they worked for the grand duke and no one else and that they only obeyed orders from the steward, his staff or the grand duke himself. On matters of security, they were to listen to Captain Finn or Lieutenant Kerisk. The staff straightened their spines and walked a little prouder.

Owen barred the doors to the grand duke's chambers, and glared at the Ascendant called Var'geris.

"You need to get your priorities straight," Var'geris hissed. "It is in your interests to assist us."

"I am a Lieutenant in the grand duke's Chevron, I don't have to do anything you say," Owen spat back.

"You will if you want your sister back in one piece. Just one word. One. Is all it will take."

Owen's stomach crawled. "I don't believe you."

"Still? Was our previous conversation not proof enough? Maybe I'll have a chat with your mother, maybe she can persuade you?"

"You hurt a hair on her head …"

Var'geris laughed and cut him off. "And what, Lieutenant Kerisk? We hold the cards here. You will do what we say or your sister, or maybe your mother will be the one to regret it."

Owen took a step forward, gritting his teeth, and Var'geris shook his head as he tutted. "Don't be hasty. Remember who is at risk. Best behaviour, Lieutenant Kerisk." Var'geris turned away. "Next time, you allow me entry, or else." The threat hovered in the air long after the Ascendant had disappeared.

Owen straightened, a scowl etched on his face as he resumed guarding the grand duke's door. His mind raced. What did the Ascendant's want of him? To go to such lengths, if indeed they had. He had no way of proving it one way or the other. There was no way to contact his father, not in time for it to be any help.

The door behind him opened and he stiffened as the grand duke stepped out of his apartment. Owen waited for the young man to precede him down the corridor and then followed as Finn's order to protect the grand duke no matter what, rang in his ears.

Randolf cast a startled glance at him and squared his shoulders as he led the way to his throne room. The courtiers bowed in a ripple as he made his way through the chamber. Var'geris scowled at both the Duke and Owen as they passed and the grand duke hesitated. He stiffened as he caught sight of his new captain standing at attention at the foot of his dais.

Randolf ignored Finn and stepped up to his throne. Moving to stand behind his shoulder, Owen stared blankly ahead of him. Randolf sat as the first petitioner stepped forward, bowed, and began speaking. "It has been six weeks since I last came. You promised to review my request ..." the man trailed off as Finn cleared his throat.

"You will address His Grace the Grand Duke as Your Grace or Your Highness," he said in a firm voice.

The man flicked a look at the captain's forbidding face and glanced up at the grand duke and blushed. "Y-Your Grace, it has been six weeks since our last audience. You promised you would review my petition to expand my holding. I have yet to receive word, if you please, Your Grace." The man flicked a nervous glance at the captain.

Owen almost laughed out loud as the grand duke coughed, was that all it took?

"Ah, yes. A holding in the Arla district. Minister Janssen, haven't you resolved this yet?" The grand duke looked across at a small man, who stepped forward, bowing.

"Your Grace," Janssen said with aplomb, his eyes twinkling, "Unfortunately, there was an issue with the documentation. But if the gentleman would like to accompany me, I am sure we can resolve it all."

"Excellent. Be so good to attend the minister."

"Th-thank you, Your Grace," the man said, bowing low, casting a look of awe up at the grand duke and his captain.

Var'geris strode forward, casting a glare at Finn. "Your Grace, I demand a private audience."

Finn tutted. "His Grace the Grand Duke of Elothia does not appreciate demands," he said, glaring across the audience room.

Owen muffled a snort as the people shuffled awkwardly. The expression on Var'geris' face lifted his spirits and made him want to cheer. He concentrated on keeping his face blank as he watched the Ascendants thwarted again. Finn was not messing about. A small disturbance at the door resolved itself to be Tor'asion entering the room, obviously arriving in haste.

Var'geris swallowed as he met Randolf's hard stare. "Ah, Your Grace, my apologies. It is quite urgent that we speak. If you would be so good to grant me a few moments of your time."

"Of course, speak to my steward, Ulfr. He has my schedule for the week. Next!" Randolf replied, waving his hand.

Var'geris had no choice but to bow and retreat, glaring at Finn as he left. Finn ignored him and stared forward. The rest of the audience passed uneventfully. Those petitioners who dared to approach did so circumspectly, and then the audience was over. The grand duke rose. "Captain, attend me," he said as he passed. Finn fell in behind his shoulder beside Owen and escorted the grand duke to his study.

Finn stood at ease before the grand duke's desk. Randolf was seated, steepling his fingers in front of him. "Captain, do you have a death wish?" he asked, his face serious.

"Not specifically, Your Grace, but if you expect your authority to be upheld, then people should treat you appropriately. My job is to protect the throne of Elothia and its incumbent, yourself. Unless, of course, you do not wish to be treated with the respect you are due?"

"Var'geris is not to be trifled with."

"No, Your Grace. If he treats you and your orders with respect, then there is no reason for strife." Finn shrugged. "If he tries to kill me, I expect you to deal with him appropriately and appoint another captain. It would not be seemly for an adviser to kill your guards, sir. Especially an advisor who is not Elothian."

Randolf frowned. "You don't think I should take advice from someone who is not Elothian?"

"Your Grace will take advice from whomever he deems appropriate, sir. It not my place to comment."

"How long can you keep him from my door?"

"For as long as you need us too, sir."

"Tempting but probably not wise." The grand duke sighed and rested his chin on his hand. He watched Finn closely. "It didn't use to be like this. I thought my reign would be peaceful and prosperous. Instead, I have strife on the borders and starvation inland. The winter looks to be harsh this year."

"Perhaps solving the strife on the borders and redirecting the resources and the food inland would solve both your problems, sir."

"If only it were that easy," the grand duke replied. "Thank you, captain, for your assistance this morning; it was timely." He nodded dismissal and Finn turned smartly and left the room. The grand duke stared thoughtfully out of the window until he was interrupted by Ulfr.

30

GRAND DUKE'S PALACE, RETARFU

Finn continued his roving patrols, keeping both his guards and the staff on their toes. He took his turn on patrol, usually guarding the grand duke's chambers, though, on occasion, in other locations around the palace. He watched everyone and everything.

Var'geris eventually got his audience with the grand duke, Finn waving him through, blank-faced. What transpired between the grand duke and his advisor Finn didn't know, but he received an icy glare as the advisor left.

One morning, Finn was sitting in the sheltered orange garden on a rare occasion when he had nothing to do, just listening to the water tinkling in the fountain when he realised he was no longer alone. He looked up from his contemplation of the water to see the scholar's attendant before him.

"Captain," Marianille said.

"Marianille, how goes you?" Finn replied easily.

"The better for your return. But where is the Lady?"

Finn frowned. "I'm afraid I don't know any Lady."

The attendant stilled and then said, "What's the plan, Captain?"

Finn frowned. "How do you know me, Marianille? No one, but you and the scholar, seem to recognise me."

"I know you because you are my Captain and I'd know you anywhere. Others do not recognise you as they never met you. When we arrived here in Retarfu, it was late at night; we met no one. Only you met the grand duke with Niallerion the next day, but not for long enough for him to recognise you now.

"You look so different in that uniform; much thinner and with a beard. Though be warned Captain, Tor'asion recognised you. He is just biding his time before he denounces you."

Finn stared at the tall woman before him; her silver eyes were familiar and yet not. "I have no choice but to hold the line," he said as his mind raced. His stomach churned at the thought of unknown enemies. It was disconcerting that others knew who he was and yet he didn't. What had happened to him to cause such complete memory loss? "We have to protect the grand duke. There is something we must do here, only I'm not sure what it was."

"Speak to Taelia; you asked her to find something. I think she has found it."

"Did I?" Finn sighed. "I don't remember her or you. I wish I knew who I was and what is going on. It is most distressing."

"Taelia told us about your memory loss. She is just as distressed. Worried about what happened to you. You really don't remember her? She is your wife. I witnessed your joining on Roberion's ship. Don't you remember that?"

"I don't, nor any of you." Finn stared at Marianille. "I have lost my way. I have no choice but to stay the course." He smiled, though it felt strained. "And hope some enemy I don't know doesn't decide to kill me for a reason I don't remember."

"I am watching your back, Captain."

"For some reason, that is reassuring. You must watch the grand duke's back as well; there is something not quite right though I haven't discovered what yet, and he is exposed."

"As the Captain commands."

"When is the best time to speak to Scholar Taelia?"

"She enjoys the sun here in this garden at about two in the afternoon when others are waiting for an audience with the grand duke."

"Advise her that I will join her tomorrow at two."

"Yes, Captain," Marianille said, turning to leave.

"Marianille, the scholar asked me if I had found Birlerion. Who is Birlerion?"

Marianille paused, a sad smile on her face. "Birlerion is my brother and your friend. He was taken by the Ascendants while protecting you at the Watch Towers. He's been missing for almost half a year."

Finn stared at her. "Birler?" he asked slowly, thinking about the terrible injuries the man was purported to have received and the systematic refusal to advance him.

Marianille stiffened. "Birler? Is he here?"

"Come with me." Finn rose and led the way to the guard barracks.

Marianille gave a small shriek as she saw her brother and rushed into his arms whilst his companions hooted at them.

"Birlerion, where have you been?" She gasped as she saw his scarred face, and his deep blue eyes. "Birler," she said, horrified, holding his face in her hands. "What did they do to you?"

Birler frowned at her. "Marian?" he asked, uncertainly.

"Yes, we've been so worried. We lost sight of you. What happened?"

Birler stared at her. "What are you doing here? Why aren't you in Vespers with Leyandrii. Did they reassign you?"

Marianille stepped back in shock as she realised Birler thought he was living in the past, that he had no idea he was a Sentinal. She stared at him and then at the Captain with a queer smile. "You know, it has some sense of symmetry. Niallerion would have it that you two are a balance, tightly aligned at all times, and I think he is right. You do seem to mirror each other." Her eyes widened. "Just as you did with Guerlaire, is that your purpose, Birlerion? To always shield the Captain?"

Birler stiffened under her hand. "What did you call me?"

"That's who you are; Sentinal Birlerion, my brother, the Captain's right hand. Still performing your duty, even though you don't know it," she breathed as the pair stared at her in shock.

"Marguerite said to wait here for the Captain. She said he needed support. I'm waiting for Guerlaire."

"Guerlaire isn't here right now. You're in Retarfu, Birlerion."

"No, yes." Birler looked confused. "Marguerite said to hold true, to stay. I have to survive to support the Captain."

"Oh Birler, what have they done to you?" she whispered, watching him with concern.

"You are supporting *me*, Birler. I am your captain. Don't worry, you are doing what you have been asked to do," Finn said, trying to alleviate some of Birler's confusion.

Marianille smiled and lightly tugged Birler's beard. "I will say I prefer you without the beard; this makes you look a lot older."

Birler blushed, and Marianille laughed even more. "Oh, Birler, I've missed you." She hugged him again. Birler's hug was more assured as he held her tight. She felt him shudder as his grip tightened. "Wait until I tell Tagerill; he will be so relieved."

"Tage? Is he alright?"

"Of course he isn't, you numbskull. He's worried about you."

"Ah, Marianille, I think Birler also has a few memory gaps, so you need to bear with us," Finn said.

Marianille nodded. "You ought to keep apart when you are around the Ascendants. If you are together, they will recognise you both. They only know you, Captain. Birlerion is unrecognisable in this uniform and with his lovely blue eyes. I'd forgotten your eyes were such a deep blue. We need to keep him hidden for as long as possible."

"*You* recognised him," Finn said.

"He's my brother," Marianille said. "I'd know him anywhere, even with a beard and more scars." She smoothed her fingers over his eye.

Birler leaned against her hand, soothed by her words. "Hidden from what?" he murmured.

Marianille looked at Finn. "Depends on what the Captain's planning."

Finn shrugged. "Protect the grand duke whilst we try to figure out what's going on."

Later that evening, Niallerion went in search of Birlerion. Birlerion! He was returned safe and well. Relief flowed through him, even though Birlerion's presence was still muted in his senses. Marianille had explained that Birlerion no longer had silver eyes, but Niallerion didn't believe it. He wanted to speak to his friend himself.

He found Birlerion on sentry duty in the main hall. Striding across the hall, he was relieved to see Birlerion's face light up as he recognised Niallerion.

"Nialler, what are you doing here?"

"I am so glad to see you, Birlerion."

"Why do people keep calling me that? My name is Birler."

Niallerion embraced him, hugging Birlerion hard. He exhaled, glad he was real and not a figment of his imagination. "Because that is your name. You are a Sentinal like I am, and your name is Birlerion. Though I think the question is more what are you doing here? Dressed as an Elothian guard?"

Birler grimaced and glanced around the hall. "Keep your voice down. I'm in disguise. Waiting for Guerlaire."

In disguise? It was certainly a good one. Niallerion wouldn't have recognised him, if Marianille hadn't warned him. Observing his friend, Niallerion gripped his shoulder and gave him a slight shake. His gut tightened at the ugly scar above his deep blue eyes.

"Guerlaire is not coming, Birlerion. He was lost with Leyandrii over three thousand years ago."

Birler stiffened. "No, that's not possible."

Niallerion tightened his grip as Birlerion tried to pull away. "Look at my eyes, Birlerion. I have silver eyes. The mark of the Lady. I am a Sentinal as are you and Marianille. Jerrol is the new Lady's Captain. You are guarding Jerrol."

"Jerrol? I don't know anyone called Jerrol. Captain Finn is my unit commander."

"Finn *is* Jerrol. They are the same person. He has Guerlaire's sword."

"No, he doesn't. I would recognise it, if he did."

Niallerion unsheathed the sword he had brought with him and held it up so Birlerion could see it. "This is Jerrol's sword."

Eyes narrowing, Birler took the sword. A flash of blue sped down the blade and it visibly vibrated in his grip. "It recognises you," Niallerion said, gently.

"Why do you have it if Finn is the Captain?"

Niallerion began explaining, summarising the last year of events as succinctly as he could. Birlerion shook his head in denial and Niallerion talked faster. "Tagerill is in Deepwater with Jennery. Jennery and Alyssa took guardianship of Deepwater. Alyssa's brother Simeon is the Lord of Greens. Versillion is with him."

"But what of my parents, Warren and Melis? And Penner? And ... and Kaf'enir?"

"I'm so sorry, Birlerion. They lived three thousand years ago. We slept in our sentinal trees all that time, only to be woken in time of need. Leyandrii needs us now."

"It can't be," Birler whispered, his eyes wide and dark in his pale face. He thrust the sword back at Niallerion as if it burned him.

"I know it's difficult to accept. A shock all at once."

"If what you say is true, what happened to me? Why don't I have silver eyes? Why don't I remember any of this, yet I know you?"

"We don't know. You were abducted by the Ascendants at the Watch Towers. You were protecting Jerrol when they overpowered you. You've been missing for nearly half a year. From the conversations I overheard, you were put to torture. They beat you repeatedly, trying to enspell you, until at some point you let go of Leyandrii."

Birler stiffened. "Never. I would never betray her so."

"Birlerion, it was not your fault. The Ascendants beat you near to death, by all accounts." A door slammed deep in the palace and Niallerion inhaled as Birlerion flinched. His friend was unrecognisable, in appearance as well as behaviour. He reminded Niallerion of when he had first met him at the academy, raw and so full of potential.

"Marguerite said to wait for the Captain; to survive," Birler whispered. "I-I thought Kaf'enir was silent because she was so far away." He fell silent, his expression withdrawn.

"Don't hide from me, Birlerion." Niallerion hurried to drag Birlerion back to the conversation. He didn't like the stark expression on his face. Losing Kaf'enir, that bond with his Darian, would be as painful as losing his parents. If Birlerion threw up his mental shields, Niallerion would not be able to get through to him. He suddenly realised how bad it must have been for the Ascendants to breach them and he swallowed. "Marguerite forgot to tell you which Captain you needed to wait for. Jerrol is the current Lady's Captain. You must protect him from the Ascendants, Birlerion. They mustn't capture him. They want him to shred the Veil."

"What Veil?"

Niallerion dragged his hand through his hair. It was impossible to explain everything at once. "The Veil Leyandrii drew down to banish all magic and the Ascendants when she destroyed the Bloodstone." Niallerion held up his hands. "And before you ask me what was the Bloodstone, I don't know. Leyandrii did something right at the very end. You were in Vespers with her. We don't know what you all did, but you destroyed the city, and Leyandrii and Guerlaire fell."

"No." Birlerion stepped back, his face grey. "They couldn't have."

Niallerion flapped his hands, trying to soothe and only making Birlerion retreat further.

Echoing footsteps interrupted them, and Niallerion cast a worried glance over his shoulder. "I have to go. I'll explain more tomorrow. Birlerion, please. Try and remember. You must protect Jerrol, I mean Captain Finn, at all costs. If anything happens, bring him to me or Marianille. The Ascendants mustn't get the Captain."

As the footsteps grew closer Niallerion cursed and then darted down the corridor leaving a shaken Birlerion to step back into position. Pausing at the base of the back stairs, Niallerion leaned against the wall and took a deep breath. He wasn't sure how much of his story, if any, Birlerion had believed.

He would have to try again tomorrow.

31

GRAND DUKE'S CHAMBERS, RETARFU

Each morning at seven, Finn reported to the grand duke's chambers. Randolf had taken to eating his breakfast as Finn updated him. "How long have you been here now, Finn?"

"Two weeks, sir."

"Two weeks? It seems longer."

"Yes, sir."

"Are you any closer to solving Elothia's problems?" he asked, a glint in his eye.

"I didn't think you wanted to hear my thoughts on the subject, Your Grace," Finn said politely.

"Did I give you short shift last time? My apologies, it all sounds so easy and yet when you try to execute it, it doesn't work."

"What did you want to achieve, sir?"

"Stop this nonsense with Vespiri. I can't get the generals to listen to me. They started a second front on the borders with Stoneford, for no reason that I can see."

"Was it as the behest of your advisors, sir? Are they directing your generals?"

The grand duke frowned at Finn. "You don't like them, do you?"

"What hold do they have on you, Your Grace? There is no reason for you to give them such free rein," Finn asked slowly.

"You overstep yourself, captain, though you surmise correctly. How to get a boot off your neck? That's the question."

"Let me help you, sir."

"You can't. That will be all," Randolf said, throwing his napkin on the table.

"Yes, sir." Finn left. He worked off his frustration on the training field before returning to change for his meeting with Scholar Taelia in the orange garden. Fortunately, for the last week he had been alternating the guards in the audience room, mostly because he didn't want to be predictable. At least his absence shouldn't be commented on, and it gave his men good experience to hear what their grand duke was being asked to solve. He wouldn't be missed while he met with the scholar, and hopefully no one would see them.

He was early. Seated in the orange garden, he listened to the water, the music soft in his ears. He looked up as he felt her presence, standing as Taelia approached. Marianille and another tall silver-eyed guard paused at the end of the path, giving them some semblance of privacy. His heart eased at the sight of her, his soul mate. He frowned at the thought. How was that possible?

"Scholar Taelia," he said.

"Jerrol." She instinctively reached for him.

He hesitated before grasping her hands and settling her on the bench.

"I'm sorry," she said, as her face dropped. She withdrew her hands. "I keep forgetting."

"Don't be," he said. "I feel I know you, and yet I don't."

He sighed. "I don't know who I am. I'm not Jerrol. I'm Finn."

"Finn was the name you used when you went into Terolia undercover; Fin'erol," Taelia said. She gripped her hands together so tight, her knuckles gleamed white. "I do hope that you will find your way back to me. I know you will, eventually. I have to be patient."

"Be patient," repeated Finn. "I seem to have asked a lot of people to wait for me."

"No doubt for a good reason," Taelia said, straightening up. She took a deep breath. "We shouldn't be seen together, so let's keep this brief. First, I discovered that Torsion is an Ascendant called Tor'asion. He tried to hide it, but he betrayed your trust. It's obvious now that we know. He was your friend, Jerrol, but no matter what, you can't trust him; don't believe anything he says. We believe he is enspelling the grand duke.

"Second, you asked me to look for something for you; something that would be hidden in the lower levels amongst the history left by the Lady. Well, I found something. It's not typical of the Lady, but I found a Guardian of the Land."

Finn raised his head, frowning. "The Land?"

"Yes, she is supposed to be here in Retarfu, helping the grand duke, but she is missing."

"She?"

"Yes, a Guardian of the Land, a follower of the sister. She keeps the balance between the seasons."

"Guin'yyfer," Finn whispered.

"Guin'yyfer?"

"The grand duke was due to be joined, but the Lady Guin'yyfer disappeared, suddenly. No one seems to know what happened to her. What would you bet that the Ascendants took her? They are holding something over his head, but he won't say what."

Taelia stared at him, her mouth open. "He wouldn't risk a guardian let alone his own heart. What a position to be in."

"One that you seem to live every day. Taelia, I am so sorry I got you into this."

"You never got me into this. I came because I had a job to do, just as you do." She gently touched his face, her fingers smoothing over his lips and hesitantly stroking his unfamiliar beard. His face was very close to hers, and she inhaled deeply, as if drawing in the scent that was uniquely Jerrol. "I've missed you, my husband. Please come back soon." Her voice wavered and then she kissed him on the lips as if it was the most natural thing ever.

His arms closed around her, his heart heady with her scent and their kiss grew more urgent, and all of his memories sifted down into his head as if they had been waiting, poised, ready for the right button to be pressed.

Stabbing pain shot through his head and he released her, groaning as the knowledge hit him.

"Jerrol? What is it?" Taelia grabbed him as he slid to the ground. She followed him down onto her knees, his unexpected weight dragging her forward.

"Just got the records back," he gasped, hugging his body as he tried to assimilate everything at once. He couldn't focus; images flew through his mind at a horrendous rate, making him feel nauseous. His mouth watered and his head pounded. He moaned.

"Niallerion? Marianille? Help me!" Taelia called as she tried to hold him. He shuddered. The reaction so strong Taelia had difficulty holding him still, and then suddenly, he went limp in her arms, and Taelia's heart lurched.

Stones skittered as the Sentinals rushed towards her. "What happened?" Marianille asked as she dropped to the gravel and reached for Jerrol's wrist. Niallerion hovered over them.

"Is he alright? Tell me he is alright." Taelia demanded. "He didn't injure himself when he fell, did he? All his memories came back and he collapsed."

"He's unconscious but his pulse is strong, if a bit erratic. I can't see that he hit his head," Marianille said as she ran her hands over Jerrol.

"Let's get him inside," Niallerion said as he knelt beside them. "Away from prying eyes." With a grunt, he lifted Jerrol and steadied himself.

Marianille and Taelia led the way, distracting anyone they met, so Niallerion could slip unnoticed back to Taelia's rooms.

Jerrol regained consciousness and lay for a moment as he remembered collapsing in the orange garden. A thrill ran through him as he remembered who he was. The uncertainty that had dogged him for months, bled away. He was Jerrol Haven, the Lady's Captain, Commander of the King's Justice and the Oath Keeper. He stiffened as he remembered the Lady had asked him to forsake her and then had sent him on this mission. Left him to be beaten senseless and then dumped in the middle of Elothia. No, that couldn't be right. She wouldn't do that to him. Something must have gone awry. Something unforeseen.

He stirred and low voices intruded, and he rolled his head towards them. His head ached, a dull ache that niggled.

"At last! We thought you were going to sleep the day out," Niallerion said as he helped Jerrol sit up.

"Where am I?"

"You are in Taelia's rooms. Rest a minute, get your bearings."

"Jerrol?" Taelia was suddenly in his arms and he collapsed back on the pillows under her weight.

"Oof! I love you too," he said with a laugh as he hugged her tight burying his nose in her curls. Relaxing in her embrace, he looked over at the Sentinals as she squirmed to get closer to him.

"How did I get here?"

"You passed out in the orange garden. I carried you here about two hours ago."

"How are you feeling?" Taelia asked, as she kissed his chin.

"Much better for seeing you," he replied and kissed her on the lips. "Though my head aches."

"Not surprising," Taelia said, as she snuggled into his side.

"How did you end up in the Third Chevron?" Niallerion asked. He spun a chair and straddled it as he sat, leaning his arms on the back.

Jerrol eyed him. He looked like he was getting comfortable. Marianille perched on the end of the bed, and Jerrol ended up recapping what he remembered about being conscripted as he lay in his wife's bed, with his wife in his arms. When he began describing Adeeron, he stiffened. "By the Lady, Birlerion. It truly is him. What he has been through for me; I don't deserve it."

"He thinks he is Birler, still back in the 1120's. He doesn't remember waking up in this time," Marianille said, plucking at the folds of the blanket. "He believes he is waiting for Guerlaire. Niallerion has been trying to tell him what happened but he's a bit sceptical."

"I'm not surprised," Jerrol said slowly. "He was in an atrocious state when I first arrived at Adeeron, and then they ..." he trailed off not wanting to tell Birlerion's sister what her brother had suffered.

"And then what?" Marianille prompted. "We know

Tor'asion beat him so badly that he lost his Sentinal, and any memories that went with it."

Jerrol shivered, remembering the poor state Birlerion had been in. A sense of betrayal sliced through him. "Torsion was our friend. How could he deceive us so?"

"I don't know," Taelia whispered. "But he isn't Torsion anymore. It is like he is a completely different person. He is cold and arrogant. Cruel."

"And they control the grand duke and his armies," Niallerion said.

"For now," Taelia replied. "I'm sure you have a plan to stop them, don't you, Jerrol? Why else are you here?"

"What happened to Birlerion?" Marianille asked.

Jerrol could see Marianille wasn't going to let it go. He sighed. "They made him fight one handed against 4 or 5 opponents at a time. He really is the most skilled swordsman in the Elothian army. They did it until they could beat him. I think they wanted to kill him, but he survived."

Niallerion shifted as Marianille's face blanched. "How could they," she said, as she ground her teeth. Jerrol's jaw ached watching her.

"We need to help him get his memories back, only I have no idea how." Jerrol rubbed his face. "I can't stay here. I will be missed. You need to warn Jason they are after the Watch Towers."

"We have already. We've been sending Stoneford and Deepwater everything we could find out. I've been eavesdropping on Tor'asion and Var'geris, so we know most of their plans," Niallerion said.

"You need to be more careful." Marianille flicked Niallerion a sharp glance as he began to protest and he stopped. "You'll get caught!" Marianille smoothed out the ridges she had made in the blankets.

Jerrol looked from Marianille to Niallerion and raised an

eyebrow. Niallerion shrugged and changed the subject. "The question is, how do we stop them? We need the duke to reverse the orders he sent to the Generals."

Taelia patted Jerrol's arm to gain his attention. "Do you think you can get in to see him?"

"I report every morning. I'll try then." He looked at the worried faces around him. "As much as I would like to stay here, I've already been here too long. Owen will be searching for me."

"Be careful, Jerrol. Please. The Ascendants are determined. They tried to kill you once, they may try again." Taelia tightened her embrace, reluctant to let him go.

"I'll try," he said, kissing her again. Then he detached himself and struggled upright. He swayed and then stiffened as a wave of nausea rushed through him.

Niallerion rose and steadied him. "I'll go with you," he said. "Until you are back with your men. You need to keep Birlerion or one of the others with you at all times. The Ascendants are less likely to attack if there are witnesses."

Jerrol exhaled. "Why did I ever think we could save the grand duke from the Ascendants?"

Niallerion grinned. "Because you like impossible odds?"

Jerrol huffed as he strode to the door. Glancing back, he saw Marianille embrace Taelia. Taelia's eyes were too big in her pale face. The expression of fear on her face tore at him but there was nothing he could do to alleviate her concerns. The door shut softly behind him.

32

GRAND DUKE'S PALACE, RETARFU

When Jerrol arrived at the grand duke's rooms the next morning, the Ascendants were already present. Jerrol paused outside the door and raised an eyebrow at Birler who was standing guard. His heart stuttered as he inspected his friend's face. His blue eyes were so disconcerting. He didn't look right without the silver eyes. And the ugly scar bisecting his eyebrow was a visible reminder of what he had been through.

Birler shrugged and displayed the clipboard. Var'geris and Tor'asion were listed. Jerrol gritted his teeth and opened the door.

"Ah, Captain Finn. I am glad you are here." The grand duke leaned back in his chair and rubbed his eyes. "I am advised that you are not who you say you are."

"I would suggest your advisors are not who they say they are, Your Grace. And they certainly don't have your best interests at heart."

"And who might they be?" Randolf asked as he inspected Var'geris.

"They are called Ascendants. They tried to poison King Benedict, and I believe they were behind your father's early demise. They hope to take control of every kingdom in Remargaren."

"Nonsense," Var'geris said. "Really Haven, your dedication astounds me."

"Haven?" Grand Duke Randolf repeated. He peered at Jerrol. "Ambassador Haven? I don't understand."

"The name is Finn; Captain Finn of the Third Chevron," Jerrol snapped. "Your plans will be the downfall of Elothia; you will kill the future of our country. Grand Duke Randolf will not agree to the decimation of our people."

Tor'asion stepped out of the shadows. "Jerrol, stop being so melodramatic."

Jerrol flinched as he met Torsion's eyes. "It *is* you," he said. An icy shiver of betrayal sped through him as he glanced between the two dark-haired men before him. "Who are you really? And what do you want with the grand duke?" He desperately looked around the room for help.

Birler peered through the open door, his eyes widening at the scene. "Lieutenant Kerisk, Your Grace," he said, opening the door wider allowing Owen to enter.

"Owen, what are you doing here?" Jerrol drew his sword as he pivoted to keep the Ascendants in view.

"I should ask you the same question! Finn, these are the grand duke's trusted advisors; what do you think you are doing?" Owen asked, raising his eyebrows in surprise.

"They are not friends of the grand duke or Elothia," Jerrol replied.

Tor'asion laughed. "Jerrol, what would you know? A spy from Vespiri. Why should the grand duke trust you?"

Jerrol watched the man he knew as Torsion flank him. "If that is the case, how did I become a captain in the Third Chevron? How did I get here?"

"You've been gone for months. You tell us. The Lady

deserted you in your time of need. You were thought to be dead. Really; you do turn out to be a good officer no matter which uniform you wear. Shame you're not on our side; we could use a man like you."

"You will destroy us all. You only see what you want. You have forgotten your purpose, to protect the people. Instead, you twist it for your own good and let down the very people you should be protecting."

Var'geris strode forward. "Enough, Kerisk deal with him."

Jerrol stared at his friend, shock immobilising him. "Owen?"

"I'm sorry Finn. I didn't have a choice."

"A choice about what?"

Owen grimaced. "Put your sword down, Finn. Private Birler, arrest this man."

Birler stepped through the open door, glancing warily around its occupants. His gaze paused on the grand duke. The grand duke raised a hand which visibly trembled. "Do it," he said. "Until we have more details about what is going on."

Birler swallowed, and turned to Finn. "Captain, your sword please."

Jerrol hesitated a moment, and then deflated as he handed over his sword. There was no way he could fight Birlerion. Not only was he family, even if Birlerion didn't know it, he would not put him in such a difficult situation. He was, after all, only following orders.

Mind racing, Jerrol stared at Tor'asion. His stomach dropped as he realised who Torsion was. The one who would deceive him; the one the Lady couldn't see. "All this time you have deceived us?" The words left a bitter taste in his mouth. "You were born deceiving."

Tor'asion preened, raising his chin and taking it as a

compliment. "I was born to deceive you. From the first breath I took, to your last. I will have deceived you. You don't know me, nor have you ever. You never really tried."

Jerrol flinched. "We were friends. For years. I looked up to you, believed in you."

"A child's response. No, I advised you, and you rarely listened. You were the most frustrating brat."

Anger flashed through Jerrol, no, not anger, a burning fury. A fury born of loss and betrayal. He gritted his teeth to keep it contained. He stood, rigid, and controlled his breathing until he was able to speak. "All things considered, I am glad I didn't listen to you. You wanted me to be a scholar, like you."

Tor'asion moved in front of Jerrol and jutted his face into Jerrol's. His eyes glittered with some emotion Jerrol couldn't name as they stood nose to nose. It wasn't anger, he had seen enough of that to know. As Tor'asion continued to speak, Jerrol realised it was something far more dangerous. "I knew when we first met, there was something about you. Something I needed to keep an eye on. It would have been much easier if you'd become a scholar. Instead you went all starry-eyed over that King's Ranger. What did he have that I didn't? Why did you follow him, instead of me?"

A tense silence enveloped them, trapping them in their own bubble of unadorned truth, thick with perceived injustices and threats. Torsion clamped his lips shut and his eyes burned with contempt.

"Compassion," Jerrol said at last, watching Tor'asion's expression as it hardened. "For me and those around him."

Tor'asion spun away, breaking the moment, his laugh harsh. "Compassion?" He circled Jerrol, clenching his fists. "Weakness you mean. You have to be strong to survive. Make hard decisions, for the good of all. Like the grand duke here, protecting his people against subversive Vespirians."

"Only because you planted the suggestion. That's what you did, didn't you? You couldn't enspell him, so you enspelled his generals and the people around him. New to the throne, he had no chance. Not with all his advisors pushing for war." Jerrol turned to Randolf, who was sitting at his desk with his head in his hands, Var'geris beside him. "Your Grace, please, Vespiri has no wish to go to war. These Ascendants have no thought for anyone but themselves."

"Shut him up," Var'geris growled, interrupting his low conversation with the grand duke.

"Finn? You are only making it worse for yourself. Do what they say and you won't be harmed," Owen said, his gaze tracking the grand duke's advisors.

"Do you expect me to believe that?" Jerrol watched Torsion and twisting his lips he said: "You've never thought of anyone but yourself, have you, Torsion? Not me. Not even She'vanne. You stole her. Did you kill her rider? Her bond mate? I bet that's why she won't speak to you."

Tor'asion hissed his breath out as he jerked to a stop. "What? The horse? You don't know what you are talking about. There are more important things to consider. Like you shredding that damn veil, once and for all." He began pacing again.

"I can't."

"Of course you can, and you will. If you don't, we will destroy Stoneford and Jason and all your friends. We will smash your home, Jerrol, and you along with it."

"Why?" Jerrol asked.

Tor'asion stopped stalking around him and faced him. "Why what?"

"Why are you so angry? At me and the people of Remargaren."

Torsion tensed, the cords of his neck standing out as he drew in his breath and released it. "You have no idea, do you? Years of injustice. Centuries! Eons! My ancestors were the rightful rulers of Remargaren as we will be now. You are all so blind. Gazing up at that seductress and believing every word she says. You let her control you and everything around you."

A low growl beside him had Jerrol glancing at Birler. The Sentinal's face was dangerously controlled, but his eyes blazed. His grip on Jerrol's arm tightened and Jerrol hurried to speak. "Seductress? You mean Leyandrii? I think you are confused. From what I've seen it is you that wants to control others, not Leyandrii."

"Look how she controls those Sentinals, marking them with those silver eyes. Owning them like slaves. Directing their every move."

Jerrol tilted his head, as he gazed at his one-time friend. The loss of his friendship, the betrayal, sat in his stomach like a rock weighing him down. "You are mistaken. We may be hers, but she is also ours. It goes both ways. One does not own the other. She wants us to live our lives to the full in a peaceful world. How is that control?"

"You know nothing about her, you let myth and legend steer your choices. She is not actually here, yet you do her bidding. You stand in my way. You have always stood in my way. If only I'd known …"

"Tor'asion, stop wasting time. You are achieving nothing." Var'geris bore down on them. "I am warning you, Haven. Shred the veil or you and the people of Stoneford will regret it." Var'geris glared at Jerrol, holding his eyes.

Birler jerked Jerrol away, breaking the gaze, and Jerrol inhaled, glad for the interruption. His mind spun as he grappled with everything Tor'asion had said. Much of his life, and his friendship with Torsion had been a lie. His head pounded with the knowledge. He concentrated as Birler spoke beside him, his soft voice grounding him.

"Captain?" he murmured. "These men are Ascendants?"

"Yes."

Birler spun on his heel. "Your Grace? Is this the Lady's will?"

Randolf struggled for a moment. His eyes glittering strangely as he rubbed his chest. He opened his mouth but no words came out.

Birler frowned. "Your Grace? Are you alright?"

"You heard the grand duke." Owen's voice was cold. "Unless you want to join Finn in the cells, private?"

Birler's face went blank. "No, sir." He gripped Jerrol's shoulder. "Captain, it would be better if you didn't resist. I do not want to hurt you."

"Owen, what could they possibly offer you that would make you side with them? The Ascendants destroy everything they touch. They want to destroy Leyandrii and Elothia," Jerrol said.

Owen shifted, embarrassed. "I can't explain."

"Try," Jerrol snapped.

The grand duke spoke, his words slurring. "The Grand Duchy supports the Lady." He lurched to his feet and Owen moved towards him, his face paling as Randolf began foaming at the mouth.

"Your Grace!" Owen caught the grand duke as he collapsed.

Birler grabbed Jerrol's arm and hauled him out of the room as the Ascendants closed in on the grand duke. Birler hurried Jerrol down the corridor, rapping out commands as he passed the sentries on duty. "Erik, get the healer, the grand duke is ill and then advise Ulfr."

"Birler?" Jerrol hurried to keep up with Birler's long strides.

"You need to get out of the palace now, captain. While

the Ascendants are distracted. Once they are in control; they will come looking for you."

"Why would you help me? You could be court martialled, sent back to the cells in Adeeron."

Birler hesitated. "The Grand Duchy supports the Lady. That means anything the Ascendants want, we do the opposite."

"But you don't remember me. Why would you let me go?"

"The Ascendants want you dead. Good enough for me," Birler said tugging him down a side corridor and then up a flight of stairs. He handed Jerrol back his sword.

"Where are we going?"

"I've been talking with Nialler. He's explained a few things that I am not sure I believe, but he does. He was always the clever one. I am more inclined to believe him than an Ascendant, any day. He said that I suffered an injury at the hands of the Ascendants and there is much I don't remember. I have to protect you as you are the Captain, not Guerlaire, even though it doesn't make sense." Birler rubbed his face and shrugged. "I don't know what to believe, but you have Guerlaire's sword and I trust Nialler and Marian. They said, if the Ascendants threatened you, then I was to take you to them." He halted outside Taelia's door and rapped on it.

Marianille opened it.

"Marian, Finn needs help. You need to get him out of the palace now or the Ascendants will kill him. He can explain. I need to help the grand duke, and delay Var'geris." Birler shoved Jerrol towards her, turned on his heel and strode off.

Marianille stood there open-mouthed. Then she lurched after Birlerion. "Birlerion, wait!"

Niallerion dragged Jerrol into the room. "Marianille,

inside now," he snapped, and Marianille spun in shock at the edge to his voice. "Now!"

"Tali," Jerrol crossed the room to Taelia and embraced her. "I have no idea what is going on," he said, as his mind spun with unease. He knew Birlerion could be decisive; he had never expected this though. "My lieutenant, Owen Kerisk, has sided with the Ascendants. The grand duke has collapsed with some malady, maybe even poisoned like King Benedict, and Birler has just completely disobeyed his orders."

Niallerion closed the door as Marianille entered glaring at him. "We have no time," Niallerion said as he pulled out a scroll from behind a chest of drawers and unrolled it on the table. "Captain. We found a secret escape route. You need to go this way." Niallerion traced a path on the map. "The entrance is off the old cells. Taelia found it. Follow the stairs, and then take the right fork at the end. It will take you through the cells. Keep going down as far as you can and then keep going; there is a door at the end of the passage. It takes you through a tunnel under the wall. Just make sure you camouflage it again when you exit. We may need it again!" He grinned with excitement, his silver eyes gleaming.

"I don't understand. What did you tell Birlerion?"

Niallerion shrugged. "The truth." He dragged another bundle out from behind the ornate piece of furniture and thrust it at Jerrol. "I found it for you."

Jerrol gasped as his sword, Guerlaire's sword, was revealed. The ornate hilt gleamed in the candle light as he unwrapped it. He belted it onto his right hip. "Thank you, you did very well." Jerrol gripped Niallerion's shoulder. "Keep an eye on Birlerion; he will need your support when all his memories return. It is an unnerving experience."

"Of course, we will."

Jerrol stared at them. "I can't thank you enough for

remaining here. For waiting. Risking your life every day, not knowing if I would return."

Marianille snorted. "Taelia knew. She never doubted you for a moment."

Jerrol's arm tightened around Taelia's shoulders.

"Taurillion and Yaserille are here in the city, somewhere. We could do with their help but we don't have time to find them," Niallerion said. "I'll send them after you."

Taelia stirred in his embrace. "Jerrol, Niallerion discovered they have Owen's mother and sister under arrest in the Summer Palace, that could explain why he is behaving the way he is, release them and you release him."

"He did say he didn't have a choice," Jerrol replied, frowning in thought. Taelia shivered as his fingers traced her lips. "What would I ever do without you," he said in wonder as he kissed her.

Her arms slid around his neck, and she kissed him back. Urgent and heartfelt. After a moment she stiffened and drew back. "We can't. Not here, not now. Follow Niallerion; he'll show you a way out." She caressed his face. "You will know me again," she whispered, placing something in his hand. "Now go." She pushed him away.

"I think they've poisoned the grand duke. See if you can help him," he called as he followed Niallerion out of her rooms.

He scurried through the palace corridors and down the servants back stairs after Niallerion. When Niallerion stopped, he stopped. He followed as close as he could, nerves jangling as they dodged the household staff. They paused at the side entrance and after a quick check, dashed across the orange garden, through the barracks and entered the stone building that housed the cells. The cells were dank and cold and he shivered as he remembered being incarcerated in one. His muscles tightened as memories of Ascendant's fists and excruciating pain followed the thought. He didn't think he could go through that again. Following Niallerion down the stone steps into the shadowy depths, he recognised when the surface changed to an older facing stone. He ran his hand over the stone. It was familiar. It reminded him of the Chapterhouse.

Niallerion left him at the bottom of the steps with a small pack and a warm cloak. A quick clasp of his forearm and he was gone; heading back to help Birlerion if he could, his concern obvious. Jerrol hesitated for a moment, but there was nothing he could do to help, except get beaten to a pulp again and that would not help anyone. He unwound the bundle of cord Taelia had given him, rubbed his finger over the smooth green stone and looped it over his head, tucking the stone in his shirt. The familiar weight was comforting.

"*Jerrol?*" Zin'talia's voice was a soothing balm to the tension constricting his gut. "*Where have you been?*"

"*I'm sorry, Zin'talia, I don't have time to explain, right now.*"

"*When did you return? Why didn't you call me?*"

"*I lost my memory. I didn't remember any of you. I'm sorry Zin'-talia, I'm going to have to leave again. The Ascendants are after me.*"

"*Not without me you're not. I didn't come all this way just to freeze in a boring stable.*"

He took the right fork and descended further, the aroma of damp stone and dirt surrounding him. "*Unless you can saddle yourself and meet me wherever this tunnel comes out, I'm not sure how you can.*"

"*Tunnel? Which direction are you going?*"

"*Under the cells, north-east, I think.*"

Zin'talia fell silent. Feeling his way, he stumbled down the tunnel as it twisted its way into the suffocating darkness. The crumbling dirt pressed down on him, and he flinched away from silky strands of cobwebs and fine frothy roots which trailed down from the ceiling and clung to his face. Taking a deep breath, he took a moment to still his racing heart and cursed. He opened his palm. He had forgotten the silvery light that the bloodstone had gifted him, and he sighed out his relief as the silver glow lit his way and revealed an empty tunnel, without any of the lurking horrors his imagination had been suggesting.

When he reached a stone wall, he stopped and searched. Niallerion said to keep going. Ah, there was a gap between the walls. Where they overlapped, he could slide behind them. The passage extended into a thick darkness and he hesitated as he inhaled the musty air. Raising his left hand, the silvery glow in his palm lit his way. The passage kept going down until the stone gave way to dirt and levelled out. The ceiling was made up of a network of tree roots that caught in his hair and cast creepy shadows that trailed after him. He ducked further until he was crawling on his hands and knees, the ground dry and crumbling beneath his fingers.

When Jerrol was beginning to think the tunnel would never end, he finally bumped into a solid wall. He felt around the wall in the oppressive darkness, the dirt crumbling under his scrabbling fingernails as he frantically searched for an exit.

The wall gave under his panicked fingers and he pushed harder and a small section gave way. Light framed the panel as he shoved against it with his shoulder and it finally fell forward and bright sunlight flooded the tunnel. He shaded his eyes against the glare and hesitantly crawled out of the tunnel.

Casting a nervous glance around him, he found the area deserted, and he pushed the mud covered panel shut and disguised the seams with more dirt, until it blended in with the mud around the base of the tree. Scattering a few crumbling leaves for luck, he brushed himself down and scanned the area. He was outside the palace walls. What was he supposed to do now?

"Come to me," a woman's voice whispered.

He stiffened as he recognised the voice. *"Marguerite?"*

Heart racing, he scrambled behind a tree at the thud of approaching hooves. Zin'talia skidded to halt. *"Jerrol? Why are you hiding behind a tree?"*

Peering round the trunk, he was amazed to see her saddled and loaded with saddlebags and a bed roll. Much like the first time he had ever seen her. *"Who helped you?"*

"Niallerion. I called him. He's been looking out for me." He sighed out a relieved breath as Zin'talia continued to ramble on about how Niallerion had been looking after her.

"I'll have to thank him later," Jerrol said as he swung up into the saddle and adjusted his sword.

"These Sentinals are quite nice, aren't they? I miss Birlerion. He always found me Baliweed."

"I'm sure he will again, soon."

As he rode away from the palace, the tension in his core eased a little as he accepted it had been Leyandrii's sister, Marguerite calling him. It wasn't the Lady. He still felt a hollow emptiness of loss that he hadn't been able to explain until now, and he wasn't wearing her uniform, so she hadn't reclaimed him. He wondered bleakly if she ever would.

Pulling the cloak that Niallerion had given him tight around him, he was thankful for its warmth. He had a purpose. Find Marguerite. She would tell him what he needed to do next.

Taelia and Marianille sat together in the parlour, both silent and tense as they waited for Niallerion. They looked up as the door opened and closed. Niallerion spoke softly. "As far as I can tell he got out safely, though they have sent out troops to search for him. Tor'asion is beside himself, so be careful."

"I can't believe you got him out," Taelia breathed. "Right under their noses."

Niallerion shrugged. "It was Birlerion. He told Lieutenant Kerisk that Jerrol was locked up, and they should look to the duke. He kept them occupied long enough. By the time they thought to check, Jerrol was long gone."

Marianille scrunched up her face. "But what of Birlerion. Will they blame him? Do they realise who he is?"

"No. He is unrecognisable in that chevron uniform. They are not expecting him to be anything other than a soldier, so they don't see anything else. The fact that Birlerion doesn't know who he is, helps." Niallerion hesitated. "I can't explain it, he doesn't have the presence he usually has. Something that is innately Birlerion is missing."

"Experience," Marianille murmured.

"What do you mean?" Taelia asked.

"Birlerion grew up very quickly. Experience and knowledge gave him a depth of understanding. He reminds me of when he was fresh out of the academy. He is instinctive, reactive. When he turned Sentinal, he would consider his response more carefully, aware he acted in the Lady's name. There was a weight to him; a power even." Marianille considered and then sighed. "He had the Lady's presence."

"He hasn't acted rashly, though, not until he helped Jerrol," Taelia said, trying to understand how Birlerion was different.

Niallerion shrugged. "I said it was difficult to explain. He is untamed. Control," Niallerion said triumphantly. "He doesn't have the control. Makes him seem younger. Different. Unrecognisable."

Taelia shook her head. "I'm not sure I agree; he seems no different to me."

Marianille gave a sour laugh. "Maybe he isn't. It doesn't really matter as long as they don't realise Birler is Birlerion."

"What of the grand duke?" Taelia asked.

Niallerion's face grew serious. "The healer is with him. He is saying it is not poison. The grand duke has been under a lot of pressure; they think it may be stress related. Tor'asion and Var'geris have their hands full struggling to get access to the duke. The healer is keeping them away."

"Good," Taelia said viciously. "Where is Birlerion?"

"From what I heard, the Third Chevron are in some disarray without Jerrol. Birlerion is back with his unit. Lieutenant Kerisk seems to be maintaining Jerrol's patrols, and it looks like he is more concerned with the duke's safety than chasing after Jerrol." Niallerion paced. "I think we should keep a low profile; we don't want to draw any attention to us. We still need to be ready for when the Captain is able to return."

Taelia sighed as she rubbed her face. "I don't think we can. We need to prevent the Ascendants from regaining control of the grand duke. This is our chance to try and help him. We need to make sure he is alright. I think we need the grand duke on our side when Jerrol returns."

Marianille groaned. "How is Tor'asion going to react to that?"

Taelia grinned. "You know what? I don't care. I am going to bombard him with questions, keep him distracted. You need to see if you can get into the grand duke's chambers. Speak to Birlerion; see if he can get you in."

Niallerion grinned. "I can help. I know the maid who cleans the barracks. She'll help us get in. There has been much talk downstairs about Captain Finn, and how things have improved since he's been here. They all like him."

"We need to be careful," Marianille warned. "The staff might not feel the same when they find out who Jerrol is."

"Let's hope the staff won't say anything," Taelia said. "We can't do anything about it, so no point worrying. Marianille, call Ari. We need to inform the king what has happened."

"Keep calm when reports come in, and remember, don't believe everything they say; they said he was dead last time, and that was obviously a lie," Marianille reminded them.

33

SOMEWHERE IN ELOTHIA

For two days, Jerrol travelled eastwards out of Retarfu. The city soon petered out into frozen fields. Odd white coated mounds loomed out of the blanket of snow, indistinct and unrecognisable. The sharp crack of a branch snapping under the weight of the snow was the only sound in the frozen landscape.

Accompanied by the muffled thud of Zin'talia's hooves, interspersed with the crunch of ice-covered mud, they struggled across the rough terrain. Snow had drifted around the margins caught by the withered bushes forming frozen barriers. A bitter easterly wind whipped around them.

Approaching a deserted barn, Jerrol slid down from Zin'talia and searched it for anything that would help keep him alive. He eyed the barn thoughtfully, but it was too early to stop; there was still had a whole day before him, and he needed to keep moving. Spotting a ragged blanket bundled in the corner, he used his dagger to cut it in half, and wrapped one piece around Zin'talia's head and the other around his, his ears and nose were freezing. Leaving the shelter of the barn, he huddled in his cloak as the icy blasts raced down the valley as they struggled onwards, shivering in the bitter wind.

"Jerrol? Where are we going? We need to find shelter."

"We will, soon." He had no idea where he was going. He had placed all his trust in the silent pull that dragged him north, as if an invisible magnet had latched onto his core and he was unable to resist its call. The unfamiliar terrain of central Elothia surrounded him. He would never have thought that he would wish for the familiar icy plains around Adeeron, and his winter gear. It was amazing how fast things could change. But his tension eased as he recognised the sheer cliffs of the Unworthy Man's drop beginning to dominate the landscape, curling away to the north.

He needed to head further south and skirt the edge. There was no way down those cliffs, but every time he veered south, his sixth sense prickled and he was forced to head north.

The grand duke's Summer Palace was due south of Adeeron on the upper tributary of what would eventually become the River Vesp. The palace was where the grand duke should have been wintering. It seemed obvious now why he wasn't using it. Jerrol mused on why no one had questioned it before, though even he hadn't thought to question why everyone was holed up in Retarfu when the climate in the south would be much better.

Saving Lady Guin'yyfer seemed the next logical step; release the grand duke from the noose that the Ascendants held him in and then see how he would act. He turned over a variety of strategies to approach the Summer Palace. Not being familiar with the layout was going to be a drawback, and he had never thought he would be on his own without support. He still couldn't believe there were no Sentinals to awaken. Surely there had been more Sentinals in Elothia? The Land, Marguerite, he corrected himself, had asked him to save her Sentinals, not to let them give up. He had failed miserably with the only two he had managed to find, but where could the rest be? He hoped Marguerite would have some ideas, but she was silent.

He thought of his Sentinals holed up in Retarfu with Taelia. He had hoped to find help within Elothia. To only find two—two so damaged they no longer functioned—was frightening. He had been convinced there would be more.

Staring out into the wintry landscape, he shuddered. The greying sky looked heavy with snow. His body ached with the cold; his muscles were so tight he thought he might seize up if he didn't keep moving. He toyed with the idea of heading north. He was sure that was where Marguerite was waiting for him, but he would never survive the conditions. Where was a well-equipped unit when you needed one?

He surprised four of the grand duke's soldiers as he led Zin'talia out of a culvert, hoping it would lead him down-wards away from the barrier of the cliffs. His cold-numbed mind barely took in the fact that these soldiers were not friendly before he released her reins and his sword was in his hand and he was backing away from them. They moved to block his retreat.

Jerrol searched the faces of the men around him. There was no sign of fear, only determination. They also looked comfortably protected from the cold. He raised his sword and one of the men laughed.

Zin'talia snorted, her breath pluming in the air. She reared, forcing one of the soldiers to flinch back to avoid her hooves. She came down with a thud, separating the man from the others.

"There is no way out, Captain Finn. You've led us a merry dance, but it ends here. The grand duke was most upset. He wanted to speak with you, but I think you're too slippery; better to kill you and be done."

Jerrol glanced behind him; the ground sloped sharply away behind him. How far, he couldn't tell. Baring his teeth, he said, "Come and get me." He wouldn't die alone, that was for sure.

The sound of swords clashing was loud in the still air. As the man to his right advanced, Jerrol turned awkwardly to better face his opponent. His foot slipped on the ice, and he shuffled back, nearer the drop. Jerrol kept an eye on the man to his left, hesitating just out of range. The soldiers knew what he was capable of by now, but he still had a few tricks up his sleeve. They didn't know all that he could do.

The fight advanced and retreated, his opponents taking turns, wearing him down, darting back and forth, in and out of range, gradually pushing him back towards the cliff edge. Zin'talia managed to knock one soldier out, but she could only herd the others closer to Jerrol, which didn't help him. She huffed as she tried to grab a soldier with her teeth, intending to pull him away, but she flinched back as his knife sliced her shoulder. *"Ow, he bit me,"* she squealed.

"Zin'talia, wait. Stay clear." Jerrol sighed out a breath of relief as she retreated, streaks of bright red blood trailing down her shoulder.

The fight was helping warm him up, at least, loosening muscles that were stiff with cold. Jerrol managed to trip the man on his right. His right hand flashed out, his dagger skimmed the man's neck as he fell, and Jerrol pivoted back to the remaining two soldiers, his left foot dangerously close to the edge. He still couldn't tell what kind of fall lay behind him.

The two men looked at each other and turned back to Jerrol, and they both rushed him together. Jerrol parried one blade with his sword, the other with the dagger, trying to push them both back, but the momentum was with them.

They forced him over the edge. Zin'talia screamed in Jerrol's head as he fell.

Yaserille skidded to a halt and clapped her hand over her mouth to prevent a squeal of horror escaping. She backed out of sight. Her blood ran cold as she tried to control her ragged breathing. She had picked up Jerrol's tracks well east of Retarfu, but she was too late; the Captain was gone. Those idiots had pushed him off the cliff.

A white horse was threatening to push the other two men off the cliff as well, rearing and screeching in anger. One shoulder was a brilliant red against her pure white hide, blood seeping from a nasty wound.

The two remaining men picked their way back from the cliff edge, avoiding the horse's flying hooves. They brandished their swords and the horse retreated. With a show of bravado, one of them dusted his hands off as if the fight had been easy. The other inspected the Captain's sword, which he had torn out of his hand as they had pushed him over the edge. They turned to their fallen comrade and shoved the body across the snow-covered ground and then pushed him off the cliff as well. Retreating from the edge, they returned the way they had come, glee at being able to tell the grand duke that his problem had been solved, clear in their voices.

Jerrol tried to still his panic. His gut roiled in terror at the memory of falling; the rush of frigid air as he flailed before he hit the rock ledge. He gasped for breath, shaking at the effort as he gripped the rock, afraid to let go. Holding himself rigid, he firmly told himself to stop panicking. It would get him nowhere. He pushed his feelings of inadequacy deep down inside and took a deep breath as he opened his eyes.

"There,' he thought, "it's not as bad as you thought it was. Not good, but not the end." His legs were dangling over the crumbling edge, his back tight against the hard rock face. He didn't remember landing there, though, as he rotated his left shoulder, it felt numb. It must have taken the brunt of the fall. He realised he had lost his sword again.

Leaning back against the rock wall, he looked up at the climb. *Possible*, he thought, as the rock gleamed gold in the weak sunlight, shadows accentuating the clefts and protrusions. The sky was the palest icy blue. He rubbed his hand over the coarse rock beside him where a coating of yellow lichen had dried out and hardened over the surface.

There were a few handholds; a few ledges. He leaned forward and then snapped his eyes shut as his stomach lurched and his head spun, frantically scrabbling for the rock beside him. He clenched the rock face, shuddering as the lichen scraped his skin.

"No, no, no," he chanted. Below him was a sheer drop; he couldn't even see the bottom, it just kept going, blurring into a grey haze far below. He broke out in a sweat as his stomach churned.

This must have been the 'Unworthy Man's drop' his troops had been so eager to tell him about. He wondered what they thought of him now, hounded out of the palace, on the run.

He'd never been particularly worried about heights before, but being suspended by one and a half hands over a bottomless drop was a different matter. Throat dry, his muscles rigid with terror, he looked up again. He couldn't tell if there were any larger ledges where he could rest or if it was one long climb to the top. The only good news that he could see was that there *was* a top. At least there was a target to aim for.

"*Zin'talia?*"

"*Jerrol! You're alive!*"

"*Are you alright? They hurt you.*"

"*I lead them away. They think they can catch me. Where are you?*"

"*Stuck on a ledge. I'm going to have to try and climb back up.*"

"*I'll be there soon. Be careful, Jerrol.*"

Jerrol grimaced, but agreed. He forced himself to let go of the rock face, which took longer than he would have wished, and flexed his right hand. It was undoubtedly stronger than he expected, but whether it was strong enough to hold his body weight as he found footholds, he wasn't sure. He sighed. Worrying about it wasn't going to make the situation any better. He might as well start climbing.

Shelving the thought about what might be waiting for him at the top, he eased his back up the wall so he could get his feet under him, and then after a few gasping breaths, he slowly shuffled around until he was facing the rock face.

He hugged the cliff and prayed. "Marguerite, if you're listening, this would be a good time for a helping hand." He searched the rock face, noting where the bumps were. If he reached for that knob, his foot would be able to reach that bump. He methodically searched the rock face as he climbed, ensuring his left hand had a secure grip before releasing his right hand and moving to the next handhold.

He wedged his right hand into a crevasse and adjusted his weight slightly to stretch for a knob a little out of his reach. He stretched, hand reaching, and his foot slipped. He lurched against the rock face; scraping his face. His heart tried to jump out of his chest as his feet scrabbled frantically, his right hand taking all his weight.

His feet found purchase and took some of his weight as he grabbed at the hard rock. His stomach was somewhere down around his ankles as the panic rose. Hissing his breath out, he tried to ease his shoulder, which was screaming with agony; his hand not much better. He gripped the rock with his left hand and hauled himself into a slight indentation and rested, trying to still his hammering heart. Clenching his eyes shut, he tried to control his breathing as sweat ran down his face.

He couldn't look down and he couldn't look up. Glued to the rock face, he was unable to move. He gradually calmed down and panted, trying to control his panic; he was the Commander of the King's Justice for Lady's sake. *Have a bit more gumption!* He grimaced against the rock. No gumption left. He was all out.

"Captain?"

He jerked and almost let go of the rock face, though not quite; some instinct kept him gripping like a limpet.

"Captain, are you alright?" The voice called down in a whisper; it didn't sound that far away. How could anyone think he was alright hanging off a sheer rock face? He didn't answer. Voices conferred above him. Was there more than one person up there?

"I'm coming to get you, hold on."

Hold on? As if he would let go! Were they mad? He must be dreaming. A short eternity later, someone was beside him, passing a rope around his waist and legs. "Let go," the voice breathed in his ear.

Let go? Were they crazy? He gripped harder, his shoulder aching dully. His hand cramped, and he whimpered.

"Captain, I've got you. You won't fall, I swear. Let go."

His body was shaking with fatigue, his grip frantic as his panic threatened to overtake him.

"Captain, it's Yaserille. I've got you, I swear by the Lady. Please, you must let go. Taurillion will pull us up."

Jerrol unclenched his eyes and stared at the face beside him. It *was* Yaserille, her silver eyes wide with concern.

"I swear, I've got you. I won't let you fall," she whispered. "Just relax." She smiled at him. He wasn't quite sure what his expression was saying, but he knew he felt disbelief. But she was there, a rope looped around her waist, one arm twisted in the rope and casually leaning away from the cliff face. After much coaxing, he finally let go of the rock face. The rope cinched around his waist and crotch, and he didn't drop; he hung limp. He was hauled up in short jerks. Yaserille guided his body around the rock face. He didn't do anything. He was exhausted, emotionally drained, done.

Yaserille boosted him over the cliff top and climbed up behind him. They both lay on their backs panting, staring up at the heavy clouds beginning to advance across the sky. Taurillion came and squatted next to him as Yaserille rolled over and sat up. She reached a soft hand and touched Jerrol's face. "Captain?"

Jerrol turned his head and looked at them. "Why are you here?" he whispered. "You went to Retarfu to warn the grand duke. You said you wouldn't help."

Taurillion twisted his lips. "Forgive us, Captain, we did not understand. We had forgotten our purpose. We had given up on the Lady, believed she had abandoned us. It's been so long."

"She never gives up on anyone," Jerrol replied. "Though I think she would forgive you for thinking so after all this time. You all amaze me, every day. Could you help me sit up?" he asked, groaning as they levered him upright. A tremor began deep in his gut and slowly spread.

Taurillion propped him up against his chest. "Where are you injured?" he asked gruffly, watching the Captain. He swallowed, his throat bobbing as he glanced at the sheer drop behind them and then back at Jerrol.

"Have you seen my horse? She was hurt."

"I'm here." Zin'talia's voice was full of concern and he peered around Taurillion as she approached.

"Thank goodness." He tried to rise, and Yaserille pushed him back down.

"Rest for a moment Captain. I'll take a look. It probably looks worse because she is so white." Yaserille went to inspect Zin'talia's shoulder, scooping up a handful of snow to press against the wound.

"Oh, it doesn't sting so much," Zin'talia said in surprise.

"Where have you been?" Jerrol's voice shook, the tremor consuming him.

"We went to the palace. It was as you said, not as we remembered. The grand duke leaves much to be desired and listens to those he should not," Taurillion replied.

"I believe the grand duke will surprise you." Jerrol winced as Taurillion prodded his right shoulder, and as he straightened his arm, Jerrol stiffened in pain. He followed Taurillion's gaze as he looked at Jerrol's hand. It was shredded, the skin hanging off in strips. His remaining fingers bled profusely, his fingernails ragged and bloody. They began to sting. His left hand wasn't much better.

Wincing in sympathy, Taurillion rinsed his hand with his canteen of water, patted it dry, and wrapped it in one of his scarves. Jerrol hissed his breath out as Taurillion wrapped another scarf around his neck and tied his arm to his chest. His shoulder was badly wrenched. He would need a healer, he was sure, but from where he didn't know.

"What a pair we are," Jerrol thought as Zin'talia crooned in his head. "Did you speak to Birlerion?" Jerrol asked as the shudder became more pronounced and his teeth chattered. He gritted his teeth, making his jaw ache. Leaning back against Taurillion, he couldn't stop shivering as his abused

body began shutting down. The horror of the drop filled his mind, and he shuddered again, his face paling.

Taurillion shrugged out of his cloak and wrapped Jerrol in it. He hugged him tight, sharing his body heat. He glanced at Yaserille. "Birlerion?" he asked. "No, I saw Niallerion. Last time we spoke, he said Birlerion was missing."

"Yes, the Ascendants captured him; he was at Adeeron. I found him there."

Taurillion tensed. "How is he?"

Jerrol grimaced. "Alive, though it seems they beat the S-Sentinal out of him. He is c-calling himself Birler. He doesn't remember being a Sentinal. Marianille is with him at the palace."

"Marianille will look after him," Yaserille said as she squatted beside him. "Your horse will be fine, though it's better you don't ride her for a day or so, let the cut heal."

"S-scholar Taelia." Jerrol struggled to speak as his teeth chattered. "Sh-she found Marguerite's g-guardian. We have t-to rescue her." He shuddered in Taurillion's grip.

"We need to get him inside," Taurillion said

"There is nowhere safe around here," Yaserille protested. "We are too far away from any town."

"What about the Tower of Leyarne? It was Marguerite's favourite tower."

"We don't even know if it's still there."

"It's better than staying out here in the open. We're asking for trouble," Taurillion replied, lifting Jerrol easily in his arms.

"I c-can walk," Jerrol protested weakly, trying to gather his reserves.

"Not just yet, Captain. Rest for a while," Taurillion replied, striding away from the cliff edge.

"It's well above the snow line; we'd be going away from help," Yaserille argued.

"Or towards it. If he's right," he said, nodding at the man in his arms, "then Marguerite will be there."

"It's got to be at least a day's ride, maybe two. Morstal would be closer."

"The duke's men will be at Morstal, looking for him. Come on, Yas, you heard him," Taurillion said. "The duke is under siege. We have to rescue him if Elothia is to be free. We must get the Captain to Retarfu and stop this war, but we can't do that in the state he is in, and he wouldn't be in this state if we hadn't deserted him. It's our fault he was on that rock face. We almost killed the Captain, Yas; we have to put it right."

Yaserille stared at him as she breathed out slowly. "You don't change allegiance by halves, do you?" she said. "All or nothing, that's you."

Taurillion grinned, his brown eyes bright, tinged with a copper gild, "When have I ever been any different?" he asked, levering Jerrol onto his horse. "I know I'm hard work. I know I make snap decisions, and yes, I admit they're not always the right ones. But this is right, I can feel it in my bones. We have to go to Leyarne." He gathered the reins of his horse.

Yaserille nodded in agreement. "Alright. Leyarne." She turned to coil up her ropes and stuff them back in her saddle bag. She gathered Zin'talia's reins, mounted her own horse and took point, checking the road ahead before leading them away from the precipitous cliff face. Taurillion followed, leading his horse as Jerrol sagged in the saddle.

34

TOWER OF LEYARNE, ELOTHIA

J errol was dreaming. A beautiful young woman stood staring at him, anxiously. She had long auburn hair, which curled around her shoulders, and vivid blue eyes, which he knew usually sparkled with laughter. She wore a long, deep-blue robe that fell in soft folds, and she was wringing her hands.

He recognised her from the vision in the temple in Pollo. Jerrol knelt. "My lady, what is wrong?"

"They can't hear me," she said. "You have to help them believe again."

"Who can't hear you?"

"My guardians. They are silent, lost, or bound by others. You have to help them."

Jerrol stared at her. "Of course, my lady."

Marguerite smiled, her face tight. "Taurillion will help you. He has the sight, if he would just use it," she said a little snippily. "I will speak to him. The Ascendants target my guardians; without them, I cannot soothe the seasons as they turn, encourage the ground to thaw, and bring forth new life. I struggle to ease the effects of winter and the ground freezes for longer as the nights lengthen. It is harder to get them to release their grip.

"It was my error; I didn't protect the Sentinals well enough. I was distracted at the end. I struggled to help Leyandrii save the others, and I overcompensated and petrified them. They cannot call for help. They are waiting, but it's been so long, few believe they will ever be released. I hardly hear their voices anymore. I need the Oath Keeper to help me. You promised. Your oath binds us as one."

"Of course, my lady, I swore to protect. Can Lady Leyandrii assist us?"

Marguerite shook her head. "You mustn't call her. Until you combine the Bloodstone, she cannot cross the Veil. With two of the crystals in your blood, you shine like a beacon to those who see. If she were to come to you, they would see you clearly. She must stay away. You must not call her; she forbids you."

"Is it not dangerous for you to be here, then?"

Marguerite's laughter pealed over him, and he smiled. "I am one with the Land. I *am* Remargaren. I couldn't possibly go anywhere else. But you are my Oath Keeper, sworn and bound to me, bound to the Liege and the Lady. I can hide you from those who must not find you until you have your shield again."

"My shield?"

Marguerite's face lost some of its gaiety. "He waits for you."

Jerrol took a deep breath; why did they always speak in riddles? "Who must I find? Where is he?"

"You know where he is. You left him behind."

"Birlerion? He is my shield?"

"Yes, he guards, even though he doesn't remember why."

"Leyandrii said I would have to help him remember."

"The time approaches, he will do what is needed. Until you can rejoin him, you must save my people. There are four towers of the Guardians: Cerne, Leyarne, Asilirie, and Teranna. They shield that which is important to us; Sentinals, Guardians and more. Our sisters and our mother watch over them for us, protecting them from desecration and ruin, sustaining those who ask, but within are those who are lost and must be found. Only the Oath Keeper can break the protections and save them."

"Taurillion and Yaserille were at Cerne, but there were no others," Jerrol said.

"No, I fear they were the only two to survive. There is one you already know of, who walks this land and cries for help; who resists the blandishments of those who should know better, but her strength fails as her hope dies. She has suffered betrayal and loss; her spirit dwindles. I cannot reach her. You must help her before it's too late. What is now Elothia will be lost to all if she cannot entwine the throne of Elothia back in line with the Land."

Jerrol stared at her. "Lady Guin'yyfer?"

Marguerite nodded her face sad.

"We are but three, if Taurillion and Yaserille truly mean to help me. We have no winter clothes or food. I have no sword. We will die in this weather."

Marguerite tutted. "Look around you. Where do you think you are?"

Jerrol looked around him as his surroundings suddenly coalesced. He hadn't noticed they had been greyed out and featureless as he spoke with Marguerite. The grey stone walls solidified into a circular room which he now realised must be the Tower of Leyarne.

He was lying in a bed which curved with the outer wall. A rectangular wooden table sat in the middle with three chairs around it. A fire burned bright in the stone hearth opposite him, logs crackling and spitting as the flames flared.

The faint thwack of an axe penetrated the stone walls and explained where the logs had come from. Taurillion must be replenishing the wood pile. Candles lit the room, revealing a row of pegs near the door.

Marguerite chuckled and drew Jerrol's attention back to her. "My Oath Keeper, you are most worthy. Remember, my mother's tower protects that which you must find. Release my guardians. Find the lost and your hand will strengthen."

Jerrol lay staring at the flower in his hand in bemusement. It was perfect: five rounded pure white petals, gilded by the silvery light of the moon and blessed by the Lady. The centre was infused with a deep pink, the colour of the deepest sunset; a colour seen only at the behest of the Land's miracle of life. Below the centre was colours of the King's robes; a deep red, gilded with gold edges. It was truly a flower of Remargaren and never seen in normal light, he was sure; he must have died and gone to the Lady's bower.

"Captain?" A soft voice intruded, and he blinked. The flower was still there. The voice altered subtly, a note of awe entering it. "Captain? Where did you get that orchid?"

"Orchid?" Jerrol whispered, looking at the impossible bloom in his hand.

"That is Marguerite's flower; very rare, never to be touched." Her voice was hushed. "It is a sign of hope, of rebirth. Taurillion, get over here," she called.

Taurillion's face blanched at the sight of the flower. "She's never going to forgive me," he whispered, dropping his head in his hands.

Yaserille reached up and clipped him round the head. "*I'll* never forgive you if you don't get a grip," she snapped. She crouched beside Jerrol. "Captain?"

"I thought I dreamt her," Jerrol replied, extending a tentative finger to touch the flower in his hand.

Taurillion choked. "You dreamt of Marguerite?"

Jerrol smiled. "Yes, she has much she needs us to do." He focused on Taurillion's pale face and sat up. "She said she would be having words with you."

Taurillion paled even more, and Yaserille laughed. Jerrol handed the flower to Taurillion. "For you, I believe, with her apologies. She did what she thought was best."

Taurillion stood staring at him, his face lost and forlorn as he held the flower as if it was the most precious thing in the world.

"She never left you. She has been here all the time, waiting for you to wake so she could welcome you back. I think you need to talk. Maybe now would be a good time whilst she is feeling penitent?" Jerrol suggested, ignoring the slight tremble beneath his feet.

"Behave," he thought. *"Remember your last meeting, and what he has been through since."*

Jerrol felt a sense of contrition as he swung his legs over the side of the bed and joined Yaserille at the table. Taurillion collapsed on the edge of the bed, staring at the flower in his hand.

Yaserille smiled as Jerrol sat at the table and a bowl of steaming soup appeared before him. "Eat," she said. "The Tower of Leyarne provides to those who ask." She leaned over to place another log on the fire, and then joined him at the table, another bowl appearing before her. She picked up the spoon and began eating, closing her eyes for a moment as she savoured the flavour.

"The Tower of Leyarne," Jerrol repeated, glancing around the small room. "Marguerite's tower."

Yaserille nodded. "There were three of them; Leyandrii, Marguerite and Asilirie. Asilirie was their older sister; she was beautiful, yet innocent. She was too nice to be a Guardian. She wasn't tough enough."

"What happened to her?"

"No one knows. She left with the Mother. One day there were three of them, the next there were two."

"Three sisters?"

Yaserille grinned. "Yes, frightening thought, isn't it?"

"Three of them," Jerrol repeated. And he had met two of them. He picked up his spoon and began sipping the steaming soup. Chicken. As he ate, warmth worked its way through his bones, bringing his body back to life. His aches and pains reported back for duty. He eased his shoulder. It ached, but was nowhere near as painful as it had been. He noticed his hand had scabbed over; the wounds healing fast. He frowned. "How long have we been here?"

"A few days; you needed the rest."

"You should have woken me."

"I doubt Marguerite would have let us."

"Zin'talia? Are you alright?"

"Oh yes, I am fine. I have been well looked after."

Jerrol smiled at her contented voice. *"I'm glad. How is your shoulder?"*

"Nearly healed. You'll be able to ride me when we leave."

"You said that Marguerite needed our help?" Yaserille said as Jerrol concentrated on his soup and then reached for a piece of bread.

"Yes, we need to find her guardians and help find the missing Sentinals. Who else was in Elothia? How many Sentinals were posted up here?"

Yaserille pursed her lips as she thought. "At least twenty. Northern Remargaren was barren when the Lady installed the first grand duke. He spent most of his time building towns and travelling between Retarfu and the Summer Palace. Retarfu and Adeeron were the farthest north anyone went. Most Sentinals were posted along the coastline or below the snowline.

"Twenty! But there are no sentinal trees. Where were you located? With the grand duke?"

"Yes, in Retarfu. I was in the palace when the world went up in smoke. Much of the palace was damaged. A terrible storm drove through the whole area, destroying much of the region. Trees were felled, rivers flooded, and there were terrible snowstorms.

"I don't remember much after that. I was caught in a twist of wind that swept me away; to Cerne, I suppose. Marguerite must have sent the wind to get us, but I don't remember. I recall a sense of time passing. I was surprised, though I suppose I shouldn't have been, to find Taurillion in Cerne. He had been in Vespers at the Lady's palace." Her eyes were distant as she stopped speaking.

"Well, we need to find the others. Ask and you shall receive. Do you think it is as simple as asking where the Sentinals are?"

Yaserille shrugged. "You're the Captain. You know best."

"I'm not. I am the Oath Keeper, bound by Lady, Land, and Liege to protect Remargaren and the Oath," Jerrol said slowly. "And I am petrified of failing all of them. I mean, look at us. We have nothing; no winter clothes, no supplies, no men."

Yaserille passed her hand over her eyes. "Oath Keeper, you will never fail whilst we are with you," she promised. Jerrol looked up in surprise as the vow was acknowledged by the trembling Land.

"Did you feel that?"

Yaserille swallowed. "Yes." Her face broke out in a wide smile. "Marguerite is listening."

"Well, that was clear enough," he said as he stood up.

"Captain?"

He looked at Yaserille and sighed. "You'd better call me Jerrol. I'm no longer a captain, just a deserter of the grand duke's army or worse, a traitor." *And I would feel less of a fraud,* he thought to himself.

Yaserille shrugged. "You are what you are; you can't lose it. You are the Lady's Captain, and I don't care what you think, or what you believe you think; no one can take that away from you. We will come with you."

"Are you sure? Maybe we ought to wait for Taurillion's opinion."

"He'll fall in line now that Marguerite has spoken to him. Our plans were not well thought through. Elothia doesn't know us, nor us it. You were right; it is much changed. Please forgive us for deserting you, Captain. We should have known better. Truly, we are the Lady's Sentinals, and we are here to do as She or her Captain bids."

"There is nothing to forgive," he said. "You had no time to adjust. The situation was extreme, to say the least." Jerrol looked around him. Thick winter coats hung on the pegs by the door, and Jerrol saw a sword in a leather sheath leaning against the wall. Standing, he went over to pick it up and unsheathed it; it wasn't Guerlaire's, he supposed that was asking for too much, but it was a finely balanced sword, and he hefted it in his left hand.

Taurillion flopped heavily into a seat at the table, an incredulous expression on his face. He stared at the fire, pinpoints of yellow flame dancing in the metallic gleam of his eyes. His usually severe expression was softened, probably by shock, Jerrol thought.

Yaserille leaned over to grip his hands. "How was Marguerite?" she asked with a grin.

"Much the same!" He looked at her as if waking from a daze.

Yaserille laughed at his surprise.

Taurillion straightened. "Captain, Marguerite explained what she has asked of you," he glanced at Yaserille, who nodded. "We are yours for as long as you want us," he said. "I swear allegiance to the Captain of the Guard, the Oath Keeper, and Guardian of the Lady, Land, and Liege."

"As do I," Yaserille said, firmly repeating his words.

Jerrol felt the oaths lock into place and sighed. "Very well. First, we need to find the Sentinals, who are hidden somewhere around here. Second, we need a distraction so we can get into the Summer Palace and rescue Marguerite's guardian, Lady Guin'yyfer, and third, we need to rescue the grand duke from the Ascendants, and that's just for starters."

Jerrol laughed at the shocked expressions on their faces. "How far are we from the Summer Palace?"

Taurillion stroked his beard, a crease between his brows. "If we avoid Adeeron to the east and head back towards Retarfu, then it will take us about four days."

"Are you sure the grand duke is still in Retarfu?" Jerrol asked.

"Definitely. From what Niallerion said, he'll be kept away from the front. His advisors don't want the generals getting too close to him, and the Summer Palace is too near the front line."

Yaserille stirred. "If we could get Deepwater to advance over the border, that would distract the generals enough for us to get into the Summer Palace. They would be so frantic, protecting the southern border, they would ignore what's happening up here."

"Yeah, right," Taurillion scoffed. "We just send a message to Deepwater and say please advance your troops."

"That's exactly what we need to do. I'm sure Jennery will be quite happy to cause a distraction," Jerrol said. "But not just yet. Are there any waystones near here? Surely there must be one here at the tower?"

"I don't remember Guerlaire creating any; he never had

time to visit Elothia in the last year or so. I think there were only waystones in Vespiri and Terolia."

"Shame. Without Guerlaire's sword, I can't create any."

"You can create them?" Taurillion asked, his eyes widening.

"I could if I had Guerlaire's sword. Never mind, we'll just have to do it the old way, on foot!"

35

GRAND DUKE'S PALACE, RETARFU

Tor'asion gritted his teeth against the curses he would much prefer to be venting. The grand duke was playing hard to get, refusing entry to all but his healer and his guards. Even Kerisk wouldn't let Tor'asion in, no matter what he threatened.

He was sure Randolf was firmly in their control, but his intractable behaviour was cause for concern. Whatever Jerrol had said to him seemed to have resonated somewhere. He hoped it wasn't a lasting effect as they couldn't reinforce the suggestions they had in place. They would have to rely on Selvia to speak to him, and her persuasive skills were not strong.

He turned away from the guard barring his entry and stalked off down the corridor, muttering under his breath.

The guard stiffened to attention as a young woman approached. She was escorted by her tall attendant. It was the blind scholar. "I'm sorry miss, the grand duke is not receiving visitors."

Taelia smiled. "I know. I hope he is recovering well. It is so terrible to hear he has been ill. I wanted to leave him the report of my findings; it might give him something to read while he recuperates."

"I'll pass it on, miss."

"Thank you." Taelia gave the guard a blinding smile, which made him blink and smile back at her in return.

Marianille's lips twitched as she led her away. "Don't overdo it," she whispered.

"It can't hurt," Taelia whispered back. "Let's hope he gets my report."

"If he does, let's hope he reads it," Marianille replied without much hope.

Birler stood by the wall and watched the grand duke poring over a map on the table, comparing a list in his hand to locations on the map and cursing under his breath.

"Do you need assistance, Your Grace?"

"Yes, tell me. If you had men positioned at these locations, what would you think?" the grand duke demanded, slapping the paper on the table and rubbing his eyes.

Birler scanned the paper and leaned over the map. "That your generals have been drinking, sir."

The grand duke gave a huff of laughter. "You could see it that fast?"

"With those positions, the Vespirians will wipe them out. There is no fallback, no defence. It's all open territory."

"They are fools," the grand duke ground out.

"Indeed they are, sir. You need to order them to retreat, at least back to Lervik. They'll draw the Vespirians straight up to the Summer Palace if they are not careful."

The grand duke bent back over the map, his eyes moving quickly. "You're right. Call Ulfr for me. I need to rescind their orders."

Birler pulled the cord and instructed the page who turned up in response. The page bowed and shot back out the door. Returning to his place by the wall, Birler observed Ulfr arrive. He looked flustered; even his moustache drooped.

"Lieutenant Kerisk has the Third Chevron, Your Grace, but he is not Captain Finn. He won't be able to keep your advisors away."

"He will if you command him too," Birler said.

Ulfr's mouth fell open as he gave Birler an incredulous stare, as shocked as if the wall had spoken. "Young man, you should not be listening to our conversation."

Birler shrugged. "The Captain said to protect the grand duke. Keeping Var'geris and Tor'asion away from the grand duke comes under that order. We can lock them up if you want?" he offered with a small smile.

The grand duke choked. "Although that is tempting, I think it will not be necessary."

Birler smiled and stiffened back into the silent sentry. He listened as Ulfr and the grand duke discussed their options, moving to interrupt before remembering his place and clamping his lips shut.

After a while, the grand duke leaned back in his chair and eyed him. "Spit it out, private, you're dying to say something."

"My apologies, Your Grace, but have you considered why the generals are positioned to attack Stoneford? What are they after? The logical route to Vespiri would be via Deepwater and Greens and then across to Vespers."

"Go on."

Birler moved to the table. "It doesn't make sense. The only targets past Stoneford are the Watch Towers. If you were going to invade Vespiri, you would take out the Lady's palace, her stronghold. So why aren't they?"

Randolf pursed his lips. "Maybe my advisors need to

explain themselves," he murmured, staring at the map. He glanced at Birler. "How come you are only a private. What did you do wrong?"

Ulfr watched the grand duke, appalled.

"I don't know, Your Grace. Never seemed to have the opportunity."

Randolf frowned at Ulfr. "Send Lieutenant Kerisk to me. He needs to step up to captain. We'll make Birler here his lieutenant. Send my orders out. Let's see if we can pull these troops back."

Tower of Leyarne

"How far down does the tower go?" Jerrol asked.

Yaserille shrugged. "If it's anything like Cerne, then at least two levels. The guardians liked to be close to the Land."

"Take the first watch while Taurillion and I go and explore. There are many Sentinals still missing. We need to find them, or at least find a sign as to where they are. This tower seems a likely place to start."

"You think you'll find them here?" Taurillion asked as Yaserille rose and grabbed a padded jacket off the peg.

"I hope so. We need the help. Come on, we have little time, and lots to do."

As Jerrol followed Taurillion down the stairs, he trailed his hand over the grey stone walls. Marguerite's excitement shivered through him, and a sense of expectation grew as they descended, the darkness wrapping them like soft velvet.

Taurillion fumbled to light the lantern, and Jerrol extended his left hand and opened it flat. A soft silvery glow revealed more stone steps spiralling down below them. Taurillion looked around him in surprise. His eyes widened as he saw where the light was coming from and, visibly awed, he began descending again. The stone walls became rougher as they descended, the stone blocks giving way seamlessly to older rock.

"Halt," Jerrol whispered as the air vibrated, caressing his skin. "Get your light out. I need my hands."

Jerrol laid his hands flat on the rock and pushed. The silver light from his hand spread in front of him and, once it had covered the wall, began to shimmer. He stepped through. Taurillion tested the wall and ducked through behind him. His eyes skittered around him as if expecting he would be refused entry. The wall continued to undulate behind them.

Jerrol searched the cavern. A natural space below the ground, once filled with water or, from the striations on the wall, ice. Jerrol stood, head bent, his senses questing through the cavern as Taurillion stared around him in amazement. Crystal formations glittered above them, refracting the light of his lantern; the result of centuries of slowly dripping water.

"They are not here," Marguerite whispered.

"Are you sure about that?" Jerrol extended his thoughts further, questing down fissures and cracks and through long-forgotten tunnels.

"It has been too long. I petrified them all, and now they are lost."

"No, don't give up, Marguerite; we have only just begun. They must be nearby. We just have to find them."

"I can't feel them, yet they are within me so I should be able to."

"You said you petrified them. That casing might be blocking your sense of them, and their sense of us. Maybe they have turned inwards to survive."

"I failed them," Marguerite said.

"Marguerite, stop it, you haven't failed them, but if you give up on them, you will. If we work together, we may have a chance."

"Together?"

"Isn't that what the Oath is about? Binding us to each other as one?"

Jerrol staggered as the ground trembled. Taurillion flung out a hand to steady him as the ground buckled beneath their feet and they dropped. Jerrol snapped his hand open as Marguerite gathered them in and brought them to a stop before a copse of tall petrified trees. Taurillion gasped out loud.

The air was soft and warm in her embrace, and Marguerite's voice resonated through Jerrol's bones. *"Together, my Oath Keeper, see what needs to be seen, touch what needs to be touched, hear those who do not call."*

Jerrol almost folded under the weight of her presence. Taurillion braced him as he flinched back. Her essence ran through him, tangling with his own, blending and searching until she finally sighed in his ear and settled, calmly waiting.

"Um, are you staying?" Jerrol asked, concerned.

"You said we were one," she said, an edge to her voice.

"True," Jerrol admitted. *"I didn't expect you to take up residence, though."*

Her laugh tingled in his ears. *"Now, feel,"* she commanded.

Jerrol reached out and touched a smooth trunk. His hands, sensitive to Marguerite's will, felt the vibrations beneath, faint and muffled but present. He tried to sink his thoughts into the trunk.

"Don't fight it. You can't separate us; we're stronger together."

"Yes, my lady."

Marguerite's laughter peeled out, and Taurillion gasped, turning his head to see her, his arms still supporting Jerrol.

"Marguerite?"

"I see why my sister likes having a Captain. She's already got one. I think you should be mine."

"I'm not sure the Lady or Taurillion will agree to that."

"True." Marguerite smiled as she caressed Taurillion's face.

Taurillion stiffened as the sensation coursed through his lean body. He twisted around. "Marguerite?" he breathed.

"Stop teasing him, now is not the time."

Marguerite sighed, but dutifully turned her attention back to Jerrol. Jerrol grinned as he sunk their combined will into the sentinal before him. *"Allarion? It is time to wake."*

Jerrol felt a tendril of thought reach for him, much diminished. He grasped the debilitated Sentinal, embraced him in the will of the Land, and drew him out of the petrified sentinal tree. He immediately knew that this man would not survive much longer. He threw their thoughts through the Land to Marchwood Watch and drove up through the roots of one of the remaining sentinal saplings in the nursery. He ever so gently laid the grey-faced man inside. Gold strands immediately began to swirl around the man and brightened as the strands thickened, and Allarion disappeared in a glowing golden cocoon.

"Laerille? I need you," Jerrol called the Marchwood Sentinal who had assisted him when he had rescued the Terolian Sentinals. Many were now close friends of his and had been trapped in a similar situation. It was fortunate that there were still four saplings waiting in the nursery at Marchwood, watched over by the Watch's forestry men.

Marguerite pulled him back, and he reached for the next Sentinal. The trees were fossilised, petrified in place, and non-responsive. It was a miracle that the men and women cocooned within were still alive; a miracle of the Lady, Jerrol assumed as he sunk their will into the next tree, shattering the casing that held it in place.

"He's not here!" Marguerite exclaimed.

"Who's not here?"

"Lorillion. Brave, brave Lorillion."

"What was he doing when the Lady sundered the stone. Where was he?"

"He was the link; the anchor for the Sentinals. He was the focus for Leyandrii. He survived; I am sure he survived. I remember pulling him out."

"I would say he never came to this sentinal. There is no sense of him having occupied it. Did you place him elsewhere? Did the Lady take him?"

"No, he should be here."

"We'll find him, Marguerite. Let's move to the next one for now." Jerrol exhaled as he felt a diminished essence languishing within the neighbouring petrified tree.

"Captain?" Laerille's surprised voice interrupted him.

"Laerille, I have Sentinals for you," he gasped as he reached. He hesitated. *"This Sentinal is more viable,"* he murmured. *"Marguerite, we need to release this tree."* He placed his hand on the trunk and sank their combined thoughts through the petrified wood. *"Livarille?"* He whispered directions to Marchwood. The tree trembled as the casing cracked, the noise rebounding off the cavern walls as the pieces fell to the floor. The sentinal's leaves spread and he began to shake. Lorillion's tree shuddered in response and then they both shimmered and disappeared.

Laerille gasped in his head. *"They just arrived."*

"They have been petrified, frozen under the ground in Elothia. They will need help."

"We'll look after them. We have space now, since the others trans-ferred to Terolia. Captain, where are you? We were told you were miss-ing, presumed dead."

"False report," Jerrol replied, gritting his teeth as he reached for the next sentinal and sank their thoughts in deep, shattering the casing.

"Davion?" he said, searching the fossilised trunk for signs of life. The tree was frozen and unresponsive, but a wisp of

interest caught his attention. Sensing a mere thought, Marguerite rushed to revive it. The thought strengthened and Jerrol's will combined with Marguerite's cocooned it as she transferred it to a sapling in Marchwood, where the sentinal tree embraced the man who had once lived in another time.

Jerrol sagged against the final tree and gasped out his breath. He frowned and broke the link to Laerille. This last one felt different. He took a deep breath as Marguerite hovered, and he concentrated one more time.

36

TOWER OF LEYARNE, ELOTHIA

"*Marguerite? This one is aware.*" Jerrol paused and then called as Marguerite hovered behind his eyes. "*Serenion?*"

The mists coalesced, and a very young Sentinal hesitantly stepped forward. He was a gangly youth, long-limbed and lean. His cheeks were hollowed and led down to a pointed chin. His long black hair was tied in a queue, and alert silver eyes inspected them. Serenion's mouth dropped open as he stared at Taurillion in confusion, his youthful face openly showing his surprise.

"Taurillion? What are you doing here? Shouldn't you be with Marguerite?"

Taurillion grinned. "I *am* with Marguerite; she needs your help."

Jerrol still couldn't get used to seeing a smile on Taurillion's face. Marguerite's talk had turned him into a different person; someone comfortable with himself, centred. It seemed she had managed to talk him into forgiving her and himself. Jerrol supposed that wouldn't be too difficult for a deity like Marguerite. He heard a petulant sniff in the back of his mind and smiled. She was a demanding taskmaster, but Taurillion seemed to like it.

Serenion shuffled back a step. "My help?" He looked around him and rubbed a hand over his mouth. "Where are we?"

Jerrol studied Serenion. He was fresh-faced and awkward as if he hadn't completely grown into his body yet. He didn't look old enough to be a Sentinal, and yet he had an air of competence about him.

As Jerrol discreetly observed him, an ash staff appeared in his hand. He looked much younger than even Birlerion when he had first met him, and he had been just nineteen, or so he had thought. He shied away from thinking about how Birlerion was faring.

Jerrol stepped forward. "We are below the Tower of Leyarne. The Lady has been protecting you for a long time, but now it is time to return to the world of Remargaren."

Serenion stared at Jerrol and then snapped to attention. "Captain?" he said.

Jerrol waved his hands. "No, no, I do not claim to be the Captain in Elothia. I am the Oath Keeper, here to help find Marguerite's missing guardians."

Taurillion smirked. "Yaserille told you; no matter what you say, you will always be the Captain."

"But, I can't be, Marguerite said ..."

"You have the Lady's mark. It is subdued, yes, but it's still there; you can't get rid of it," Serenion said, his gaze jumping between Taurillion and Jerrol.

"But the Lady forsook me and instructed me to forsake *her*. I can't be the Captain."

"Well you're doing a terrible job of forsaking her, then," Taurillion chuckled.

"It's not as easy as it sounds," Jerrol bit out.

Serenion held his hand up. "I don't understand. Why would you want to forsake the Lady?"

"Because she told me too."

"But why?"

"Because the Ascendants are searching for me and I need to hide."

Serenion grinned. "It's not working." He raised an eyebrow at Taurillion as Jerrol groaned. "Yaserille? Is she here too?"

Jerrol waved a hand in permission as Taurillion began explaining to Serenion the current situation.

"Three thousand years?" Serenion repeated numbly, when Taurillion had finished.

"Yes, it is the year 4125. Remargaren is now comprised of four Kingdoms. Grand Duke Randolf the fourteenth rules over Elothia, King Benedict rules over Vespiri and Terolia, and Emperor Geraine rules over the Island Empire of Birtoli."

Serenion blinked. "Island Empire?"

"Yes, much has changed."

"So it seems," he said, gazing into the distance.

"I'm sorry, Serenion, but we have little time; we have to get moving," Jerrol said.

Serenion nodded. "Of course." His brief grin was strained. "At least they can't accuse me of being a kid anymore."

Jerrol grinned. "Not at all," he agreed. At least the boy was trying. *"Just how old is he?"* he asked Marguerite as they began climbing the steep stone stairs leading back up to the surface.

"Seventeen, but he is so good! It would have been a shocking waste to make him wait," Marguerite murmured.

Jerrol led the way up the stairs, pausing at the top to catch his breath. Serenion pushed passed him, drawn to the fire. He hesitantly spread his hands before the heat, mesmerised by the flames. Jerrol glanced over the neatly stacked provisions on the table. He wished there were self-stocking towers located across the other territories as well. He collapsed into a chair and waved his hand at the table, dropping it as it shook and exhaustion overtook him.

"Take what you need," he said to the Sentinals, as a flush of warmth spread through him and he straightened as Marguerite restored him. *"Thank you,"* he thought.

"My apologies, I should have realised it would have taken a lot more effort." Marguerite replied. *"Please my tower provides to those who ask."*

Standing, he selected what he needed and stuffed it into a rucksack and then lifted a fur-lined coat off the peg. "Tauril-lion, go get Yaserille. We're leaving. Serenion, your friends have been transferred to Marchwood to recover. Your sentinal ought to relocate, but until we know where he should relocate to, will he be alright remaining where he is? Or we could give him directions to Marchwood if he can transfer and prefers to wait for you there. At least he will feel the sun on his leaves."

Serenion's youthful face froze as he communed with his sentinal. And just as fast, his face firmed and refocused on Jerrol. "Once we have left, he will transfer to Marchwood with the others and wait for me there, if you would be so kind as to give him the directions."

Jerrol nodded. "Consider it done," he said as Marguerite's voice whispered to the sentinal. He sent a warning to Laerille to expect another sentinal tree to appear.

Serenion's face lit up as he heard her voice. "Mar-guerite?" He blushed as she whispered a soft welcome in his ear.

She was interrupted as Taurillion and Yaserille returned, bringing a gust of cold air with them. Yaserille engulfed the boy in a heartfelt hug. She stood back, holding him by his shoulders. "By the Lady, let me look at you," she grinned, her silver eyes shining.

She was slightly taller than him, but he laughed at her scrutiny. "I'm not far off now, Yas; I'll catch you soon."

She nodded ruefully. "That you will, but not today at least."

"Lorillion is missing. Do any of you know where he was near the end?" Jerrol asked, watching the three tall Sentinals.

Yaserille frowned in thought, her brows creasing. "He was in Vespers with you, Taurillion, wasn't he?"

Taurillion grimaced. "Yeah, he was at the palace with Leyandrii, last I saw. Birlerion and I were ambushed and got trapped in the basement of the administration building in Vespers. I didn't see what happened to him." He faltered. "Marguerite, you only saved *me*. Why didn't you take Birlerion too?"

"Leyandrii needed him," Marguerite said sadly. *"But he managed to escape on his own. He did what was asked of him, and he did it well. As he will again."*

"What did he do?" Jerrol asked.

"What was needed."

Jerrol could tell from the tone of her voice that she wouldn't say anything more. Why would no one say what had happened?

"We will meet again, my Oath Keeper." Jerrol felt a soft kiss on his cheek and her presence faded from his awareness. He exhaled a relieved breath as the weight lifted from his mind. Taurillion's face fell as she whispered her farewell.

Jerrol cleared his throat and stared at the Sentinals. "Well, we need to go to the Summer Palace." He glanced around the room. "I think it's time to arrange our diversion." He looked at Yaserille. "Travel with us as far as Morstal and then cut down through Tierne to the border. You'd better go and tell them what we need. Ask for Tagerillion. He'll take you to Lord Jennery."

"Why can't you go? They are more likely to do what *you* say."

"If I go, they won't let me come back."

"But you're the Lady's Captain," Taurillion protested.

Jerrol looked at him and Taurillion grimaced. "Yas, you'll have to go. They won't believe me, I haven't got the silver eyes! You do."

Yaserille cursed under her breath. "You know Tagerill better than I do. And anyway, what makes you think they'll let *me* come back?"

"Tell Jennery that if they prevent you from returning, Commander Haven will be most angry with him and he'll hit him over the head with a ladle. Got it?"

"Umm, are you sure that's what you want me to say to a Lord Guardian of the Watch?" Yaserille asked.

Jerrol nodded. "Word for word."

Rolling her eyes, Yaserille sighed. "Alright. When do we want them to attack? And where?"

Jerrol leaned over the map. "It will take us a week to get to the Summer Palace, a day to get in position, so eight days from now along the Tierne pass south of the Summer Palace. It will draw attention from both Adeeron and Retarfu. Make sure you warn them that the Chevrons are at full strength in Adeeron. They must ensure their east flank is reinforced.

"This is only a diversion. They mustn't overplay their hand, and they need to have a retreat strategy. If the Chevrons are engaged, it will be full out war. Make sure they warn Stoneford what they are doing; we don't want Jason piling in as well."

Yaserille looked at him, bright-eyed. "Are you sure we can stop them? The incursions have been going on for months, and they are just waiting for an excuse. This might not be the best strategy."

"You got any better suggestions?" Jerrol asked, as he straightened.

Yaserille looked at Taurillion and shrugged. "We'll do it your way, but I reserve the right to make an alternative suggestion when I think of it."

Jerrol grinned. "Deal," he said. He folded up the map and took a moment to kneel before the fire. "We give thanks to Lady Marguerite for all that we received and thank you for your gift of fire and shelter." The fire flared briefly before it began to die out. Taurillion replenished the wood basket and refilled the jugs with water. Yaserille filled a vase with green foliage, and the orchid stood resplendent against the rich backdrop.

Jerrol stood, checking the sword at his belt and the daggers sheathed next to it. He shrugged into his rucksack and followed the Sentinals down the stairs, thanking Marguerite for his warm winter coat as the bitterly cold air blasted him as he left the Tower. They all hunched against the icy wind and began the long trek along the top of the Unworthy Man's Drop and down towards Morstal.

The horses were sturdy and familiar with travelling in the snowy conditions, all except Zin'talia who slogged onwards without complaint. Serenion doubled up with Yaserille until they could purchase another horse. They found derelict barns to shelter in overnight, and once, a shallow cave which at least protected them against the vicious wind. Any exposed skin was scoured by the frozen snowflakes swirled by the icy blasts of wind.

The journey took four exhausting days to reach the plains below the sheer cliffs which loomed before them in the early darkness. The lowering clouds threatened yet more snow. They hunkered down as best they could before gratefully brewing a can of coffee over a tiny fire to thaw the extremities before starting again at first light. The following morning, Yaserille waved farewell as she left for Tierne.

Jerrol tucked his scarf tighter across his face and slogged on, Taurillion and Serenion close behind him. They travelled all day, following farm tracks and cutting across frozen fields and streams. They found easier going on a rutted track that Jerrol thought led into the small village of Morstal halfway between the Tower and the Summer Palace. The track sunk below the fields and provided some protection from the icy winds.

Jerrol followed the track down out of the fields and hesitated as a more significant road came into view. He dismounted and dropped to the frozen ground as he heard the echoes of marching feet; not particularly regular marching feet, but feet all the same.

The Sentinals dropped beside him. For tall men, they were light on their feet. Jerrol eased up the side of the bank to peer over the edge, recognising the outskirts of Morstal in the distance. The horizon was covered by heavy grey clouds rolling across the sky. A storm threatened more sleet and snow, and it wasn't far away. Both he and the troops on the road below would need to find some cover before it hit.

37

MORSTAL, ELOTHIA

E ven though a mounted officer tried to hustle his men along, it was clear that this column of soldiers was in some distress. Several ragged-looking men helped the walking wounded keep up with the main column. Jerrol's breath caught as a ragged bunch of what looked like Vespirian prisoners stumbled behind. They were chained to a slow horse-drawn wagon, loaded with more wounded, which pulled up by a barn on the edge of town.

It looked like this was the remnants of one of the Elothian hit and run units; one that had managed to capture some trophies from behind the lines. Why were they dragging them all the way back up here? Surely, they weren't heading for Adeeron? Didn't they have any forward posts set up?

Jerrol cursed the Elothian generals under his breath. How could they not have supply posts behind the lines with healers and camps for the men to rest and recuperate? How could they start a war whilst being so unprepared? It would take weeks to get these men reorganised and back to the front. He was suddenly glad his men were safe in Retarfu, though he knew if things went badly, they wouldn't be there for long. Well trained men would be at a premium.

He waited until the slow-moving column pulled up on the outskirts of Morstal. The officer's sharp voice carried on the night air, and the men began setting up tents in the lea of the barn. The officer dismounted and opened the doors of the reasonably well-kept building. At least the man had some weather sense and some idea of how to prepare for it. He ordered the wagons to be pulled up on the other side of the tents, providing a shelter of sorts.

The wounded were unloaded and carried into the requisitioned barn as chickens burst out of the door, squawking loudly as a couple of men chased after them. Jerrol frowned. They were low on supplies as well, then.

The biting cold began to penetrate his winter clothes as he lay on the frozen ground. Frost sparkled on his gloves as he slithered back down onto the track and began stamping his feet and swinging his arms, trying to ease the stiffness that was creeping over him.

He considered their options. They would not be able to circle Morstal, it was too open, but they couldn't reach the village without passing through the soldier's encampment. The approaching storm may help him pass himself off as one of them. They would know their officers, but maybe in the confusion of a storm, they would be able slip by. It all depended on whether they were from the same unit. At this distance, he couldn't tell.

He crawled up the bank for one last look. Tents were going up fast; it looked like the prisoners were being herded into one of them. Small campfires were tended, glowing beacons in the dim light. The land was frozen. There wasn't much to burn; enough to boil some water and to make a thin gruel to warm the insides, and then they would be wrapped in their blankets and hunkering down as the approaching storm hit. He wished he could take advantage of the storm to slip passed them, but he knew the blizzards of Elothia; he needed to find somewhere to shelter, else they would be frozen corpses in the morning. He eyed the barn.

"*Jerrol, we have to move. We can't stay here,*" Zin'talia murmured.

"*I know. We have to wait until the guards turn in.*"

Zin'talia shifted beside him. "*If we wait much longer the storm will overtake us.*"

In the end, they had no choice. As the storm crept closer, the soldiers all battened down, dousing the fires. One sentry ducked into the prisoner's tent and tied the flap down securely. With no one in sight, Jerrol and the Sentinals rode their horses out of the sunken track and hastened towards the village before the snow hit. They didn't make it.

The outer tents of the encampment were still some distance ahead of them when icy winds swept across the snowy plains and obscured everything around them. The dizzying snowflakes swirled, disorienting them. They had to dismount, unable to see the ground before them. The howling wind buffeted Jerrol as he blindly staggered forward, until he tripped over a pile of discarded supplies and landed on one of the tent's guy ropes, pulling the canvas down with him.

Voices rose in protest as Jerrol tried to disentangle himself. The sentry poked his head out, and Serenion knocked him out with a sharp jab of his staff. As Serenion eased the man's limp body down onto the snow, Jerrol peered into the tent. About to push the unconscious guard inside, he paused when he heard a voice from inside that he thought he recognised.

"Landis?" he called.

Oscar Landis slowly sat up. "Who's there?" he replied, straining to see in the gloom. His chains clanked, a dull echo as he moved.

"Haven," Jerrol said, moving further in, knowing it was unlikely that any of the other prisoners would recognise him hooded and with a beard.

Landis gasped. "Commander Haven? What are you doing here? The last report we had said that you were dead."

"Huh, don't believe everything you hear. I could ask the same of you. What are you doing so far north?" he asked as he eased off his gloves and patted down the guard for the keys. Finding them, he unlocked the manacles around Landis' wrists.

"We fell foul of a decoy, got sucked up the valley and cut off. They've been dragging us up here for the last three days or more." Landis struggled to get his stiff fingers to work as Jerrol moved on to his ankles.

"Is anyone injured?"

"Nothing that some warmth and rest wouldn't sort."

"What happened to your boots?"

"They take them away every night, make sure we don't try to run away."

Jerrol passed the keys on to eager hands and crouched next to Landis. He could just make out the pale face of the man sitting next to him. Jerrol grinned, his teeth gleaming in the dull light. "I think I found your boots outside. They haven't taken them far." He leaned out of the tent and brushed the snow off the strange lumps he had tripped over. Sure enough, they were a pile of boots.

"We need to be quick. The storm is passing. I could use your help, but I am short of supplies myself; no food, not enough horses, and no extra weapons."

"I'm sure we'll find some, sir. They piled our swords on

the wagon. Maybe they're still there. The storm hit pretty quick; not much time to prepare anything."

Jerrol cast an eye over the men; they looked sunken-eyed and exhausted, though they were shedding their manacles fast enough; no one was dawdling. None of them had coats or cloaks. Landis was worst off, having been stripped off his jacket. Jerrol tugged the coat off the unconscious guard and handed it to the grateful Landis. The snow was beginning to thin, but it was still bitterly cold. Landis' lips were blue, and the rest of the men were not better off.

"Let's see if we can get you away before the snow eases." He passed more boots inside and then went to check the wagon. Beneath the snow, he found a cloth-wrapped bundle and distributed the swords as the Vespirians came up behind him out of the gloom.

"At least the snow should cover our tracks," he said, as Taurillion materialised out of the haze before them, Serenion close behind. Taurillion lifted an eyebrow; a silent question.

"Troops," Jerrol muttered as he led them away from the village of Morstal continuing south, back the way Landis and his men had already come. It looked like another front was sweeping in behind and would keep the Elothians contained for a little while longer. He needed to get his men under cover if they were going to survive the night.

"Is that an Elothian uniform you're wearing, Commander Haven?" Landis asked through chattering teeth. His blue eyes glinted with a touch of humour as he eyed Jerrol.

Jerrol grinned. "Captain of the Third Chevron, I'll have you know."

"That will be a story to hear," Landis chuckled as the men muttered behind him passing on the news that it was

Commander Haven who had rescued them. They straightened their backs and tried to look more alert.

Jerrol cast an eye at the heavy sky. "We have to find shelter; the front is almost on us. I'm sure there was a farm down here. We're just not prepared for this weather," he muttered under his breath, frantically trying to remember where the small farmsteads were on the map.

He struck off down a small track, following an instinct he wasn't sure was his own, and sure enough, a small grey stone tower loomed ahead of him. He didn't hesitate before opening the arched wooden door and pushing the men inside. "Up the stairs, don't stop," he called urgently as the snow began to fall again and the night closed in around them.

Fourteen men. Jerrol wondered where the rest of the unit was as he followed them up the spiral stairs. His fingers trailed the wall as he rose, the words filling his mind, '*Welcome to the Tower of Asilirie. Ask and you shall receive. Rest your head, warm your body, replenish all before you leave.*'

Jerrol entered the room at the top of the tower. The men were standing awkwardly along the wall, staring at the roaring fire and the strange Sentinals in disbelief. The room was much larger inside than it had appeared outside.

Ask, and you shall receive, he thought hopefully. "Landis, sit by the fire, you're frozen." He looked at the men, and chose those with the bluest lips to join the shivering captain. "There should be blankets and furs in here. Ah yes," he said as he reached for the pile of thick fleeces stacked beside him.

"Wrap these around you; you need to get warm first," he said, handing them out.

Landis was pushed towards the fire by his men; he was visibly shaking, and they wouldn't listen to his protests. One side of his thin face was covered in colourful bruises, and his lip was split and swollen. Some of the other men sported similar contusions, though none were seriously injured. As the seats around the wooden table were taken, bowls appeared before them full of a hearty stew. "Eat. The Lady watches," Jerrol said. Taurillion paused long enough to grab a mug of coffee before heading out on watch. Serenion stood watchful and alert.

Jerrol unfolded his map on the table and called Serenion over. "How far do you think we are from the Summer Palace?"

"A couple of hours, no more. The road follows the valley. To reach the Palace, we will have to cross the river. There are two crossings, one above and one below the palace; both will probably be guarded, but the northern crossing at Kerrit is nearest. The southern crossing is down near Tyrsil, quite a way south. Well," Serenion paused, "that's where it used to be."

"From this map, I'd say it was still pretty much as you remembered. You take point in the morning, Taurillion will help break a trail. We'll head for the northern crossing, a new unit fresh from Adeeron. That should get us up the approach, at least. Try to get some sleep; you get the early watch."

"Yes, sir," Serenion said and turned towards the fire.

The men slowly thawed. Their ragged uniforms steamed as the heat from the fire warmed the air, and full stomachs eased the worst aches. Bedrolls with more blankets appeared on the floor, and gradually, the men relaxed enough to hang their outer clothes up to dry and wrap themselves in the blankets. They were soon asleep.

Landis and Jerrol were the last seated at the wooden table, a bowl of stew before them.

"We give thanks to the Lady for all that we receive," Jerrol said, before digging in.

"What has happened to you, Commander? I would never have recognised you in that uniform, nor with that beard."

Jerrol scowled at his stew. "Many things have befallen me, too many to explain, but all will be well in the end."

"What can we do to help?"

Jerrol stared at Landis bleakly. This unassuming captain had been in the thick of things ever since he had been assigned to help rescue Lady Alyssa from Lord Aaron of Deepwater, Alyssa and Jennery's predecessor. After that, he and his men had been blooded at the battle with the Ascendants at the King's Palace in Old Vespers. Since then, they had been on the frontline, defending Deepwater against the Elothians. Landis would be a handy man to have around. At least he looked like he was more comfortable now that his lips were pink, and he had stopped shaking. A blanket was tucked tightly around his narrow shoulders.

"I need to rescue someone from the Summer Palace," he said.

Landis nodded. "And the plan?"

Jerrol smiled at Landis' calm acceptance. "We walk up to the front door. Feel like joining the Third Chevron?" He pointed at the clothes hanging on the pegs; the winter uniform of the third chevron.

Landis' grin widened as he inspected the uniforms. "Where did you get those? And all of this?" His hand indicated the sleeping men bundled in warm furs. Soft snores drifted on the air.

"The Lady Asilirie provides all. Lady Leyandrii's sister watches over us tonight. Get your men to replenish the wood stock and water in the morning, will you?

"Elothia is fortunate in its Ladies. As you can see, they offer comfort and solace to those who ask, only many have forgotten as the time passes and these Towers are left untended and unseen. Fortunate for us, the Lady

Marguerite knows where they all are and guides my feet. But enough of history. What happened to the rest of your men?"

Landis stiffened. "We were ambushed just south of Harstad. Lord Jennery had us guarding the East Bank to make sure they didn't flank us into Stoneford. They have been driving sorties into the plantations for weeks, but this last one was more determined. I should have known better. They pulled us out of position and had us surrounded before we knew it. And then, instead of driving further in, they pulled back, taking us with them. I'm hoping the others managed to retreat, but the fighting was fierce, even if they didn't take advantage of it. But why didn't they? It doesn't make sense."

"I think the generals are just toying with us. They are severely undermanned and lack organisation. They have no supply chain behind the front. Look at how far they are taking you inland. All the way back to Adeeron.

"The Ascendants have them on a tight leash, and they are using the units to keep our forces occupied. I believe they are after Stoneford; the Watch Towers, in particular. So once you've helped me take the Summer Palace, I need you to report to Lord Jason and tell him so.

"There is a unit of the Third Chevron at Retarfu. Their troops are top-notch, so don't underestimate them. Birlerion is with them." He paused as Landis exclaimed. "I know, don't ask me how, but he is currently guarding the grand duke against the Ascendants. The second and fourth Chevrons are not so well trained but can bite just as well. The first is on its way to reinforce the front.

"The grand duke has no idea what is going on. He is young, untried, and completely browbeaten by the Ascendants and his generals. We are about to take one of the boots off his neck. Let's hope it's enough to help him breathe. If we can give the grand duke room to manoeuvre, he may be able to rein in his army."

Landis nodded as his pinched face creased into a feral grin. "They won't know what hit them nor where we came from."

"Let's try to keep it that way."

38

CENTRAL ELOTHIA

The next morning, they continued their journey south, following the river embedded in a deep gorge. The track wound along the cliff edge of the narrow river valley until it reached a point where a rockfall blocked their way and a makeshift bridge arched over what was now a rushing torrent. The water roared as it tumbled over the rocks; a white foaming mass that would charge towards Deepwater and smooth into the deep green water of the River Vesp.

"Captain, you can do this. The bridge is sturdy; it's quite safe," Taurillion reassured him.

Jerrol's heart raced as he looked at the sheer drop below. He broke out in a sweat as he hesitated at the edge of the bridge; there were no railings or ropes to guard the edges, just the rough cut timber planks extending over the deep gorge. The tremors built in his limbs, and he drifted a couple of steps away.

He felt physically ill at the thought of crossing that bridge. It was mesmerising the way he was drawn to the side of it; the seductive impulse to step off the edge and fall to his death. He clenched his teeth and shut his eyes, his heart raced and he took a deep calming breath.

"Did he just run across that bridge with his eyes shut?" Serenion asked in disbelief.

"Yep, that's our Captain." Taurillion grinned as he followed.

Jerrol gasped for breath as he leaned against a tree on the other side of the bridge. His limbs were trembling furiously, and he tried to bring his ragged breathing under control as the men crossed, eyeing the deep drop below them. A few threw friendly taunts at him and at those who had been reluctant to cross. Taurillion approached behind them.

"It affects people sometimes," he said as if making conversation. "It may fade, it may stay; the Unworthy Man's Drop takes its toll on everyone. I think it's more the fact that there is no bottom, so it plays on the mind even more."

Jerrol shuddered as the image filled his mind.

"What you have to remember is the fact that you climbed back up, even though you knew death was below. You didn't freeze; you didn't give up." Jerrol heard the smile in Taurillion's voice. "You beat it. Most men don't. Very rare is the man who survives the Unworthy Man's Drop." His voice was loud in the sudden silence.

Jerrol straightened as the jeering men fell silent and stared at him wide-eyed. Taurillion turned to face them. "Yes, beware who you insult. This man climbed the Unworthy Man's Drop, which is that ridge over there." Taurillion pointed to the sheer cliffs dominating the horizon behind them. "As you see, he still lives. When you have climbed it, you can claim your right to jeer. Until then I suggest you keep your big mouths shut!" He glared at the men, who shuffled and dropped their gaze to the floor.

"Taurillion, don't, it's fine. Everyone is fair game in the military."

"Not the Captain," he said.

Jerrol grinned, easing his aching shoulders. "Especially the Captain, when he displays weakness."

"Is it true, sir? You climbed them cliffs?" a grubby private piped up.

Jerrol laughed. "Not by choice, you know. I was thrown over first, and to be fair, I did have help up the last ten feet. Otherwise, who knows …." He shrugged. "I likely wouldn't be standing here today. I do seem to have an aversion to heights now though lads, so if you could avoid putting me in a position where I have to deal with it, I would appreciate it."

The soldiers laughed, a few clapping him on the shoulder as they dispersed. A couple lingered. "Sir, according to the map there's another crossing up ahead, worse than this one. We could go around it, but it'll take another day," the soldier suggested.

Jerrol swallowed. "No, we cross. Thank you for your concern, but don't worry about me. We have to get to the palace as fast as we can."

The soldier nodded and turned away. "You got any spare rope in that pack of yours?" he asked his mate as they joined the end of the column.

Taurillion grinned at Jerrol. "I don't know how you do it, but they are all looking out for you."

Jerrol grimaced. "Unfortunately, not all."

"Enough of them are, though," Taurillion said under his breath as they strode up to the head of the column to join Captain Landis.

Deepwater

"My lord Jennery, there is a—a strange Sentinal here to see you, sir."

Jennery looked up from the papers on his makeshift desk and frowned. "Strange?"

"Um, no one knows her. It's a she, sir, and she's asking for Sentinal Tagerill; says she's from Captain Haven."

Jennery straightened up abruptly. "Then don't dawdle. Get her in here, now. And send for Tagerill."

"Yessir," the man backed out with alacrity and a tall, slender, silver-eyed woman with long platinum blonde hair was escorted into Jennery's command tent under guard.

Jennery eyed his men. "Since when have Sentinals been escorted under armed guard?" he inquired.

"Since she managed to penetrate our front lines and didn't know any of the code words, sir."

Jennery stared at the Sentinal. He didn't recognise her either, but if she was from Elothia, it was possible that Jerrol, if he was still alive, had awoken her.

"I'm afraid I don't know your name."

"Yaserille, from Retarfu. The Captain needs your help."

"How did you get through our lines?"

"The Captain advised me of your protocols. They are excellent," she said, her silver eyes gleaming in appreciation.

"Tell me about this captain. Where did you meet him?"

Yaserille smiled. "I first met him in Cerne when he awoke myself and Taurillion. We were a bit shocked at the awakening and didn't believe who he was. He was travelling to Retarfu at the time with a woman. Later we helped rescue him from the Unworthy Man's Drop. Some Elothian soldiers pushed him over the cliff."

"They did what? Is he alright?"

"Yes, a little battered, but he is well. We found him climbing up the sheer rock face. Marguerite was watching over him that's for sure; a more worthy man there can't be. He needs your help."

"Describe him," Jennery said.

"Lord Jennery, we don't have time for this. He said to tell you that if you didn't help him and prevented me from returning to him, he would hit you over the head with a ladle."

Jennery's face broke out into a broad smile, and Yaserille smiled in response as his rugged face lit up. "That sounds like the Captain," he agreed. "Where is he and what does he need? The last we heard he had been killed protecting the duke."

"He has been protecting the grand duke as a captain of the Third Chevron. Right now, he is descending on the Summer Palace, attempting to rescue a guardian that the Ascendants abducted. But he needs you to create a diversion to draw their attention south. We are few and need all the help we can get."

Jennery pulled out a map of Elothia. "When does he intend to infiltrate the palace?"

"In two days. It took me two days to get here, so he should be in position here." She pointed at the map. "He intends to attack at dawn with two other Sentinals. The Summer guardian is restrained there. We have to get her out."

"Two other Sentinals?" Jennery looked up at her.

"Taurillion and Serenion. He sent three others to a nursery in Marchwood to recover. They were in poor shape."

"He found six more Sentinals?"

Yaserille smiled. "Yes, and we serve the Captain and his needs."

Jennery sighed deeply. "Thank the Lady. Keep him safe; we need him."

Yaserille nodded. "He told me to give these papers to you. It contains all that he has collected so far."

Jennery took the papers and collapsed in his chair. He

spread the maps out and looked up. "How do you feel about helping the enemy?"

"I am a Sentinal of Remargaren, in service to the Lady and the Captain. Their enemies are my enemies."

Jennery nodded. "Well said." He leaned back in his chair as Tagerill arrived. Jennery's lips tightened at his friend's haggard face, concern for his brother and the Captain taking its toll. Injecting a note of enthusiasm in his voice, Jennery introduced Yaserille. "Ah, Tagerill, this is Yaserille, a newly awoken Sentinal from Elothia. She has news of Jerrol."

Tagerill clasped Yaserille's arm in greeting. "Yas, glad to see you. What news? Is Jerrol alright?"

"The Captain is fine." Yaserille replied as she gripped his arm in return.

A slow smile spread over Tagerill's face. "That is good news. Is there any news of Birlerion?"

Yaserille smiled. "Apparently, Birlerion is in Retarfu disguised as a member of the Third Chevron. The Captain was alone when we found him. I left him with Taurillion and Serenion. I understand Marianille was commanded to stay and protect Scholar Haven. Birlerion is with them in Retarfu."

Tagerill hissed his breath out and shielded his eyes with a shaky hand. He cleared his throat and Jennery's chest tightened at the gruffness of Tagerill's voice. "Is Birlerion alright? Why didn't he send word? We've been worried sick."

Yaserille shrugged. "I don't know. I haven't seen him, but he is alive. From what the Captain said they found each other in Adeeron."

Jennery sat back down with a thump, his chair creaking in protest. He looked up at the Sentinals filling his tent. Tagerill screwed up his face and ducked back out of the entry. Jennery hurried to fill the gap and give Tagerill time to collect himself. Relief coursed through him as he grinned at

Yaserille. "News has been slow. It's been a worrying time. Taelia and Jerrol were joined? We weren't sure if that was the case."

Tagerill re-entered the tent and after a swift glance at him, Jennery ignored the Sentinal's flushed face and over-bright eyes. "I'm surprised Taelia is still out there. I would have thought the king would have brought them home by now."

Tagerill shrugged. "My sister keeps refusing to leave, she can be stubborn like that, which is fortunate considering the information they are sending us." He paused, and then muttered under his breath. "At least she will be there for Birlerion." He turned to Yaserille. "Did Jerrol explain how Birlerion became a soldier in the grand duke's army? Because last we heard he was in bad shape."

"I'm sorry, he didn't. I assume they are waiting for the Captain to return."

Shuffling the papers on his desk into a pile, Jennery heaved a deep sigh. "Too many unknowns. What we do know is that Jerrol needs a diversion. Fill Yaserille in on our situation, will you? She needs to get back to Jerrol as soon as possible."

Tagerill looked back at Yaserille. "How is he?" he asked again, the concern plain on his face.

"He's fine. Planning to infiltrate the Summer Palace. There is a guardian he intends to rescue. He needs your troops here to cause a distraction; only a distraction. He warns against a full engagement. Adeeron has reserves that they could send down on you, and the Captain believes the true target is the Watch Towers at Velmouth."

"Who else is awake?" Tagerill asked.

"Taurillion and Serenion. The Captain sent the others to Marchwood to recover. All the details are in the information I gave Lord Jennery."

Jennery waved the papers, and Tagerill nodded. "Very well, I'll be back shortly. Yaserille, if you come with me, we'll get you reprovisioned and on your way. I'd send some men with you, but I think you'll be less conspicuous and travel quicker alone."

Yaserille nodded. "The Captain intends to return to Retarfu. There is no point taking a squad of Vespirian soldiers deeper into Elothia."

"Agreed; they have enough of our men already. What do you need?" Their voices faded as Tagerill led her away.

When Tagerill returned to Jennery's tent, he was engrossed in the papers and maps spread out before him. He looked up and inspected his friend for a moment. "Did she get away alright?"

"Yes, no problem."

Jennery sighed and indicated the maps. "We have all their positions, numbers, units; you name it."

"At least we know he is well and guarded," Tagerill said, his mind obviously still on Jerrol.

"He *was* well, but he is about to enter the hornet's nest. The Summer Palace will not be lightly defended, and he has only three Sentinals?"

Tagerill grinned. "You'd be surprised how much damage three Sentinals can do."

Jennery gave a huff of laughter. "I'm sure. What else did she say?"

"Lady Marguerite rides his shoulder. Her sister offers succour. The Lady is hidden, removed. The Captain struggles to forsake the Lady. That's why he's muted in our senses. It's not that he is injured. He is trying to hide."

"But why?" Jennery asked.

"Because the Lady told him to."

Jennery stared at him. "For what purpose?"

Tagerill shrugged. "There are deeper currents at play than even we know."

Jennery sighed. "No doubt. What about this diversion. What do you think we should do? Everything I can think of is more likely to trigger a strong reaction."

"Maybe it's time. I was going to suggest we strengthen the defences around Velmouth. If that is their true target, we should support Jason. They will react to us bolstering the defences. If we make it seem like we have reduced the defences here, it may draw them in, and they might take the bait."

Jennery nodded, frowning at the map. "We can buy them time. But at what cost?"

Tagerill leaned over the table. "We try to mitigate the cost where we can, hold the front line as long as possible, then fall back to the true defensive position."

Jennery stared at him steadily. "And who is going to lead that suicide mission?"

Tagerill smiled, a glint in his eyes. "Well, it won't be the Lord of the Watch, now, will it?" he said as he pulled the maps closer and sat down.

39

GRAND DUKE'S PALACE, RETARFU

Taelia gave the guard outside the grand duke's chambers a blinding smile as she handed over her report for the fourth day in a row. She halted in surprise as the guard failed to take it. Instead, he turned to open the chamber door. "The grand duke is expecting you, Scholar."

Taelia recovered and promptly entered the chambers. She paused on the threshold, unsure where the grand duke was, and Marianille hovered close behind her.

The aroma of musty books and fresh coffee lingered in the air. The rug was soft under her feet, her shoes sank into the deep pile but she hesitated, straining to hear who was in the room.

"Ah, the persistent Scholar Taelia of Vespiri." The grand duke's voice sounded tired.

Taelia turned towards the sound of his voice off to her left and curtsied. "Your Grace, thank you for seeing me."

"It seems you were determined to give me your report. I thought it might be easier if you explained it yourself; it wasn't making a lot of sense to me."

"It would be my pleasure, Your Grace, after all, you asked me to find your Guardian of the Summer."

The chair creaked as the grand duke moved. "I did?"

Marianille pushed Taelia forward so she could enter the chamber. "Your Grace," she murmured, bowing. The grand duke was still unnaturally pale. He was dressed informally in shirt and trousers and seated behind his desk, his dark blue jacket slung over the back of a chair near the table.

"The Scholar's faithful attendant." The grand duke nodded his head, his eyes alert.

Marianille's eyes darted around the chamber, alighting on Birler standing against the wall. "Are you alone, Your Grace? You should not be unattended."

The room seemed empty but for the grand duke and Birler, and spoke tellingly of his lack of trust in the people around him.

The grand duke smiled. "I thought this conversation might be best held privately, for I don't believe I have heard all that needs to be told, and for some reason, I don't believe that the companions of Captain Finn or, for that matter, Commander Haven will harm me. He could have killed me any time this last month if he had wanted to. Instead, I find he has been trying to protect me and my country." He indicated the chairs in front of his desk. "Please sit. Why don't you begin by telling me who you really are?"

Marianille led Taelia forward. Taelia's hands fluttered over the chair as she spoke. "My name is Taelia Haven, and I am a scholar of the Lady's Order of Remargaren."

"Haven?"

"King Benedict's Ambassador, Commander Jerrol Haven, is my husband."

"Your husband?" Taelia heard the surprise in his voice. "Did you realise he was also Captain Finn? Or so my advisors said, eventually."

"Immediately, Your Grace," Taelia admitted. "Once I got over the shock, I knew he wasn't dead. It was only a matter of time before he found a way to return."

"And you were the only one who recognised him," the grand duke said.

"No, Tor'asion and Var'geris knew who he was straight away. No one else really had a chance to see him when we first arrived."

The grand duke winced. "Yes, my apologies for your reception, though as it turns out, maybe it was for the best. And you?" The grand duke looked at Marianille.

"I am a Sentinal, your Grace. The Captain awoke me in Terolia. My name is Marianille."

The grand duke's eyes widened. "A Sentinal? Truly? I thought they were a myth."

Marianille smiled. "Obviously not, Your Grace. And Private Birler behind you is my brother, Sentinal Birlerion. Only, the Ascendants attacked and injured him. He ended up at Adeeron like the Captain."

"Lieutenant Birler, have you been keeping secrets from me?" the grand duke asked, staring at Birlerion.

"I am sorry, Your Grace, but I don't remember being a Sentinal. My name is Birler, and I am as you see."

"Why are you here?" The grand duke turned back to Taelia.

"To be brief, Your Grace," Taelia said. "The Ascendants are trying to take over Remargaren. They tried to overthrow King Benedict, they set the Terolian Families against each other, and now they are trying to cause unrest in Elothia. Your generals have caused tensions along the borders, sending incursions into Vespiri. We came to try to stop you from going to war with Vespiri."

"But I have not ordered any such action."

"The Ascendants have, Your Grace."

"The Ascendants?"

"Tor'asion and Var'geris; they are direct descendants of the Ascendants who tried to destroy the Lady and Remargaren over three thousand years ago."

Birler stirred by the wall, and Marianille cast him a worried glance.

"They are but two men. How could they possibly tell my generals what to do?"

"They have powers over the mind. They influence those who cannot defend themselves or threaten those who try to."

The grand duke stilled. "Captain Finn tried to tell me something similar. Is that why they are ignoring my recall orders?"

"Yes, Your Grace." Marianille's calm voice continued, "The Captain believes that the Ascendants have Lady Guin'yyfer of Tierne held against her will; he intends to free her."

The grand duke galvanised to his feet. "They'll kill her."

"They are already killing her. She is the Summer Guardian and Lady Marguerite needs her, just as Guin'yyfer needs Marguerite," Taelia said. "She is being suffocated, tortured without her connection to you and the land. She should be by your side; she's written in the walls of your palace. I find her everywhere, except where she should be. The Land mourns her loss, and your rule suffers."

Birler moved forward as the grand duke swayed. "Your Grace, please sit. You are still recovering. They shouldn't have sprung so much on you all at once."

The grand duke sat. "No, it's alright. I should have known all along." He rested his head in his hands and massaged his temples. "I thought I was protecting her," he said, his voice muffled.

"I'm sorry, Your Grace, please don't worry. Jerrol will bring her back."

"You have great faith in your husband, Scholar. How is one man going to rescue her?" His voice was subdued as he took the glass of water that Birler offered.

"He'll find a way, Your Grace. He always does."

The silence was interrupted by the ornate clock on the shelf behind the grand duke, chiming eight. He sighed and leaned forward. "Come back the same time tomorrow. We'll talk more then."

"It may be best if the Ascendants don't know that we spoke," Taelia suggested as she rose.

"I'm trying to avoid them. Though without Captain Finn to guard my doors, I'm not sure how much longer that will work."

"Birlerion will protect you, and the Lady protects those who ask, don't forget," Taelia said as she left.

The grand duke sat at his desk, staring at the closed door for a long time.

40

RETARFU, ELOTHIA

B irler knew Owen wasn't enamoured with his on-the-job promotion. He hadn't stopped complaining about filling in for Finn, or the extended conversations he was expected to have with the grand duke about his sister. Being interrogated by the scholar of all people about Captain Finn and his sister Guin'yyfer had Owen fuming.

All of the men tried to avoid him, though Captain Finn had put in place such rigorous processes that they didn't really need to speak to him. They continued as Finn had intended.

Birler observed the Ascendants trying to importune Owen, making threats against his sister if he didn't let them in to see the grand duke. But Owen stood firm and they gritted their teeth and left him alone.

Birler was the only member of his unit that the grand duke allowed to enter his rooms and stand behind his shoulder. He wondered what the regime at Adeeron would make of his promotion to lieutenant, and then shrugged the thought off.

Interestingly, the scholar was permitted entry regularly, and subsequent requests to recall the generals began to be sent out. He watched with interest as the Ascendants tied themselves in knots trying to delay or redirect the requests. At least it kept them busy and away from him.

The day that two soldiers arrived during the grand duke's daily audience to say that they had killed the rogue captain was fraught for everyone involved. Owen stood to the side of the platform, trying to glower at anyone who chose to approach the grand duke with a petition. He had kept most away, but two palace guards approached, too excited to notice his scowl. The petitioners peered over the courtier's shoulders with interest at the sudden interruption.

Grand Duke Randolf sat on his throne and inspected the soldiers before him. He glanced at Taelia, seated beside a bored Selvia, off to his left. Tall, silver-eyed Sentinals stood behind the scholar. His gaze paused on them before moving to Taelia. "Scholar?" he asked. She shook her head.

Birler stepped forward and took the sword with shaking hands. He recognised it. "It is the Captain's," he said, his gut churning. He turned on the guards. "Where did you say you killed him?" His voice whipped across the room and they flinched back.

"We pushed him off the cliff; off the drop."

"But you didn't see his body?"

"He went off the drop. No one survives that."

Birler smiled in relief, the cramp in his gut easing. "You'd be surprised," he said, his voice low. "Marguerite has a soft spot for the Captain, and if he's not worthy, then no man is. I'm sure you are mistaken." He returned to his post behind the grand duke, unsheathing his sword and sliding the Captain's home in its place. It vibrated gently and he relaxed at its familiar hum.

Tor'asion stepped out from behind one of the marble statues lining the room and peered at Birler behind the throne. As he approached the dais, his jaw squared and the cords in his neck stood out as he clenched his fists. "What are you doing here, Birlerion? How did you escape from Adeeron? Your Grace, you have a Vespirian Sentinal standing behind you. He was imprisoned in Adeeron. He is not to be trusted."

Owen moved towards the duke. "Lieutenant Birler is as trustworthy as I am, Your Grace."

Tor'asion snorted. "That's not saying much."

"And who made you the expert on the Elothian Army?" Owen asked, ice in his voice. Offended that they dare question his or any other soldier's commitment to the grand duke. "I would question your loyalty before Birler's," he bit out.

"Randolf, you must arrest him, he is masquerading as an Elothian soldier," Selvia ordered. "You can't trust him."

Birler felt a sense of inevitability as he watched Tor'asion approach the throne. He had the Captain's sword. One of the Ascendants who had tortured him approached the throne. A calm settled over him as he waited.

"Birler?" the grand duke said.

Birler stepped forward and stood in front of the grand duke.

Var'geris spoke as he joined Tor'asion at the foot of the dais. "Birlerion, Leyandrii commands you to kill the grand duke. You will do it now," he intoned.

Much of the throne room faded as Birler focused on the two men who had made him suffer, though he was aware of his sister moving around the throne room, as if she wasn't sure how he would react.

Birler drew the Captain's sword; the swish of metal loud in the silent room.

"Marianille, what's happening?" Taelia turned, her hands searching. "I do not believe they could ever enspell Birlerion."

"Of course they haven't," Niallerion said as he grabbed

Taelia's hand. His voice rose as he described the scene. "Birlerion's facing two Ascendants in the middle of the throne room. He's standing between them and the grand duke. Marianille has gone to help."

Birler spoke over his shoulder. "My apologies, Your Grace, for what I am about to do."

"And what is that?" Randolf asked calmly.

Birler walked down the steps as the Captain's sword vibrated in his hand. A sense of recognition permeated through him, and he gripped it tighter. He spoke to Tor'asion, though his eyes were on Var'geris. "You have been training me for this very moment, and you should know that Leyandrii would never command me to kill one of her guardians."

His eyes flickered as two more Ascendants arrived, moving to surround him. Ain'uncer and Sul'enne. "You have never commanded me. Only the Captain and the grand duke do that," he said, rotating. He moved so fast, blocking their approach to the dais, that Ain'uncer didn't have time to react. The Ascendant fell on the steps of the grand duke's throne, a wheezing groan his last breath. A rising murmur raced around the room as courtiers and petitioners alike watched, riveted to the unfolding drama. Birler forced Sul'enne back away from the grand duke towards Var'geris, spinning between the remaining three. Tor'asion cursed and retreated as the shining sword flickered with a blue light as Birler disarmed him.

Birler bore down on him, his blue eyes flashing with silver. Tor'asion grimaced before he swirled his cloak and disappeared. The courtiers gasped and flattened themselves against the walls out of the way. Birler spun and blocked Sul'enne's blow, the clash of swords ringing through the room.

The grand duke sat on his throne and watched. Selvia

stood beside him, eyes wide, her hand over her mouth. She gripped her brother's shoulder. "You must stop him, Randolf. He's one of those Sentinals. Why won't you stop him? We need the Ascendants, can't you see?"

"Why would I trust those who plot to kill me?" Randolf asked, his gaze fixed on Birler. "And anyway, what do you know of the Sentinals? They are just myth. Children's stories."

Selvia snorted and gestured at the fighting men. "Can't you see the difference? Even without the silver eyes it is obvious."

"So you confirm he is a Sentinal?"

"Confirm, deny. What difference does it make? There were lots of them in Old Vespers. It's their fault Kharel died. If they hadn't interfered …."

"Prevented your attempted coup, you mean? Is that what you attempt here, Selvia? Have you not learned your lesson yet?"

"Uncle Samuel understands. He sees what needs to be done."

Flicking his gaze back to Selvia, Randolf wrinkled his brow. "Kabil? Selvia! What have you done?"

"Nothing, that father wouldn't have. You are too indecisive, too weak. We must make a stand."

Randolf's gaze returned to the fight in his throne room as Var'geris cursed as he flinched back from Birler's sword which had caught him; he switched hands, his arm hanging limply.

"You'll pay for that," Var'geris spat.

"I've already paid," Birler replied, and cast a desperate glance around the throne room. Spotting his sister flanking him and Niallerion hovering at the edge of dais, he stiffened as memories teased him, but he didn't have time to sort them. Var'geris reclaimed his attention, and forced him to give ground.

Marianille tried to move between the fight and the grand duke, but Birler was there, blocking the way. "Birlerion, it's me, Marianille. I'm here to help." Marianille stepped back at the grand duke's signal.

Birler didn't hear her; his focus was on protecting the grand duke. He bore down on the two remaining men, and Sul'enne resorted to defence. The fury and power of the Sentinal were astonishing as he forced them away from the throne. Var'geris dropped his sword and grabbed Sul'enne, and they both disappeared in a swirl of black material. Birler was left alone in the centre of the room, breathing heavily.

Stiffening, Randolf glared at his sister. "I will deal with you later," he said, his voice sharp. The threat unspoken. "I am the Grand Duke and you will abide by my decisions."

Selvia backed away, her gaze skittered around the throne room and she paled as she saw the fallen Ascendant crumpled on the steps and only the Sentinal left standing in the centre of the room.

Birler slowly controlled his breathing, sheathed the Captain's sword with a trembling hand and flexed his shoulders. He turned back to the throne and faced the grand duke. The room was silent; everyone was watching him.

Randolf rose from his throne as Selvia scuttled off the dais and he let her go. Birler took a step towards him as exhilaration flooded through him; the flush of battle still rushing through his veins. Randolf walked down the steps and met Birler in the centre of the room.

"Birlerion?"

"My apologies for fighting in your throne room, Your Grace," Birler said, and taking a deep breath, he dropped to one knee and bent his head, trying to regain his composure.

A deep sense of loss gripped him, draining his exhilaration and leaving him exhausted.

Randolf raised him to his feet and Birler couldn't help but sway. The grand duke's grip tightened and Birler stiffened, concentrating on remaining upright. "Thank you, Sentinal Birlerion. I thank you for your care, your protection, and your sacrifice." Randolf gazed around at the shocked people in his throne room, and his voice rang out. "See this man. Birlerion, Sentinal Birlerion. Let his name spread throughout our country. Know this one and all; Sentinal Birlerion has the Grand Duchy of Elothia in his debt. Let it never be forgotten."

A low murmur spread around the throne room as the courtiers recovered from their shock and began discussing the events with excitement. They had witnessed history, and they were quick to share it.

"Your Grace, please." Birler was appalled. He raised a trembling hand to his temple. "I-I don't remember being a Sentinal."

"You will. I have no doubt about that. The Lady sent you to us in our time of need, and we thank her for it." Randolf grinned. "Come, Birlerion. We have much to discuss, but I think there are some people who want to speak with you first." Randolf steered him towards Marianille.

She flew into his arms. "By the Lady, Birlerion. You could have been killed!"

Owen stepped forward. "Not likely," he said with a snort as he slapped Birlerion's shoulder. "A Sentinal, huh? You kept that quiet."

Taelia pushed her way through, her hands questing. "Birlerion? Are you alright?" Her concern was evident.

"I'm fine," he murmured, stiffening as she hugged him and unsure how he was supposed to respond. Marianille had said she was the wife of Captain Finn, no of

Commander Haven. He shook his head, confused. Whoever she was, he doubted she was supposed to be hugging him.

Her hands patted him down. "Are you sure? They didn't hurt you, did they?"

Randolf smiled at her concern. "He's fine. They didn't touch him."

Taelia heaved a sigh of relief as she cupped Birlerion's face, her turquoise eyes shining with tears. "We've missed you, terribly. Jerrol will be so relieved."

Niallerion gripped Birlerion's shoulder. "Four of them!" he said. "You were amazing."

"Nialler," he murmured as Taelia released him. "I'm not Birlerion."

"You are and you'd better get used to it, because that is who we all know you as. Maybe your memories will return as you get used to answering to your name. Leyandrii herself gave you the name, Birlerion, accept it."

Randolf herded them all back to his apartments, leaving Owen to clean up his throne room. He watched Marianille and Taelia hover over Birlerion with amusement, both wanting to reassure themselves that he was there and unharmed.

Birlerion flushed with embarrassment, not used to all the attention, but the hollow ache in his chest was soothed at the fervent concern for him. They had been worried about him and *for* him. It warmed him through, thawing the last frozen emotions he had so diligently suppressed, melting away the fear of being abandoned and forgotten.

Birlerion looked across at the grand duke. "They will have retreated to the front. They will drive the generals even more now that they know they have no chance of controlling you."

Randolf nodded. "We'll remove to the Summer Palace.

If the generals don't abide by my orders, then I will go to them."

He instructed Ulfr to send a messenger to the Summer Palace staff to prepare for their arrival and drove his steward to have everything organised within a week of his decision. The grand duke would brook no argument, and for once, his staff seemed to realise that he meant what he said.

Birlerion spent time with Marianille and Niallerion, swapping stories, catching up on events, and filling in the blanks. Relief was uppermost in his mind, to be back where he was supposed to be.

All the Sentinals wore smiles. Marianille barely let her brother out of her sight, berating him for worrying her and hugging him tight, in turn. Niallerion kept slapping his shoulder and then pulling Birlerion into a hug as tears welled in his eyes.

Grinning, Birlerion soaked it all up. Warmed by everyone's concern, he slowly relaxed, accepting that if Leyandrii had named him so, then he must be Birlerion. Marianille and Niallerion would not lie to him about Leyandrii, and they both used their Sentinal names as naturally as if they had been born with them. He hoped given time, he would too.

The horrific memories of Adeeron, he put to one side; they were still too painful to be prodded. He skimmed over the details of his treatment, distracting everyone with stories about Jerrol's rise to captain. If he was honest, he was not surprised he had a few memory lapses. Considering what he had suffered, he was amazed he was still alive.

The next day, Owen ordered Birlerion back on duty. "We're already a man down, I need you. The grand duke trusts you." Owen huffed as he glowered at Birlerion. "We've had word King Benedict arrived in Stoneford with more troops. The grand duke is even more determined to travel south. In this weather!" His voice was aggrieved as he gestured towards the window, where a blizzard of snow swirled in the grey afternoon gloom as any remaining light disappeared under the heavy clouds.

Moving his court meant moving Taelia, Birlerion and the other Sentinals as well. When the grand duke mentioned the carriage, Taelia asked permission to ride a horse instead.

Randolf was offended. "What's wrong with a carriage? It is a perfectly acceptable form of transport."

"But they are so uncomfortable, Your Grace. I'd much prefer to ride if possible."

"Nonsense all the carriages have great suspension. My mother would accept no less."

"Maybe not all your carriages have been maintained as you expect, Your Grace," Taelia replied.

Randolf snorted. "You shall ride with me and then you shall see."

Taelia had no choice but to give in gracefully. At least the grand duke's carriage should be in much better condition than the last one; even so, she would much prefer to be travelling in the arms of her husband.

She very much hoped he would be waiting at the Summer Palace to greet her.

A few days later, Birlerion handed Taelia into the grand duke's carriage. "Calm down," he murmured. Taelia was starry-eyed at the thought of being with Jerrol, and as he settled her, he muttered a warning. "I'll tell your husband you were flirting with the grand duke if you don't tone it down."

Taelia gasped, though she nodded. "I'm sorry, I'm just so happy."

"Well, wait till you see him. He might not even be there."

"He will be. Jerrol was sure Lady Guin'yyfer was being held at the Summer Palace. That is where he would have gone," she replied, demurely smiling as she heard the grand duke arrive.

Birlerion stood away from the door and stiffened impersonally as Randolf passed. Randolf's lips twitched, but he refrained from comment and Birlerion breathed a sigh of relief. The Grand Duke had gotten to know them quite well the past few days, between Taelia and the Grand Duke, Birlerion wasn't sure his position as a lieutenant in the Elothian army would hold for much longer. Owen acted as if he was still under his command, and to be honest Birlerion was most comfortable as a Chevron lieutenant. He didn't remember being a Sentinal. The conflicting memories confused him, and although he answered to Birlerion, Leyandrii's absence and the growing sense of loss threatened to consume him and he avoided thinking about what that meant. Marianille and Niallerion were here, that was enough to anchor him, for now.

The Duke and Taelia both seemed to think the Captain would be waiting for them at the Summer Palace ready to hand them what they both wanted on a plate, and probably tied up in a nice bright ribbon.

Birlerion sighed as he mounted his horse and fell in behind the carriage. Owen scowled at him as he passed to the front. They hadn't even left yet and he was already in a foul mood. Birlerion made sure Marianille was perched on top of the baggage carriage, and then he tugged his cloak tighter around him as he settled in for what he trusted would be a peaceful journey to the Summer Palace. He cast a glance up at the brooding clouds, and hoped they would reach their overnight stop before the snow began to fall.

41

SUMMER PALACE, ELOTHIA

The Summer Palace seemed to hover above the early morning mists clinging to the river that lazily looped around it. The sheer, grey stone walls were more reminiscent of a fortified castle than a palace, especially with the serrated edging around the battlements connecting the four round towers, which guarded each corner. The only way in, was, as Jerrol had said, to walk up to the front door. Jerrol didn't stop. He kept his column marching up to the river crossing where he arrogantly demanded the ferryman transport them over, refusing to pay the toll. The grand duke's army never paid a toll.

Cursing his luck, the ferryman unhooked the rope and ferried them over, glowering silently at Jerrol. Jerrol ignored him and observed the palace instead. It looked deserted. The stone walls towered over them as they reformed on the other side of the river. He glanced back at Landis. "Remember, lieutenant. Third Chevron, unit three, lately from Retarfu. Leave the talking to me."

Landis nodded, happily relegated to a lieutenant.

Jerrol searched out the Sentinals. "Try to blend in; let's not alert them to the fact that we have Sentinals in our midst." Yas made a face at Serenion. She had rejoined them at the ferry crossing, slipping into the ranks unnoticed. Their silver eyes didn't always attract attention, though they both studiously looked at the floor and bowed their shoulders slightly. Taurillion grinned and stuck close to Jerrol; he hadn't let the Captain out of his sight, and he wasn't going to start now.

Jerrol marched straight up to the palace and halted his column at the gate. He strode forward, alone. "Captain Finn, Third Chevron, unit three, reporting for duty," he snapped to the guard on sentry duty.

The guard almost dropped his logbook in shock. "I-I'm sorry, sir, but we are not expecting anyone."

"That is not my problem," Jerrol said. "I have a unit of the Third Chevron here to take over the security of the palace, in preparation for the visit of His Grace, Grand Duke Randolf the fourteenth."

"W-what? The grand duke is coming here?" the guard squeaked in horror.

"That's what I said," Jerrol said, glaring at the guard.

"Y-Yes, sir, if you would follow me, sir."

Jerrol stared at the guard. "You would leave the gate unattended?"

"Yes, sir, there's only me. I need to let you into the palace."

"What is your name?"

"Private Mattison, sir."

Jerrol turned to his unit and glared at Landis. Landis struggled to keep his face straight. "Lieutenant, assign two guards to man the gate; the rest of you, follow me." He turned back to Mattison and gestured for him to lead the way. "Who else is here?"

"A housekeeper and the steward, a few maids and foot-men. Oh, and an aunt of the grand duke and her retinue are staying in the East Tower. They keep themselves to themselves. We don't really see them as she has her own cook and servants." The private struggled with the lock in a small door set in the larger gate. Jerrol watched in resignation. *Oh, how the mighty are fallen*, he thought as he stepped through the palace defences.

"What happened to the rest of your unit?"

"They were recalled, sir. A relief unit was supposed to have been sent months ago, but they never arrived. I guess you must be it, sir?"

"I suppose I must be," Jerrol said, barely a quiver in his voice. "Very well, show us the barracks so my men can settle in, and then lead me to the steward."

Mattison led them to the barracks on the outer edge of the west tower, where Landis began blandly assigning beds.

"Mattison, give Lieutenant Landis the gate key. I think you've been on gate duty long enough. It must be time for you to have a rest."

"Yes, sir," Mattison gladly handed Landis the key. Jerrol turned away from the expression on Landis' face and glared at Taurillion. "Taurill, with me," he said, gritting his teeth.

"Yes, sir." Taurillion stepped up to his shoulder.

Jerrol looked at the eager young guard. "Do you have a map of the palace? My lieutenant needs to assign posts."

"Yes, sir," he rifled through some papers on a shelf and held out a shaking hand.

"Excellent." He inspected it before handing it to Landis. "Where do you sleep, private?"

"In there, sir."

Jerrol peered into what looked like a small storeroom. He looked at the private and nodded and then led the way out of the barracks. "The steward. What is his name?" he asked as they mounted the steps to the main entrance hall.

"Bracken, sir, and the housekeeper is Mrs Stokes."

"Well, Private Mattison, let's hope they are better at withstanding shocks than you are," Jerrol said as he followed the boy down the corridors and into the palace kitchens before dismissing him back to the barracks.

They were not. Bracken had to catch Mrs Stokes as she half fainted when she heard the grand duke was arriving.

"He's not arriving today," Jerrol snapped, losing his patience. "I am here to prepare for when he *does* arrive. You need to stock the kitchens, open the state apartments, lay the fires, clean the house," he said, wiping the dust off the sideboard.

"We don't have the staff, sir," the steward stuttered.

"Who do you have?"

"Apart from us, six maids and four footmen, and the guard," he added as an after-thought.

"How many staff does the duke's aunt have? And what is her name?"

"Lady Agatha has two maids, her cook, a page, and two guards."

"I see. Well, I will speak to her about borrowing her staff, as well. But I would suggest it is about time that your staff earn the money His Grace pays them."

Bracken started at the bite in Jerrol's voice and nodded, his eyes bulging with fear.

"I have sixteen men in the barracks. They will be on roving patrols on six-hour shifts. I assume you have enough supplies to feed us? I expect you to have meals available for those who are off duty. It will be cold enough outside without them going hungry. Am I understood? They will eat in the staff hall. The grates in the barracks need preparing, and the beds need linen and blankets."

"Yes, sir," Bracken replied, in a daze.

"I suggest your footmen start chopping wood and preparing the grates. It will take some time to warm this palace up. I imagine we have two weeks to prepare, if we are lucky. If you have staff you can call on, then I suggest you get them here, now. Advise my lieutenant of anyone you expect to arrive at the palace; if they are not approved, they will not be allowed entry, even if it is a routine delivery of milk. If they are not on the list, they will not be granted entry, do you understand?" Jerrol softened his voice upon seeing their terrified faces.

"Yes, sir." Bracken was incapable of saying anything else, and Mrs Stokes looked like she was about to swoon again.

"Where is the captain of the guard normally based? Are there rooms near the grand duke's apartments?"

"Yes, sir, in the south tower."

"Prepare those first. I will move in tonight."

"Yes, sir," Bracken whispered.

"Thank you. I know this is a shock, but I am sure you will all manage fine. After all, the grand duke has been in residence before, hasn't he?" His words did not seem to reassure the staff as he had hoped. "Very well, I will leave you to it," he said as he turned and left, Taurillion behind him. He let his breath out in a whoosh. "Well, that didn't go so well, did it?"

"Once they get over the shock, things may improve," Taurillion replied.

"What do you reckon on the aunt? Real or not?"

Taurillion pursed his lips. "I would think not; the staff would know if there were any other captives in the palace."

"I'm not so sure, with so few to guard them?"

"Ascendants rely on their powers to restrain. They don't believe they need very many people, Captain."

"True. Let's check out the south tower, see what view I have."

"Yes, sir."

Jerrol laughed as they left the kitchens and crossed the

empty dining hall. Their footsteps echoed as they skirted what looked like a private temple. Carved wooden screens guarded the temple entrance, and the scent of lilies drifted on the air as they passed. Peering into the small chambers that lined either side of a narrow passage they arrived at the base of the stone stairs that spiralled up the south tower. "Keep your eyes open for any of Lady Agatha's people," Jerrol murmured as he led the way up the stairs. The first landing opened into an airy study, across from which sat an empty office. A library extended between the duke's study and the east tower.

Continuing to the second floor, they reached an ornate door which led to an opulent bed chamber, and across the hallway were the captain's rooms, comprised of a small bedroom and a tiny office with a desk and a chair. Jerrol shivered. The rooms had not been aired in months. He walked back into the grand duke's bed chamber and gazed out of the window. The tower looked south over the river; he could just see the gleam of water curving off towards Vespiri.

He rotated, figuring that the north tower would have a view of the ferry crossing, and the west tower would overlook the other river crossing, and the east tower looked towards the ridge; no roads, rivers, or sight of visitors. He hoped they hadn't noticed the arrival of the grand duke's new guards. All the same, he would have Landis position guards in all four towers. With two on the gate and one roving per floor, that was nine guards per shift. They would all have to pitch in for twelve-hour shifts and not the six he had hoped for.

He descended the stairs in deep thought. Lady Agatha and her people were bound to notice the sudden activity. If it *was* Lady Guin'yyfer being detained, then they needed to ensure that the Ascendants didn't make off with her before he could rescue her. He was the most likely person an Ascendant would recognise if they were familiar with Vespers.

Arriving in the barracks, he called Landis over. "This place is bigger than it looks. We need two guards on the gate, one in each tower, and one roving for each floor. Oh, and guests are in the east tower. Go careful; we don't want to scare them away. Split the Sentinals. You know the drill."

"Got it," Landis turned away to issue instructions.

Glancing around the barracks, Jerrol realised that the fires were lit, and the beds were made. "My rooms are in the south tower; office on the first floor, bed on the second. Both you and the Sentinals can use my office when I'm not on duty."

Landis nodded. "Yes, sir."

"Have you got that map? We need more copies."

"I've got young Perks copying it out for us."

"Is he now?" Jerrol eyed the lad conscientiously copying at the table. "You found some paper?"

"Yeah, the steward came by with some when he got the lads to clear the fires. He said he would leave some in your rooms."

"Good, I'll leave you to it. I suggest you put Mattison in with the lads and take his room."

"Already done, sir. The lads already moved him. Yaserille has the other room." Landis grinned as Jerrol raised his hands in surrender.

"I'll be in my office. Put me as a roving for the night shift."

"Yes, sir."

"Avoid the east tower, for now. We'll deal with them tomorrow."

"Yes, sir."

42

SUMMER PALACE

I n the end, it was Jerrol who first met the Ascendant Pev'eril in the deep of the night as he patrolled the second floor. The explosive exclamation as Pev'eril rounded the gallery had Jerrol swinging around in response, sword drawn.

"Who are you? Where is Mattison?" Pev'eril peered through the gloom, his once plump face pinched and drawn and nothing like the assured man who had led the young lord of Deepwater astray.

"Your worst nightmare," Jerrol replied.

Pev'eril flinched at the sound of his voice. "Haven," he exclaimed in shock, beginning to back away. "How did you get here?"

Jerrol advanced on the Ascendant who had caused so much trouble in Deepwater. "Those who kill guardians have to pay the price in the end," he said.

"We'll kill her, with just one word."

"No, you won't," he replied as he swung his sword at the unprepared man. His blade penetrated cloth and skin and he twisted, thrusting his sword deeper. Jerrol stood, frowning over the crumpled body. The man was pale and gaunt, a shadow of his former self. Whatever they had been doing here had drained his power and his health. Jerrol had not expected to overcome him so easily. He hoped the second Ascendant would be just as easily overpowered.

Serenion burst out from the top of the stairs of the north tower. "I heard voices," he said as Jerrol pivoted to meet him. Serenion had been patrolling the floor below.

"Ascendant Pev'eril and I were having a short discussion," Jerrol replied, relaxing his grip on his sword as he rolled the body over with his foot.

Serenion crouched and searched the man. He held up an ornate key, and Jerrol looked at it thoughtfully before slipping it in his pocket.

"Let us deal with the second Ascendant, before he realises his companion is missing. We need to speak to him first, though, find out what they have done to Lady Guin'yyfer. Check the rest of the chambers on this floor." Serenion darted off down the corridor, silently opening doors while Jerrol dragged Pev'eril's body into the shadows.

Once Serenion confirmed the floor was deserted, they silently traversed the galleries to the east tower. On reaching the ornate double doors which led into Lady Agatha's suite, Jerrol paused and listened intently. All was silent behind the wooden doors. According to the floor plan, there would be an antechamber which led off to three bed chambers and then the main suite. He lifted the latch and eased open the door as Serenion followed behind him, his staff at the ready. The chamber was lit by the soft glow of a candle. Signs of occupation, an open book, a half-empty glass, indicated that Pev'eril had been standing the night watch. A hollow cough from a room off to the left had Jerrol raising an eyebrow, and Serenion drifted over to investigate.

Jerrol tried to lift the wrought iron latch on the more ornate door and released it as it resisted. He eyed the keyhole before moving to check the door of the next chamber. The latch lifted, and he eased the door open. An older woman wearing a lacy nightcap was snoring gently in the moonlight. He shut the door without disturbing her.

Serenion silently returned. "Looks like a sick room, pasty-looking dark-haired man in bed, asleep but restless. There's a whole apothecary next to his bed."

Jerrol nodded at the ornate door. "The Lady Guin'yyfer is locked in. The maid is asleep in there. The other servants must be upstairs. Let us have a quiet chat with her protector."

Serenion flashed a quick look at the Captain's face, noticing the edge in his voice, but he followed.

Jerrol paused by the bedside of the sickly man and stiffened, his face darkening with anger. "You," he snarled as he grabbed the man's neck. The Ascendant gasped awake, choking, his fingers scrabbling at the hand viciously squeezing his throat. His eyes bulged as he recognised the man standing over him.

"He needs to breathe," Serenion cautioned, and Jerrol reluctantly eased his grip.

The man coughed, trying to draw breath, and then he began babbling. "It wasn't my fault, they made me do it. I didn't have a choice."

"What did they make you do?" Jerrol asked his voice cutting.

"They made me subdue the Lady Guin'yyfer; we only used the gentler drugs; trealt, valenia, nothing permanent."

"You used trealt on the Lady Guin'yyfer?" Jerrol said, and the man flinched at the expression on his face. "This is Isseran, the ex-Chancellor of Vespiri," he said, as if introductions were needed. "Though I suppose that's not your name, is it? Who are you really?" Jerrol gritted his teeth and tightened his grip as Isseran hesitated.

Isseran blanched at his expression. "Alright, alright. It's Iss'aren."

"Ascendant Iss'aren. You tried to kill King Benedict using trealt."

"No, no, it wasn't me."

"Really?" Jerrol said, curling his lip as the man flailed. "What else did you do?"

"N-nothing, honest, just the drugs. The lady is well."

"Maybe we ought to let the grand duke be the judge of that?" Jerrol snapped. "Who else is here?"

"N-no one. It's just me. The lady sleeps; no more is needed."

"You lie."

"No, honest, Haven, it's just me." Iss'aren's lips tightened. "It's all they trust me with," he said, his voice bitter.

"That's about the only true thing you've said tonight. Take us to Lady Guin'yyfer."

"Now?"

"Yes, now. I want to see that she is alright." He released Iss'aren's throat and stepped back. "Get up."

Iss'aren wheezed as he rubbed his neck, livid red marks marring his pale skin. He swung his thin legs over the side of the bed. They looked incongruous sticking out under his nightshirt. Jerrol watched the man consider his options. He was quite sure Iss'aren only had powers of persuasion, but he flicked his fingers at Serenion, who closed in, his staff at the ready.

Iss'aren flinched back from the looming Sentinal. "I- I don't have the key," he mumbled. "The guard does."

"You mean this one?" Jerrol asked as he held up the ornate key that Serenion had found on Pev'eril.

The Ascendant's shoulders slumped. He coughed hollowly and suddenly lunged towards Jerrol, a knife appearing in his hand. Serenion's staff whipped up and caught him under his chin. The Ascendant flopped back unconscious and slid off the bed onto the floor, the knife clattering beside him.

"They really don't like you, do they?" Serenion said, kicking the knife towards Jerrol.

"It seems not," Jerrol agreed as he retrieved the knife. "I am sure there is a dank cell somewhere under this castle suitable for him. Tie him up and cover his eyes, and tell the guards to keep his face covered. If he can see, he can transport himself elsewhere. The grand duke can decide his fate; hopefully, it will be something very permanent, and if it isn't, King Benedict will bring him to justice, I'm sure." He looked around the room. "I'll send someone up to clear these rooms. We don't want trealt lying around."

"And the lady?"

"Let her sleep. She doesn't need to worry about all this until the morning." Jerrol paused to unlock her door before slipping the key back in his pocket.

He was turning away from the door when a young lad skidded into the room, his bare feet slipping on the rug. "You leave her be!" he shouted, brandishing a sword that looked too big for him. He held it with both hands. His brown hair flopped into his eyes, and the boy tried to flick it away while holding on to the unwieldy sword.

"I mean your lady no harm," Jerrol said, holding his arms away from his body.

"Move away from her door," the boy demanded, his brown eyes large in his face.

Jerrol moved away and allowed the boy to take his place in front of her door. The sword wavered as Serenion appeared behind Jerrol. Serenion grinned at the boy, tipped his staff against his temple in salute, and left, dragging the unconscious Pev'eril behind him.

The boy stared after Serenion and flicked his eyes back to

Jerrol. "What did you do to the guard?" His voice broke and he cleared his throat.

"We mean you no harm. We came to help. I'm a soldier in the grand duke's army."

The boy's eyes flickered over Jerrol's uniform, and his sword wavered. He stiffened as the latch clicked and the door opened behind him. A young woman, with masses of blonde curls and glazed blue eyes, appeared in the doorway, hastily wrapping a deep blue shawl around her. She took in the scene and tensed, her hand resting against the door frame. "Joren, come here. Stand behind me."

"Nay, my lady. I'm here to protect you."

She looked across at Jerrol. "Please, don't harm him," she pleaded. "He's just a boy."

Jerrol raised his hands again. "I mean neither of you any harm," he said. "I am a captain of the Third Chevron. I am here to help you. Your guards have been relieved, my lady."

"Relieved?"

"Another soldier dragged that Iss'aren man out; he was dead!" Joren exclaimed.

"Unconscious," Jerrol corrected. "He was only unconscious."

"And the other one?" Lady Guin'yyfer asked, her face pale. Her hand gripped the doorframe so hard, her knuckles whitened.

"I'm sorry, my lady, but he *is* dead."

"Show me," she said as she swayed in the doorway.

"It's not a sight for a lady's eyes. I assure you, he is dead; I killed him myself."

"I need to see." She stepped out of her room. "Where is he?"

Joren squeaked as she pushed him aside, but he was as eager to see a dead body as the lady was.

Jerrol bowed. "Of course, my lady, this way." He indicated the door and led the way out into the gallery. "I left him by the north tower, unless my men have removed him already." He led the way around the gallery and stopped as he saw two of his men lifting the body. "Hold a moment, Lady Guin'yyfer wishes to ascertain if he is dead."

His men unceremoniously dropped the body back to the floor and stepped back, eyes dutifully staring at the carpet after a swift glance at the informally dressed lady. Jerrol rolled the body over with his foot.

Guin'yyfer's gasp was masked by Joren's enthusiastic, "Cor!"

"As you see, my lady, he will trouble you no more. Please let me escort you back to your rooms. Private, send up some hot tea to Lady Guin'yyfer's room, will you?"

"Yes, sir." The burly soldier grinned at Joren and stooped to grab the dead man's ankles again.

"Where are you taking him?" Joren's voice followed the soldiers down the stairwell as he peppered them with questions, his need to guard the lady forgotten.

"Shall we?" Jerrol asked, waving his hand back towards her chambers.

Lady Guin'yyfer stood rigid, staring at the empty doorway.

"My lady? I assure you. No one here means you any harm."

She shuddered and then turned back to her chamber. Jerrol followed and then busied himself with the grate in her room, giving her a chance to recover her composure. Once the fire was going to his satisfaction, he stood and, spying a jug and glasses, poured her some water. He sniffed it first, to make sure it was just water.

He sat in the chair opposite her. "It's alright. Seeing a dead body is very upsetting."

"It wasn't that; I'm glad he's dead," she said, gripping

her hands together. "If I could have, I would have killed him myself, and that other snivelling little toad."

Jerrol was a little surprised at her bloodthirsty response, though he smiled at her description of King Benedict's ex-chancellor. He couldn't agree more. "How are you feeling? I understand they may have dosed you with some sedatives. It will take some time for them to work their way out of your system."

"I am feeling much better already, Captain, and I thank you for your timely intervention." She looked at him with a slight frown on her face. "What did you say your name was?"

"Captain Finn, my lady. Third Unit of the Third Chevron."

"How came you here?"

"It's a long story, my lady, but suffice to say, the grand duke asked me to find you."

She lifted her eyes in surprise. "He did?"

"Yes, my lady." Jerrol paused as a housemaid entered the chamber with a tray. He stood and pulled over a small table. "Just leave it, we'll manage," he said as he took the tray. The maid bobbed a quick curtsey and bolted.

"Oh dear," Guin'yyfer held a hand to her head. "I must look a mess."

"Not at all, my lady." He handed her a cup and saucer.

"Thank you, please call me Guin'yyfer. I keep thinking you are speaking to my mother."

"Is that your mother asleep next door?"

"Yes, she won't wake. They've been dosing her too, though to be honest, I think she has had enough. She would rather sleep through this mess than face it." She paused, and began folding her handkerchief between her fingers. "I was beginning to think the grand duke had had enough of me as well. It has been so long."

"They have been holding the threat of your safety over him to ensure his co-operation," Jerrol said.

She reared back in shock. "He's the grand duke! He shouldn't put anyone above the best interests of his people."

"I think he loves you very much."

"Still, a man in his position has to be above such a thing as love."

"He wasn't the grand duke when you first met. I think he is still struggling to understand his role in the world, and his advisors are not much help."

"I suppose not." She stared at him. "What happens now?"

Jerrol shrugged. "That's up to you. I'm preparing the Summer Palace for the grand duke's arrival."

"He's coming here?"

"I believe so, my lady."

"Am I free to leave?"

"If that is your desire. We will escort you to wherever you wish to go," Jerrol promised, falling silent as Guin'yyfer concentrated on folding her handkerchief as she considered her options.

The wood spat and hissed in the grate, and Jerrol sipped his tea, relaxing back into the chair as he watched her. The firelight teased out reddish highlights in her hair. Her high cheekbones were accentuated by the shadows and rose over a very decided chin. He didn't think Guin'yyfer was one to suffer fools gladly.

He wasn't surprised when she raised her head and looked him straight in the eye. "I think maybe I should wait for him. His palace needs a woman's touch."

"That it does, my lady," he agreed and he couldn't help the smile that spread over his face in response to the brilliant smile she gave him. He wasn't at all surprised that the grand duke had fallen for her so heavily.

He leaned forward and placed his cup and saucer back on the tray. "Your key, my lady."

She took the ornate key from him with raised eyebrows. A dimple briefly appeared in her right cheek, and she looked as if a mighty weight had been lifted from her shoulders.

"There are a few hours yet left for sleep. I'll see you in the morning, and we can figure out what needs to be done. My men patrol the castle and the battlements. They will not disturb you; they are very well behaved. I will introduce you to my Lieutenant, Landis, and he will assist you if I am not around."

"Are you leaving?" Panic rose in her eyes.

"I have to sleep as well, you know," Jerrol said with a grin, and she gave a shaky laugh as she nodded. "Sleep well, my lady," he said in parting as he rose. He closed the door behind him and took a deep breath before leaving the antechamber and returning to the gallery. Serenion was waiting for him on the landing. "Everything cleared up?"

"Yes, Captain. The Ascendant is in the dungeons. Are you sure you don't want him to have an accident before the grand duke arrives?"

"Tempting, but I think the grand duke needs to see who has been acting against him. Maybe he will shed Tor'asion and Var'geris as a result."

"Well, I think that influence is in decline if the grand duke is coming here."

Jerrol hesitated. "I don't actually know that Randolf is coming. It seemed like a good excuse to give the staff," he owned as they walked down the stairs.

Serenion's crack of laughter echoed up the tower behind them.

. . .

It was late the next morning when Jerrol was awoken by Taurillion frantically shaking his shoulder. He blearily looked around his unfamiliar surroundings before latching onto the worried face of his Sentinal.

"Taurillion, what's the matter?"

"A messenger arrived with orders from the grand duke." Taurillion handed him the sealed paper.

Jerrol levered himself up onto one arm and took the envelope. He flipped it over; it was the grand duke's seal sure enough. He slid his nail under the wax and broke the seal. Unfolding the paper, he gave a huff of laughter and lay back against his pillow. "Sometimes, you get what you wish for!" His grey eyes twinkled up at Taurillion, and Taurillion's shoulders began to relax. "The grand duke will be with us within the week. He expects his palace to be ready to receive him."

Taurillion blanched. "What? What are we going to do?"

"Have the palace ready for him, of course."

43

SUMMER PALACE

When Jerrol made his way down to his office on the first floor, he found Lady Guin'yyfer already in control of the Summer Palace. He gladly handed over preparations for the arrival of the grand duke into her capable hands, and Mrs Stokes and Steward Bracken fell on her with delight.

The days passed as the palace came back to life; flowers appeared in tall vases and meals vastly improved. The staff were noticeably happier, and Lady Guin'yyfer took to cornering Jerrol, asking about the grand duke and conditions in Retarfu. Jerrol answered all he could and trying to distract her suggested she talk to Taurillion. He dropped subtle hints that Taurillion was an expert on ancient history and knew quite a lot about Lady Marguerite, but that backfired when she returned with even more questions about Sentinals and Guardians.

He was seated in the library, researching ancient palaces of Elothia, when her voice spoke behind him. "Since when has a captain in the Grand Duke's Chevron had three Sentinals reporting to him?"

Jerrol twisted in his seat, rose, and then smiled at her.

"Since the Lady Marguerite assigned them to me," he replied, deciding honesty was the best course of action in light of the determined expression on her face.

"Why would Marguerite assign them to you? Are you a Guardian?" she asked, her voice hushed.

Jerrol nodded. "Yes, in a way."

"There are no Sentinals in Elothia. I was talking to Yaserille, and she said there used to be many. She said that you woke them up from a long sleep."

"Yes, they are the Lady's Guards. Marguerite stirs; she has missed you. The Ascendants try to curb the Lady's influence. We are here to prevent that from happening," Jerrol said.

Guin'yyfer watched him, tilting her head to one side. "Some of your men have strange accents."

"Have they been bothering you, my lady?"

"No, not at all, they are exquisitely polite. I could only wish all of Randolf's men were so well mannered." She hesitated. "Who are you really, Captain?"

"I am what you see; just a man trying to do the Lady's work."

She tapped her lip, watching him. "I will find out," she warned.

Jerrol sighed. Once the grand duke arrived, it was unlikely that any pretence could be continued. "I don't doubt it, my lady, but for now, a captain I am."

The advanced guard arrived precisely a week later, warning of the grand duke's imminent arrival. Though Jerrol already knew. Two hours later, Captain Kerisk and the rest of his men led a stately carriage under the portcullis and into the central courtyard. The household staff waited on the steps, along with Jerrol, Lady Guin'yyfer, and a guard of honour.

The rest of Jerrol's men patrolled. Taurillion stood behind Jerrol's shoulder, watching and alert. Yaserille stood behind Lady Guin'yyfer's. Jerrol had assigned her as Guin'yyfer's bodyguard, and she had accepted the orders with delight.

Jerrol tensed as he watched Birlerion, Marianille, and Niallerion dismount, and then the grand duke emerged from his carriage and glanced up the steps. His eyes widened as he saw who stood before him, but he turned and held a hand out to help his companion descend. Guin'yyfer glanced at Jerrol as he inhaled sharply.

Taelia reached the ground and looked towards him with a brilliant smile on her face. Guin'yyfer nudged him, and he started. Taking Guin'yyfer's proffered hand, he led her towards the grand duke.

The grand duke smiled. "Ah Captain Finn and my Lady Guin'yyfer." He lay a slight emphasis on the pronoun, and Guin'yyfer stiffened.

"Your Grace, Scholar Taelia, welcome to the Summer Palace. I hope you find everything as you expected," Jerrol said smoothly. Guin'yyfer frowned at him. He couldn't quite disguise the shiver that made his hand tremble. She glanced between him, the grand duke, and the young woman holding the grand duke's hand.

"It is exactly as we were hoping," Randolf replied with a smile.

Guin'yyfer's frown deepened as if she sensed an under-current in his words.

"I think we ought to swap," Randolf said with aplomb, as Taelia's hand trembled in his.

"Of course, your Grace," Jerrol murmured, handing Guin'yyfer to him with a slight bow and grasping Taelia's hand in return. Guin'yyfer watched the young woman lean into the captain and the captain slide a discreet arm around her waist. He dropped his face to her hair and inhaled deeply.

Guin'yyfer looked at the grand duke in shock and was surprised to see a small smile playing about his lips. His smile broadened as he looked at her.

Randolf cleared his throat. " I think we ought to go in. Captain Finn, Scholar Taelia, please accompany us."

"Of course, Your Grace," Jerrol murmured. He nodded at Taurillion, and he smoothly stepped behind the grand duke's shoulder as Yaserille shadowed Guin'yyfer as they entered the palace. Jerrol paused as Owen approached. "Owen, welcome to the Summer Palace."

"Finn, what is going on?"

"I'll explain later. Landis here will show you the ropes; I need to attend the grand duke."

"How did you find Guin'yyfer, is she alright? And my mother?"

"They are both fine. Later, Owen. I'll find you later," Jerrol promised hastily as he led Taelia inside, jerking his head at Birlerion to follow.

The grand duke eyed his shadow with concern but led the way to the receiving chamber on the ground floor. Here, he turned and waited until the door had closed behind them. He raised an eyebrow as Birlerion slid behind Jerrol.

Birlerion flushed. "My apologies, Your Grace. It just seemed the right thing to do," he murmured.

Jerrol inspected Birlerion's face, and his lips pinched at the blue eyes. "It's where you're supposed to be, Birlerion. I know it doesn't make sense at the moment, but I'll explain everything, later. I promise. Just stay with me."

"Commander Haven, I think it is time you reclaimed your wife and returned to your interrupted life as a Vespirian Ambassador."

"With pleasure, Your Grace," Jerrol murmured as he tightened his grip on Taelia.

"In that case, my dear Lady Guin'yyfer, may I introduce Commander Jerrol Haven, Ambassador to King Benedict of Vespiri and his wife, Scholar Taelia Haven. Scholar, Ambassador, Lady Guin'yyfer of Tierne."

"A pleasure to meet you, Lady Guin'yyfer," Taelia smiled, dropping a curtsy and holding out her hand. Jerrol guided it towards Guin'yyfer's.

"The pleasure is mine, Scholar Haven." Guin'yyfer glared at Jerrol. "I knew you weren't a captain! Why didn't you just tell me? And here are *more* Sentinals. Who are they?"

Taelia smiled happily "Oh, he *is* a Captain; the Lady's Captain. He just happens to be an Ambassador as well. And this is our very good friend Sentinal Birlerion, and his sister, Sentinal Marianille, and this is Sentinal Niallerion."

"Sentinal Birlerion saved my life. We are indebted to him." The grand duke looked at Jerrol. "As we are to you, Commander Haven, for saving Lady Guin'yyfer."

Jerrol bowed. "Behind you is Sentinal Taurillion and Sentinal Yaserille of Retarfu. They are of the Lady's Guard but loyal to the throne of Elothia. If you will have them, they will guard you with their lives," Jerrol said. "Marianille, Birlerion and Niallerion are of Vespers and loyal to King Benedict and the Lady's Captain. Birlerion has been much missed," he said as he gripped Birlerion's arm, trying to reassure his friend who was looking drawn and strained amidst the introductions of people he knew by different names.

"The Lady's Captain?" Guin'yyfer spoke sharply.

Jerrol grinned. "Yes, my lady."

"I think we have a lot to discuss. But first, I need to speak to the Ambassador and get a status report. Why don't you ladies go on ahead? We'll meet you upstairs shortly," the grand duke suggested.

"Of course," Lady Guin'yyfer smiled, her gaze holding Randolf's for a moment. "Taelia—may I call you Taelia? Let me show you to your room, and you can freshen up after your journey." She arched an eyebrow at Jerrol. "I'll request your things to be moved to the green suite. I believe you know where that is." She smiled wickedly and drew Taelia away, closely followed by Yaserille and Marianille.

The grand duke let out a sigh and rubbed his eyes. He gestured to the chairs. "Sit. Now tell me how you happen to be here and how you rescued Guin'yyfer. Where are the people who held her?"

Jerrol released Birlerion's arm, his chest still thrumming with a combination of concern and relief to have his friend back. He sat as directed, and Birlerion stood behind him. Niallerion stood by the door and watched the room. "Your Grace, when I realised that the Summer Guardian and the Lady Guin'yyfer were the same person, I knew she had to be here. There was no other reason why you had not removed south."

"But even before that, how did you end up in the Third Chevron of all places?"

Jerrol grinned. "I got conscripted. I was asleep in an inn someplace, and the next thing I knew, I was being marched into your army. At the time, I had no memory of who I was or where I was." Jerrol shrugged. "Apparently, I was in a bit of a mess when they found me."

The grand duke winced. "And then?"

"I went through your training regime and met Birlerion, who was in a similar state. We were assigned to the Third Chevron, and I ended up at your palace as Captain Finn."

"All that in three months?"

"I'm afraid your recruits have much to be desired. I think your commanders were rather desperate."

"I think they were very fortunate," the grand duke said.

He looked at Birlerion. "And how did you end up in Adeeron?"

Birlerion eased his shoulders. "I don't know."

"You were defending me at the Watch Towers. Ain'uncer and Tor'asion dragged you with them when you wouldn't let them pass. We now know they took you to Adeeron. You've been missing for months, only we didn't know where they had taken you," Jerrol said.

"How did you become ... well," Randolf faltered, "as you are now."

"Let's just say that Tor'asion is an angry man and leave it at that," Birlerion said, his face darkening in memory.

After a slight pause, Randolf turned to Jerrol. "And when did you realise you weren't Captain Finn?"

"Just before the Ascendants chased me out of your palace, Your Grace."

"Yet you still came and rescued Lady Guin'yyfer?"

"I came to Elothia to stop the Ascendants' plans, whatever they were trying to do. Part of that was removing the hold they had over you. Truly, Your Grace, Vespiri has no desire to go to war with you. Your generals threaten the peace between our countries. It doesn't have to be that way."

"So I understand, and I apologise, Ambassador Haven, for your treatment whilst you have been in Elothia. I thank you for your continued assistance." The grand duke paused. "Who is actually guarding my palace right now?"

Jerrol laughed. "I am afraid you are being guarded by half a unit from Deepwater, Your Grace."

"Deepwater?"

"Yes, your Grace. I stumbled over them in the middle of a snowstorm. At the time, I had few resources. It seemed opportune that I found them, and they came with me here to rescue Lady Guin'yyfer."

The grand duke sighed. "It seems I have much to thank

King Benedict for when we finally meet. I think maybe you should hand over the guard to Captain Owen and regroup your men as the Ambassador's honour guard."

"Certainly, Your Grace. But I would suggest their time would be better spent supporting your guards to protect you and this palace."

"Very well. And what of the Ascendants who you said were holding Lady Guin'yyfer against her wishes?"

"One is in your dungeon awaiting your judgement. A man named Iss'aren; he used to be King Benedict's chancellor. If you don't want to pass judgement on him yourself, I can assure you, King Benedict will be very grateful if you hand him over. He would be a very good peace offering, I think. The other, a man called Pev'eril, is dead."

The grand duke stared at Jerrol. "A peace offering," he repeated in a voice of disbelief.

"I would recommend that you don't tell Tor'asion or Var'geris of his whereabouts if they are still attending you; they would probably kill him outright for his failings. They weren't too pleased with him."

"Ain'uncer is dead," Birlerion said, his voice cold. "That's one less to worry about."

Jerrol cast him a glance. "You must tell me how that happened, later," he murmured.

The grand duke bared his teeth. "They didn't seem to be enamoured with the idea of me coming here."

"Why *are* you here, Your Grace?"

"As you once so eloquently said: If I stop the strife on the borders and redirect the resources inland, that would solve both my problems. I need to get control of my army, and my generals are not responding to my orders."

Jerrol frowned in thought, he knew the Ascendants would be desperate to keep the generals focused on their warmongering. "I imagine that is where the Ascendants have gone, then; to try to and whip up the war."

Randolf sighed. "We'll talk more later. Sentinal Birlerion, I thank you for your care, but I think your Captain needs you more right now."

Birlerion nodded. "Yes, Your Grace."

The grand duke looked at Taurillion. "Welcome back, Sentinal Taurillion. I hope the Grand Duchy meets your expectations after all these years."

"You have a low bar to cross, Your Grace. Your ancestors left much to be desired," Taurillion said with a grin.

Randolf laughed. "That does not fill me with as much pleasure as I once would have said. Very well, let's join the ladies upstairs."

44

SUMMER PALACE

It was much later by the time Taelia and Jerrol managed to slip away to their rooms. They were exhausted with all the questions and happily shut the door on all their troubles. Jerrol finally turned to take Taelia in his arms. She shivered as he dipped his head into her neck.

"I've missed you," he whispered, his voice thick with emotion as he kissed her neck, her face, her lips. He shuddered as he took a deep breath, suddenly relaxing as if a convoluted knot of tension within him had unravelled.

"Not as much as I've missed you," Taelia whispered back, attacking his jacket buttons, wanting to get as close to him as she possibly could.

She raised her face in concern as she felt warm tears on her neck. "My love, we are together now," she said, smothering his face in kisses. But it was if a dam had broken within him, and he couldn't stop; his shoulders began to shake. Taelia led him to the bed, where she laid him down and drew him in close as she let him cry away his pain and despair.

It was much later when he spoke. "I'm sorry."

"Hush, there is nothing to be sorry for." She kissed him

as her fingers smoothed his unfamiliar beard. "You can only take so much. Sometimes, you need to cry it out."

"When I saw you descend from the carriage, I thought I was going to lose it. You looked so beautiful, so serene." His voice shook.

"I wasn't serene at all. Birlerion threatened to tell you that I had been flirting with the grand duke, if I didn't calm my excitement," Taelia admitted. She was relieved when he gave a watery chuckle in return. She levered herself above him and began studiously undoing his buttons. "What you need, my dearest husband, is for your wife to show you how much she loves you." She gently kissed his chest as she pushed his shirt apart. Smoothing her hands over his skin, she felt a tremor deep within him, and she slid her hands up his chest and over his shoulders, working his arms out of his sleeves. She dropped his shirt on the floor with his jacket. She pushed him back down as he reached for her.

"I said I was going to show you how much you are loved," she murmured.

"And you can, if you take your clothes off too," Jerrol whispered into her hair, and she smiled.

She shivered in delight as he kissed her ear and his warm breath caressed her skin. She allowed him to unbutton her dress, and she released him long enough to step out of it. She heard his sigh of pleasure, and she leaned into his hand as he trailed it across her chest and cupped her breast. The heat from his hand sent her southwards, kissing her way down his body as she smoothed his skin in a loving caress.

She kissed a newly found scar as she removed his trousers, continuously caressing as her lips explored him. Jerrol groaned as her touch became firmer, his body responding to every caress. His back arched as her lips and hands showed him how much she loved him until he could hold it no more. He shuddered his release as she soothed him, relieving him of his horrors and replacing them with her love.

He pulled her back up his body and cradled her in his arms. He kissed her eyes, her nose. His lips caressed her cheeks and chin, and then he found her lips and his tongue quested deeper, tasting her mouth, and as his kiss became more demanding, she gave herself up to the man who was determined to show her that he loved her as much as she loved him.

They lay in the shadows cast by the moon. Jerrol smoothed her skin, swirling his fingers around her belly button, watching his hand flicker from light to dark; soothed as her hand massaged his neck. He suddenly sat up and looked at her stomach. "Have you been eating too much fruit?" he asked, frowning at the gentle swell of her tummy.

"Only the fruit that you gave me, my love." Taelia smiled, secretively.

He rested his hand on her stomach and looked at her face. "You mean ...?" He paused in wonder, and before she could speak, his head dipped and gently kissed the soft mound.

He lay back down beside her and tucked her into his chest, twining his legs with hers. The fall of soft tears against her skin made her nestle closer, but this time, they were tears of happiness and wonder. She reached up to wipe his cheek and lovingly kissed the father of her child.

The grand duke observed Jerrol closely the next morning as they gathered for the morning meal. He looked like a different man, and not just because he was no longer wearing an Elothian uniform. He looked relaxed and very happy. Birlerion was different too, his face softer, not so severe. As if he was relieved to be back at his Captain's shoulder, even if he still didn't understand what had happened to him. Randolf hadn't realised how much strain these men had been under until it was removed.

He subtly observed the Sentinal, seeing how Birlerion shadowed Jerrol's every move. Jerrol had adapted to the change without comment. It looked like they had slipped back into a familiar routine as Birlerion responded to his slightest gesture and often pre-empted him. They were both very attentive to Scholar Taelia, and she was blooming under their care, Birlerion seamlessly including her in his sphere of protection.

Randolf eyed Taurillion discreetly and was surprised as Taurillion leaned forward. "Yes, Your Grace?"

"I was just wondering if you could be as attentive as Birlerion over there."

Taurillion smiled. "Birlerion has been protecting the Captain for some time. They are used to each other. Give us time, Your Grace, and we will be just as strong."

"Just as strong," Randolf murmured, suddenly hopeful as he turned to the beautiful woman sitting next to him. His table was full, and he smiled in pleasure to be surrounded by people who meant him no harm. He suddenly realised what it could be like to have a family.

After the meal, Guin'yyfer and Taelia retired to the library, discussing Lady Marguerite and the guardian's duties. Jerrol pulled Marianille aside and asked her to watch Taelia. He explained why.

She cast a bright eye at him. "Congratulations, Captain. Maybe it's time to look to your own family now."

Jerrol's heart clenched. "I wish I could," he said. "I wish we could go home and set up house like any other couple, but we're not finished yet." He sighed. "It's hardly begun." He turned away but paused as Marianille caught his arm.

"Captain, it will be well, you'll see."

Jerrol tried to smile and patted her hand. "Of course it will," he agreed. Marianille joined the ladies in the library, casting an informed eye over Taelia. She sat at the table and listened to them interrogating Yaserille on the history of the Summer Palace.

"You have the history in the books around you," Yaserille complained. "You don't need to ask me."

"But you lived it. You can tell us which bits are original and what has been added," Taelia retorted. "And anyway, I can't help with that, so tell us. Which is the oldest part of the Palace?"

Yaserille smiled. "I would have thought that was obvious; the temple, of course."

"There's a temple?" Taelia sat back in surprise.

"Yes, I'm surprised the Captain didn't tell you; it's off the courtyard."

Taelia considered. Jerrol had struggled to forsake the Lady. He would have avoided her temple at all costs; he would never have been able to resist her there. She knew he would openly speak of her if he had embraced her again, but he hadn't. Her heart ached for him. "Are his eyes silver?" she asked hesitantly.

"Yes, they changed when his memories returned."

"What is so important about his eyes?" Guin'yyfer asked, listening with interest.

Yaserille spoke quietly. "It's a side effect of swearing your Oath to the Lady. When she accepts you into her guard, your eyes turn silver. No one knows why, and the Lady never explained. We weren't concerned. It was like a badge of honour. We are proud to be of the Lady. When we were first awoken by the Captain, his eyes were silver. When we rescued him from the 'Drop', his eyes were grey and didn't change back to silver until his memories returned. He tried to tell us the Lady no longer rode his shoulder, that he wasn't the Captain anymore, he was the Oath Keeper. But he is the Captain," she finished, a touch of defiance in her voice.

Guin'yyfer gasped in surprise. "The Oath Keeper? He holds the Land's Oath as well as being the Lady's Captain?"

"He holds the King's Oath," Taelia corrected. "He is responsible for ensuring that the king protects the people of Remargaren, the Lady's Guardians protect the Land, and the Land sustains all. Thrice entwined, the Oath stands before us, and we need to help him keep it."

The library was silent, then Yaserille spoke. "We should start in the temple. Its foundations date back to the time of the Lady. If there is anything to be found, we'll find it there."

"Then that's where we need to go," Taelia said as she rose. The need to visit the temple grew stronger and Taelia let the feeling draw her out of the library. Taelia paused in surprise as they were about to descend the stairs, hearing a voice she recognised explaining the guard positions in the Summer Palace. She halted and swung towards his voice, pulling Guin'yyfer with her.

"Captain Landis?" she called. "Is that you?"

There was a short silence, and then Landis approached her. "Ah, Scholar Taelia, how nice to see you again. It's, ah, actually, I'm Lieutenant Landis, seconded to the Elothian Third Chevron."

"Seconded?" Taelia asked with a laugh. "I'm assuming this is something to do with Jerrol?"

"Yes, Scholar. He needed troops, and we were all he had."

"I see. I expect to hear the whole story later. You do realise that Captain Finn has retired and that Ambassador Haven has taken his place?"

"Yes, Scholar. But the grand duke's guard is a bit depleted, and the ambassador said we should bolster them, so to speak, seeing as we were already in situ."

"Well, I think the ambassador could have at least reinstated you as a captain," she said with a laugh, relieved that Jerrol hadn't been surrounded by strangers all these months.

Guin'yyfer suddenly stiffened beside her. "Owen? Is that you? What are you doing in a Chevron uniform?"

"Owen?" Taelia's head swung around. "Your brother? Owen, have you been with Jerrol all along?"

Owen frowned at his sister. "And why shouldn't I be in a Chevron?"

"Because you always said soldiering was for fools and you had better things to do," Guin'yyfer replied dryly. "How did they manage to snare you?"

"I joined at the same time as Finn," he said, glaring at his sister.

Yaserille gave a bark of laughter. "You mean you were conscripted."

Owen had the grace to blush, and Landis chuckled. "Well, he may have been conscripted, but he is the head of your security now, my lady. He was Captain Finn's second."

"So the grand duke needs to make you a captain, then, Lieutenant Owen?" Taelia suggested.

"He already did," Owen responded, rolling his eyes.

Taelia laughed as she heard the disgust in his voice. "Well, we will leave you to your work, gentlemen. We are off to visit the Lady's temple. Captain Landis, I truly am glad to know that you and your men are here."

"It's lieutenant, Scholar, just a lieutenant," Landis replied with a laugh.

"You know, it's probably good that we only have one captain," Guin'yyfer's voice faded as they walked down the corridor. "At least we know who we are talking about."

45

GRAND DUKE'S STUDY, SUMMER PALACE

Randolf paced in front of Jerrol in agitation. "Benedict has moved to Stoneford bringing reinforcements. A direct response to my army's posturing. I've lost control of my generals, and I don't know how to stop them."

"It's not completely their fault. The Ascendants have the power to control minds; they persuade people to do what they want. They use *Mentiserium*, and it is tough to resist without help." Jerrol looked at the worried man before him. "Who do you trust?"

Randolf looked at him. "You?"

Jerrol laughed and gave him a slight bow. "Thank you for your vote of confidence, Your Grace, but who else is amongst your trusted advisors? Who would you promote to general if you had to fill the position?"

"Apart from Captain Finn? He is sorely missed, you know." Randolf sighed as he frowned in thought. "I would bring Henrik out of retirement. My father trusted him completely, and he isn't that old."

"Good. Who else?"

"Maybe transfer the Interior Minister, Janssen. He is a good man and an excellent organiser."

"Do it then, Your Grace."

"But they're not going to believe me. The generals have done their warmongering well."

"You are the grand duke; explain your rationale. You received an ambassador from King Benedict, offering a peaceful resolution. Any sensible person would prefer that to war. And anyway, if they are as intelligent as you say, they will know that Benedict doesn't want Elothia."

"Why wouldn't he?"

Jerrol laughed as the grand duke took offence. "He doesn't have enough hours in the day to manage the countries he already has, let alone another. He was furious when I annexed Terolia for him."

"Why didn't he give it back then?"

"Because the Families asked him to honour the accords. They knew they were vulnerable and needed protection. They knew about the Oath."

"The Oath?"

"The King's Oath. He is bound by the Lady and the Land to protect his people. The Guardians complete the circle and protect Remargaren. The Lady gave us life, and her guardians to protect us. The Land offers us sustenance. The king provides the safety to live our lives." Jerrol smiled at the grand duke. "Randolf," he said. "You have Lady Guin'yyfer, Marguerite's Guardian. She is the link between your rule and the Land; embrace it, understand it. She will guide you well. Propagate the belief in your people and your country will thrive."

"But that won't stop the generals."

"Give your people the power to stop them, Your Grace. Position them above the generals. The generals need to be removed; they are lost, but the rest of your army isn't. A very wise man once said to me that we can't save everyone, but we should do our best to save the ones that we can."

The grand duke stared at him.

"Trust your instincts, Your Grace. Those you trust will have men and women they trust, your reach will grow, and they will enact your will. You will get your power back, and I am quite sure you won't let it go again."

"By the Lady, you are right. Thank you, Ambassador, for your wise advice."

"My pleasure, Your Grace." Jerrol bowed himself out of the grand duke's presence and, collecting Birlerion, led him to the library. He turned and waited for Birlerion to shut the door.

They stared at each other across the room, and Jerrol exhaled. "Birlerion, please forgive me. I never meant for any of this to happen."

"Captain, don't. You don't have to do this."

"Yes, I think I do. You are like a brother to me. You are family. I sometimes forget that I have a responsibility of care as much as you do. I should take more care of you. What you have been through, are still going through, is because of me. You don't remember me, or what happened to us, yet you act as if I am your Captain. I don't deserve that."

Birlerion sighed and moving away from the door, he spread his hands. "I'm sure Leyandrii had a good reason for all that happened." He smiled grimly. "I know she never intended us to suffer what we did, but she can't control everything, much as she would like to." He cleared his throat. "I believe this is yours," he said, beginning to unbuckle his sword belt.

Jerrol grinned and stayed his hand. "I keep losing it. I think you will look after it better than I," he said. "I think you may make better use of it."

Birlerion shook his head, unsheathed and handed the

sword to Jerrol. As Jerrol gripped the hilt, a flash of blue light shot down the blade and Birlerion shuddered. He jerked back, releasing the sword and staggered as his memories cascaded into his brain. He gasped for breath as he tried to assimilate them.

Jerrol leapt to catch him, cushioning Birlerion's head as he collapsed to the floor. His eyes rolled back in his head. Embracing his friend, Jerrol beseeched the Lady to help her faithful Sentinal. Birlerion had already suffered enough, he didn't need to lose his family and friends a second time.

As Birlerion's eyelids fluttered, Jerrol prayed he would wake in full possession of his memories and able to accept all that had happened. He would not be surprised if Birlerion struggled. Awakening to the knowledge that his family had died three thousand years before was going to be a painful memory.

Molten silver eyes stared up at him, swirling with a moonlit glow before they settled, and a fleeting expression of anguish and loss was replaced by resigned acceptance.

"I'm so sorry," Jerrol whispered as he rocked Birlerion in his arms. His own intense experience of regaining his memories overwhelming him.

Birlerion cleared his throat. "None of it was your fault," he said and sat up out of Jerrol's embrace. He rested his head in his hands for a moment.

Jerrol rose, observing him in concern. He had no idea how Birlerion would react. "Do you remember being a Sentinal?"

Birlerion twisted his lips. "I remember everything. It's giving me a headache."

"I'm sorry," Jerrol said again.

"For what? You woke me. I should be thanking you."

Jerrol gaped at him. "How do you feel? It's a bit of a shock I know." He hesitated and then said, "I'm so sorry,

Birlerion. If I listened to you, we wouldn't get into so many scrapes that you have to get us out of."

"That's what I'm here for. I would prefer to be awake. To be living, experiencing every moment instead of sleeping the centuries away." Birlerion winced. "Well, maybe not every moment."

Running his hands through his hair, Jerrol began pacing across the room. "I'm so used to everyone expecting me to have the answer, to know everything, to be the one making the decisions that I don't always pay attention when I should."

Regaining his feet, Birlerion sat in the nearest chair. He closed his eyes for a moment and then opened them again as he said, "You can't change that, Jerrol. You are the Captain and you must make decisions. You can't falter, I know that. I also know that you will listen in the end. You are not Guerlaire, thank the Lady, who would never listen to anyone. You don't need to change, and I know you will listen to me when it matters."

"But it was my fault you ended up in Adeeron, and I know there is much more that happened there than you are saying. I saw you there, remember? I saw what they did to you, your injuries." Jerrol stopped, his throat thick with emotion.

Birlerion rose and gripped his arm. "It's over, forgotten. We survived. We move on."

"It's not. I'm sorry Birlerion, it is not in me to leave my men to fight my battles. It was my fault; my error thinking that we could cope without guards. I am to blame."

Birlerion's grip on his arms tightened. "It's not your fault. You're not to blame for any of this, not Terolia, not Adeeron, not now. If anything, *I* failed *you*. Look what they did to you."

Jerrol shifted restlessly. "I put you in that position. You were against impossible odds."

"We didn't know, Jerrol."

"We should have known."

"Yes, we should have known. We learn from our mistakes. I followed *you*. I didn't think that the Ascendants would have taken over the rangers. It is not your fault. You can't take the blame for everything. You're overreacting, Jerrol."

"I know. But I should have listened to you about Torsion. You were right."

"You knew him for a long time; you trusted him. He hid it well."

"He was my mentor. He shaped most of my life. With what I now know, I'm amazed I turned out so well. Even from the beginning, he was twisting everything." Jerrol broke away and sat down, clenching his fingers in his hair.

He exhaled and looked up. "When I was a kid, I killed a man," Jerrol said, his voice low. "He was attacking Taelia. I was just trying to protect her; I didn't mean to kill him. I was trying to stop him." He faltered and then continued. "The man I killed was her father. Torsion joked about it, you know, said I was a cold-blooded killer, starting young, that I had taken her family from her. I was only a kid."

Jerrol paused. "It made me want to learn how to fight so that I would know how *not* to kill a man. Instead, I learnt how to kill in more ways than I can say." Jerrol's voice was devoid of emotion as he continued. "And now I am in a position where I could put even more men and women in harm's way. And I do. I put you in harm's way; you could have died, Birlerion."

"But I didn't."

There was a moment of silence, and Jerrol closed his eyes. It was broken as Birlerion stirred. "I killed my father," he said, moving away and staring blindly out the window.

"What?" Jerrol's eyes flew open as he hastily suppressed

his gasp. The dull light entering through the window leached the colour from Birlerion's skin. He stood as still as one of Randolf's marble statues in the halls below them, barely breathing.

"At Adeeron, it brought it all back. I thought I was back in that time. I remember it as if it was yesterday. My mother died when I was a kid; six or seven, I think. My father took to the bottle, his way of dealing with it, I guess, but he was a vicious drunk, so I ran away. Lived on the streets," Birlerion said as if it meant nothing, "until Guerlaire found me and sponsored me into the cadets."

Jerrol made a soft sound of encouragement just to let Birlerion know he was listening. Birlerion shifted uncomfortably. "I was just skin and bone when I arrived at the garrison. They tried to feed me up. Of course, I just threw it all back up again, not used to it. I'd never seen so much food all at once," he said with a slight smile; the smile faded. "Serill said I hadn't been living on the streets; I was dying on the streets. He was right, of course." Birlerion's face was stark with memories.

"There was a faction led by a man called Clary, Dominant Clary, that believed only those with ancient lineage, those with family names should be in the cadets. He always said I wasn't good enough, no respected family, a gutter rat. My existence seemed to annoy him. The fact that Leyandrii supported me galled him even more, he couldn't stand it. They tried to get Serill expelled; me, they just tried to kill, even after Warren and Melis formally adopted me into their family." His face softened. "To have a family that loves you is a blessing."

"So Tagerill and Marianille are truly your family," Jerrol murmured, enlightened.

Birlerion smiled. "His parents said they adopted me from the first moment they saw me. They always said I was the making of Tage." He laughed, flushing. Jerrol was glad to see some colour return to his face. The scar bisecting his eyebrow stood out, and Jerrol remembered the ugly wound when he had first seen him at Adeeron.

"But it wasn't enough. I was seen as worthless by those who thought they knew better. I got in their way. The Lady accepted me, and that wasn't right." He took a deeper breath. "They paid my father to waylay me. He tried to kill me with my own sword. He stabbed me with it whilst they held me down. For money." His voice was deathly quiet, and Jerrol strained to hear him. "I killed him instead. I thought that made me a cold-blooded killer. Good for nothing. No one would want to know me." His voice trailed off into silence; his shoulders were stiff, his back rigid. Jerrol saw the gleam of tears in his eyes.

"But you defended yourself; you had no choice," Jerrol said, desperate to ease the anguish in his friend's face. He flexed his aching fingers. He had unconsciously clenched them into a fist.

Birlerion turned towards him, his eyes bright. "As did you. You were but a child, defending an innocent girl. You did what you had to do. You protected someone who couldn't protect themselves. It doesn't make you a cold-blooded killer. It makes you someone prepared to put another's safety before your own, a Lady's guard, a Sentinal."

Jerrol stared at him for a moment in silence. "It's a hard lesson to learn," he said, eventually.

"I know," Birlerion replied, turning back to the window.

He stiffened when Jerrol gripped his shoulder. "Thank you," Jerrol said, turning Birlerion towards him and gripping his other shoulder. "Maybe we can help each other remember that we are not to blame." He gave Birlerion a little shake. "I promise I'll listen. I'll take more care."

Birlerion's lips twitched. "Just help me keep you alive. That will be enough," he said, his voice gruff.

Jerrol embraced him, and Birlerion hugged him back. "Thank you," Jerrol said as he released him, his colour a little heightened. He offered his sword to Birlerion. "Keep it safe. You'll make better use of it than I will."

Birlerion silently accepted it and Jerrol wasn't surprised when the sword began to glow in his hands. Birlerion stood staring at the sword and a flicker of blue silhouetted him for a moment and he relaxed as it sank into him, smiling as he accepted the Lady's blessing.

Throat tightening, Jerrol watched. It felt like an intrusion, but Jerrol couldn't tear his gaze away. The raw emotion on Birlerion's face as the Lady embraced him, tore at his heart. The pain Birlerion had suffered, deprived of the Lady's love because of him. Jerrol wasn't sure he would have coped as well as Birlerion had.

Clearing his throat and hesitant to interrupt the moment, Jerrol said, "We'll be here for a few days. Take some time, spend it with Marianille. You're due it. You're due so much more."

Birlerion shook his head. "You need me."

"Yes, I will need you. It will get worse before it gets better, so, Birlerion, don't make me order you. Take the time you can get. We will all need to be at our very best."

Birlerion stared at Jerrol before nodding. "You may be right," he said quietly, before sheathing the sword and turning to look out the window as Jerrol left.

46

LADY'S TEMPLE, SUMMER PALACE

J errol went in search of his wife. He traced her to the Lady's temple and taking a deep breath, entered the vaulted chamber. He sighed as he felt nothing. The Lady wasn't here. He had a feeling, or at least he hoped, she was still with Birlerion. Dust motes swirled in the beam of light slanted across the small nave as he crossed in front of the altar decorated with white lilies; the gentle perfume permeated the air and eased his spirit. He followed the muffled sound of voices coming from a far corner.

Stone spiral steps led down. He paused on the steps as Taelia's voice floated up to him.

"I'll tell him tomorrow."

"No, Taelia, you have to tell him now; if you don't, I will." Yaserille's voice was determined.

"Can't we have one more day? He's so happy, finally relaxed. We've had so little time together."

"Taelia, you can't keep something of this magnitude from him."

Guin'yyfer's voice interrupted them. "But how do you know it refers to Jerrol?"

Jerrol spoke above them. "Keep what from me?" His

heart clenched as Taelia flinched and Yaserille and Guin'yyfer melted away after one look at his face.

"Sweetheart, keep what from me? You know you can tell me anything." Jerrol descended the remaining steps as Yaserille dragged Marianille up the stairs and out of earshot. He grasped Taelia's hands and pulled her into his arms.

"It's not fair; why does it always have to be you?" Taelia's voice was muffled as she pressed her face into his chest.

"Because we wouldn't trust anyone else. I remember you once telling me that sometimes we don't have a choice; no matter how we try to change it, we will end up where we are supposed to be anyway," Jerrol said.

"I know, but I don't want to let you go. You only just came back," Taelia said, tears welling in her eyes.

"But I am meant to be held in your arms, my love. You know I'll always come back to you. Come, show me what you found."

"I was drawn to the temple. By the Lady I think. She wanted me to find this for you. I wish I had ignored her," Taelia said, screwing her face up in an attempt not to cry.

Jerrol hugged her. "You know you don't mean that. The Lady is being busy. Birlerion's memories just returned…"

"Oh, I am so glad," Taelia exclaimed, interrupting him. "Is he alright?"

"… and I left her reassuring him. Now she's showing you what I need to do next. Hopefully, how to stop a war," he said, kneeling before the section of wall Taelia indicated.

"Guin'yyfer, what's the matter?" Randolf was surprised to find Guin'yyfer seated on the steps outside the temple, Yaserille standing beside her. Marianille hovered at the door to the temple, glancing inside frequently.

"It's so unfair."

"What is?

"We found an engraving in the Lady's temple. It foretells what is to come."

Randolf lifted Guin'yyfer off the floor and led her up to his study. He sat her in a chair and crouched beside her with a growing sense of foreboding. "Tell me," he said.

She began quoting, her voice low and clear,

> 'Keep the compact, the shroud to tame
> 'til dominant fist doth snuff the flame.
> Suffer thy plight the marke to surveye
> 'neath yonder stars cleave ye may.
> Keep thy course as stillness creeps
> Bide thy time lest maidens weep.
> Await the watch and make the leap
> Her sacrifice will heal the breach.'

Randolf scowled. "What? What does that mean? If this is about you at all, I will not allow it. Darling, I won't let them take you."

"I-it's not me; the keeper of the compact is Commander Haven. He has been touched by the Lady; he is the Lady's Captain, and he holds the Oath. He is the keeper of the promise."

"What? No, he can't be."

"He is. Taelia is telling him now down in the Lady's Temple. She didn't want to tell him, but he overheard us talking."

"But what does it mean?"

"I'm not sure about all of it, but Taelia says there will be a final confrontation. The Ascendants are trying to bring their ancestors back from beyond the Veil. The only way they can do that is if they force Jerrol to split the Veil; he has to submit to the Ascendants power and tear the Veil in order to find the location of the final meeting. Until now he has resisted their demands, but I fear for him. That's how he lost his fingers, the Ascendant Var'geris, your advisor," she said bitterly, "tortured him by cutting them off, trying to get him to tear the Veil. They tried to kill Taelia, using her to force him to breach it."

Randolf gasped and said, "You mean he is supposed to tear the Veil?"

"I don't know."

"But," Randolf spluttered, "he never said anything about the Ascendants threat."

"Would you have believed him if he had?"

"Maybe not at first, and then I suppose, it would have made no difference," Randolf admitted. "But wait, if he has withstood all they've tried to do, why would the Lady sacrifice him now? It doesn't make sense."

"The Veil is voracious; it will eat you alive," Jerrol's voice was conversational, absent of emotion, and Randolf raised his head. Jerrol was alone, and Randolf wondered where Taelia was.

"It seems the Lady has given me my marching orders and it's time to return to the fray." He smiled, though Randolf couldn't see why.

"Those words are ancient. How can you truly know what they mean?" Randolf protested. "You can't meekly give yourself up to them, not after everything that's happened. The Lady won't betray her Captain."

Jerrol shrugged. "She already has. She has forsaken me, and I can no longer reach her."

Guin'yyfer shivered at the lack of expression in his voice. "What can we do?"

"Look after Taelia for me. I can't take her with me in her condition. I would ask Roberion to take her home, but she won't go."

"Condition? What condition?"

"Randolf, keep up. Taelia and Jerrol are having a baby."

"They are? You are? Congratulations my friend." Randolf smiled with pleasure, though his smile faded as he realised this may not be the time. "How can we help you?"

"Keep doing what you are doing. Stop your generals or our people will die for nothing. The Ascendants will waste hundreds of lives trying to distract us. The final meeting is the key. We have to stop them from breaching the Veil or we will all be destroyed, and if it takes my body to protect my family, then that is what I will give."

Randolf stared at him in amazement. "What do you intend to do?"

Jerrol smiled grimly. "Well, first of all, I need to speak to the king; update him on the situation here, and then—well, it seems we need to plan a sacrifice."

Randolf gaped at him, horrified. "A sacrifice? You can't mean you? I won't allow it!"

"I don't think you can prevent it," Jerrol said with a twist of his lips.

"Then you'll take Taurillion with you. You're not going alone."

"You need him. I'll have Birlerion with me."

"Then take Yaserille. I mean it, Jerrol, we're all in this together."

Jerrol nodded slowly, warmed by the duke's words. "Very well."

47

SUMMER PALACE

Armed with Randolf's assurance that he would continue to work on his generals to halt their advance and stand down his troops, Jerrol prepared to leave for Stoneford. Randolf did not want to go to war with Vespiri any more than Benedict wanted to go to war with him. Jerrol needed to advise the king and attempt to avert the approaching tragedy.

Guin'yyfer had refused to remain at the palace and Randolf had finally agreed as long as she stayed back from the frontlines. Taelia would accompany Guin'yyfer, and they would help the healers prepare for the impending battle. They all knew Randolf was unlikely to succeed in pulling all his troops back in time to prevent hostilities.

Informing the Sentinals remaining in Elothia that he had created a new waystone outside the palace gates, Jerrol, Birlerion, Yaserille, and Niallerion discreetly used it to travel to Stoneford. The instant transition from one place to another via the waystone, one of the few remnants of ancient magic still to be found in Remargaren, was a convenience Jerrol was getting used to.

Jerrol had agreed with Landis that he and his men would

stay seconded to the duke. Marianille stayed with Taelia, giving Jerrol some reassurance that Taelia had protection that he could trust. Having made what preparations he could, Jerrol enfolded Taelia in his arms and breathed in her precious scent in case it was the last time.

He left Taelia wrapped in Guin'yyfer's arms. The memory of her brilliant turquoise eyes full of unshed tears haunted him as they made their way up to Stoneford Keep. Jerrol grimaced as he heard the faint shouts of the sentries as they passed word down of their arrival.

Lord Jason was waiting for Jerrol as they passed under the gate. "Jerrol, we had almost given up hope. I thought the sentries needed their eyes checked when word of your arrival came down and that Birlerion was with you. Where have you been? We've been so worried."

Jerrol closed his eyes as Jason engulfed him in a hug. For a moment, he felt safe, but then he had to open his eyes again.

"Birlerion, welcome. Where have you been? How did Jerrol find you? Where is Taelia?"

"Is the king still here?" Jerrol interrupted Jason's perplexed questions.

"Yes, yes, I suppose it will be easier to tell everything all at once. He has taken up residence in my study."

Jerrol laughed. "Poor Jason, you've lost your bolt hole."

"At least he didn't bring the whole court. I don't know where we would have put them all."

"This is Yaserille of Retarfu, and you know Niallerion," Jerrol introduced Yaserille as he followed Jason down the familiar corridors. It felt like coming home, and he relaxed in response. He tensed back up at the explosive greeting from the king.

"Jerrol! Thank the Lady. Where have you been? What news from Elothia? Their troops are massing north of

Lervik. Jason and I were just discussing placements. What happened with Randolf? Why did he say you died? Are you alright? We've had no news of you for months." He paused long enough to glare at Niallerion and then he saw Birlerion.

Jerrol held up his hands to fend off the torrent of questions. Fonorion grinned in sympathy and took the opportunity to give Birlerion a fierce hug.

"And you," the king continued as he glared at Birlerion, pausing trying to find a word strong enough without cursing. "We were concerned about you. Where is Scholar Taelia?" The king finally wound down. "Jerrol, where is your wife?"

Jerrol smiled. "My wife is under the care of the grand duke at the Summer Palace."

"What? Is he still holding her? Jerrol! What does he want?"

"To not go to war with you."

"Holding Taelia is not going to help with that."

"He isn't holding her; he is looking after her for me. I couldn't bring her through the waystone, so she stayed with him and Lady Guin'yyfer. I left Landis and his men guarding her."

"Lady Guin'yyfer? Landis? What is Landis doing in Elothia?" The king exhaled. "You've been missing for over four months, Jerrol, where have you been?"

Jerrol passed his hand over his face and cast his mind back to arriving in Elothia all those months ago. "I'm not sure what reports you received, but when we arrived in Elothia, we found out the old duke had died and his son had been in power for a few months."

"They had kept that quiet." Benedict murmured, not wanting to interrupt but unable to keep quiet.

"We didn't even get presented at court. My audience with the grand duke was just an opportunity for Tor'asion to pounce. He had inveigled his way into the young duke's confidence, and he and Var'geris have subverted all his generals."

"What?" Benedict jerked upright.

"As I said, the grand duke has no intention of going to war with us, but his generals have other ideas. The grand duke is currently trying to recall them. He will attempt to replace them and stand down his troops. Unfortunately, the Ascendants are going to be driving them to attack, but we have to delay engaging as long as possible to give Randolf time to regain control."

The king sighed. "We can't. Deepwater is already engaged, and we have to hold the line into Stoneford else they will just sweep behind us all the way to the towers."

"We still control the Watch Towers?"

Jason was quick to reassure him. "Yes, though they did try to take them. We managed to hold them off. It was fortunate you sent your Sentinals. Venterion realised what they were doing, so we were ready," he said with satisfaction.

"Where have you been?" the king asked again.

"I ended up being conscripted into the grand duke's army and taken to Adeeron, where I finally came out of their training program as a captain in the Third Chevron, and I was sent to Retarfu to guard the grand duke." Jerrol grinned at their shocked expressions. "Of course, one tiny problem; I had lost my memory and didn't know who I was."

The king inspected Jerrol more closely. "And how did you lose your memory?"

"Tor'asion packs a punch," he said.

Benedict was aghast. For Jerrol to be beaten so badly as to lose his memory ... he shuddered at the thought. "Do you need a healer now? Are you alright?" he asked in concern.

"I'm fine. My memory returned when I met Taelia after I returned to Retarfu."

"I imagine that was a shock for both of you."

"She knew. She had been waiting for me."

Benedict scowled at Birlerion. "And what about you?" he growled.

Birlerion smiled, his face bland. "The Ascendants took me to Adeeron. I was waiting for the Captain there." He ignored Jerrol's splutter.

Jerrol glared at Birlerion and then continued. "After that, when I had nearly gotten through to the duke, the Ascendants hounded me out of Retarfu again. By then though, I had found out that they were holding hostage the woman Randolf was pledged to marry, and she's a guardian to boot. Oh, and I awoke some Sentinals on our way. This is Yaserille." He indicated the distinctive Sentinal standing by the door, "and also Taurillion and Serenion. I stumbled over Landis during a snowstorm, and between us, we managed to rescue the guardian, Lady Guinyyfer. Randolf joined us at the Summer Palace and brought Taelia, Marianille, Niallerion and Birlerion with him."

"I get the feeling he's left a lot out," Benedict said his voice thoughtful as he observed Jerrol.

"That is a certainty," Jason agreed. "Why are you here now, Jerrol? What's happened?"

The king gave a bark of laughter. "You mean what else has happened? I assume you have returned Lady Guin'yyfer to the grand duke?"

"Yes, she is Lady Marguerite's Summer Guardian. She is connected to the land, and she is the conduit between the Grand Duchy and the Lady."

"So, part of the Ascendants plan is foiled and the grand duke is himself again. We now need to defeat the generals," the king said.

"If only it were that simple," Jerrol hesitated. "The Lady led Taelia to an inscription at the Summer Palace. The generals are not the end game. They are just a distraction. As

I said, they could be a very costly distraction if we are not careful. If it wasn't for the Watchers, I'd suggest we just keep falling back; delay them enough to make them think we mean it and let them have the towers. Save our people."

"We can't do that," Jason exclaimed

"Jerrol, you can't be serious!" the king said at the same time.

Jerrol closed his eyes briefly as the king's horrified voice override Jason's. He took a deep breath. "I said: 'If it wasn't for the Watchers'. It's the towers the Ascendants want. They aren't going to invade Vespiri. They won't need to if they manage to breach the Veil and bring their ancestors here."

"But if they have the towers, they'll breach the Veil."

"Not without me," Jerrol said. "We need to find the location of the Ascendants. I need to confront them."

"Absolutely not." King Benedict's response was immediate. "You just said they can't breach the Veil without you. We're not handing you over. You've had too many close calls."

"I don't think we have much choice."

"Of course we have a choice. As your king, I forbid it."

"We need them to tell us the final meeting place."

"Meeting place? That would be the Watch Towers, wouldn't it? That's why they are so eager to reach them!"

"No, I don't think so. They believe the Watchers may help them breach the Veil. That's why they want the towers. But the Lady is more thrifty. Sometimes, you just have to use the tools you have, and sometimes, no matter what you try, it will happen anyway," Jerrol said as he pulled a piece of paper out of his pocket. He stared down at it, and King Benedict watched him in concern.

"You said Taelia found something. Is that it?"

Jerrol unfolded the paper and handed it to the king. "Guin'yyfer wrote it out for me."

The king's face paled as his eyes moved down the paper. "This had better not mean what I think it means," he said slowly as he raised his eyes to Jerrol's. From the expression on his face Jerrol knew he could see that it did.

"What? What is it?" Jason's worried voice broke the extended silence. Benedict handed him the paper.

"I assume you believe this means you and that this is why you have to find the Ascendants?" Jason said after a quiet pause. "How does a Dominant fist snuffing a flame mean you? It could mean anything!"

"'Dominant' was the old term for Ascendants. And well, the flame," Jerrol opened his left hand and a soft glow filled the room.

"How long have you been able to do that?" the king asked.

"A while." Jerrol was non-committal as he closed his fist.

"But the only way to extinguish that would be to kill you …" Jason's voice faded away in shock.

"Maybe not. We need to know where they are going to perform their summoning. We need to find the marke, the place, and it seems I can only get to it by submitting to Tor'asion's fists." Jerrol shivered. "And the reference to yonder stars, I think is beyond the Veil, so I must breach it. Otherwise, why reference it? There's more …" He looked at the king.

"I don't understand," Jason said, the worry clear in his voice.

"I'm not sure I do either. The shroud is the Veil?" the king asked. Jerrol nodded. "You said once that the Veil sucks the life out of a person. Is that what it means? It will take your blood to heal it? But you said it was sealed; you sealed it when …" Benedict hesitated, "when you saved Saerille."

"The Veil is sealed," Fonorion confirmed, watching Jerrol

with an expression of horror on his face. "Why would you deliberately breach it?"

"To save our people and to stop them bringing their ancestors here."

"You're not making sense, Jerrol. If you tear the Veil, they will be able to bring them here. Surely we just keep it sealed."

"The only way to finish this once and for all, and remove this Ascendant threat, is to get their ancestors to cross the Veil so we can destroy them, and that will only happen if I breach it for them." The room was silent as they all digested his words. "It will happen. The words were carved into the wall of the Lady's temple at the Summer Palace. Don't you think I wish it were otherwise?"

Birlerion gripped Jerrol's shoulder at the harshness of his voice. Jerrol ignored him. "The only thing I can do is at least try to do it on my terms, and then maybe …" his words were muffled as he covered his face with hands, "just maybe, I'll have a chance."

No one spoke as they stared at Jerrol's bowed shoulders; there was nothing to say.

48

ELOTHIAN FRONT

Tor'asion watched as another unit of men marched passed, followed by a rumbling wagon loaded with tools and canvas: materials for the command post being built a safe distance from the battlefield. The troops were gathering for a major assault across the plains north of Stoneford. They would flank the Vespirian units and draw them away from the Watch Towers. Tor'asion was prepared to throw all the grand duke's men into this battle. If he couldn't capture Jerrol, then he had to get to the towers.

His face was stern and forbidding as he watched the men march though the compacted snow, their breath misting the air as they passed. It was their last chance and he would drive Elothia to war to grasp it. He looked around as a bluff, red-faced man puffed his way up to his side. He glared at the man, hoping to drive him away, but the general was immune to sharp glances and began speaking. "We'll all move up to command post two once the men have it in place, then we can see how the land lies. These maps you gave us said it was all open plains, but the plains butt up to that range of mountains. How are you expecting us to get around that? Stoneford lies directly in our path."

"Annihilate them," Tor'asion growled.

"What? No, it's Stoneford. They won't lie down for us. Lord Jason is a wily fox. They'll have traps and all sorts prepared for us. They must know we are coming. You can't move these many men and not be noticed."

"I don't care how you do it, General Kabil, just get me to the Watch Towers."

"I'm not sure this is the right way to go about it," Kabil said, nervously twitching his maps. "We'll lose too many men with a frontal assault."

Tor'asion gripped the man's arm, a tremor of annoyance rippling through him, and Kabil let out a nervous squeak. "You've been paid handsomely for your services. I'm trusting you to make good on your word. Don't make me change my mind. I'm sure your adjutant will be more than happy to take your place. Your choice, General. Selvia said you would do it. Don't return without good news." Tor'asion released the man's arm and turned away as his brother approached. He tried to control his temper. Why couldn't the idiot just do as he was told? Controlling the spurt of anger, he raised an eyebrow as Var'geris halted beside him. Var'geris looked pleased with himself. His grin an unusual expression on his normally intense face.

"Haven's been seen on the borders. He returned to Stoneford as you said he would." Var'geris' grin widened with relief, his black eyes bright with anticipation. "How do we draw him out?"

"We don't, you go and get him. I'll meet you at the ruins." Tor'asion cracked his knuckles. "I'll be ready for him; he won't escape this time."

49

STONEFORD KEEP, VESPIRI

Jerrol paced liked a caged animal. He knew time was running out, and he didn't know how to divert the tragedy that was about to happen. News from Deepwater was not good. Units of the second Chevron had already forced them back to their first holding position. This ripple of news along the front line had Stoneford's commanders and the Sentinals out rallying the men and reinforcing their west flank. The king had split Nikols' men between the two watches, reserves standing at the ready. Jason had them reposition in case the Elothians managed to break through the lines.

Saerille and Adilion were prominent, as was Royerion, who had appeared through the waystone earlier, pale-faced but determined. Niallerion was busy concocting some surprises with an enterprising corporal he had found in the keep. They were now distributing the results of their endeavours with very clear instructions on how to use them, piling the strange objects behind the network of earth mounds where the archers were positioned.

Jerrol had Birlerion create a waystone on the ridge above the plain, hoping it was far enough from the front that it wouldn't be overrun, but it was the only way the king was prepared to wait at Stoneford, though Jerrol knew he wouldn't stay there.

Jason strode through the ranks and nodded at Jerrol. "Well?"

"I'll walk the line once more and then I'll report back to the king."

Jason gripped his arm before he returning to his command tent, Chryllion close behind him.

Jerrol was halfway down the line when the Elothians began their charge. He grabbed a young soldier. "Private, report back to Lord Jason, the third unit is engaged, line holding, go!" He swung round, expecting Birlerion to be at his shoulder. He cursed as his faithful Sentinal was obeying his orders and keeping out of sight.

"Your weakness, Haven, has always been the people around you. You worry what happens to them." Jerrol turned as he heard Var'geris' voice behind him.

"Some would say that was a strength," Jerrol replied as he drew his sword.

Var'geris laughed. "How can it be a strength when it fails you every time?"

"It hasn't failed me. It has failed you."

Var'geris scowled. "I have succeeded where others failed; after all, I have the Captain. You will do as I command."

"Oh?" Jerrol smiled grimly and struck.

The clash of their swords startled the men in front of them. They paused to stare before returning to their own fights.

Var'geris broke away and glared at Jerrol. "You will not win. I will kill you first."

"You could try," Jerrol replied, watching him carefully. "You are finished, Var'geris. No great leader is coming. The Ascendants are no more; your cause is lost."

"Never," he hissed, his eyes flashing with anger.

Jerrol shrugged calmly and advanced on Var'geris. "Your numbers dwindle; I heard Ain'uncer is dead."

Var'geris stumbled back. "That Sentinal; I should have killed him."

"You missed your opportunity," Jerrol said with a vicious grin as he forced Var'geris to give ground.

"I won't the next time," Var'geris said, recovering and jerkily blocking Jerrol's thrust.

"What makes you think you'll get a next time?" Jerrol asked, flicking the tip of his sword across Var'geris' face.

Var'geris hissed as he touched the cut with his fingers. "It makes no difference; I'll end your life before the end of the day."

Jerrol nodded solemnly. "You can try. What made you want to destroy all that is good in the world? What was it? A desire for power? Money? Or is it adulation that your heart desires?"

Yaserille lifted her head. What was the Captain doing? She frantically looked around for Birlerion. She caught his eye, and he slithered around the ditch towards her. "Birlerion, are you hearing this?"

"Don't interrupt them; it must happen. We can't stop it."

"But why?"

She felt his shrug in the gloom. "You know why. Var'geris has to take Jerrol. It's the only way we can find out the final meeting place. We're hoping Jerrol can get him to reveal the Ascendant's location before they go."

The blood drained from Yaserille's face. "Hoping?" she squeaked.

"Hush, listen."

"So, you found the seat; did it salve your conscience? You failed at the Watch Towers, didn't you?" Jerrol asked.

"Our ancestors will step over the threshold, and you will

all bow before our leader's overwhelming presence. You will become his first disciple, you ..."

"Surely not," Jerrol interrupted him, lazily swinging his sword. "Aren't you the first disciple? After all, you have given up everything for him. Aren't you expecting him to sweep you up into his arms and pat you on the head as soon as he arrives?"

Var'geris paled, rigid with anger. "I will be his high priest, ready to escort him to his rightful throne at Oprimere. The Tower of Teranna will call him, and you will do the calling. You will be his first sacrifice."

"Oh? So not his disciple, after all. You disappoint me."

Var'geris hissed at Jerrol. "You will regret your arrogance. You will plead for mercy, plead for the honour of serving him." He charged Jerrol, wrapping his arms around him as he drove him to the ground. He swirled his cloak, and they were gone.

Yaserille rose in horror. "Oprimere? That is a myth; the long-lost cathedral to the Lady's Mother. The location was lost when it was decimated in a land shift. It was lost thousands of years before the Lady broke the stone; no one knows where it is."

"What about the Tower of Teranna? Is it a Watch Tower?" Birlerion asked.

Yaserille frowned off into the distance. "I know the name, but it too was destroyed. It used to mirror the towers at Velmouth. It is not far from there, though I don't know the exact location."

"The grand duke might know. Come on, we need to get back. We need to speak to him."

"What about all this?" Yaserille cast her hand around the battlefield.

Birlerion smiled sadly. "They'll still be fighting when we come back."

Summer Palace, Elothia

Birlerion and Yaserille stepped out of the waystone at the Summer Palace. They hustled the guards to open the gate and rushed into a confusion of people preparing to leave. "The grand duke? Where is he?" Birlerion demanded.

"His study of course." The footman stared after the Sentinals as they ran down the corridor towards the stairwell.

"Birlerion," Landis caught his arm. "Status report, quick." He kept pace with the tall Sentinal as Birlerion briefed him, and the captain let him go. He started issuing instructions, sending his men running.

Yaserille reached the study door first and paused long enough to rap on it, before opening it anyway. The grand duke looked up from his desk in surprise, and then he was on his feet. "You have news? What happened?"

"We need to find the location of the Tower of Teranna," Birlerion gasped out, hurrying in behind Yaserille.

The grand duke snapped his fingers. "Go fetch Lady Guin'yyfer; she is in the library," he ordered, and a young page shot out the door.

Taurillion stepped around the grand duke. "Where is Jerrol?"

"The Ascendants have him; they have taken him to Teranna. We have to find him," Birlerion replied.

"Teranna? That's the Mother's tower. But it's been lost for centuries," Taurillion said.

"As has Oprimere; that was the location of the Mother's cathedral, destroyed long before the Lady sundered the stone." Yaserille started searching the duke's shelves before pulling down a rolled-up parchment. She discarded it and pulled down another.

Lady Guin'yyfer entered the study. "Oprimere will not be

on any map," she said. "It is a far deeper memory than any we will have recorded here."

Yaserille reached for more scrolls. "We need to find Oprimere. That's where the Ascendants will take him." Yaserille stopped tugging scrolls off the shelves and frowned at Birlerion as Guin'yyfer's words registered. "Birlerion, that time you came up here, what were you searching for? Marguerite had to pry you off the frozen ground. What did you see? You never said."

"The Land; he shared many images," Birlerion said slowly. "He was trying to persuade me to stay."

"The Land?" Yaserille asked as she gripped his arm. "The Land tried to coax you to stay? You mean the Land wanted you to take over from him? Not Marguerite? What did he show you?"

Flicking a glance at Taurillion, Birlerion chose his words carefully. Taurillion had never fully forgiven him for not sacrificing himself in Marguerite's place. Taurillion had tried to persuade Marguerite not to bond with the Land, but she had felt it was her duty. "Leyandrii forbid it. She said my purpose lay elsewhere. But he showed me the wonders of Remargaren." Birlerion fell silent as he trawled through his memories, so fresh and clear in his mind being so newly returned.

Birlerion froze. A shudder passed through him and Guin'yyfer steadied him. Yaserille reached for Birlerion and in turn stiffened. Flanked by a guardian and a Sentinal, Birlerion's eyes widened as he retrieved his deepest memories. "Teranna lies due north of Velmouth," he said, his voice vibrating with power. "Its position will mirror that of the Watch Towers. High above a lake, surrounded by pine trees." Birlerion lurched, steadying himself against the table as he inhaled.

Yaserille pulled a map of Elothia closer. "Here, Birlerion, show us where."

Randolf opened his mouth to protest that he couldn't, when Birlerion placed his finger on the map. "Jerrol is there."

Yaserille peered closer and then nodded. "We'll find him," she promised before turning to leave. Birlerion on her heels.

"I'll take you, Birlerion," Zin'talia said. *"Ride me."*

Birlerion nearly tripped over his over feet. *"How can you speak to me? How did you know?"*

"You've been open to me ever since your memories returned. I've been able to hear you since Terolia. You always seemed hesitant so I didn't like to intrude, and I understand why now, but Jerrol needs me, please take me with you."

"Of course."

"Birlerion," Randolf's voice halted him. "We are leaving for the Chevron encampment. I fear I am needed to curtail my general's activities. You will find us there."

Birlerion held the grand duke's eyes and then nodded. He and Yaserille left. The grand duke stood beside Guin'yyfer and looked down at the map. A line of faint arrows divided Vespiri from Elothia; the Stanton mountains. They stopped just short of Stoneford, curving protectively around Velmouth and the Watch Towers. He shuddered as he envisioned the rampage his men would be on if they forced their way through Stoneford; not a man or woman would be left standing.

He looked up as Landis appeared at the door.

"The Chevrons have engaged at Deepwater, it's started." Landis reported, his face pale. "They have begun advancing across the plains towards Mendel."

Randolf blanched. "The fools, what are they doing? Get

us moving. We'll head for Lervik first, pull back the troops where we can before we head east."

Landis nodded. "We're ready to leave, Your Grace."

Tower of Teranna, Elothia

Jerrol watched the sun set behind the jagged mountains ranges which edged the plains of Oprimere. *Such a beautiful view*, he thought as Tor'asion coldly circled him. Such fragile beauty in the world yet men like Tor'asion didn't even see it. Stiffening in the grip of two large Elothian guards, Jerrol tried to prepare himself for Tor'asion's fury. It simmered behind his eyes, in the corded lines of his neck, the rigid shoulders. Could he survive a second beating? He wasn't sure and he repressed the shiver of fear that coursed through him.

Trying to bolster his wavering courage, he reminded himself he had saved the king and destroyed their hold on the Watches, and in Terolia, he had protected the Families and revealed their plans. Now in Elothia, he had undermined their influence on the grand duke and the chevrons. He had managed to capture or kill five of their brothers. Only three of them were left; would they still be able to open the way for their ancestors? They obviously thought so, though they needed him. They couldn't kill him until he tore the Veil for them.

Tor'asion unleashed a ferocious punch and Jerrol folded like a burst paper bag, pain engulfed him as he desperately gasped for air, groaning into his knees as he heaved.

Concentrating on his breathing, Jerrol sagged in the guard's grip until Tor'asion gripped his hair and raised his face. Jerrol staggered under the blow, his vision faded as darkness consumed him. As he came to, Tor'asion's voice was battering him, demanding he do something, but he couldn't make sense of it. His head lolled, and the guards strained to hold him up.

"We don't have time for this, Tor'asion. I've told you before." Var'geris' voice faded in and out as Jerrol tried to concentrate. "You need to go and prepare. I have a better way to persuade him to do what is needed."

Jerrol sagged between the guards, his head buzzing, his body aching. Tor'asion would douse the flame; he would kill him. He knew it. Having suffered Tor'asion's fists, he wondered how Birlerion had survived. He tensed. Birlerion had survived and so would he.

He peered at Var'geris through sore eyes; the tone of Var'geris' voice made his skin prickle, and Taelia's gasp had him struggling against the guards' hold. His heart raced as panic bubbled up. Where had he found her? She should have been safe with Randolf and Marianille.

"Let her go," Jerrol said, trying to keep his voice calm. Flickering anger burnt his fingertips. He flexed his hands, and the guards tightened their grip.

"The people around you aren't a weakness? I thought we could test your theory," Var'geris said, cinching his grip around Taelia's neck. Var'geris' knuckles whitened, but Taelia didn't flinch as she stared blindly at Jerrol. "Go, Tor'asion. I will follow when we have what we need."

Tor'asion shifted restlessly, observing Jerrol's reaction. His gaze lingered on Taelia, and then he said, "Don't fail, Var'geris, you know what's at stake." He took a step and swirled his cloak, and he was gone.

Jerrol inhaled, steadying his breathing as he flicked a glance around him; the stone ruins of the Tower of Teranna stood behind Var'geris. It was eerily similar in construction to the Watch Towers above Velmouth. Narrow arched windows were cut into the stone at odd places around the shattered tower.

They were on a small plateau overlooking a steep valley that led down between a gorge, spindly trees and bushes clinging to the limestone cliff faces, dark shadows hiding clefts and hollows. A small lake gleamed below them through the broad-leafed trees that skirted the plateau, flashes of dancing sunlight reflecting off the surface.

It was a beautiful day.

He brought his gaze back to Var'geris, who hadn't moved.

"Var'geris. Look at yourself, see what you are doing." He cleared his throat as his voice wavered.

"I know what I'm doing. If she is your heart, then you'll do anything to save her, won't you?" He shifted his grip and Taelia teetered on her toes, her hands gripping Var'geris' arm.

Jerrol stilled as the gleam of a knife rested against Taelia's pale skin. The world fell silent, not a breath of wind; even the trees were still, waiting expectantly.

Var'geris shattered the silence as he burst into laughter, his broad shoulders shaking. The knife pressed deeper, lined with red. "Your face!" Var'geris laughed louder. "If you could only see yourself; such fear, such determination, such indecision. You must know the outcome today can only go one way. You know you will do what I say. Inside," his voice dropped, cold and serious, as he pointed the reddened knife towards the tower.

The guards pushed Jerrol towards the small wooden door at the base of the tower, and he reached for the black iron ring. It tingled under his hand, and the door opened smoothly. He was confronted by deep stone steps leading up in a spiral and downwards into shadow.

"Up," Var'geris commanded from behind him. "Wait here. Make sure no one disturbs us," he said to the guards as he followed with Taelia still in his grasp.

Jerrol rested his hand on the wall as he climbed the steep steps. Narrow windows relieved the darkness. His fingers trailing over the wall felt indentations and grooves; the wall was engraved. As he climbed, the words filled his mind.

Welcome to the Tower of Teranna. The Mother blesses you and all of Remargaren. Ask and you will receive.

Jerrol reached the end of the stairs and entered the room. There was no roof. It was open to the skies. He turned and watched Var'geris enter behind him, moving further into the room as he saw the blood running down Taelia's neck. He swallowed against the fear that coursed through him. The room was empty but for a chair in the corner and a coil of rope on the floor.

"Kneel," Var'geris commanded.

Jerrol knelt.

"What do you hope to achieve by this, Var'geris? No one needs to get hurt," Jerrol said as Var'geris came towards him. He struggled to stay still, his instincts driving him to launch himself at Var'geris' neck, but the knife was still biting into Taelia's throat, and he stayed where he was.

"Tie his arms behind him," Var'geris instructed Taelia, shifting the blade as he moved her behind Jerrol. Taelia's fingers trembled as she tugged Jerrol's arms behind him. Jerrol gripped her hand as Taelia struggled with the rope; her fingers were cold, so very cold.

Var'geris moved Taelia into Jerrol's view. Her expression was determined, her jaw firm as if she was gritting her teeth. She was trying to work her fingers under his arm but he tightened his grip and she hung on to him to keep her balance.

"Now what?"

"You *know* what. Shred the Veil," Var'geris said, his voice calm and reasonable.

"You know I can't."

"Not even to save her life?"

Jerrol eased his shoulders as his mind raced. Taelia had done her job too well. His heart rate rocketed as he fumbled the slender hair clip she had slipped into his palm and rotating it, he levered it open. Who would have known he would be the one in need, instead of her. He was just glad he had given her the hair clip in the first place. He began to saw at the rope.

"The Lady no longer sits at my shoulder," he said as he glanced up at the blue sky. The criss-cross of the grid tracing the air above him made his words a lie, and he began to sweat. "How did you find this place?"

"We've had plenty of time to search. We knew there had to be such a tower to the Lady here in Elothia; after all, it was once all one, as it will be again." Var'geris' eyes glittered. He looked down at Jerrol. "Shred it or the girl dies."

Jerrol strained to snap the rope as the knife bit deeper into Taelia's neck. Ruby red blood ran down her pale skin, the metallic tang sharp in the air. Her back was arched unnaturally against the tall man's chest.

"Is this your idea? Where did Tor'asion go? I'm surprised he's not here to finish the job." Jerrol taunted the Ascendant, his voice so sharp it should cut the ropes binding him. Taelia waited.

"Attacking you will not work. Your threshold for pain is quite surprising. If you can withstand mutilation, thumping you a bit isn't going to make that much difference, is it? But challenge your protective streak and what do you get? So, I found your weakness. Shred the veil. I won't ask again." Var'geris shifted the blade against Taelia's throat, the cold steel biting her skin as he drew it across her neck. Taelia flinched and hissed through her gritted teeth. She struggled against his hold, but the Ascendants grip was like a vice.

Taelia sucked her breath in as the Ascendant repeated

the action. Her neck was coated in red, stark against her paling skin, the cloying scent of her blood filled his nose. The blade scored her skin for a third time and Taelia gripped Var'geris' arm and tried to twist out of his grip.

"Stop," Jerrol gasped. "Just stop." The agony of each bite of the knife was like it scored his own skin. He couldn't keep his anguish out of his voice, and he knew Taelia would hear it. He made his decision as more blood ran down her throat and soaked into her robe.

"Shred it."

Jerrol gave Var'geris a vicious glare, he would make him pay for this, but he kept his voice soft as he spoke. "Taelia, all will be well," he said as he reached for the Veil and ripped it apart.

"Jerrol, no," Taelia shouted. She took a deep breath and stamped on the side of Var'geris' foot, he flinched and she dropped her body, all her dead weight pulling the Ascendant off balance and she pushed hard as they careened into the wall behind them. Var'geris loosened his grip in surprise and Taelia squirmed away. Jerrol tossed the rope aside and barged into Var'geris.

Taelia rolled out of the way, desperately scrabbling for a weapon as Jerrol and Var'geris grappled on the floor. The chair skittered away as they rolled into it. Taelia followed the sound and, grabbing the chair, hovered, trying to discern who was who.

"Now," Jerrol grunted as Var'geris heaved his body above Jerrol's and Taelia smashed the chair down as hard as she could.

Var'geris roared and spun, his knife skimming the air and across her exposed side. Taelia staggered away from the knife's bite as Jerrol cried out. "No!" He desperately wrapped the rope around Var'geris' neck, trying to get a purchase as the larger man struggled beneath him. Var'geris snarled and twisted, forcing Jerrol to release the rope.

They rolled near Taelia as she swayed and then crumpled to the floor, her robes reddening with horrific speed. Var'geris rose, his knife poised, and Jerrol launched himself at him, gripping his wrist, forcing it down. He twisted Var'geris' wrist and came up with the knife, and in one smooth thrust, buried it in Var'geris' rib cage. He tried to pull the knife back out but it was stuck hard.

Var'geris howled in agony and curled in on himself as Jerrol scuttled over to Taelia on all fours, his chest heaving desperately as he gathered her in his arms. He pressed his hand hard against the wound, trying to stem the flow of blood, begging the Lady, Marguerite, anyone, for help, but the blood seeped around his hand in a never-ending draining of life.

"Taelia," he whispered as he rocked her in his arms. "I am so sorry. I should never have brought you to Elothia."

Taelia stared up at him, her blood-stained hand reaching for his face as the light faded from her brilliant eyes.

50

STONEFORD FRONT, VESPIRI

King Benedict stared out over the battlefield and scowled. Their east flank was guarded by the Stanton mountains and gave some protection to the Watch Towers from the north. The threat would come from the north-west, but there was no sign of it yet.

The open plain was a killing field. Although Jason had reassured him that they had a few surprises ready, he was not convinced it would be enough. They had no fallback position. The battlefield was open all the way to Stoneford itself. There was no protection.

Jennery was already engaged in the Vesp valley, trying to block advances from the north-west through the open river plain. Reports had already started to arrive. They were holding, but for how long? The Elothians had to begin advancing soon, especially if they expected to take the Watch Towers. They had to neutralise Stoneford first; it was the only way to gain access.

He stopped frowning at the horizon as Fonorion appeared beside him. "We have movement on the west flank, Your Majesty. We need to move to the rear."

"I need to see what is happening," the king protested.

Fonorion shook his head. "We are too exposed. There is no point making you a needless target. We can't afford to put you at risk."

"The men need to see me."

"They do not need to see you fall," Fonorion said. "They have seen you. They know you are here, and they will fight to their deaths for you. Let that be enough." Fonorion was determined.

"Any word from Commander Haven?"

"Not yet. Birlerion and Yaserille will find him, Your Majesty."

"I shouldn't have agreed to it," King Benedict said, staring past Fonorion.

Fonorion shrugged. "You use the tools you have. It was the only thing you could do. We have to fight them on all fronts; we can't let them destroy our world."

"I know, I just wish … never mind, where are you taking me?"

"Stoneford for now, Your Majesty."

Fonorion led the king back down from the plateau and behind the lines of soldiers waiting to advance. Sentinals were strategically positioned throughout the ranks, and many a soldier had surreptitiously inspected the tall, heavily armed men and women and straightened in pride to be standing beside such warriors. Surely, the Lady was with them. Archers were positioned behind hastily dug earth mounds, ready to fire swathes of lethal arrows.

Fonorion nodded to Adilion, standing beside the reserves, trying to hold the men together. He kept the king moving. If he decided to stay there would be little Fonorion could do about it except grit his teeth and try to defend him.

Tower of Teranna, Elothia

Birlerion veered into the stables and saddled Zin'talia. The images of the Tower of Teranna tumbled in his mind, giving him an idea. Leading Zin'talia through the courtyard and out of the main gate, he met Yaserille nervously pacing near the waystone.

"Hurry up, Birlerion. I thought you were behind me."

Birlerion's eyebrows rose. "Where were you intending on going? There is no waystone near Teranna."

Yaserille froze, the blood draining from her face. "I never thought …"

"Yet," Birlerion finished as he drew the Captain's sword. Flickers of blue light traced the blade and it hummed in Birlerion's hand.

"You can create waystones?" Yaserille asked, backing away from the shining sword.

"It seems so." Birlerion gripped the sword tighter and swirled it above his head, concentrating on the sparks of energy pooling around the tip. He pictured the Tower of Teranna and commanded the waystone to coalesce outside the grey stone walls. Staggering as the energy released him, Birlerion inhaled as a rich ringing chime called to him.

"Did it work?" Yaserille asked, wringing her hands

"Sounds like it," he replied. Leading Zin'talia towards the waystone, he reached out and clasped Yaserille's arm. "Let's see shall we?" he said with an impish grin and stepped into the waystone before she could release her squawk of protest.

They appeared outside the ruins of a grey stone tower guarded by two soldiers who gaped at them. It must have seemed like they manifested out of thin air, Birlerion supposed, but it gave Yaserille enough time to rush them.

Zin'talia's concerned voice filled his head. *"Hurry, Jerrol believes Taelia is dead. He won't listen to me. He is blocking me out."*

"Keep trying," he replied as he raced into the tower, Yaserille having drawn both guards away from the wooden door. He braced himself against the wall as the tower trembled and understood Zin'talia's concern.

Birlerion stumbled into the chamber and his heart quailed at so much blood. His glance took in the dark mound lying to one side as he skidded onto his knees beside Jerrol, who was numbly rocking back and forth, tears streaming down his face.

"Jerrol?" Birlerion tried to ease his grip on Taelia, but Jerrol tightened his embrace and began keening. "Jerrol, let me see her."

"It's all my fault," Jerrol moaned, his eyes wide with fear, his face bruised and strained. Birlerion hissed his breath out at the sight of him. He was battered and bloody, his clothes torn. Taelia was bleeding out in his arms, the red stain on her robes spreading as he watched.

"No, it isn't. Let go of her."

"Never," he hissed, folding over Taelia.

"It *will* be your fault if you don't let me see to her," Birlerion snapped as the building began to tremble. "Control your emotions, Jerrol. Now is not the time. If you don't control yourself, you will collapse this tower." Birlerion glanced around in concern and then down back at Taelia.

"If not now, when?" Jerrol asked, anguish in his voice, his face drenched in tears.

"When she is actually dead," Birlerion replied, his voice cutting.

Jerrol relaxed his grip in shock. "What?"

"She's still bleeding; we need to staunch the wound. Help me." Birlerion tugged Taelia out of Jerrol's nerveless grasp.

"What?" Jerrol said again, an expression of hope warring with despair on his face.

"She's not dead, you idiot."

"Var'geris stabbed her."

Birlerion concentrated on padding the wound. "Looks like he sliced her, not stabbed."

Jerrol smoothed Taelia's curls off her pale face. "But she's so cold."

"Shock, I expect," Birlerion muttered, shrugging out of his jacket and covering Taelia. "Keep her warm. Yaserille will be here soon."

"But the baby," Jerrol began, as he clasped Taelia close.

"Don't even go there," Birlerion said, gripping his shoulder. "One step at a time. Let's help Taelia; *she* will look after the baby."

Birlerion gently cupped Taelia's face, "Taelia, can you hear me?" Her eyes fluttered open and closed again. "Taelia, I need you to walk to Marianille."

"What?" Jerrol jerked upright.

"We need to get her to a healer. The fastest way is for her to transition herself."

"Transition?"

"Yes, that's what she's been doing. Leyandrii used to do it. She could transfer people from one place to another. Leyandrii had Guerlaire create the waystones as she wasn't always available. The Ascendants have developed a version of it, they've figured out how to transfer themselves. It's all based on the same core magic."

Jerrol stared at him. "Can you do it?"

Birlerion huffed out a laugh and shook his head. "Taelia!"

Taelia stirred in Jerrol's arms. "Sweetheart?" Jerrol whispered. "I need you to find Marianille."

Taelia stared up at him, her eyes glazed with pain and confusion, and he kissed her. "Love? You need to go to Marianille; she will help you." Taelia blinked, her eyes clearing.

"Jerrol? Are you alright?" She cupped his face and he turned his head so he could kiss her palm.

"I'm fine. I'm so sorry Tali. I never meant for you to get hurt. This is my fault." He rested his face in her palm and tried not to weep.

Taelia laughed and then winced. "Always blaming yourself," she whispered.

Jerrol grimaced. "Do you think you can transition to Marianille? That would be the quickest way for you to reach help."

"Transition?"

"That walking through air thing you do."

"What about you?"

"I need to clear up here."

"I suppose so. Can you help me stand?" She gritted her teeth as Jerrol helped her upright and she leaned against him. "I don't think I can take you with me."

"Concentrate on yourself. Birlerion and I will use the waystone." Jerrol held her until she began to shimmer and she disappeared.

Birlerion glanced out the narrow slit in the wall and saw Yaserille dragging the guards' bodies aside. Zin'talia watched her with interest, her ears pointed forward. Turning back to the room, he approached the silent mound by the wall. Reluctantly, Birlerion used his foot to roll Var'geris over onto his back. He had died angry, his mouth was drawn back in a hideous grin. Grimacing, he knelt and searched the body. The knife was well and truly lodged under his breastbone and wouldn't budge. Jerrol had driven it with such anger, Birlerion was surprised it hadn't come out the other side.

Removing a wad of papers from an inside pocket, he took his findings back to a table that had appeared in the centre of the room. Two chairs sat beside it and a glass fronted lantern sat on top. He turned up the wick on the lantern and thanked the Mother.

"It wasn't supposed to be like this," Jerrol said, as he joined him, his voice tinged with exhaustion.

"No," Birlerion agreed.

"I should have shredded the Veil when he first demanded it, and this would never have happened."

"You don't know that," Birlerion replied, skimming the documents. He unfolded a map and inspected it. "Ah," he murmured. "Here we are, Oprimere." He pushed the map towards Jerrol, but Jerrol ignored it.

"I saw the way in. I could have done what he asked. Why did I wait?"

"It wouldn't have stopped him."

"I waited too long," Jerrol said, looking up. His face was stiff, his eyes cold.

Birlerion shivered at the pain in his eyes, the guilt etched on his face. "You know it wasn't the right time, so why do you suggest it?"

Jerrol flinched as if struck, and Birlerion made soothing motions with his hands.

"I shouldn't have waited," Jerrol said again.

Birlerion frowned at him. "Zin'talia is outside. You should speak to her; she is upset."

"Zin'talia? Where did you find her?"

"At the palace where you left her," Birlerion replied as Jerrol exhaled and then his eyes went distant. Birlerion studied him and after a moment said, "You have nothing to feel guilty for."

Jerrol jerked as if the word had burned him. Guilt. Birlerion saw it in eyes. He felt guilty for placing Taelia in danger in the first place, and now he felt guilty for not protecting her. Jerrol's guilt flashed across his face; Taelia, Serillion, the Terolian mines, even what had happened to Birlerion. Jerrol blamed himself for all of it.

The tower trembled around them, stone grating against each other as dust and grit showered them. The building groaned, and Jerrol bowed his head as he struggled to contain his emotions. "I failed her," he said, staring at his blood-coated hands.

"No, you didn't. Taelia will be fine, Jerrol. The healers' will fix her up."

"I failed them all, even you," Jerrol whispered, his voice muffled as he dropped his head in his hands. The tower trembled, and Birlerion peered around him in concern.

"Jerrol …?" he began as the floor buckled. "Jerrol, no, wait," Birlerion shouted. The stone floor split with a resounding crack and they fell into the dark depths below.

Marianille cursed as Taelia lurched into her. "By the Lady, Taelia where have you been? I've been searching everywhere for you." Marianille's voice tailed off as she took in the state of scholar. "Taelia, what's happened?" Fear sharpened her voice, and Marianille's arms tightened around Taelia as she wavered.

"Jerrol and Birlerion …" she began.

"Healer first, you can tell me on the way," Marianille murmured and she led her through the ranks of tents and steered her into a much larger tent. The air warmed imperceptibly, and Taelia's nose twitched at the aroma of emollients and linen.

"Var'geris abducted me. He wanted Jerrol to shred the Veil. They fought, and Var'geris caught me with his blade."

Taelia flinched as someone began undoing her robes.

"The healer needs to get to your wounds." Marianille said, a reassuring presence beside her.

"Var'geris had a knife," Taelia whispered, her eyes gleaming with a sheen of tears. She bit her lip. "He was threatening me with it to get Jerrol to shred the Veil." Her side stung as it was wiped down, and then it went numb and she relaxed against Marianille, who was gently swabbing her neck clean. The chill air was cool against her bare skin and she shivered.

"They are shallow cuts. They shouldn't scar," Marianille murmured in her ear.

Taelia shrugged. "I'm more concerned with Jerrol and Birlerion. I left them in the tower. What if the Ascendants return?"

"Which tower? Where are they?"

Taelia screwed her face up at the urgency in Marianille's voice. "It was a stone tower, with spiral steps. Ancient. Marianille, I don't where it was. Jerrol said they would use the waystone."

"Don't worry, I'm sure they'll be here soon."

"Jerrol was upset."

"I'm not surprised. Your robes are covered in blood. It looks much worse than it was. But it no doubt frightened the life out of him."

The healer began wrapping Taelia in long thin, bandages. "Eight stitches. The wound was not deep, but you must rest, give it time to heal," the healer said. He handed Taelia a sachet. "When the salve wears off, it will hurt. Take that in a glass of water." He smeared more ointment over the wounds on her neck and began wrapping more bandages around them. "More for protection against the rubbing of your collar," he said, patting her shoulder as he finished and moved off.

Marianille helped Taelia into clean shirt and trousers, discarding the robes as a lost cause. "Rest for a moment, Taelia. We can do nothing for now." Marianille forced her down on a cot, and Taelia scowled at her, but she ached, she hurt, and exhaustion ambushed her as she closed her eyes.

51

DEEPWATER WATCH, VESPIRI

J ennery was having a nightmare; at least he hoped it was a nightmare, as he saw Jerrol pummelled to his knees by Torsion. He launched himself at the guards holding Jerrol, shouting he wasn't sure what, and he was forced to the ground, the two burly guards taking pleasure in face-planting him into the stone-flagged floor. They wrenched him to his feet as Torsion swirled his cloak and disappeared. Var'geris revealed Taelia, and Jennery gasped. He tried to take a step, and then he was watching Jerrol keening over Taelia's body, and ice ran through his veins.

He stiffened in shock as Birlerion rushed into the room. It was true; Birlerion was alive.

Birlerion stared across the room at Jennery and spoke: "We need time. You have to delay them." And then the floor collapsed.

Jennery woke up on a bedroll in his command tent. Heart racing, he jerked to his feet in shock, his head spinning. "Birlerion?"

"Jennery! Thank the Lady. We need you. The Elothians are breaking through the lines. We can't stop them." Tagerill strode towards him and gripped his arm. "The second unit is falling back. This position will be overrun. We have to move."

Jennery shook his head and gripped Tagerill's arm to steady himself. "Regroup to the fallback position; use the reserves to delay," he said, frantically trying to adjust.

Tagerill looked at him closely. "What has happened?"

"Jerrol's in trouble. Torsion captured him and Taelia." He looked at Tagerill his face bleak. "Birlerion is with him."

Tagerill hissed his breath out. "Birlerion?"

"We need to get into a defensive position. They need time to recover. We have to delay the advance."

"Right, I'll take the reserves. You fall everyone else back and dig in," Tagerill commanded, ducking out of the tent. He looked back at Jennery. "It's been an honour," he said, nodding at Jennery before striding off in the direction of the fiercest fighting.

Jennery watched him go in dismay, understanding Tagerill's intention to hold the line at all costs. Minutes later, he was reeling off instructions; runners departed as he began co-ordinating a strategic retreat to buy the Captain time. But could they buy him enough time? And what was it for?

Ruins of the Tower of Teranna, Elothia

Yaserille stared at the pile of rubble in horror. The only sign that the tower had once stood there. Dust and grit hung in the air and she and Zin'talia retreated further eyeing the stones with caution as they continued to shift and settle.

"Ascendants balls," Yaserille gasped.

Zin'talia snorted in agreement.

What had happened? Yaserille checked her sense of Birlerion and the Captain and they both sparked in her mind. *Not crushed to death then.*

Inspecting the mound, Yaserille selected a rock and

began shifting some of the rubble, tossing the smaller stones aside and struggling to lever the larger slabs up. The edges bit into her hands; the gritty surface abraded her skin. She paused for a moment with a slab of stone balanced against her back as she tried to pivot it off the pile and knew she was wasting her time.

"This is hopeless," she said at last as she gasped for breath and rubbed her sore fingers on grubby trousers. Lifting her face to the clear blue sky, she sat back on heels and absorbed the weak heat from the sun which was slowly being encroached upon by thick grey clouds threatening more snow.

Zin'talia approached her, and rubbed her head against Yaserille's and Yaserille rose to her feet. "I can feel them, so they're still alive, the question is are they trapped, or have they found a way out?" She rubbed her temple, trying to ease the ache. "We need more help. But from where?" She racked her brains for a moment. "Let's try Stoneford." Leading Zin'talia away from the ruins they entered the waystone and stepped to Stoneford.

Birlerion grabbed Jerrol as they fell, twisting in the air as he pushed his transparent shield around them. The air pulsed as stone fragments ricocheted around them. They landed with a jarring thump that rattled their bones, both gasping for air, choking in the dust-filled darkness.

"What did you do?" Birlerion gasped.

"Me?" Jerrol's voice was strained. "I didn't do anything."

"Yes, you did. The floor collapsed, along with everything else."

"It must have been you; I don't have this sort of power," Jerrol said, feeling around him.

"You're the Lady's Captain, of course you have power,"

Birlerion said through gritted teeth. "You just need to control it."

Jerrol digested that for a moment and then asked, "Why aren't we dead?"

"There's still time," Birlerion said, flexing his shield as the weight of the stone pressed down on him. He shuddered, and Jerrol opened his left hand, releasing the soft glow to see where they were. He looked up into Birlerion's strained face and the rock suspended above them. Birlerion was on his hands and knees, back braced as if he was holding the rock up with his shoulders.

"What are you doing, Birlerion?"

"Giving us a chance. But you need to find a way out fast. I can only hold this for so long."

Jerrol stared at him, understanding slowly dawning. "You're the Lady's shield," he whispered.

"As the Captain is the sword," Birlerion replied, gritting his teeth. "But neither of us will be of any use if you don't find us a way out." Birlerion's voice shook, and Jerrol scrabbled out from beneath him.

Jerrol's eyes widened. "You protected the people of Vespers, didn't you? At the end? That's why there were so few people lost. That's why you were so exhausted and confused at the end."

"This is not the time for a history lesson, Jerrol," Birlerion growled.

Jerrol chuckled, surprising himself and Birlerion. "But you will tell me when we get out of here; all of it," he said as he began searching the small space. "Marguerite? Can you help us?" he asked as he opened himself to the Land, and slowly sank his senses into the dirt below them, much as he had done when searching for the Sentinals in Terolia. The Land embraced him as Marguerite responded to his plea.

"You do manage to find some interesting predicaments," Marguerite murmured in his ear.

Filtering through dirt and stones, Jerrol grimaced as he followed tiny fissures down through the soil. "Not through choice, I assure you," he replied.

"Less chit chat, more speed," Birlerion gasped.

Jerrol reached an opening, which widened out into a large cavern. He heard water dripping and drifted towards it, a mere thought. A tiny glow appeared in the cavern ceiling, a blue-green light suspended on the finest gossamer thread, followed by thousands of tiny pin-pricks of light illuminating a way out. He felt the slightest breath of air against his cheek, and he inhaled deeply, wincing at the pain in his chest. A flash of light caught his eye, and he flowed towards it. He reached for the crystal, for that was what it was, the last piece. The edges sliced his skin and it greedily absorbed his blood, merging with him as the other pieces had and fading into his palm. Heat flashed through him, and he stilled as he assimilated it.

"You have to return," Marguerite whispered. *"I cannot enter the tower, but I can give you this."* He felt a jolt of energy wrapped around a host of sensations and images, which he absorbed. His aches and pains faded.

Jerrol curled the fingers of his left hand into a fist, feeling the bite as the edges cut into his skin. The crystal had absorbed his lifeblood just as fast as he absorbed the crystal. His hand was a bloody mess, but he could still feel the crystal as if he was holding it, though it was gone from sight. The final crystal: he had found all three. They just seemed to appear out of nowhere as no doubt the Lady and the Land had planned.

He suddenly jerked, his body stiffening as the crystal entered his bloodstream, rushing through his veins. His heart stuttered as the bloodstone became one with him and the

Lady's arms cradled him, holding him tight. "All will be well, my Captain," she whispered. "All will be well." He closed his eyes in acceptance of what would be, listening to the Lady's voice sing through his body.

When Jerrol opened his eyes he was once again laying at the foot of the largest sentinal tree he had ever seen. He slowly sat up. His hand hurt. The final crystal was working its way into his system. Changing him. He hoped whatever it was doing would be for the better.

The Lady approached and smiled brilliantly at him. She cupped his face. "The final step is yours to take," she said. "You will know what to do when the time comes. My shield is at your side. Know that I will always be with you both. You are the hope of Remargaren."

His vision shimmered, and Birlerion's anxious voice was demanding he wake up. Birlerion awkwardly gripped his hand, trying to stem the blood.

"Ow," he said out loud, and Birlerion flinched back.

"For Lady's sake, Jerrol, what are you trying to do to me?"

"Sorry. When duty calls, it seems I don't have much choice but to listen."

"Well, tell Leyandrii to at least patch you up better!" Birlerion snapped, his voice cracking.

"I'll tell Her next time I see Her," Jerrol promised and wadded a piece of his shirt in his palm.

"What did you do?" Birlerion asked.

"I'm not sure," Jerrol replied, frowning at his hand. "I saw something flash, and I picked it up, but I don't know where it went."

Birlerion's sigh was resigned.

"I think I have found a way out," Jerrol murmured, focusing back on the floor. He slowly pushed further, creating a tunnel, deliberately not thinking about what he was doing.

Time passed as he gradually tunnelled down to the cavern below. He eased back into Birlerion's arms, aware of the effort they were both expending, and Jerrol looked up into his taut face. "I learnt how to tunnel," Jerrol said as he opened his hand to reveal the silver light that flared and sparkled in his hand. Birlerion's eyes widened at the sight and his gaze followed the light over to the wall, and his mouth fell open at the sight of the gaping hole sloping downwards.

"I think we'd better leave sooner rather than later," Jerrol said, wheezing like an old man. His body ached, a reminder of Tor'asion's fists. "You can't hold this for much longer." He eased himself feet first down the man-sized tunnel. It was very narrow, but the edges were smooth. The stone crowded in on him and he tried not to think about getting stuck.

Jerrol's feet flopped as empty space opened beneath them, and he frantically felt around for the ground. Easing forward, he balanced on the rim of the tunnel, his arms braced either side, and heard the shingle slide beneath his feet. He let out a relieved breath and eased down on to the shelving stones and then turned to help Birlerion down.

He watched as Birlerion gingerly inched his way down the tunnel, an intense look of concentration on his face. His grimy shirt was in tatters, revealing his emaciated frame and the scars that marred his skin. Adeeron would be haunting them both for the forseeable future, they both needed to put some weight back on. A strengthening breeze rose from below and cleared the dusty air.

There was a creaking groan and a rush of dust and grit as Birlerion suddenly relaxed and slid out of the hole. The stone collapsed onto the rock strata above them with a dull thud that shook the cavern. Jerrol steadied Birlerion as he took a deep shuddering breath and shook out his arms as if they had been physically holding the stone up above them.

"You got that light?" Birlerion asked as the sound of a

loud plop hitting the water nearby made him jump. "What was that?" He flinched as the shale shifted under his feet and Jerrol held up his hand.

"This is a limestone cavern; water seeps through it where there are weaknesses in the rock, dripping into the lake below. That's the sound of the water dripping. The echoes make it sound very loud," Jerrol said as he rotated, lighting up the cavern. Together, they staggered down to the water's edge.

"Are you sure this is the way out?" Birlerion asked, peering into the darkness. The air was damp and chill and smelt of old stone.

"Just follow the lights."

There was a pregnant pause. "What lights?"

"The lights in the ceiling, like twinkling stars of blue and white," Jerrol replied, closing his fingers to shut off the glow. He looked up at the swathe of tiny points of lights above them.

The darkness was filled with the sound of sliding shale as it shifted under their feet and the lapping of water as the stones disturbed the smooth calm. The water looked very deep, dark, and uninviting and, once the ripples from the sliding shale settled, very still. The cavern ceiling extended high above them, and the plops of water dripping from the heights echoed loudly in the silence.

Birlerion hesitated, then as his eyes adjusted to the dark, and, taking a deep breath, he took a step forward into the inky river. His breath caught as the icy cold water bit his legs. "Any chance you could magic up a boat for us?" he gasped as he edged deeper into the water.

Jerrol chuckled through chattering teeth. "Not on such short notice." The water was deathly cold, and Jerrol cringed as the water crept over his cuts and bruises. His ribs ached in the cold, which stole his breath. The water was freezing and sapped what little strength their weary bodies had left. The cavern was silent except for the gentle ripples they made as they swam and the occasional heavy plop of water echoing through the tunnels. The darkness was thick and consuming. The damp tang of minerals filled their nostrils.

"It's very peaceful, isn't it?" Jerrol said as he gazed at the twinkling stars above him.

"Yes," Birlerion replied, concentrating on blindly swimming into the inky darkness. He hesitantly reached out in front of him. "The water level doesn't rise up to the ceiling at any point, does it? I don't want to knock myself out."

"Don't think so," Jerrol said, his voice soft and remote. "You know, these rocks are quite amazing. They must have been here for thousands of years. Look at the columns up there, hanging from the ceiling. I wonder if any of them fall."

"Don't," Birlerion spluttered. "We have enough problems already. I've picked up a bit of a current. It goes off to the right, I think."

"Yes, too the right, that's right," Jerrol muttered.

"I can see a light up ahead," Birlerion said, his voice loud in the echoey darkness. "We're nearly there."

Birlerion swam steadily towards the faint light, the cavern above him taking shape as the dim light alleviated the inky darkness. Limestone columns rose around them, disappearing into the shadows above.

The current helped them drift towards the gaping hole ahead of them. Moonlight drew them towards the entrance which was covered with long strands of greenery and vines, subduing the light and screening the cavern from view. The only evidence that the cavern was there was the cloudy water, full of sediment from the caves, rushing out into a lake, swirling into the clear water and dissipating along the edges.

Jerrol peered through the fronds, blinking in the bright

glare of the moon flickering through the trees. All he could see was moss-covered trees, trailing more vines. Trees covered the lakeside as far as he could see. There was a strong smell of leafy ferns and vegetation which was welcome after the dead mineral-infused air they had been breathing underground.

They dragged themselves out of the water onto the bank and lay there shivering for a moment. Jerrol opened his eyes as he felt Birlerion stir. Marguerite stood before them.

Birlerion rose, his clothes dripping, and a slow smile spread over his tired face. His boots squelched as he walked towards her and opened his arms. "Marguerite," he said as he hugged her. "I didn't expect to see you here."

Marguerite leaned back in his arms and grinned up at him. "I've missed you too," she said, rising on tiptoe to kiss his cheek. She wrinkled her nose at his wet clothes. "Leyandrii, you need to dry them out," she said with a small smile.

Jerrol rose trying not to think of Leyandrii. He had forsaken her as best he could, and her absence ached in his chest. He wondered how much longer she would see the need to forsake him.

"I have never forsaken you, my Captain," Leyandrii breathed in his ear, and he jerked back in shock. His left hand throbbed in time with his heartbeat. There were two of them before him; one dark, one fair. Their presence was a physical disturbance in the air and he stared at them in awe. He swallowed as he straightened his shoulders.

Birlerion gasped. "Leyandrii." Jerrol winced at the anguish in Birlerion's voice. His voice sounded so tight, he was surprised he had managed to speak at all.

Masses of golden hair framed her exquisite face, her green eyes sparkled as she approached them and smiled. "My dearest Birlerion, you have done so well." Leyandrii embraced him and Birlerion relaxed in her arms. She drew his head down to kiss his forehead. Releasing him she turned to Jerrol. "As have you, my Captain. You know there is only one other Sentinal that is as stubborn as you, and he is standing right beside you. You have never failed me, my Captain," she said. Her love spread through him like a wave of pure emotion and belonging, and he curled into the sensation as she held him tight, the aroma of roses teasing his nose as she soothed away his distress and exhaustion. "After all, I asked you to forsake me. Thank you for trusting me, and for welcoming me back."

Marguerite tutted as she watched them. "I've never known two men find such difficult paths," she said with a small smile. She embraced her sister. "It has been too long," she murmured.

They turned to face the Sentinals, their beauty mirrored. Jerrol's mind grappled with the fact that two of their world's deities stood before him. They could have been twins, though Jerrol knew Marguerite to be the younger.

Leyandrii pouted. "Are you saying I am old?" she asked as Marguerite laughed.

"N-never, my Lady," Jerrol stuttered, inordinately soothed by their gentle teasing. Birlerion watched, amusement softening his face.

"I think I'll have to steal him. You have a Captain already," Marguerite baited her sister.

"No, you won't. I only said you could borrow him."

Marguerite chuckled. "I thank you for your service, Oath Keeper, but the Lady's Captain is needed to finish the job."

Jerrol bowed. "My Ladies," he said, overwhelmed.

"He's good. You sure I can't have him?" Marguerite suggested slyly.

The Lady smiled. "Welcome home, Captain. You cannot shoulder the burden of saving everyone; that is my burden to bear and my grief when we fail, and do not mistake, we will fail. We can but try our best to make this world a place for all to live in peacefully." Leyandrii held her hands out to Jerrol and Birlerion. "Come," she said as Marguerite completed the circle.

Leyandrii smiled and their surroundings shifted and they reappeared under Chryllion and Saerille's tall sentinal trees in the Stoneford Grove. Leyandrii released their hands and peered up at the trees, trailing her fingers across the bark of the nearest tree. The canopy shivered in response and she whispered a greeting.

"Did it work?" Jerrol asked after a long moment.

"Oh yes, my Captain. The way is open, and now for the final act. The Ascendants make their way to Oprimere. They intend to welcome their ancestors now you have breached the Veil. They seem to have forgotten that if their Ancestors can return, then so can I." The Lady's smile was sharp. A soft chime resonated through him, and he knew the new waystone Leyandrii had just created would take him to Oprimere if he so desired. "My sword and my shield united once more. I thank you both for your trust, your dedication and your belief. Together we will rid this world of this terrible threat."

"Why bring us here, to Stoneford, then?" Birlerion asked. "Shouldn't we be in Oprimere too?"

"You have time to catch your breath." Leyandrii inspected him. "And a bath."

"And even eat," Marguerite interjected. "Why is it that you never find time to eat?"

Leyandrii chuckled. "Rest for a few chimes, Birlerion, before you return to the battle. There is nothing more either of you can do until the Ascendants reach Oprimere. You have both done enough." She patted his cheek and turned to Jerrol. "More than enough. Know that I will always be with you," she said, and she and Marguerite were gone.

Jerrol and Birlerion stared at each other for a moment. Their pristine uniforms shimmering in the fading moonlight as the sun began to breach the night. Leyandrii had obviously thought they wouldn't take the time to bathe.

The flush of the bloodstone and the comforting weight of the Lady encompassed Jerrol. Leyandrii's blessing hovered in the air, and he smiled grimly. It was time to finish this.

52

STONEFORD KEEP, VESPIRI

Jerrol and Birlerion hurried up the road to Stoneford Keep. Jerrol had forgotten how far the waystone was from Jason's home, and he idly thought about moving it but forgot the idea as Saerille blocked his way. Her eyes gleamed in the torchlight. She had her broadsword strapped across her back and a short sword at her waist; she looked ready for battle.

"Captain, I couldn't reach you, and the king is about to explode. The Veil, Captain, it's been breached. We need to patch it up."

Jerrol's smile was a little strained. "I'm sorry, things have been a little hectic. We'll deal with the Veil in due course. Don't worry about it, and don't try to fix it on your own. First, take us to the king. I need to speak to him."

Saerille grabbed Birlerion and then pulled him into a heartfelt hug before she let him follow Jerrol.

Jerrol paused on the threshold of Jason's study. Even at this early hour of the morning, there was a mass of people all talking at once; how anyone could think in all that noise was beyond him. The voices began to die out as the people inside caught sight of him in the doorway. Jerrol dreaded to think what they saw. Their stunned faces didn't bode well.

King Benedict slowly stood. "Everyone out. I need to speak with Commander Haven alone."

Jerrol moved out of the doorway, but he caught Jason's arm. "Stay," he murmured, saddened at the sight of his friend's careworn face.

Jerrol moved to the table and pulled the map towards him. "Oprimere is here," he pointed to a spot to the west of the plains. "According to Niallerion, the Elothians will funnel down the Vesp valley and try to swing behind us. The grand duke has sent relief to replace the generals and withdraw his troops, but it will take time, and the generals are eager."

"Jerrol," the king said.

"The second advance will be on the Watch Towers. They intend to sweep through Stoneford and up behind the Stantons. There is no way to prevent it even though the Ascendants no longer need the towers."

"Jerrol stop; what has happened to you?" The king's voice was soft, and he stared at him as if he didn't recognise him. Jason was watching him, his concern also obvious.

"It doesn't matter. I'm so sorry, Your Majesty. I couldn't stop the generals. The grand duke has ordered their removal, but it won't happen in time to stop their advance. I must get to the front, see what we can do. But we found the location of Oprimere."

"Jerrol, of course it matters. Stop a moment, sit down."

"There isn't time. I have to get to the front. Jason …"

"Enough, sit down." The king glared at him until he stilled and silently sank into a chair. Even then, he fidgeted, driven by a need that was beyond King Benedict's understanding. "Tell us," he said, his voice gentle.

"It makes no difference. I'm here now. We need to make plans."

"We know what we need to do. The men are in position. Tell us." The king was implacable.

Jerrol sighed, his resistance suddenly fading. He dropped his face in his hands, and the king's eyes widened as he caught the sparkle beneath Jerrol's skin.

"It has happened as was foretold," Jerrol said. "Var'geris tried to kill Taelia. The flame was extinguished, just not the way I was expecting. I found the final piece." He opened his hand and what was once a steady glow now sparked and spangled in the air in front of him, making his skin sparkle brilliantly in response.

He closed his fist as Jason gasped. "What final piece? Jerrol?"

"The Bloodstone, it sits within me, runs through my veins, desperate to reach the Veil. But it's not time," he said, his silver eyes distant. He shimmered before them, his body blurring a little around the edges.

"Jerrol?"

King Benedict's sharp voice brought him back to the room, and he looked at the king. "I tore the Veil."

The king nodded. "Saerille and Fonorion said."

"We have to go to Oprimere. It is the final meeting place. Tor'asion will already be there. It's the only way to stop this senseless fighting." He suddenly stilled, and his luminous eyes widened as the solution came to him. "I have to stop them all." He stood. "I know what I have to do. I have to get to Oprimere."

The king rested his hand on Jerrol's arm. "Take care if you can," he said simply.

Jerrol nodded, gave Jason a swift hug, and he left the room, calling his Sentinals. His voice issuing instructions echoed down the hallway as Benedict followed him to the door. He turned as Jason spoke behind him. "We're going to lose him, aren't we?"

"I fear we already have," the king replied, turning back to the empty door.

"Birlerion with me, we're going to Oprimere," Jerrol commanded.

"Leyandrii said wait," Birlerion protested as he followed. "We should wait, eat. Just one chime, Jerrol. We haven't stopped. We'll be safer waiting here than in the middle of a battlefield."

"True," Jerrol sighed and rubbed his face. "It doesn't seem right though. We should be doing whatever we can to stop this."

"And we will, when the time is right," Birlerion replied. He coaxed Jerrol down the passage towards the kitchens and pushed him into a seat at the kitchen table.

The aroma of fresh baked bread made Jerrol's stomach growl and he flushed. He didn't think he would be able to eat but once the food was in front of him, he realised he was starving.

Birlerion was on his second bowl of stew before Jerrol had finished his first. "When did you last eat, Birlerion?"

"Don't remember. Using magic makes you hungry. It drains you if you use it for too long."

"Have you always used magic? What is it that you can do?"

"Leyandrii taught me how to use my shield. It's defensive, for protection."

"So I saw. What else?"

"It's all connected to the control of magical energy. I can compress the energy into a flame, or the onoffs, things like that. Once you seal the Veil though, I expect I won't be able to do it anymore. We'll see."

Jerrol eyed Birlerion as he shivered. He wondered if

Birlerion was as confident as he made himself out to be. He had been through this once before and come out confused and he thought, probably traumatised. Without argument, he was about to do it again.

Jerrol sighed out a breath, his stomach beginning to regret the food he had eaten. There was no point worrying about it. The confrontation would happen, and they would face it, together. Finishing his stew, he saw Birlerion had finally stopped eating and gave him a tired grin. He rotated his shoulders to ease the aches and pains he was slowly collecting. His back muscles twinged in protest, and he tried not to wince.

Birlerion leaned back in his chair and met Jerrol's eyes. "Ready?" he asked, some of the strain dropping from his face as he gave Jerrol an encouraging smile.

Love for his friend rushed through Jerrol. Birlerion was prepared to stand by his shoulder without question. He was so thankful. He didn't think he would be able to succeed without him. "Do I have a choice?" Jerrol asked with an equally tired grin.

Birlerion laughed. "Suppose not. One more time, eh?"

Jerrol rose and gripped his shoulder. "One more time," he agreed. "Thank you, Birlerion."

Birlerion's eyes flickered at the emotion in Jerrol's voice but he just nodded and rose. "Let's get out of here before the king realises we're still here."

Jerrol and Birlerion entered the Stoneford waystone without being accosted and stepped out in the middle of a battlefield. The noise was horrendous as men fought on the open plains. The thunder of hooves preceded the darting runs of a Vespirian mounted regiment. Horses squealed, swords clashed, officers yelled orders and in the confusion Jerrol and Birlerion managed to skirt the worst of the fighting.

A raised plateau ran down the middle of the battlefield, adorned by broken plinths and columns, collapsed walls and fragments of grey rock. Some of which Jerrol was sure had been used to bolster the array of barricades the Vespirians had erected to slow the Elothian advance.

The Vespirian engineers had been busy, instead of trying to dig into the frozen ground they had built barriers of snow and ice to force the Elothians away from Stoneford and towards the mountains. The mounted regiments were herding them away from the open valleys leading into Deepwater and Stoneford.

The plateau acted like an island in the middle of a river with the battle flowing down either side and the island ignored. Climbing the frozen slopes took a matter of moments and they hid behind the broken masonry on the southern end.

Jerrol focused his thoughts and brought the image Leyandrii had given him to the fore, and the land began to tremble. Large blocks of grey stone began to rise from the ground, pointing skywards at various angles as they formed a ragged rectangle. The ruins rose into the Mother's cathedral in Jerrol's eyes, the towers and spires rising above him, crowned by the gilt-covered dome. A sense of soothing peace enveloped him, and he sighed as the vision faded, leaving the remnants of the magnificent cathedral before him on the raised plateau.

Jerrol's face tightened at the sight of the battle raging in the pre-dawn gloom, the king's army in their grey uniforms and the Chevrons in their red and blue. He couldn't stand aside and let them kill each other. They were all good men. They should be living together in peace, returned to their everyday lives, instead of being conscripted into the industry of death.

He racked his brains desperately, his desperation fuelling

the anger simmering within him. He turned to Birlerion, his voice tight. "Can you erect a barrier? Keep them apart?"

Birlerion stared at him for a moment and then out over the battlefield. "There will be some that get caught on the wrong side but it should keep most of them apart." His shoulders tensed as he raised his hands and twisted his wrists before compressing his palms. As he rubbed them together, a blue sparkle flickered over his skin, and the Captain's sword still strapped around Birlerion's waist, vibrated on his hip in acknowledgment of whatever Birlerion was doing.

Jerrol observed the glow emanating from Guerlaire's sword as Birlerion lovingly caressed the sparkle between his hands and shaped it into a ball and then stretched it between his hands. He threw the ball of energy at the battlefield. A shimmering blue haze appeared, separating the two armies from Stoneford all the way to Deepwater.

"Now, Marguerite," Birlerion murmured.

The battling men halted in surprise, trying to keep their balance as the ground beneath them buckled and forced them apart. The rising ground pushed the barrier up into the air, and then the men stared at each other through the barrier as it slowly cleared. They found themselves frozen, unable to move; Elothian and Vespiran alike glaring at each other, unable to do anything else. The ground began to tear apart as the soil was forced upwards, forming a wall. If the barrier failed, the men would still not be able to reach each other, but it remained glimmering before them.

Jerrol was aware that their losses were horrendous. Sentinals had fallen; he could feel their loss, though he didn't know who had gone. There was no time to check, no matter how much he wanted to; he needed to keep focused.

A blinding light shot into the night sky, and the fabric of the air was torn apart. Jerrol stiffened as Tor'asion stepped out onto the middle of the plateau. He was followed by Sul'enne, the last remaining brothers of the Ascendants.

Birlerion shifted next to him, and Tor'asion's black eyes caught sight of them as they approached. Tor'asion's face was pale and haggard; deep lines grooved either side of his mouth and between his eyes, permanently etching a frown on his face. He lifted his finger and pointed at Jerrol, his attention exclusively focused on the man who had disrupted all their plans.

"You," he snarled. "I should have killed you the first time I met you."

Jerrol faced him. "And spoil such a good friendship? Surely not."

"If I had realised who you were and what your survival would mean …" Tor'asion paused and then smiled. His eyes glinted with his anger, but he controlled it.

"Then what?" Jerrol asked, watching him. Birlerion slowly drifted towards the second Ascendant poised behind Tor'asion.

"It doesn't matter. The Veil is breached, and you won't be sealing it again."

"Don't you think I could have sealed it by now if I wanted to?" Jerrol asked.

Tor'asion frowned. "You would have if you could, but you obviously can't. Leyandrii must be so disappointed in you."

"I should think your ancestors must be much more disappointed in you. Two acolytes left; not much of a welcome is it?"

Tor'asion bunched his fists, the cords in his neck standing out as he braced for an attack. He relaxed at a soft word from his companion, though Jerrol saw it took effort.

"You know, Var'geris was right about me. I have compassion for others. My purpose is to protect. You never got that, did you? He was just too late. Did you feel it when he died? Along with Pev'eril? Even Ain'uncer?" Jerrol asked.

Tor'asion raised his arms, his face livid. "You will pay. I will kill you many times over. You will regret you ever lived." His eyes glazed as he focused elsewhere, searching, and Birlerion raised his hand, drawing a barrier around them.

"I think not, you will not find Taelia or anyone else to threaten; your fight is with me. And anyway, don't you have more important things to do?" Jerrol gestured towards the luminous sky above them.

Tor'asion hesitated.

"Aren't you going to call them? They must be growing impatient. Do you think you and Sul'enne are powerful enough to call them here?"

Tor'asion's gaze darted around him. The battlefield was littered with bodies. A shimmering barrier on top of a small ridge prevented those still standing from reaching each other. The soldiers stood shocked, watching the outcome of the tableau above them. Small movements indicated that not all were dead though, and the sound of weakly calling voices stirred some to help.

Jerrol watched the Ascendants, waiting calmly.

From the grand duke's encampment far to the north, Taelia stuffed a fist in her mouth to avoid shrieking out. She could see Jerrol standing tall in her mind's eye. There was an otherworldliness about him, the Lady's glimmer bright in his eye; he was something more than just a man. His brother in arms was standing in his shadow. "Birlerion," she breathed in horror. The two most important people in her life stood between them and the Ascendants' final act. Marianille stiffened by her shoulder, her gaze on her brother.

Taelia turned as the grand duke exited his tent behind her. "Do something," she pleaded, her blind gaze taking in Taurillion, Serenion and Landis behind him.

Serenion stepped forward to steady her. "It's too late. We won't be able to breach the barrier. Now it is in the hands of the Lady."

The grand duke shivered as an icy breeze swept around them. "I think it's time I had words with my generals. They have much explaining to do." His gaze swept the battlefield and lingered on the stalemate before them. "Serenion, get a triage set up. Let's get as many of our men off this field as we can."

"Yes, Your Grace."

"But we have to help Jerrol and Birlerion," Taelia said.

"I'm sorry my dear, it is out of our hands now. Come."

"We can't just leave. We have to watch."

"Watch?" Randolf repeated, bemused. "There are enough watching for all of us. We need to prepare, just in case."

"Just in case?"

"Yes, in case your husband is unable to defeat whatever it is he thinks is about to arrive. I am sure we will hear about it as soon as anything happens."

"I'll go," Landis whispered in her ear, squeezing her shoulder before setting off across the battlefield towards the plateau.

Jerrol stood, waiting. The sky shimmered above them as dawn arrived, and the sun rose, bathing the battleground in its golden light. A new day; an ongoing fight. On the horizon, darkening clouds roiled as if an impending storm was about to break.

The breach in the Veil grated on his senses as if it was a wound on his body. The tang of power filled his mouth as the crystal in his blood stirred, responding to the needs of the

Veil. The murmur of voices grew louder in his ears as the breach tore further and Tor'asion worked his magic.

Birlerion waited at his shoulder. A comforting presence, observing Tor'asion. Jerrol's skin began to glow in response to whatever Tor'asion was trying to do and he felt the Veil give. Birlerion was suddenly in motion, responding to the threat as Sul'enne tried to strike out at Jerrol.

Birlerion blocked the blow, forcing Sul'enne back. Jerrol watched. He would have been cleaved in two, but for the Sentinal.

Jerrol focused on Tor'asion as he reached for the Veil, for the voices calling him. He breached the Veil and gasped as a confusion of thoughts swirled around him, entwined with the fabric of the Veil, caught as securely as Saerille had been. The Veil swirled around him, the torn ends reaching for him, seeking his body, seeking sustenance, seeking life. He sensed Birlerion in the outer weave, part of the original creation with the Lady, his song steady and true, woven with the Lady's. He hadn't realised Birlerion had been part of the creation of the Veil. He suddenly wondered what else his reticent Sentinal had been involved in that he wasn't aware of.

Sul'enne's gaze flicked towards Tor'asion, but he was as absorbed as the Lady's Captain was, and Sul'enne focused his attention on the lethal Sentinal in front of him. He seemed indestructible, always wherever Haven was. It was time to dispense with him. Sul'enne began to mutter under his breath but stopped as Tor'asion hissed. Tor'asion needed his power.

Birlerion bared his teeth. "Time to see if you can fight like a real man," he said, his voice a low growl. He lifted his glowing sword. The soldiers below watched transfixed, as the two men circled, testing each other. Sul'enne reacted swiftly, and the clash of swords and the ring of metal echoed over the battlefield. The two men were evenly matched, fighting each other and yet hampered by the need to protect the two men frozen beside them in concentration.

Serenion instructed the Captain's unified unit of men to begin retrieving the fallen, Elothian and Vespirian alike, and then drifted towards the barrier, his gaze drawn to the men on the plateau above him. He mentally reached towards the Captain and gasped as he was buffeted by a swirl of energy and desperate voices. Jerrol pushed him away.

"I can help," Serenion insisted and reached again; he felt Jerrol's hesitation before he accepted their connection and he swirled into the maelstrom that was the Lady's Captain.

"Serenion? What's wrong?" Taurillion shook his shoulder, but Serenion was unmoving, fixated on the Captain. His silver eyes were luminous in the growing gloom as the sky continued to darken above them. Tendrils of black hair escaped from his normally neat queue and rose around his waxen face as a strengthening wind began to swirl around him.

Taurillion looked up at the Captain and reached.

"No, my love, protect Randolf. He is not safe yet." Marguerite's voice settled in his mind. He could feel her sense of urgency and concern. Taurillion looked at the nearest soldier. "Denning? Isn't it?"

"Yes, sir."

"Stay with him. Make sure he doesn't come to harm."

"What's wrong with him?"

"He's with the Captain," Taurillion said as he returned to his post at the grand duke's shoulder.

Deepwater

Jennery raised his head above the edge of the ditch he had been sheltering behind and stared at the barrier shimmering in the distance. All sounds of fighting had stopped, and the silence was unnerving. Around him, men rose from the ground like toddlers on unsteady legs, staggering in the unexpected stillness and gazing at the barrier in shock, hands previously bent on killing hanging limp at their sides.

The rising sun lit the battlefield in streaks of golden rays revealing men both littered on the ground and standing. Discarded weapons glinted in the morning light. Bodies were shadowed, until the sun slowly peeked over them, revealing their colours, mostly marred with bright red blood.

He climbed out of his ditch and began to walk towards the barrier, stepping over discarded weapons and makeshift defences. He began to run as he neared the area of fiercest fighting where Tagerill had last been seen holding the line. Bodies lay sprawled in ungainly positions. A few low groans disturbed the silence. "Call the healers," Jennery shouted as he began his frantic search.

A brave soul hesitantly reached for the shimmering divide and his hand met resistance. He stood back and looked up. The brilliant blue sky above was being encroached on by a roiling mass of dark clouds.

Oprimere

The voices grew clearer as Serenion began to help Jerrol unravel the threads. *"Mind you don't get trapped; the Veil is greedy,"* Jerrol murmured as his fingers worked fast, his mind working faster. He had found the lost Sentinals, but if, and it was a big if, he could get them out before Tor'asion completed his work, where would he send them?

He was dimly aware of Birlerion moving around him, a glowing light pulsing in his peripheral vision, but he feverishly concentrated on the Veil. It was insidious, constantly reaching for him, needing him and what he contained within. "Not yet," he soothed, "not yet."

Part of his mind was monitoring Tor'asion and another part, he had to admit was gawping at the brilliant beauty beyond the Veil. The expanse of possibility and opportunity, the seductive pull of unending power and unknown futures; the essence of what could have been or what might still be if the Lady had never pulled down the Veil around them.

He was drawn back as Serenion gasped in pain as he pulled the threads free from his skin. Jerrol realised he had freed his captives and he pushed them into Serenion's arms before the threads could burrow back in. "Take them to Marchwood," Jerrol said pushing Serenion away as his attention skittered elsewhere. Laerille reached. *"I'll take them,"* she breathed as Serenion collapsed. Corporal Denning caught him before he hit the ground.

Jerrol moved onto the next presence caught in the Veil. There was a weight about this one that was familiar, and he frowned as the Veil expanded and contracted beneath his hands. "Lorillion," he breathed, recognising the lost Sentinal and he furiously slashed at the threads, pulling the Sentinals to him, indiscriminately grabbing them as they reached for him, directing their thoughts at the Veil and ignoring all else.

Birlerion's sword penetrated Sul'enne's guard, and Sul'enne faltered before him, his agonised eyes wide with shock. Birlerion yanked his sword out of Sul'enne's chest and watched him collapse to the ground. He breathed in deeply, trying to catch his breath. His gaze flicked out over his barriers, checking that they were still holding. He fed his dwindling energy into the barrier stretching to Deepwater, allowing the wall around the plateau to flicker and fade. Sweat gleamed on his face as he turned to Tor'asion.

A shimmering form began to coalesce between them. The indistinct outline of a man began to firm as Tor'asion's arms shook with the effort, his jaw jutted out as he gritted his teeth and continued his chanting.

"No!" Saerille shouted as she reached Chryllion at the foot of the plateau, her sides heaving from the run from the waystone the Captain had created at Oprimere. Chryllion was staring up at the Captain and Birlerion. She gripped his arm. "I'll help him, you help Birlerion protect the Captain."

Chryllion stirred as her words reached him. "Are you sure?" he asked in concern. The last time she had tried to patch the Veil, she had got trapped inside it and another Sentinal, Serillion, had died protecting her and the Captain.

"I'll do it. You must protect them long enough to finish this. Help them," Saerille said firmly, turning towards the Captain and the subtly glowing Sentinal beside him. Taking a deep breath, she reached for the Veil and froze in turn as she connected to the Sentinals assisting the Captain trying to save those trapped in the Veil.

Chryllion climbed the icy slope and drew his broadsword as the shimmering form coalesced into a shrouded figure, slowly straightening between the Captain and the Ascendant. More shapeless figures began to form behind it, stepping onto the plateau. The Ascendant Tor'asion gasped out his breath in heaving gulps as he slowly lowered his hands and gazed at his ancestors in awe.

Jerrol slowly raised his hands in supplication, and Tor'asion laughed. "It's too late now. Clary will rule all. Our ancestors have returned, and you will all bow down before them. You will be first," he said, holding Jerrol's gaze. "You will submit to his will and accept Ascendant rule. You will have no choice, you will ..."

Birlerion made a sudden movement and struck, and Tor'asion instinctively blocked his strike. Distracted, he released Jerrol from his hold. Unnoticed, Landis crept up behind the Ascendant and he drove his dagger into Tor'asion's back with all his strength. Tor'asion screeched in agony as he twisted, instinctively striking Landis away from him, and as he turned back towards Jerrol and Clary, Chryllion was there. His broadsword decapitated the Ascendant before he could react.

Jerrol straightened as power rolled off the figure before him.

"You dare to get in our way." The voice hissed and bubbled, not quite fully formed.

"Yes, I dare. You are not welcome here," Jerrol said. "The Lady has already told you once. This world is not for you. Your acolytes are gone; you stand alone. There is nothing for you here."

"This world is mine, as are you." The figure reached for Jerrol, and a brilliant white light engulfed him as his touch encircled Jerrol's throat. Clary hesitated, though his grip tightened. "What is this?"

"My Captain already told you; this world is not for you, nor is he or my Sentinals." The Lady stepped out of the light, her green robes flowing around her. Long blonde hair swirled around her face as if alive. Her emerald eyes were hard as stone. The Lady's voice rang out over Oprimere, and everyone stopped and looked skyward in amazement. Light swirled in the roiling clouds, streaks of all colours blending and twisting, flashes of lightning cutting through the air, and the land trembled in response.

"My people are not for you. Begone and never return," Leyandrii said.

The figure hissed, drawing Jerrol closer. Jerrol struggled to relax, his instinct to fight an overpowering impulse. A soft kiss caressed his cheek, and he stilled as he remembered the line from the prophecy:

'Keep thy course as stillness creeps
Bide thy time lest maidens weep.'

He had to wait for all the Ascendants to arrive.

"This cannot be." Clary lifted his face as if testing the air. He swung around, taking Jerrol with him, and he negligently struck Chryllion out of the way. The force of his touch sent Chryllion flying over the heads of stunned soldiers. He hit the ground with a muffled thump, and many eyes turned back to the plateau, watching the shining Lady and her Captain and his shadow held in the grip of a creature from another time.

More shrouded figures formed behind him.

Birlerion stepped around Jerrol and into the light, a glowing nimbus of power in Jerrol's eyes, and Clary flinched back. "You!" he hissed.

Birlerion smiled, his eyes exultant. "Yes. There is only one truth. I belong to only one purpose, and that purpose is not yours." Birlerion smiled viciously. "Clary, you just aren't good enough," he said, his voice full of satisfaction.

Clary's hand shot up into the air, and it seemed to grab and twist before his black eyes focused on Birlerion. He roared his anger, striking out at Birlerion as the Lady whispered, "Now, my Captain." Birlerion shielded them, feeding what was left of his power into the transparent barrier until the Ascendant lord's power hit him in the chest and he fell. Leyandrii absorbed his shield as she wrapped herself around Jerrol and he drove his hands into the creature's chest, reaching up and through, Jerrol grasped the Veil in both hands and pulled.

The bloodstone exploded out of his body, shooting himself and Leyandrii skywards and beyond, dragging the remnants of the creature and his companions with him. Jerrol spread to fill the gap, and the Veil caught him and buried itself in his skin, driving down into his bones, humming in delight as it made him its own. The wail of the Ancestors was lost as the Veil devoured them, never fully formed, and now silent forever.

Birlerion failed to draw breath as his lungs collapsed and fire seared through his soul. He struggled to reach for Leyandrii one last time, knowing he had lost her as his sight faded and he lost consciousness.

His desolate cry was lost as he collapsed. Unresponsive, his body flew through the air landing in a senseless heap beside Chryllion's. An appalled Landis stopped slapping Chryllion's slack face and moved towards Birlerion's smoking body in horror, shouting for help. The grand duke's soldiers came running, and between them, they dragged the unconscious Sentinals away.

The Veil throbbed. The insidious threads reached deep and pulled Jerrol apart as the crystal in his blood sealed the exposed ends for all time. His mind expanded as he encapsulated the world of Remargaren, and he sighed as he merged with the protection that would keep them safe forever.

The air sparkled as the sky cleared. The stormy clouds melted away and the brilliant blue sky arced overhead. The barrier shimmered and disappeared with a slight popping sound, leaving tiny bubbles floating in the air, glistening with the colours of the rainbow as they descended.

The plateau stood empty and silent.

53

PLATEAU OF OPRIMERE

King Benedict drew a shaky breath and looked down across the open plain towards the plateau of Oprimere. He had forced Fonorion to bring him through the waystone to the ridge north of Stoneford when news of the barrier arrived. He had watched from the ridge in horror as the action unfolded on the plateau below them. Some of the men around him were weeping, over-whelmed at the sight of the Lady. Others stood in shock, horrified at the loss of their captain and commander.

He gazed across the land barrier at the men gathering at the foot of the plateau, knowing that the young man with the bright blonde hair was the grand duke. Randolf slowly raised a hand in acknowledgement, and then they both turned away, surrounded by their retainers, as they attempted to assimilate what had just happened.

The sky was a blaze of orange and crimson and the Lady's moon was just visible as she began her ascent when six tall sentinal trees shimmered into view on the plateau. Their silvery trunks were burnished blood-red by the dying rays of the golden sun and the canopies were haloed by an iridescent glow that only touched the trees. They stood silent, still, searching.

Taelia faced the trees, staring across the plateau as if she could see them. The air was oppressive, the anguish heavy. The trees stood clear in her mind's eye, but none of them waited for Jerrol. She shuddered as the names of the fallen Sentinals chimed through her body. Her breath caught in her throat, no, it wasn't true. "Taurillion!" she shouted as she shuffled back to the healer's tent, desperately calling Ari.

Stoneford Keep, Vespiri

"Find out which six Sentinals fell, now!" King Benedict ordered as he sat in Lord Jason's study. His fearful gaze touched on Fonorion who stood at his shoulder as always. Niallerion stood by the door, his face pale and anguished. Both the Stoneford Sentinals were missing, and he caught his breath as he saw Jason's strained face, somewhat diminished without his familiar Sentinals standing behind him. "What news from Deepwater?" he asked slowly, not wanting to acknowledge the possibility.

Niallerion shook his head. "There is much confusion, not all Sentinals have been found. Tagerill is missing, as is Frenerion. The Captain has not been seen since …" his voice trailed off. He struggled on. "Chryllion and Saerille have yet to return. Birlerion fell, but the Elothians have him. We haven't heard if he survived. There are reports that more Sentinals were seen to fall. We don't know who or where they are."

"But you know when one of you falls, so surely you know who they are?"

Niallerion shook his head. "There are too many. It is not clear."

"Go, find out," the king instructed as another messenger entered the study, his hands full of missives.

Niallerion rushed to the waystone and stepped into Oprimere. He faltered as the trees came into view, his chest tight as he slowly circled the plateau. The trees would not have traveled if their Sentinal had not fallen. They had come in search of their companions. He took a deep breath and climbed the mound, and, stopping before the first tree, he hesitantly extended a hand.

Anguish tore through him. "Birlerion," he cried as he collapsed to his knees hugging the tree. "No, Lady please, not Birlerion." He rested his forehead against the trunk. He couldn't believe Birlerion was one of the fallen. That he would never see his friend's face again.

Inhaling deep, he tried to control the tears that blurred his vision. Throat tight, he forced himself to rise. Blindly, he staggered to the next tree. Ari popped into view above the trees, shrieking at the top of his voice, and Birlerion's tree shuddered violently before fading from view. Ari disappeared in its wake.

Niallerion swayed, his eyes widening as the ramification of Birlerion's tree leaving hit him. Was there a chance? Could Birlerion still be alive? Ari had come to get Birlerion's tree. He grasped at the possibility like a drowning man grabbing a life belt. His hand descended on the trunk and Lorillion's name struck him deep inside. He moaned as he gripped the tree, his body shaking uncontrollably as he grieved for the man who had never truly been awoken. He swallowed, trying not to heave. His stomach roiled as he tried to control his grief. The ground trembled as a final tree appeared in the gap left by Birlerion's tree, completing the circle, and Niallerion knew it was Serillion's, come to join his grieving brethren.

"Birlerion," he muttered. Hanging on to an impossible

hope, he pushed himself away from Lorillion's tree. He slid down the hill and staggered towards the Elothian encampment, tears streaming down his face as he searched.

His way was barred by Landis, who displayed an impressive array of bruising down the side of his face.

"Where is Birlerion?" Niallerion demanded.

Landis winced and placed his hands on Niallerion's chest.

"You need to prepare yourself," he said, his voice thick with emotion. "The healer says there is no hope."

Niallerion brushed passed him and paused in the entrance of a large tent, his thin face grey and pinched as he took in the scene. Birlerion lay on a table, unnaturally pale and still. His chest was exposed, revealing horrific burns. The remains of his clothes were still smoking on the floor. Marianille and Taelia were arguing furiously with a healer, Taelia's arms flying in the air with agitation.

"He needs his tree." Niallerion's voice cut through the tent. "Now," he said as he strode up to Birlerion's body.

The healer barred his way. "It's too late. He's gone. No one could survive the blast he received. His chest is crushed; his lungs collapsed. He cannot breathe."

"We are not losing one more Sentinal," Niallerion hissed, forcibly moving the healer, who cringed away from the expression on the Sentinal's face.

"Niallerion?" Marianille turned toward him. Her silver eyes filled her face. "I need your help. I can't carry him on my own."

Niallerion scooped Birlerion up in his arms. He staggered under his weight, but he steadied and marched out of the tent, his silver eyes blazing. The aroma of scorched skin and roses tickled his nose as he strode through a crowd of milling soldiers, who parted before him. Marianille hurried beside him. Niallerion raised his head, his senses questing.

"This way," Taurillion stood before him. "His sentinal is this way. Let me take him."

"I'm fine." Niallerion tightened his grip and Taurillion gave way. He led the way to the newly seated sentinal just behind the encampment and Niallerion shimmered into the tree without stopping, closely followed by Marianille. They didn't come back out, and Taurillion took up a sentry position, waiting, staring unseeingly before him.

Taelia rested a soft hand on his arm as she stopped beside him. "Taurillion, I am so sorry."

Taurillion slowly stiffened as he stared at her, realising she didn't refer to Birlerion. "No, I don't believe it."

"Her tree is waiting at the plateau."

"No, it can't be." He strode off into the deepening gloom, leaving Taelia alone outside the sentinal.

She took a deep breath and hesitantly reached for the trunk. It warmed briefly beneath her touch. "Marianille?" she called. She knew the pain the Sentinals were suffering. She felt it herself. Her only consolation was that there was no tree waiting for her husband. Then again, he didn't have a tree.

Healer's tent, Oprimere Plateau, Elothia

Serenion woke up in tears. He was laying on the floor of a tent full of injured soldiers. Generille hovered over him and gathered him in her arms as he shuddered. "Hush, dear boy. It wasn't your fault. He pushed us all away. Lad, you didn't want to be going where he was."

Serenion stiffened in her arms. "Where's Yas?" His voice was muffled, and Generille glanced at her husband.

Royerion reluctantly shook his head, and Generille's eyes filled with tears. Her grip tightened on Serenion, and he knew. He reared out of her arms, overwhelmed with shock and loss. He blundered out of the Elothian tent and stopped in horror at the sight of the glowing sentinal trees crowning the Oprimere plateau, as it was being called. Six trees, six Sentinals. He breathed a sigh of relief as he saw Taurillion's tall form striding through the tents and past the flickering torches, and he hurried to catch up with him. He seemed the last link to normality, to the past.

"Taurillion." Serenion grasped his sleeve, and Taurillion's severe face softened at the sight of the distressed boy. He wrapped an arm around his shoulder.

"Thank the Lady, you are alright," he breathed, giving the boy a slight hug.

"What happened?"

"The Captain gave his life to remove the threat and seal the Veil, and some of our friends did too." He squeezed Serenion's shoulder again and turned back to the trees. "Can you give me a moment?" he said, his voice faltering as he stared ahead.

"Of course. I'll be with the grand duke." Serenion turned away. He didn't think Taurillion had heard him. When he looked back, Taurillion was crouched beside a tree, his shoulders bowed in grief.

Serenion entered the command tent and found the grand duke surrounded by people and looking harassed. He positioned himself behind the grand duke's shoulder, and Randolf looked up in surprise. At the sight of his face, he cleared the room and peace descended for a moment.

"Tell me."

"Yaserille's sentinal is on the plateau," Serenion said simply, and Randolf closed his eyes. Guin'yyfer would be inconsolable.

"And Taurillion?"

"He went to the plateau."

"And you?"

"What about me, Your Grace?"

"You were knocked unconscious. You're supposed to be in the infirmary."

"There are others who have a greater need for healers than me."

Randolf nodded, watching him. The boy's eyes looked wild, though he was manfully trying to control his grief. Maybe keeping him busy was best. "Very well, keep me informed." He rubbed a hand over his face. "We recovered another Sentinal. Chryllion, I believe. Niallerion came searching for Birlerion and is around somewhere with Taelia and Marianille. I hear Birlerion's condition is not good, and there has been no word of Commander Haven."

"I'll stay with you until Taurillion returns. Where is Lady Guin'yyfer, Your Grace?"

"Helping the healers; they are overwhelmed."

Serenion stepped to the flap of the tent. "Generille?"

Two Sentinals stepped forward out of the mass of people waiting outside, and Serenion introduced them to the grand duke. "Royerion and Generille of East Watch, Your Grace. May I suggest Generille accompanies Lady Guin'yyfer for now? And Royerion guards your door. They don't all need to be in here at the same time."

Randolf's lips twitched, but he said: "East Watch? How came you to be here?"

"The Captain called, and we came; he needed help with the Veil," Royerion's calm voice replied.

"Do you know what happened to him?"

Generille sighed. "He pushed us away, trying to protect everyone except himself. We need to teach him better."

"He lives, then?" the duke asked, the strain on his face easing.

"He lives until we know otherwise. And at the moment, he is only missing," Generille said firmly.

"Very well, then, Sentinal Generille. I would appreciate it very much if you would accompany Lady Guin'yyfer and ensure she comes to no harm. Serenion, I think you are right; a guard on the door seems most sensible if we are to have any peace to figure out how we clear this mess up. If either Captain Landis or Captain Owen arrive, show them in immediately."

"Of course, Your Grace," Royerion bowed and escorted Generille out of the tent. He took up the position outside the flap. His silver eyes glinted at his wife as she smiled sadly and patted his face before heading off towards the infirmary.

Generille bowed over in grief. She honestly hadn't expected to find her friend in the rows of dead being prepared for burial, but here he was, his body laid out, long and lifeless, his wounds hidden beneath the canvas shroud in which he was wrapped. She laid a gentle finger on his face and breathed his name. "Adilion."

For such vitality to be laying so still, it was unnatural, and the tears fell. She looked up as someone stopped behind her. She heard a soft curse as the man crouched beside her. "Do you need help? To get him to his tree."

Generille looked at the wiry man dressed in a blue and red uniform and blinked away her tears. "L-Landis?"

Landis nodded. "He shouldn't be here. Taurillion said his tree is on the plateau. We've been searching for him."

Deepwater Watch, Vespiri

Alyssa shoved her hair out of her face and looked up into the night sky. The Lady's waxing moon lit the landscape with her brilliant silver light; it seemed blindingly bright, throwing their two sentinal trees into stark relief. Her eyes teared up as she remembered her husband returning with two Sentinals laid out among the many injured soldiers.

Heart constricting, she remembered the sight of Tagerill lying next to a woman they named Yaserille. She had thought he was dead, too; he had been so still and pale. Her mother, Miranda, Tagerill's wife, had fainted on the steps before Jennery had a chance to tell her he was still alive, just.

He was lying within his sentinal now. She thanked the Lady that Denirion had been with them. They would not have been able to get him into his sentinal so fast otherwise, and she knew deep down that Tagerill would not have survived if there had been any delay.

One piece of good news was that Frenerion had appeared out of the gloom, dazed but whole. Denirion had escorted him back to Greenswatch with orders to stay in his tree until told otherwise.

Alyssa took a deep breath and exhaled slowly. Her stomach cramped as she considered the number of losses and those still missing. Their infirmary was overflowing though her husband said they were better off than he had expected. She shuddered at the thought that he had expected their losses to be much worse.

They had no news from Stoneford; no word from Commander Haven. Alyssa knew her husband was frantic. She also knew conditions had been worse at Stoneford. There could be little good news from there. Jennery had sent Denirion through the waystone desperate to know what had happened. Denirion had yet to return.

The sudden appearance of the barrier had to mean that Jerrol had been involved. She recognised the Lady's work, and she blessed him fervently for trying to limit their losses. The cessation of all fighting even after the barrier had disappeared and the skies had cleared, indicated that whatever was wrong had been resolved. She prayed to the Lady for good news, and she prayed for Jerrol and Taelia, as well as the king and those at Stoneford.

The tears slowly dripped down her cheeks as a sense of foreboding crept over her. They had lost a Sentinal, and a second hung by a thread. How many more were they going to have to say goodbye to?

She looked up as Denirion slowly walked up the steps to the house, his shoulders stiff as if he were forcing himself to remain upright, and she turned towards him in despair. Jennery came clattering down the steps, his face taut in the moonlight.

"Tell me," he said, his voice rough.

"In total; five Sentinals dead, two critical including Tagerill, and one missing," Denirion said, staring blindly at them. "Lord Jason lost over half his men. Many are still missing. His Watch is ..." Denirion's voice failed him. "The grand duke remains encamped at the battlefield of Oprimere. His losses are just as severe."

"Who did Jason lose?" Jennery asked, his voice painfully controlled.

Denirion closed his eyes. "Chryllion and Saerille."

Jennery swallowed, his face paling alarmingly. "Both of them? How is Jason?" He knew how he would feel if he lost Tagerill and Denirion.

"Coping. The king remains at Stoneford, as does Fonorion. King Benedict plans to meet with Grand Duke Randolf tomorrow. The threat from the Ascendants is no more. The Veil is sealed."

"Who else did we lose?"

"Adilion, Yaserille and Lorillion."

"Commander Haven?"

"Missing. He's not been seen since..." Denirion failed to get the words out, and Jennery gripped his shoulder in support. "Lady Leyandrii appeared on the plateau. She and the Captain attacked the Ascendants, and swept them away. The Veil is sealed and the Ascendants are no more, but the Captain hasn't returned."

Jennery forced the words out. "Anyone else?"

"Birlerion," Denirion replied as he exhaled. "Apparently, he caused the distraction, enough for the Captain to attack, but he took the full brunt of the Ascendant lord's power. The healer pronounced him dead, but his sentinal says otherwise."

Alyssa's tears overflowed. "Lea." She reached for her husband, and he wrapped his arms around her.

"I know, sweetheart, I know."

"What can we do?"

"Wait. All we can do is wait."

"What about Taelia?"

Jennery looked at Denirion. "Where is Taelia?"

"She is with the grand duke. Marianille is with her. They watch over Birlerion." Denirion paused. "She waits for news of the Captain, but it doesn't look hopeful."

Jennery sighed. "Come, let us go in. We have much to discuss and much still to do."

54

ELSEWHERE

"So many lost. Was it necessary?" Jerrol asked as he stood beneath the Lady's sentinal, idly staring up into its branches. A soft green light illuminated the glade, soothing and calm.

Leyandrii sighed. "Man is impatient. They use force and pain to solve what the mind could solve easily, but the power of the mind, as you have also seen, is a danger unto itself. It is a drug, a seductress that lulls man into thinking they are supreme and don't require governance. They believe that, because they have power, they must, therefore, be ascendant over all others. But power needs control, and in a world such as Remargaren, such power is not required."

"What happens now, then? I couldn't save Lorillion. He was tied so tightly that even as I released him, he wrapped himself around me and came too."

"My poor Lorillion. He was my locus, he was used to linking. I expect it was as natural as breathing to link to you. Don't berate yourself, my Captain, it was meant to be. His role was ordained before you were even born. And the twins, Ellaerion and Elliarille, you'll need to keep an eye on them;

they'll need some help to come to terms with what happened to them, trapped in the Veil all these years.

"As for the others, you released Serenion, Generille, and Royerion. Chryllion, I think, saw a need and filled it. He was always there when you needed him," she said fondly. "And my dear Saerille; the Veil recognised her, I think."

Jerrol stirred restlessly as he looked at his hands. His skin glittered with the crystal pumping through his veins. "I thought we would find more. I was sure of it when I heard their voices."

"I think some were only echoes. It has been a long time, and as you well know, the Veil does not give anything up easily."

The Veil caressed his skin as gentle and as jealous as a lover. It tried to call him away, tempting him to merge as one with his lost friends. Serillion's name lingered in the air, and his heart constricted as the Veil coaxed him to wrap the world in their protection. Offering him two perfect hands to hold the world in. He shook the temptation away and met the Lady's sympathetic eyes. "What about Birlerion? Who is he really?"

"Ah, Birlerion," the Lady's face grew pensive. "He never deserved any of this. He never asked for it, yet there was never anyone else. As you have found, my Captain, you can't do it alone. There is a balance to everything. You need the unvarnished sight to achieve the impossible; without it, you just deceive yourself and everyone else. He hid much, kept his abilities safe until it was needed. He has always been my shield, as my Captain is my sword."

"What about me? Can I return? I am no longer what I was. The Veil calls to me."

The Lady smiled, her exquisite face sad. "Change happens to us all. You will always be part of the Veil as you are the Bloodstone. You are my Captain; you are the Oath

Keeper, and you have a choice as always. You will always be my anchor and treasured as such, no matter what you choose. We would live in a very different world but for your bravery, your fortitude, your belief. You are the soul of Remargaren."

"I am but a man."

"The greatest miracle on this word is man. Man will always find a way. My Sentinals were once but men and women." She shrugged, her eyes bright. "We would not be here but for them. They kept the Ascendants at bay long enough. We lost so many, and as the few awaken, those we never found, it's like losing them again."

Jerrol smiled in sympathy. He shared the pain she felt. "What happened to Guerlaire?"

"He chose," the Lady said with a glittering smile. "He chose to stay with me, and no matter what, I am only a woman, and I cannot fault his choice."

"What of me?"

"You have a choice as all men do."

"You would leave it up to me?"

She gave him an amused glance. "But you make such good choices, my Captain."

Jerrol grimaced. "This is going to hurt, isn't it?"

"Birth always hurts, but the rewards are so great. I will be watching; take care of them for me."

"Always."

She reached out to touch his face in parting as the king's throne room in Old Vespers began to coalesce around him. The king and his court were caught in silent tableau. The king's mouth open to issue a command.

Jerrol looked around him. Time had passed since the final confrontation. Benedict had returned to Old Vespers, and Randolf to Retarfu. Taelia stood beside the king, her face sad but composed, the life they had created together still hidden within. He stooped to kiss her, and her eyes widened in shock. Her hand began to rise towards him.

He knew Birlerion and Tagerill still convalesced in their sentinals, and he sent a silent blessing to them both and to those whom he had lost.

He saluted the king and his frozen court as he walked across the room and stood in front of the Oath. He laid his left hand flat against the words. His palm pulsed sending a shaft of pain through his veins as he began to push. He heard a despairing wail behind him as the Oath began to pulse red as he sank further into the wall. The crystal expanded through his body, the edges stinging as they cut; his blood welled and seeped into the grooves of the letters. Pain spiked through his veins and made his arms tremble as he forced himself forward. His skin glittered, causing flashes of light and colour to spangle around the room.

Taelia launched herself at him, wrapping her arms around his waist as if she could pull him back. Her sudden movement broke the stasis as the king shouted in horror and voices crashed around them. The throne room was a blur of horrified motion until a brilliant flash engulfed the room stunning the occupants to silence and Jerrol and Taelia were gone. The echo of Taelia's wail combined with Jerrol's voice raised in agony gradually faded to silence as the Oath pulsed a brilliant red before finally settling into a warm golden glow, bathing the king and his court in its light.

The shocked silence was interrupted by a nervous courtier dashing into the throne room and skidding to a breathless halt in front of the king. "S-sire," he stammered, "there's a tall tree in your courtyard. I-it just appeared fully grown."

The court rushed out of the throne room and into the courtyard, gasps of wonder and dismay arising as they stared up at the tall sentinal tree towering over the palace walls, the subtly glowing trunk a twisting dance of two trees entwined, the bark emitting a silvery hue.

King Benedict solemnly bowed his head and placed one hand against the bark. His other hand rested over his heart. He shivered as the sentinal's acknowledgement tingled through his palm, *Jerrolion*. He turned and swept the court with a searing glance. "Our peace has been bought with many lives. It is our duty to guard that peace for the good of all, in the name of our Lady." His eyes rested on the awed faces of Jennery and Alyssa, openly clutching each other in shock, before passing on to the Sentinals standing tall.

"The Captain will be watching," he said.

The Sentinals knelt. The king watched them nervously. Only Jerrol had seemed able to keep them under control. They struck their chests with their fists. "The Captain sees all," they chanted. "In the sight of the Lady, at the command of the Liege, to protect the Land and its people."

Niallerion stared up into the leafy canopy overhead, the pointy leaves intertwining so much that one couldn't tell which tree they belonged to. And he smiled.

The Captain's sentinal had arrived.

EPILOGUE

A slender young man with gleaming silver eyes and shoulder-length brown hair strode into the throne room. He was dressed in a somewhat archaic-looking silvery-green uniform. His high-necked tunic glimmered as the Oath flared a brilliant white in welcome before settling into its more usual golden glow. The man nodded an acknowledgement and bethought the king. He waited patiently, staring up at the Oath, his hands clasped behind his back.

He didn't have to wait long. The king came puffing into the throne room, stopping as a grin of pure delight spread across his face. "Jerrol," he exclaimed as he strode forward, hands outstretched. "At last! Or should I call you Jerrolion?"

Jerrol smiled wryly as he dropped to one knee. "My liege," he murmured.

"Rise, rise, thank goodness you are alright. I am glad you came."

Jerrol quirked an eyebrow at the king as he rose. "Did you think I wouldn't?"

The king laughed. "I wouldn't have blamed you," he said, inspecting him. "You look, ah, a little different," he said, observing the threads of silver in his hair, the slight sparkle to his skin, and the luminous eyes that saw everything.

"The Lady's influence. You know how she likes to meddle, even Taelia didn't escape. Once she got over the shock of seeing me and receiving the Lady's Blessing, she settled down quite nicely as the wife of Captain Jerrolion."

"Well, congratulations!" the king said, an appreciative smile on his face. "Before your lovely wife arrives, I need to tell you about the trouble we're having." The king began explaining as the Captain of the Lady's Guard, Commander of the King's Justice, and Keeper of the Oath, listened.

The End.

The adventure continues in Book Three dot five: Sentinals Recovery. A novella following Birlerion's recovery and his bonding with his Darian. There was no physical way to include this story in Sentinals Justice. Birlerion never had the chance to return to Greenswatch before the final confrontation, but I thought it was a story worth telling. Available December 2021. A surprise Christmas bonus for those of you have reached the end of Sentinals Justice and to tide you over until the next book in the series releases! Keep reading to find the first chapter.

Sign up to my newsletter via the link on https://linktr.ee/helengarraway to find out first when it is available, and to download a free novella in the same world.

Novella: Book 0.5: Sentinals Stirring

. . .

If you have a moment and you enjoyed reading Sentinals Justice, then please do leave a review and tell other fantasy readers what you enjoyed. Reviews are so important to independent authors to drive visibility and to help us to continue publishing our books.

Thank you for your support.
Helen Garraway
www.helengarraway.com
September 2021

Other books in the series:
Book One: Sentinals Awaken
Book Two: Sentinals Rising
Book Three: Sentinals Justice
Book 3.5: Sentinals Recovery (December 2021)
Book Four: Title TBC: Spring 2022

ACKNOWLEDGMENTS

I can't quite believe that I am writing these words, but I have finished the third book in the Sentinal series and with the release of Sentinals Justice I will have published three books in one year. Don't expect three books every year!

I have some very special people to thank who helped me on my self publishing journey.

First, my wonderful daughter Jennifer who has supported all my dreams to write and publish my novels.

My very good friend Kaye Adams who is my sounding board, and keeps me sane when I go off track.

Michael Strick, my ever faithful beta reader and Jill Wells who helped hunt down those darned typos. If you do still manage to find any, the fault is all mine!

Maddy Glenn, my editor who asks those probing questions and makes me look more closely at some of my 'darlings' that really need to go, and encourages me to expand rather than cut!

My wonderful team of ARC readers, who grow with each book. Thank you for joining me on this journey, I really appreciate all your support, comments and feedback.

Jeff Brown of Jeff Brown Graphics (jeffbrowngraphics.-

com) designed my gorgeous cover and Tom from Fictive Designs (https://fictive-designs.com/maps) drew the wonderful map of Elothia.

Thank you all,
    Helen

BOOK 3.5
THE SENTINAL SERIES

SENTINALS
RECOVERY

HELEN GARRAWAY

CHAPTER 1

Birlerion woke in a panic. Gasping for air, he struggled out of the constraining blankets. He couldn't breathe. His mouth was full of dirt, clogging his throat, suffocating him. He coughed and choked, and tears trailed down his cheeks as he dragged in a desperate gulp of air. His chest ached at the effort.

Warm arms embraced him. "Hush, you're safe, Birlerion. Concentrate on your breaths, one at a time."

Birlerion writhed, inhaling more noise than air. His face darkened as his lungs failed to take in enough, and he shuddered as the stench of burning flesh filled his nose. He clutched the material beneath his fingers, and the arms around him tightened.

"You're safe in your sentinal. You can control it. That's right. One breath, two breaths …"

Birlerion collapsed, exhausted, his throat raw, his chest heavy. He inhaled, chest heaving, and exhaled a wheezing sigh, concentrating on the effort. He relaxed as the soft touch of his sentinal embraced him, and then darkness claimed him.

Much later, soft voices woke him, and he lay concentrating on the simple mechanics of getting air into his lungs. In and out. Why was it so difficult to breathe? His chest was tight, uncomfortable. Voices percolated into his awareness, and his brow wrinkled as he tried to place them.

"He needs more time. We can't move him yet. He's not stable enough."

"The grand duke has recalled all his men; the plateau is deserted. It's been nearly two months since the battle, Marguerite. How much longer will it take?"

"As long as it needs to. He nearly died, Taurillion. His chest was crushed. It takes time to rebuild, to heal."

"Then how did he survive?"

The light changed above Birlerion as a soft hand smoothed his forehead. Marguerite sighed. "Birlerion?" She leaned over him, and he opened his eyes. As her precious face hovered above him, her vivid blue eyes were full of concern, though she was quick to hide it. She smiled at him.

"Hi," she said. Birlerion stared at her, an impossibility. She had bonded with the land, hadn't she? "Marguerite?" he croaked, raising a shaky hand. By the Lady, he felt weak. He rested his hand on her arm, rubbing the auburn curls between his trembling fingers. She was real. "How are you here? Did we win?"

"Of course we won. You did it. You shielded the Captain long enough for him to strike."

Birlerion flinched against the flood of memories: the terrible winds, Leyandrii and Guerlaire falling as the ground ripped apart, being consumed by the Land ... "Leyandrii fell. Is she alright?"

"She's fine."

"And the Captain?"

"He had to leave. He is in Old Vespers with the king."

Birlerion dropped his hand, exhausted by the effort. He cleared his throat; the taste of rain and fresh soil filled his mouth. "King? What king? Where are Leyandrii and Guerlaire?"

Marguerite hesitated and exchanged glances with Taurillion. She reached for a glass. "They are fine. Here, drink. You must be thirsty. Just take small sips."

Taurillion helped Birlerion sit up, and he sipped the water while resting against Taurillion's solid chest, catching his breath in between. If he took the gulps he wanted, he thought he might drown. He lay back on his pillow, breathless, his chest wheezing.

"What happened to me?"

"You got in the way of an Ascendant, and he blasted you in the chest," Taurillion replied.

Birlerion stared at the copper-eyed Sentinal as the memories filtered in. "It was Clary, wasn't it? He just won't stop hounding me."

"I think that's enough talking for now," said Marguerite. "Rest, Birlerion. We'll talk more later."

Obediently closing his eyes, Birlerion relaxed into the soft embrace of his sentinal. The hum deepened in concern, and Birlerion hurried to reassure him that he was fine. Then his awareness melted away, and he slept.

Marguerite looked down at him. His black hair had grown and now curled around his neck, accentuating the translucence of his skin. His face, relaxed in sleep, was all hollow angles and curves, with dark lashes hiding mesmerising silver eyes. Once, they had been an equally mesmerising indigo. His cheeks were sunken and he had lost weight, a result of the huge discharge of magic he had made; too much.

On top of that, he had taken the full brunt of an Ascendant lord's anger. It was amazing that he lived. She wasn't sure how it was possible. The healer had proclaimed him dead, but Ari, the little Arifel, and his sentinal had refused to believe it.

As his chest rose, she knew that, although the horrific burns had been healed by his sentinal, his lungs were struggling to fill the space that his newly rebuilt rib cage provided. If that was not enough, he was also confused. Unsurprising, she supposed. She should have anticipated it.

The next morning, Birlerion tried to get up. He paused, resting on the side of his bed, his hands gripping the edge as his head swam. A soft exclamation had him peering up. Marguerite stood before him, her hands on her hips. "What do you think you are doing? You don't have the strength to get up by yourself."

"You said I've been here for over a month. I should be healed by now."

"Your sentinal brought you back from the brink of death. That's no mean feat and certainly not an overnight job," Marguerite snapped, pushing him back onto the bed. "Why aren't you keeping him in bed?" she asked the air above her, scowling up at the sentinal that surrounded them.

Birlerion chuckled. "Because I told him not to. I want to get up." The air around him warmed, and a flush of energy rushed through his body. He straightened. "Only for a few minutes to look outside and breathe the fresh air." He shuddered as his words reminded him of the tragedy in Terolia, one of many memories and experiences he hadn't had time to process, and that still grated on his nerves.

Marguerite placed a hand on his chest. "I wasn't going to say anything yet, but you need to know what happened." The reluctance was clear in her voice, and she sighed as she sat next to him. "I'm sorry, Birlerion. There is no easy way to say this, but we lost some friends in that final battle."

Birlerion tensed as his heart raced in his aching chest.

Marguerite stroked his arm as his sentinal hummed with concern. "Tagerill, Versillion, and Marianille are all fine," she said in a rush, "but we lost Chryllion and Saerille."

The pain hit him, and Birlerion shuddered. "No," he whispered as their faces swam before his blurring eyes.

"I am so sorry," Marguerite said helplessly.

"Who else?" he asked, knowing there were more.

"Adilion."

Birlerion closed his eyes. No. Adilion had been one of his closest friends. They had been at the academy together.

"And Yaserille and Lorillion."

Birlerion's heart twisted, and he panted as his chest constricted and tears leaked down his cheeks.

"Their trees are on the plateau; you'll see them as soon as you go outside, along with Serillion's sentinal."

"I want to see them."

Marguerite heaved a sigh. "If you fall over, it won't be my fault," she said, though she helped him up and shoved her shoulder under his armpit to steady him. He wavered and then, stiffening, staggered to the edge of the room and out into the sunshine.

He inhaled. The scent of fresh grass and meadow flowers tickled his nose, and he sneezed. He held his chest as the ache spiked. Marguerite helped him to the bench and he thumped down with a groan as he tried to inhale again. His breath caught twice but still didn't grab enough air, and he concentrated on his breathing, in and out, until his rising panic subsided.

Marguerite tucked a blanket around his shoulders. The air had a chill bite to it, even though most of the snow had melted, leaving a slushy mire behind.

Releasing his grip on the bench, Birlerion looked around. A canvas tent stood beside his sentinal. The tall tree arched protectively over them, its silver bark glistening in the sunlight. A fire pit had been dug between them. The smoke from the crackling fire drifted in the still air and teased his nose with the scent of resin and burnt wood. The plains of Oprimere stretched out before him: grassy knolls interspersed with slashes of deep brown soil, torn open to the sky. Ditches crisscrossed the plain, and discarded weapons glinted in the sunlight.

He scowled at the scene. "You haven't healed the land," he said, stilling as his gaze reached the raised plateau to the east. Six tall sentinal trees crowned the top, their silver trunks burnished by the golden sun.

"It will heal on its own. I thought you were more important. And anyway, I don't think that final confrontation should be forgotten so soon. Healing the scars will only hide the wounds; people need to understand and accept what happened. Many a pilgrim will come here, trying to find peace out of loss."

"True." There was a small silence. "Five. We lost five more."

"Yes."

Tears filled his eyes as their names chimed through him, all friends who would be much missed. "Doesn't seem real, does it?" he said, blindly staring at the sentinal trees. "If it wasn't for them, in time, all this would be forgotten."

Marguerite sat on the bench and gently embraced him. "It will never be forgotten."

"Of course it will. It will fade into history, much as it did the last time. The grass will grow," he smiled briefly, "if you allow it, and it will all become myth and legend." He sighed carefully and took a shallow breath before looking up at the brilliant blue sky. "Leyandrii's really gone this time, hasn't she?"

"She is still watching."

Birlerion smiled, crinkling the corner of his eyes. "Good."

Sentinals Recovery will be available December 2nd, 2021. Sign up to my newsletter via www. helengarraway.com to receive all the latest news.

Printed in Great Britain
by Amazon

74933222R00296